RED
RIVER
VENGEANCE

*Look for these exciting Western series from
bestselling authors*
WILLIAM W. JOHNSTONE
and **J. A. JOHNSTONE**

The Mountain Man
Preacher: The First Mountain Man
Luke Jensen: Bounty Hunter
Those Jensen Boys!
The Jensen Brand
MacCallister
The Red Ryan Westerns
Perley Gates
Have Brides, Will Travel
Will Tanner, Deputy U.S. Marshal
Shotgun Johnny
The Chuckwagon Trail
The Jackals
The Slash and Pecos Westerns
The Texas Moonshiners
Stoneface Finnegan Westerns
Ben Savage: Saloon Ranger
The Buck Trammel Westerns
The Death and Texas Westerns
The Hunter Buchanon Westerns

AVAILABLE FROM PINNACLE BOOKS

RED RIVER VENGEANCE

A PERLEY GATES WESTERN

WILLIAM W. JOHNSTONE

AND J. A. JOHNSTONE

PINNACLE BOOKS

Kensington Publishing Corp.

www.kensingtonbooks.com

PINNACLE BOOKS are published by

Kensington Publishing Corp.
119 West 40th Street
New York, NY 10018

Copyright © 2021 J. A. Johnstone

All rights reserved. No part of this book may be reproduced in any form or by any means without the prior written consent of the publisher, excepting brief quotes used in reviews.

This book is a work of fiction. Names, characters, businesses, organizations, places, events, and incidents either are the product of the author's imagination or are used fictitiously. Any resemblance to actual persons, living or dead, events, or locales is entirely coincidental. To the extent that the image or images on the cover of this book depict a person or persons, such person or persons are merely models, and are not intended to portray any character or characters featured in the book.

PUBLISHER'S NOTE:
Following the death of William W. Johnstone, the Johnstone family is working with a carefully selected writer to organize and complete Mr. Johnstone's outlines and many unfinished manuscripts to create additional novels in all of his series like The Last Gunfighter, Mountain Man, and Eagles, among others. This novel was inspired by Mr. Johnstone's superb storytelling.

If you purchased this book without a cover, you should be aware that this book is stolen property. It was reported as "unsold and destroyed" to the publisher, and neither the author nor the publisher has received any payment for this "stripped book." All Kensington titles, imprints, and distributed lines are available at special quantity discounts for bulk purchases for sales promotions, premiums, fund-raising, educational, or institutional use. Special book excerpts or customized printings can also be created to fit specific needs. For details, write or phone the office of the Kensington sales manager: Kensington Publishing Corp., 119 West 40th Street, New York, NY 10018, attn: Sales Department; phone 1-800-221-2647.

PINNACLE BOOKS, the Pinnacle logo, and the WWJ steer head logo are Reg. U.S. Pat. & TM Off.

ISBN-13: 978-0-7860-4739-0
ISBN-10: 0-7860-4739-9

First Pinnacle paperback printing: June 2021

10 9 8 7 6 5 4 3 2 1

Printed in the United States of America

Electronic edition:
ISBN-13: 978-0-7860-4740-6 (e-book)
ISBN-10: 0-7860-4740-2 (e-book)

CHAPTER 1

"Reckon we'll find out if Beulah's cookin' tastes as good as it did when she called her place the Paris Diner," Sonny Rice announced as he drove the wagon carrying supplies behind Perley, who was riding the bay gelding named Buck.

"How do you know that?" young Link Drew asked. "He just said he wanted to see the new hotel."

"I know 'cause he always eats at Beulah's place when he comes to town for supplies," Sonny replied. "Why do ya think I volunteered to drive the wagon in?"

"I bet the food won't be a whole lot better'n what Ollie cooks," Link said. It was his honest opinion. The gangly orphan had never eaten as well as he did now, ever since Perley brought him to live at the Triple-G after his parents were killed. Although most of the crew at the Triple-G complained good-naturedly about Ollie Dinkler's lack of compassion, they had to admit that he had taken a special interest in the welfare of the young lad.

"It'll be a whole lot fancier," Sonny said, "and it'll look better comin' from a pretty woman, instead of an old man with tobacco juice in his whiskers."

Ahead of the wagon, Perley reined Buck back to a halt and waited for Sonny and Link to come up beside him. "They built it right next to the railroad tracks," Perley stated the obvious. "That'll be handy, won't it? Get off the train and you can walk to the hotel." He nudged his horse and rode up to the rail in front of the hotel and stepped down to wait for the wagon. "Park it on the side, Sonny," he directed. "You and Link go on in and get us a table. I'm just gonna walk through the hotel and take a look." The hotel had been completed while Perley and Possum Smith were down in Bison Gap, and he was curious to see what kind of place it was going to be. According to what his brother Rubin told him, the fellow who built it made his money in cotton. Amos Johnson was his name, and he thought the little town of Paris was ready for a first-class hotel. Rubin said he had talked Beulah Walsh into moving her business into the hotel. Perley figured what Rubin had told him must have been right because the little Paris Diner building was vacant when they had ridden past.

When Sonny drove the wagon around to the side where the outside entrance was located, Perley walked in the front door. He was greeted by a desk clerk, smartly dressed in a coat and vest. "Can I help you, sir?"

"Howdy," Perley replied. "I'm on my way to your dinin' room and I just wanted to get a look at the hotel. My name's Perley Gates. I work at the Triple-G, and your hotel opened while I was outta town."

"Pleased to meet you," the young man said. "I'm David Smith. If you're looking to see the owner, that's Mr. Johnson. He's in the dining room eating his dinner."

"Oh no," Perley quickly responded. "I don't need to

bother him. I just wanted to see what the hotel looked like on the inside. It looks like a first-class hotel."

"Would you like to see what the rooms look like?" David asked. "I'd be glad to show you one."

"No, no thanks," Perley replied. "I won't have much occasion to rent one, anyway. I'll just go on to the dinin' room, but I thank you for offerin'." He pointed to the entrance to a hallway. "That way?" David nodded. "Much obliged," Perley said, and headed down the hall.

The first door he came to wore a sign that said it was the entrance to the dining room. Perley stepped inside and stood there a moment to look the room over. Still looking and smelling new, it was about half again bigger than Beulah's original establishment. Unlike Beulah's original location, there was no long table in the center of the room, only little tables with four chairs at each one. He saw Sonny and Link sitting at one of them over against the outside wall. He started toward them but stopped when Sonny waved his arm and pointed to a table beside the outside entrance, holding several weapons. Perley nodded and unbuckled his gun belt, looking toward the kitchen door as he walked over to leave his weapon with the others.

He was curious to see if Becky and Lucy had come to the hotel with Beulah, but if they had, they must all be in the kitchen right now. He rolled his holster up in his gun belt, and when he put it on the table, he noticed there were three others there. One he recognized as Sonny's six-gun. It was easy to guess who the other two belonged to. He glanced at a table near the center of the room where two men were attacking the food in front of them as if they were afraid someone might try to take it away from them.

One of the holsters caught his eye. It was a well-oiled fast-draw holster. He glanced again at the two strangers and tried to guess which one belonged to that holster before going over to join his friends. "I thought you would already be eatin'," he said when he sat down at the table.

"It's on the way," Sonny replied, and nodded toward the kitchen just as Lucy Tate, carrying two plates, came out the door. "We're havin' the pork chops, since we don't get much pork at the ranch. It's either that or stew beef today. You don't usually have a choice at the midday meal, but Lucy said today you do because it's Beulah's birthday."

"Well, how 'bout that?" Perley replied. "Don't reckon she said how old she is today."

"Nope, and I sure ain't gonna ask her," Sonny responded. Perley had to laugh at his response. Beulah had reached the age where she was no longer young, but she didn't consider herself old. And only she knew how many notches she had actually acquired.

"Well, there you are," Lucy Tate greeted him. "You haven't been to see us in so long, I figured you'd found someplace else to eat."

Before Perley had time to answer, one of the men at the table in the center of the room blurted, "Hey, Red, where the hell's that coffeepot?"

"Keep your shirt on, cowboy," Lucy yelled back at him. "Got a fresh pot workin' and it'll be ready in a minute." Back to Perley, she said, "I heard you had been gone for a while. You back to stay?"

"Far as I know," he answered. "At least I ain't plannin' to go anywhere right now." He looked at Link and winked. "I expect my brothers are thinkin' it's about time I did my share of the chores at the ranch." Back to Lucy, he said,

"Those pork chops look pretty good, I expect I'll try 'em, too."

"Right," Lucy replied, "I'll tell Becky to bring you a cup of coffee." He hadn't asked, but she figured he was wondering where Becky was.

As she walked past the table with the two strangers, one of them stated loudly, "The coffee, Red."

"I told you," she replied, "it's making. And don't call me Red. I don't have red hair, and my name's not Red."

"I reckon she told you what's what," Leonard Watts japed, and reached over to give his partner a playful jab on his shoulder.

Not to be put down by the cocky waitress, Jesse Sage called after Lucy as she continued on to the kitchen. "What is your name, Sassy Britches?"

There were only a few other patrons in the dining room, but Lucy didn't respond to Jesse's last attempt to rile her, sensing an air of discomfort among those diners already. When she went into the kitchen, she met Becky Morris on her way out with a cup of coffee for Perley. She knew the young waitress must have recognized Perley's voice when he joined Sonny and Link. "He wants the chops," Lucy said.

"I heard," Becky said, "but I thought I'd take him some coffee while Beulah's fixing up his plate."

Lucy chuckled, unable to resist teasing her. "You do have good ears," she japed. "I could have waited on him."

Accustomed to her friend's joking, Becky didn't respond while she went out the door, hurried over to Perley's table, and placed the cup of coffee down before him. "I know how you like your coffee," she said, "so I brought it right out. It's the first cup out of a new pot. Beulah's fixing your plate right now."

The warm smile she always caused to form on Perley's face blossomed into a beaming grin of embarrassment as he tried to think of something intelligent to say. Failing to come up with anything, he settled for, "Howdy, Becky."

His response was not loud, but it was enough to be heard at the table several feet away. "Yeah, howdy, Becky," Jesse demanded, "where the hell's my coffee? If anybody got the first cup, it oughta been me. Hell, he just walked in."

Leonard chuckled. "I swear, Jesse, you sure are feelin' ornery today, ain'tcha?"

"Damn right I am," Jesse said. Then to Becky, he ordered, "Tell that other gal, Miss Sassy Britches, I want some fresh coffee right now."

It had already gone too far. Perley was not happy with the obvious disrespect shown the two women, and now he could see that same resentment building in Sonny's eyes. Afraid Sonny might get into an altercation with the two drifters, he thought he'd better try to see if he could defuse the situation before it blew up. "Hey, there ain't no problem, friend," he called out to Jesse. "Becky, here, didn't know you were supposed to get the first cup. You can take this one and I'll wait for the next one. We don't talk to the ladies here in the dinin' room like you might talk to the ladies in the saloon, so it doesn't set too well with 'em. Whaddaya say? You want this cup of coffee?"

Both drifters looked at Perley in disbelief for a long moment before Jesse responded. "Mister, in the first place, I ain't your friend, and it ain't none of your business how I talk to a woman anywhere. So you'd best keep your mouth shut and mind your own business. I don't want your damn cup of coffee. If I did, I woulda already come over there and took it. Whaddaya say about that?"

Remaining unruffled, Perley paused and shrugged. "Well, I'd say that wouldn'ta been necessary, since I offered to give it to you, anyway."

Jesse looked at Leonard and asked, "Do you believe this mealymouthed jasper?" Looking back at Perley then, he warned, "Like I told you, keep your nose in your own business and stay the hell outta mine."

"Don't fret yourself, Perley," Becky said. "I'll run get the man some more coffee. There's no reason to have any trouble."

Jesse didn't miss hearing the name. "*Pearly*, is that what your name is?" When Perley nodded, Jesse declared, "Well, it sure as hell suits you. *Pearly*," he repeated, laughing. "What's your last name? Gates?" He looked over at Leonard and gave him a playful punch on the shoulder.

"Matter of fact, it is," Perley said.

That caused Jesse to pause for a moment. He was so surprised to find he had guessed right when he thought he had made a joke of the fellow's name. He looked at Leonard again, then they both howled with laughter. "*Pearly* Gates," he repeated a couple more times. "If that ain't a perfect name for a jasper like you, I don't know what is." He paused then when it occurred to him that the innocent-looking cowhand might be japing him. "Or maybe that ain't really your name and you're thinkin' you're pretty funny." He was about to threaten Perley but was interrupted by Lucy, who came from the kitchen at that point, carrying two fresh cups of coffee.

"Sorry to make you boys wait," she said. "I had to clear

my throat first." She glanced at Becky and winked. "Now, I hope you two will settle down and act like you've been around decent folks before."

Having caught Lucy's quick wink at Becky, Jesse was at once suspicious. "I don't reckon there's anything in that cup but coffee, right?"

"Of course, that's right," Lucy answered. "Did you want something else in it?"

He looked at his friend and gave him a wink. "Then I don't reckon you'd mind takin' a little drink of it first," Jesse said.

Lucy shrugged and without hesitating, picked up the cup and took a couple of sips of coffee. Then she graced him with a broad smile as she placed the cup back on the table. "Fresh out of the pot," she said. "Satisfied?" She turned to Becky then and said, "Come on, Becky, let's let 'em eat so they can get outta here. Perley's plate is ready now, anyway."

Becky started to follow her to the kitchen, but Jesse grabbed her wrist and pulled her back. "To hell with Perley's plate. You can stay here and keep company with me and Leonard."

That was as much as Perley could abide. "I reckon you've gone far enough to make it my business now," he said as he got up from his chair. "We don't stand for that kinda treatment to the ladies in this town. Let her go and we won't send for the sheriff. You can just finish your dinner and get on outta here and let decent people eat in peace."

Jesse gave him a big smile as he released Becky's wrist. She shot one worried look in Perley's direction before running out the door to find the sheriff. "Well, well," Jesse asked Leonard, "did you hear what he called me?"

"He called you a dirty name I can't repeat in front of these citizens settin' in here eatin'. And he said you was a yellow-bellied, scum-eatin' dog," the simple man answered, knowing what Jesse was fixing to do. Judging by the foolish grin on his face, it was easy to guess he possessed mere childlike intelligence.

"I'm thinkin' a man ain't no man a-tall, if he don't stand up to a yellow snivelin' dog callin' him names like that. Whaddaya think I oughta do about it?"

"I reckon you ain't got no choice," Leonard said. "A man's got a right to stand up for his honor. If he don't, he ain't got no honor. Ain't that what Micah always says?" They both got to their feet and stood grinning at Perley. "Maybe if he said he was sorry and admitted he was a yellow dog and crawled outta here on his hands and knees, you could let him get by with what he said," Leonard added, excitedly.

Perley patiently watched their little parody for a few minutes before responding. "You two fellows are puttin' on a good little show over one cup of coffee. If you think I'm gonna participate in a gunfight with you, you're mistaken. I came in here to eat my dinner, just like the rest of these folks. So why don't you sit back down and finish your dinner? Then you can go to Patton's Saloon and tell everybody there how you backed me down. That way, nobody gets shot, and we can eat in peace."

Since it was fairly obvious that Perley was not inclined to answer his challenge, Jesse was determined to force him to face him in the street or acknowledge his cowardice. He was about to issue his ultimatum when Sheriff Paul

McQueen walked in with Becky right behind him. "What's the trouble here?" McQueen asked as he walked up to face the two strangers still standing.

"Ain't no trouble, Sheriff," Jesse answered. "I ain't got no idea why that young lady thought there was and went and got you for nothin'. Me and my friend, here, was just tryin' to enjoy us a nice dinner. Then this feller"—he nodded toward Perley—"came in and started bellyachin' about a cup of coffee."

"That ain't exactly the way I heard it," McQueen replied. "I heard you two were disturbin' the peace. We don't stand for any rough treatment of the women who work in this dinin' room, or any rough language, either." He looked at Perley then, knowing he hadn't started any trouble. "Perley, you got anything to say?"

"Not much, Sheriff," Perley replied. "I think these fellows just forgot their manners. They're new in town and don't know how to act in a peaceful place of business. But there ain't any need to lock 'em up, if they'll just finish their dinner and get on outta here. That oughta be all right, wouldn't it, Beulah?"

Beulah Walsh, who was witnessing the confrontation from the kitchen door, shrugged and answered. "I reckon, if they agree not to cause no more trouble."

"Seems to me you ain't hearin' but one side of this argument," Leonard Watts declared. "That feller, there, is the one oughta go to jail. He as much as called Jesse out, but we'll finish up and get on outta here, anyway. Ain't no need to put us in jail."

"Leonard's right," Jesse added. "We ain't gonna start nothin', but I ain't gonna back down if he calls me out."

McQueen couldn't suppress a little smile. "Well, that

would be a different matter. If Perley called you out, you'd have a right to defend yourself." He looked at Beulah to see if she was satisfied to let them remain.

She nodded and asked, "You wanna sit down and have a cup of coffee or something, Sheriff?" He had already eaten there earlier, but she figured it would ensure the peace if he stayed awhile.

"As long as I'm here, I might as well," McQueen said. "I'll just sit down over here." He walked over and sat down at a table near the one that held the weapons. "I'll make sure Perley don't call one of your customers out," he couldn't resist saying.

"I'll get you some coffee," Lucy sang out, and went into the kitchen with Beulah and Becky.

Beulah fixed up a fresh plate for Perley, since the first one had begun to cool off. While she dished it out, Becky stopped Lucy on her way out with the sheriff's coffee to ask a question. "I thought I knew why you winked when you said you had to clear your throat. Why did you take a gulp of that coffee when that man dared you to?"

Lucy laughed. "'Cause it was just my spit in it. I was just glad he didn't want me to taste the other fellow's coffee. Beulah spit in his."

"That fellow was really puttin' the challenge out on you," Sonny said to Perley, his voice low so as not to be overheard at the table where the two strangers were rapidly finishing up their meal.

"It's just mostly big talk," Perley said. "He probably owns that gun on the table in the fast-draw holster, so he's always lookin' for some excuse to shoot somebody. I didn't want it to be one of us."

"I reckon it was a good thing Becky went to fetch the sheriff," Sonny said. "You mighta had to meet him out in the middle of the street."

"I wasn't gonna meet anybody out in the middle of the street," Perley insisted. "That's one of the dumbest things a man can do."

"I reckon you're right," Sonny allowed. He had heard rumors of how fast Perley was with a six-gun, although he had never witnessed it, himself. And he once overheard Perley's brother John telling Fred Farmer about an incident he had witnessed. Fred was older than the rest of the hands at the Triple-G and had been with the Gateses the longest of any of the men. John told him that Perley was like chain lightning when backed into a corner. He said Perley didn't know why he was so fast, something just fired in his brain when he had to act. John figured because he didn't understand that "gift," he was reluctant to use it. Thinking about that now, Sonny thought he would surely like to have been there with John to see for himself.

"Ain't you afraid they might go braggin' around town that you were too scared to face that bigmouth?" Link asked. Perley was his hero, and he didn't like to think there was a flaw in his hero. The man called Jesse had openly laid down a challenge to Perley, and Perley just tried to talk his way out of it.

"Doesn't make any difference to me what they say," Perley told him. "It's just words, and words get blown away by the first little breeze that comes along. Sometimes you might get caught where you ain't got no choice. There ain't much you can do then but try to do the best you can.

Anyway, it ain't nothin' but tomfools that pull a gun on another fellow just to see if he can get his out quicker. The folks that count are the folks you see and work with every day. And they know who you are, so it doesn't matter what some stranger passin' through town thinks about you. You understand that, don'tcha?"

"Yeah, I reckon so," Link answered, but he was still thinking he would have liked to have seen how fast Perley really was.

Chapter 2

When the two drifters finished eating, they left money on the table and walked toward the door. As they passed by the table where the three Triple-G hands were eating, Jesse reached down and knocked Perley's coffee cup over, causing him to jump backward to keep from getting his lap filled. He just managed to catch himself from going over backward with his chair. "Damn, Perley," Jesse mumbled. "Sorry 'bout that. That was kinda clumsy of me, weren't it? I'll be down at the saloon if you wanna do somethin' about it."

Perley reached over and grabbed Sonny's elbow when he started to jump to his feet. "No need to get excited," he said. "I didn't get any on me, and it needed warmin' up, anyway." He looked at McQueen and shook his head when the sheriff got to his feet.

As a precaution, the sheriff walked over to stand beside the weapons table while Jesse and Leonard picked up their guns. "You two are gettin' close to spendin' the night in my jail. You're damn lucky the man you been pickin' away at is a peaceful man or you mighta been sleepin' in the boneyard up on the hill."

"We ain't gonna cause no more trouble, Sheriff," Leonard was quick to assure him. "Come on, Jesse, we don't wanna spend the night in jail." They went out the door and McQueen followed them to watch them as they walked away.

When the two troublemakers reached Patton's Saloon and went inside, McQueen returned to the dining room. He was met at the door by Becky Morris. "You should have put them in jail," she said, "especially when that dirty-looking one knocked Perley's cup over."

"Perley's after the same thing I am," the sheriff told her. "And that's to keep from havin' gunfights in our street and endangerin' the good folks in this town. I'm beholden to him for not answerin' that saddle tramp's challenge." He glanced at Perley and nodded his thanks. He was well aware of Perley's skill with a six-shooter, but he also knew that the young man's lightning-like reflexes were not something Perley liked to display. He slowly shook his head when he thought about Perley's dilemma. McQueen had never met a more peaceful man than Perley Gates. His father had placed a tremendous burden on his youngest son's shoulders when he named him for the boy's grand-father. McQueen could only assume that God, in His mercy, compensated for the name by endowing the boy with reflexes akin to those of a striking rattlesnake.

When he realized Becky was still standing there, as if waiting for him to say more, he thanked her for the coffee. "I'd best get back to shoein' that horse," he said, referring to the job he was in the middle of when Becky came to find him. It brought to mind a subject that had been in his thoughts a lot lately. The town was growing so fast that he felt it already called for a full-time sheriff, instead of one who was also a part-time blacksmith.

"Thanks for coming, Sheriff," Becky said, turned, and went back to the table where Lucy and Beulah were already warning Perley to be careful when he left the dining room. "They're right, Perley," Becky said. "Those two are just looking for trouble."

And like John and Rubin like to say, if there ain't but one cow pie in the whole state of Texas, Perley will most likely step in it, was the thought in Perley's mind. To Becky, however, he said, "Nothin' to worry about. We've already got the wagon loaded with the supplies we came after, so we'll be headin' straight to the ranch when we leave here. Besides, I've got Sonny and Link to take care of me. Ain't that right, Link?" Link looked undecided. Perley continued, "So, I'm gonna take my time to enjoy this fine meal Beulah cooked. By the time I'm finished, those fellows probably won't even remember me."

"I hope you're right," Becky said, and turned her attention to some of the other customers, who were waiting for coffee refills. The room returned to its usual atmosphere of peaceful dining.

Just as he said he would, Perley took his time to enjoy his dinner and some idle conversation with Becky and Lucy, plus a pause to stick his head inside the kitchen door to wish Beulah a happy birthday. Unfortunately, it provided enough time for his two antagonists to think of another way to entertain themselves at his expense. "We saw them two fellers ol' Perley met with when they drove that wagon around to the side of the buildin'," Jesse recalled as he and

Leonard walked out on the porch of the saloon. "But he came from that inside door from the hotel."

"Yeah, he did," Leonard replied, wondering what that had to do with anything.

"Look yonder at that bay horse tied out front of the hotel," Jesse said, a grin slowly spreading across his unshaven face. "I'm thinkin' that's ol' Perley's horse. I bet you he ain't got a room in the hotel. He just tied his horse out there."

Still not quite sure what his friend was driving at, Leonard asked, "Maybe, so what about it?"

"I'm thinkin' about borrowin' his horse for a little ride," Jesse answered, his grin spreading from ear to ear now. "See if that don't get his dander up enough to make him do somethin' about it."

"Damned if you ain't got the itch awful bad to shoot somebody, ain't you? How do you know how fast he is?"

"I know he ain't faster'n me," Jesse crowed. "I just don't like his attitude—like he's too good to have to stand up like a man." He continued to grin at Leonard, waiting for him to show some enthusiasm for the caper. When Leonard remained indifferent, Jesse announced, "Well, I'm gonna take that bay for a little ride up and down this street a few times, till ol' Perley shows his yellow self."

"What if it ain't his horse?" Leonard asked.

"Then I'll just say, *Beg your pardon, sir,* and if whoever owns him don't like it, we can settle it with six-guns." Jesse didn't wait for more discussion but headed straight for the hotel. Thinking it was bound to provide some entertainment, no matter who owned the horse, Leonard followed along behind him. He didn't think it was a good idea, and Jesse's brothers wouldn't like for him to draw any more attention to them. But he knew better than to tell Jesse not to do something.

When he walked up to the hitching rail, Jesse took a quick look toward the front door of the hotel. Seeing no one, he untied Buck's reins from the rail and turned the bay gelding toward the street. "You're a good-lookin' horse for a jasper like that to be ridin'. It's time to let you feel a man on your back." He put a foot in the stirrup and climbed up. While he was throwing his right leg over, Buck lowered his head toward the ground and reared up on his front legs, causing the unsuspecting Jesse to do a somersault in midair and land hard on the ground in front of the horse. "Damn you!" Jesse spat as he tried to gather himself. "You like to broke my back!"

It only made matters worse when Leonard whooped and hollered, "Hot damn, Jesse! You never said nothin' about flyin'. Looks to me like that horse don't wanna be rode."

"Well, he's gonna be," Jesse announced emphatically and got back up on his feet. "C'mere, you hardheaded plug." Buck didn't move but stood watching the strange man as he advanced cautiously toward him. "You fooled me with that trick, but I ain't gonna be fooled this time." The horse remained stone still as Jesse walked slowly up to him and took the reins again.

Leonard bit his lip to keep from laughing, urging Jesse on. "Watch him, Jesse, he's waitin' to give you another flip."

"He does and I'll shoot the fool crowbait," Jesse said. "He ain't as ornery as he thinks he is." Buck continued to watch Jesse with a wary eye, but he remained as still as a statue. Trying again to approach the stone-still horse, Jesse kept talking calmly. "You just hold still, ol' boy, till I get settled in the saddle. Then I'll run some of the steam outta you." With his foot in the stirrup again, he took a good grip on the saddle horn, then stood there on one leg before attempting to climb into the saddle. Still he paused, waiting to catch the horse by surprise. When he was ready, he suddenly pulled himself up to land squarely in the saddle. Buck did not flinch. He remained still as a statue. "Now, you're showin' some sense, horse." He looked over at Leonard and grinned. "All he needed was for . . ." That was as far as he got before the big bay gelding exploded. With all four legs stiff as poles, the horse bounced around and around in a circle while Jesse held on for dear life. When that didn't rid him of his rider, the incensed gelding started a series of bucks that ended when Jesse was finally thrown, landing on the hotel porch to slide up against a corner post.

With the fuse on his temper burning brightly now, Jesse rolled over on the rough boards of the porch, his hands and knees skinned under his clothes. He scrambled on all fours to recover his .44, which had been knocked out of his holster when he landed on the porch. When he had the pistol in hand, he turned to level it at the offending horse. "Damn you, you four-legged devil, I'm sendin' you back to hell where you came from!" He cocked the pistol at almost the same time his hand was smashed by the .44 slug that knocked the weapon free.

Jesse screamed with the pain in his hand as he turned to see Perley standing in the doorway, his six-gun trained on him. "I'm willin' to ignore your childish behavior when it ain't doin' any harm," Perley said. "But you're goin' too far when you mess with my horse." He glanced over at Leonard, standing in the street, to make sure he wasn't showing any signs of retaliation. He wasn't, after having witnessed the swiftness of the shot just fired. Perley looked back at Jesse. "I'm sure Sheriff McQueen heard that shot and he'll be up here pretty quick to find out who did the shootin'. My advice to both of you is to get on your horses and get outta town before he gets here. If you do, I'll tell him it was just an accidental discharge of a weapon. If you don't, you're goin' to jail. So, what's it gonna be?"

"We're gettin' outta town," Leonard said at once. "We don't want no more trouble." He hurried over to the edge of the porch. "Come on, Jesse, he's right, it's best we get outta town. You can't go to jail right now."

Jesse was in too much pain to argue. He picked up his pistol with his left hand and let Leonard help him off the porch. "I might be seein' you again, Perley," he had to threaten as he went down the one step to the street.

"Come on," Leonard urged him. "Let's get outta here and find a place to take a look at that hand."

Perley stepped out into the street to watch them hurry to the saloon, where their horses were tied. They galloped past the blacksmith's forge just as Paul McQueen came walking out to the street. He paused to take a look at the two departing riders. Then, when he saw Perley standing out in front of the hotel, he headed that way. By the time he walked up there, Sonny and Link were there as well. "Wasn't that those two in the dinin' room before?" the sheriff asked.

"Yep," Perley answered. "They decided it best to leave town before they wound up in your jailhouse." When McQueen asked about the shot he heard, Perley told him he fired it and why. "I did the best I could to avoid trouble with those two, but that one that kept pickin' at me was fixin' to shoot my horse. So I had to keep him from doin' that."

"You shot him?" McQueen asked.

"Just in the hand," Perley replied. "I told 'em you'd be on your way to most likely put 'em in jail, so they decided to leave town."

"Good," the sheriff said, "'cause it don't look like I'm ever gonna get done shoein' Luther Rains's horse."

"Sorry you were bothered," Perley said. "If you do get called out again, it won't be on account of me. We're fixin' to head back to the Triple-G right now."

"I know it ain't your fault, Perley. You don't ever cause any trouble," the sheriff said. To himself, he thought, *but damned if trouble doesn't have a way of finding you*. He turned away and went back to finish his work at his forge. He had put his wife and son on the train the day before for a trip to visit her family in Kansas City. So he was trying to take advantage of the opportunity to catch up with some of his work as a blacksmith. Maybe if Perley stayed out of town for a while, he could get more done. As soon as he thought it, he scolded himself for thinking anything negative about Perley.

"He was gonna shoot Buck, so you had to shoot that feller, right, Perley?" Link was eager to confirm. His admiration for Perley had wavered a bit after having witnessed Perley's reluctance to fight before. But now his faith was restored.

"That's right, Link. There wasn't any time to talk him

out of it. It's too bad it takes a gun to talk somebody outta doin' something stupid." He glanced down the street to see a few people coming out into the street, curious to see what the gunshot was about, so he climbed up into the saddle. "Let's go home before Rubin sends somebody after us."

When they reached a small stream approximately five miles south of Paris, Leonard Watts said, "Let's pull up here and take a look at your hand." He dismounted and waited for Jesse to pull up beside him. "Is it still bleedin' pretty bad?"

"Hell, yeah, it's still bleedin'," Jesse complained painfully. "I think it broke all the bones in my hand." He had bound his bandanna around the wounded hand as tightly as he could, but the bandanna was thoroughly soaked.

"Come on," Leonard said, "let's wash some of the blood off and see how bad it is." He helped Jesse down from his horse and they knelt beside the stream to clean the hand. After he had cleared some of the blood away, he said, "The bullet went all the way through."

"Hell, I know that," Jesse retorted, "you can see the mark on the grip of my Colt. And I can't move my fingers."

"Well, quit tryin' to move 'em. That just makes it bleed more. Lemme get a rag outta my saddlebag, and I'll try to bind it tight enough to hold it till we get back to camp. Micah can take a look at it and see what we gotta do. You might have to ride down to Sulphur Springs. They got a doctor there."

"That sneakin' egg-suckin' dog," Jesse muttered. "I oughta go back and call him out with my left hand."

Leonard shook his head. "I don't know, Jesse, that was a helluva shot that feller made, comin' outta the doorway when he done it. You weren't lookin' at him when he shot you, but I was lookin' right at him when he opened the door. And his gun was in the holster when he started to step out. I don't know," he repeated.

"I reckon that was the reason you never thought about pullin' your gun," Jesse grunted sarcastically. "He was just lucky as hell," he insisted. "He was tryin' to shoot me anywhere and just happened to hit my hand."

"I don't know," Leonard said once again, thinking he had seen what he had seen, and knowing he had never seen anyone faster. Finished with his bandaging then, he said, "Maybe that'll hold you till we get back to the others." Jesse's two brothers were waiting at a camp on the Sulphur River and that was fully ten or eleven miles from where they now stood. Leonard didn't raise the subject with Jesse, but he was thinking Micah and Lucas were not going to be very happy to learn of the attention he and Jesse had called upon themselves in Paris. Their purpose for visiting the town was to take a look at the recently opened bank while Micah and Lucas rode down to Sulphur Springs to look at that bank. Their camp was halfway between the two towns and the plan had been to go to the towns in the morning, look them over, and meet back at the river that afternoon. It was easy for Leonard to forget his part in encouraging Jesse's behavior and then blame him for causing them to be one man short in the planned robbery. *I reckon he can at least hold the horses while we do the real business,* he thought. "We'd best get goin'," he said to Jesse.

Leonard was right on the mark when he figured that Jesse's older brothers were not going to be happy to hear the cause for his wounded hand. "What the hell were you two thinkin'?" Lucas demanded. "We told you to lay low while you were up there and not attract any attention. So you decided to challenge somebody to have a gunfight out in the middle of the street? I swear, no wonder Ma and Pa decided not to have no more young 'uns after you popped out." He looked at the eldest brother, who was busy examining Jesse's hand. "Whaddaya think, Micah? Think we just oughta hit that bank in Sulphur Springs? It's been there a lot longer than the one they looked at, but there is a damn guard."

"Yeah, and they got a pretty tough sheriff, too," Micah replied. He turned to Leonard and asked, "Tell me what you did find out when you weren't tryin' to get everybody to notice you."

"I swear, Micah," Leonard responded, "we did look the town over. It didn't take long. It ain't a big town, not as big as Sulphur Springs. The bank's new, and they ain't got no guards workin' there. It'd be easy to knock it over. They got a sheriff, but he's just part-time. Most of the time he works in a blacksmith shop. I don't think they'd be able to get up a posse to amount to much. And there weren't but a few people that got a look at me and Jesse. Besides, we'd be wearin' bandannas over our faces, anyway."

"Right," Lucas scoffed, "and one of the bandannas would be blood soaked on the feller with a bandaged-up hand. How 'bout it, Micah? Is he gonna have to go see a doctor about that hand?"

"Well, it ain't good, but it coulda been busted up a lot worse. Just feelin' around on it, I think it mighta broke one of them little bones in there but not all of 'em. It just went straight through. If he can stand it, I think a doctor can wait till we get the hell outta Texas." He turned to Jesse then. "What do you say, Jesse? Can you make it?"

Jesse took a look at his bandaged right hand and cursed. "Yeah," he decided. "I can wait till we get our business done here and get gone."

Micah studied him for a long moment before deciding Jesse was not just blowing smoke. Considering what he now knew about the two possible targets for bank robbery, he made his thoughts known to the others. "Right now, I'm thinkin' that Paris bank is the smartest move, especially since we're short a man. It's smaller, not well guarded, and they've got a part-time sheriff. There's one other thing I like about it, it's a lot closer to the Red River, only about sixteen miles and we'd be in Indian Territory. I'm thinkin' that right there would discourage any posse they might get up to come after us. Sulphur Springs is more like fifty miles before we could slip into Oklahoma Indian Territory. It's been a while since we were up that way, but ol' Doc O'Shea is most likely still over at Durant Station. If your hand don't show signs of healin', we can let him take a look at it."

"If the old fool ain't drank hisself to death by now," Lucas said. Dr. Oliver O'Shea was a competent physician when he was sober, so it was said. They knew that he was adequate even when drunk, since that was the only state in which they had ever seen him.

There was no disagreement on the plan from any of the four after they discussed it a little further. They decided Micah was right in his opinion that there was less of a gamble on their part if they struck the smaller town. "All right, then," Lucas declared, "I reckon we'll ride on up to Paris tomorrow, camp outside of town tomorrow night, so the horses will be rested up good. Then we can go to the bank the next mornin' to make a withdrawal. That'll be a Friday. That's a good day to go to the bank."

Chapter 3

"What's Sonny talkin' about—you shootin' somebody?" Possum Smith wanted to know. He had had some second thoughts about not going into town with Perley. It was only natural that he would, since they had been constant companions ever since Perley accompanied him and Emma Slocum to Bison Gap. He counted himself fortunate to have crossed paths with Perley and he had not hesitated to go back to Perley's home at the Triple-G Ranch with him.

"Oh, it was just a little discussion with a couple of saddle tramps in the dinin' room at the hotel," Perley said. "Didn't amount to much."

"Sonny said you shot some fellow," Possum insisted. "That sounds like more than a discussion."

"I shot a fellow in the hand 'cause he was fixin' to shoot Buck," Perley said, knowing Possum would whittle away at him until he got the whole story. "That was the end of it. They got on their horses and left town."

Possum just shook his head, knowing that Perley had stepped in another cow pie, just as Rubin and John always predicted. He admitted that it often seemed the case, but he thought most of the time it was Perley's father's fault for naming him what he did. "I shoulda gone into town with you instead of Sonny," he finally said. During the last couple of years, it had been his lot to partner with Perley in some dangerous business while they were down in Bison Gap. It had served to form a bond between the older Possum and the young Perley. Consequently, Possum felt a certain responsibility toward Perley. Perley appreciated Possum's concern, but he felt he was getting to be like his guardian or something, and that was the last thing Perley needed. "Why was he gonna shoot your horse?" Possum asked, refusing to give up until he got the complete story.

"'Cause he tried to ride him and got thrown," Perley replied. "At least, that's what a fellow who was standin' in front of the saloon told me. I was still in the hotel when that happened. So that's the whole story."

"I swear, trouble follows you like stink follows a hog," Possum declared before he finally let the incident rest.

"Talk to Buck," Perley replied. "He's the one who wouldn't let him ride."

Friday morning dawned in Paris with the arrival of four riders, two of whom were strangers to the little Texas town. One of the other two wore a heavy glove on his right hand. They led two packhorses casually along the wide main street past the hotel at the lower end, across from the railroad tracks. Wilford Taylor, president of the First National Bank of Paris, paid them no particular mind as they walked their horses past the bank, which was just beyond the hotel. James Bedford and Thomas Deal, his two tellers, were standing at the door, waiting for Taylor to unlock it. "Good morning," he offered cheerfully as he inserted his key in the heavy lock.

"Good morning, sir," both men replied, almost as one. They anticipated a busy afternoon following a growing trend for the new bank on Fridays. The bank had been well received by the merchants of the little town as well as many of the farms and ranches close around. Taylor had invested heavily in his banking enterprise, counting on the potential of the little town. He could already foresee the need to employ a full-time custodian, but for the time being, his tellers took care of cleaning up the premises when they were not busy with customers. With the sign on the door still turned to CLOSED, Taylor went in the back to get the cash drawers out of the safe while his tellers went about the business of raising the shades in the windows and front door. They were still in the process when someone tapped on the front door.

Thomas Deal glanced at the big clock on the wall as he went to the door. "It'll just be five minutes before the bank opens," he announced loud enough to be heard by the smiling man on the other side of the glass.

"Five minutes?" Micah Sage responded. He held a pouch up that looked to be stuffed quite full and showed it to Deal. "You mind if I wait inside?"

"I reckon that would be all right," Deal answered, thinking the man wanted to deposit some cash. He looked over at Bedford and got a shrug of indifference from him, so he turned the key in the lock. Micah went inside, holding the door open behind him for Lucas and Leonard, who had been waiting at the corner of the building where they couldn't be seen from inside. Not realizing what was happening, Deal blurted, "Wait! We're not open quite yet."

"That's all right," Micah said, "they're with me. We won't be long." Deal stared down in shocked disbelief at the .44 handgun now in the hand of the intruder.

When Bedford realized what was happening, he froze in his tracks, not knowing what to do, and stared at the pistol in Leonard Watts's hand. "Now, let's go around to your cages, little birds, and we'll see what you got in those cash drawers," Leonard said.

They walked the two tellers around the partition in time to meet Wilford Taylor coming from the safe, carrying the two drawers. Like his tellers, he froze when confronted with the bank robbers, one with a gun pointed at him. "Just set 'em down right there on the counter," Lucas Sage instructed. "Then me and you can go see what you've got in that safe."

"You're making a big mistake to think you can get away with this in broad daylight," Taylor was finally able to sputter.

"Well, we woulda waited till after dark to do it, but you ain't open at night," Lucas responded, grinning broadly. "What you need to worry about is to just do like I tell you, so I don't have to use this gun on you. Now get your ass back there to that safe." Since the safe was still open, Lucas had only to order Taylor to empty the money into the canvas bank sacks beside the safe. "Damn, there's more in there than I figured on," Lucas said. "How much is it?"

"I don't know the exact amount without looking at my ledger in my desk drawer," Taylor claimed. "I can get it for you."

"Well, now, that's mighty accommodatin' of ya," Lucas said. "Which drawer is it in?"

"Right there in my desk. I can get it for you."

"You just keep fillin' that sack," Lucas directed, and took a few steps backward until he felt the desk against the back of his legs. Then he looked down quickly and opened the top desk drawer. "Good thing I looked for you. There's a Colt Peacemaker in this drawer. You mighta shot yourself by accident when you reached for this book." He took the pistol out and stuck it in his belt. "Now, why don't you give me a rough estimate of how much is in that safe? You don't need to look in the ledger. You know how much you've got."

"There's roughly forty-eight thousand dollars," Taylor sadly admitted when there was no use not to. When he saw the look of surprise on Lucas's face, he made a desperate request for mercy. "Most of that money is mine, that I invested to start up this bank until it can generate enough on its own. I beg you to leave me some of it to operate the bank."

Lucas studied the desperate man for a long moment before responding. "I'm not an unreasonable man. I can understand what a fix this is gonna leave you in, so I'll work with you." He looked at the safe, now empty of cash money. He took the sack from Taylor and peered in it. "Yep, there's plenty for us. I'll leave you a little to operate the bank on." He slipped a twenty-dollar bill out of a pack of bills and put it on the desk. "There you go, you can operate on that." He favored Taylor with a wide grin then called out, "You done out there?" When Micah answered, saying they were ready to go, Lucas said, "Bring 'em on back here."

When the two tellers were herded back in the office, Lucas pointed to a supply closet in the corner. "That's as good a place as any," he said, and they put the three of them inside. Since the closet door opened to the outside, Micah propped a side chair under the knob, figuring that would hold long enough for their escape.

"I swear, this whole thing was awful easy," Micah declared. "Too damned easy, as a matter of fact."

"That ain't the best part," Lucas replied. "Wait till I tell you how much money he had in this scrawny little bank."

Becky Morris took a few steps inside and stopped. The sign on the door said the bank was closed, but the door was standing open. She could hear voices in the back office behind the cages, but it was strange for no one to be in the teller cages. Suddenly, three strange men carrying canvas bags walked out. Then she recognized Leonard from the other day and immediately turned to run, only to be met at the door by Jesse Sage. She screamed.

"Shut up!" Jesse commanded. "I'll put a bullet in your head!" He grabbed her by the front of her blouse with his left hand, pushing her on inside. Well aware of what was happening, she screamed again, forcing him to release her blouse in order to backhand her, knocking her to the floor.

"What tha . . . ?" That was all Micah got out before he heard the chair holding the closet door give way, apparently in response to the young woman's screams. He turned and fired two quick shots through the door of the office to stop any heroic attempt by the three men. "First one through that door gets a round in the belly," he warned. It served to stop any attempt to come to the lady's rescue, but it also sounded an alarm to prevent their quiet departure from town. Seeing Jesse standing over Becky, Micah demanded, "What are you doin' in here? Where are the horses?"

"They're right out front," Jesse replied. "Everything was goin' good until she showed up. She'd seen Leonard before, so I came in to keep her from runnin' to the sheriff."

"Well, we'd better get the hell outta here now," Lucas said, "since we woke the whole damn town up." He went to the door and looked up and down the street. When he saw someone running toward the sheriff's office, he exclaimed. "We've got to go now! Bring her!" he said to Leonard. "We may need her!" Once he was up in the saddle, with the sack of money secured, he said, "Put her up behind me." And when Leonard put her up behind him, Lucas told her to wrap her arms around his waist. "You'd best hold on to me, sister, 'cause if you let go, I'll put a bullet in you for sure." To encourage her, he added, "I'll let you go, soon as we get outta town." Too terrified to resist, she did as he directed.

Sheriff Paul McQueen came out of his office door with Bill Simmons, the barber, right behind him. Simmons pointed toward the bank. "They're holdin' up the bank!" he cried. "Look yonder!" McQueen ran toward the bank, his six-gun drawn, but could not get there before the four robbers galloped off past the stable on the north road.

"Don't shoot!" James Bedford exclaimed. "They took Becky Morris!" McQueen checked his shot just in time when he realized it was Becky holding on behind the last rider galloping away. Wilford Taylor and Thomas Deal ran out in the street and frantically began telling the sheriff about the robbery and the abduction.

Within minutes, the dining room in the hotel emptied onto the street, with Beulah and Lucy among the crowd. Since she didn't see Becky anywhere, Lucy ran over to the sheriff. "Paul, have you seen Becky? She just went to the bank to get money for the cash drawer."

"They took her," McQueen answered. "Sat her down behind the last rider, so I couldn't take a chance on shootin' at 'em." He shook his head slowly in sympathy with Lucy's immediate look of despair. "Maybe they'll let her go, since they got outta town okay." There was nothing he could do to comfort her, so he turned his attention back to what he could do.

"I need volunteers right now!" McQueen announced. There were not many to volunteer. Walt Carver, who owned the stable, was the first, then Simmons and Luther Rains, but at least they all hustled to saddle up as quickly as possible. They managed to get under way in less than thirty minutes. "They took off on the north road," McQueen said, "so it figures they're countin' on headin' for Injun Territory. The Triple-G's between here and the Red River. We'll stop there and see if some of their hands will volunteer to go with us."

"I'm volunteerin', Paul," Walt Carver commented. "And that's because they took the little Morris girl, but I don't know how good a chance we have to catch 'em. They got a pretty good head start, and the Oklahoma border ain't but sixteen miles from here."

McQueen agreed with him but didn't say so. They had to make an effort to catch them, hoping maybe they would stop somewhere to count the money. Knowing what a sweet and innocent young woman Becky was, he prayed they had not taken her with any intent beyond keeping anyone from shooting at them. He sincerely hoped they would release her right away, after she had served her purpose as a shield in their escape. When they were all ready, the four-man posse rode out the north road after the four outlaws, with McQueen lacking confidence in the matchup, should it come to a confrontation. He counted heavily on offsetting the outlaws' advantage with the addition of some of the Triple-G hands, although it would add more time to the head start the outlaws already had.

There were only two of the Triple-G Ranch hands at the headquarters when the sheriff rode in with his three-man posse. Sonny Rice and Fred Farmer were working on some stalls in the stable that were in need of repair. Ollie Dinkler came out of his kitchen next to the bunkhouse when he saw the posse ride in. "Howdy, Sheriff," Ollie greeted him. "What you boys doin' out this way? Some-body burn the town down?" He recognized the business-men riding with the sheriff, so he figured there was something unusual going on.

"Howdy, Ollie," McQueen responded. He knew Ollie from a couple of overnight drunks Ollie had slept off in the jail. He wasted no time explaining his purpose.

Ollie was properly sorry to hear of the bank robbery, but like the members of the posse, he was especially con-cerned for the fate of Becky Morris. "I swear, Sheriff," he said, "there ain't nobody here right now but Sonny and Fred. I expect they'll go with you, though. I can't go 'cause I'm just gettin' started to cook some grub for the boys to eat for dinner."

"Where's Perley?" McQueen asked, thinking there wasn't a better shot in the county. With his posse made up so far with the likes of the barber and the older men,

Luther Rains and Walt Carver, he could use a little more firepower.

"Him and Possum are workin' with his brother John and Charlie Ramey over toward Widow Creek, roundin' up some strays," Ollie said. "They won't be back till in the mornin' sometime, most likely."

That was disappointing news to McQueen. "How 'bout you two?" he asked Fred and Sonny, who had joined the discussion by that time.

"Sure," Sonny said right away, "I'll go with you. I got a look at two of those fellows you're talkin' about and they were bad news." Fred volunteered to go as well, so they saddled a couple of horses and the posse returned to the north road to resume its pursuit of the bank robbers.

Back on the road, the posse picked up the tracks they had followed up to the trail to the Triple-G and started up again from there. Due to a recent rain, the fresh tracks left by Micah Sage and his party were easily picked up on the narrow wagon road, so they continued following them. It soon became obvious that the outlaws were intent upon driving their horses without rest until they crossed the Red River. So there was really no careful tracking to be done.

The posse moved along the road at a steady pace, hoping to make up for some of the time already lost, but it was noontime by the time they reached the Red. They had to stop there to rest the horses, since they had pushed them pretty hard. There was plenty of grass for the horses, but there were no provisions for food for the riders. Ollie Dinkler had just been in the process of starting to fix dinner when they left the Triple-G, so he didn't even have any biscuits or bacon ready to send with them. Empty bellies soon began to dominate stout hearts as the men sat around waiting for the horses to rest up. The best they could do was to build a fire to sit around and discuss their possibilities.

"You know, I feel as bad as anybody about that woman bein' kidnapped," Walt Carver declared as he poked at the fire with a dead limb. "And I don't want to discourage anybody, but once we cross this river, there's trails leadin' every whichaway. It's gonna be damned hard to figure out which one they took."

"I reckon you're right about that," Luther Rains commented. "We might as well be whistlin' in the wind. They ain't been goin' to no trouble a-tall to try to hide their tracks, but you can bet it'll be a different story once they cross the river."

"I'm thinkin' about some responsibilities I've got back at the stable," Carver continued. "There's folks thinkin' that I'm takin' care of their horses. I'm afraid I'm gonna have to leave you fellers here and go on back. I hate to say it, but we ain't got a chance in hell of catchin' up with those outlaws." He looked at the sheriff. "I hope you don't hold it against me, Paul, but I've got customers to think about."

"I reckon that's up to you, Walt," McQueen said. "Anybody else think there ain't no use in goin' on?"

"I didn't think we had much chance at the start," Bill Simmons replied. "I was just gonna go along with everybody else, just in case we got lucky."

"How 'bout you boys from the Triple-G?" the sheriff asked.

"I'll go over and scout around for some sign with you, if you want, Sheriff," Fred Farmer offered. "They're most likely right, I expect, if the men we're chasin' have got any brains a-tall, they'll ride up or down the river before they come outta the water. Then they'll go to some trouble to hide their tracks. It won't be as easy as it was followin' their tracks on the road. So, what we're lookin' at is a long time tryin' to track these buzzards down. And we ain't got food, beddin', or nothin' else for a long time out on a scout."

"It's pretty plain to me that Fred's right," Luther spoke up. "We had good intentions and every man here would keep goin', if it made any sense to. But those four outlaws are gone and we ain't got a prayer of catchin' 'em. I'm sorry for the girl, but I expect I'll head on back home when my horse is ready to go. It's a long ride back to town."

They all looked at the sheriff after Luther's statement, waiting for his reaction. "I reckon I can't really disagree with anything you said," he responded. "My responsibilities are back in the town as well. And I'll tell you the truth, if I thought we had just one chance in hell of catchin' those outlaws, I'd try to talk you out of turnin' back. But the truth is, they got away. They had too much head start on us, but we did what we could. When the horses are ready to go, we might as well all go on back home." His statement was followed by a long moment of silence, filled with some solemn nodding of heads and the general feeling that they had answered the call, but it was just not in the cards for any success. So they turned around without so much as a look on the Oklahoma side of the river and returned home.

It was a not a happy return for the sheriff's posse. Wilford Taylor waited in the hotel dining room with the owner of the hotel, Amos Johnson, who was also the new mayor of the town. It was suppertime, and Beulah helped Lucy serve the guests in Becky's absence. Raymond Patton, owner of Patton's Saloon, came to the hotel to let them know Sheriff McQueen's posse had just returned. He said he told McQueen they were in the dining room and the sheriff said he would be there as soon as he left his horse with Walt Carver.

Beulah and Lucy stood by the table while Paul McQueen made his sad report. Wilford Taylor did not make a sound when he heard of the robbers' clean escape, but he bit his lip until blood was seen in his beard. Beulah hung her head and muttered a prayer over and over in her grief for Becky Morris. Lucy Tate, who had often teased the young girl, sometimes to the point of cruelty, wept openly. When it was done, the two women, as women will, pulled themselves together and fixed some supper for the sheriff, since he had not eaten since breakfast.

"I shoulda took that damn check over to the bank, myself," Beulah moaned as she filled her big coffeepot at the pump. "Those bank robbers woulda played hell tryin' to tote me off on a horse."

CHAPTER 4

"Hell, ain't no tellin' where this old Injun trail leads to," Jesse Sage complained as he followed along behind his older brother Micah. His hand throbbed constantly, making sure he didn't forget his wound for a moment. He was the only one of the four outlaws harboring any negative feelings at all after the successful robbery of the bank. The other three were downright cheerful, considering how well everything had gone for them. All three were of the opinion Jesse deserved to suffer for the stupid attempt to shoot the bay horse just because he couldn't ride him.

"It don't matter where it leads to," Micah responded to Jesse's complaint about the trail they had chosen to follow. "It's goin' in the right direction, due west, so we might as well stay on it till we wind up in Durant or somewhere close to it. If this trail changes direction, we'll just leave it and keep headin' west." He was not concerned about any pursuit. If there was a posse after them, they would likely have caught up to them when they stopped to rest the horses, so now he knew they were in the clear. It was no longer necessary to push their horses hard. Leonard had expressed concern about a posse while they were taking their ease while the horses rested. Micah had assured him that, if they even formed a posse, they wouldn't follow them across the Red. And he was smug now in the knowledge that he had evidently been right. The knowledge that they were rich was a comforting thought as well. They had counted the money during the rest stop to see if Wilford Taylor had been accurate in his estimate of the amount. It was hard to believe there had been that amount of cash money in the little bank, still in its birth stages, but it was all there, a little more than the forty-eight thousand Taylor had said.

Micah turned to look back at the one negative he saw in their holdup of the bank. Perched on top of the packs on one of the packhorses now, her eyes still red from crying, sat the young woman named Becky. He had tried to persuade Lucas to release her back at the river, but he and Jesse both insisted on keeping her. "Holdin' a young girl like that ain't gonna be nothin' but constant trouble," Micah had said. "Hell, you're rich now. You can buy all the women you want."

"Yeah, but this little heifer ain't never been rode, I bet," Lucas said. "And that ain't somethin' money can buy." He looked back at the captive girl. "Ain't that right, darlin'?"

Having pleaded for Lucas to let her go ever since they were successfully away from town, Becky was certain her hopes were in vain. All thoughts of a posse coming to rescue her were abandoned after hearing their confident talk that any posse would turn back at the river. Almost struck helpless in her fear for what was to be her fate at the hands of these outlaws, she tried desperately to think of some way to escape. The only thing she could think of that might save her was something she wasn't convinced they would believe. But she was desperate to the point where she would make an attempt. "You'll be sorry if you mess with me," she managed to force out.

"Is that so?" Jesse replied, at once amused. "What makes you say that?"

"'Cause I was rode once and I got the sickness down there. If you ride me, you'll get it, too, and then you'll wanna kill me."

No one responded to her claim at first. Then Micah asked, "You mean you're dirty down there?"

"Yes, sir," Becky sobbed. "It wasn't my fault. I didn't wanna do it and now I get those terrible pains and nasty cleanups."

"Hell, I don't believe that," Lucas said. "You're lyin'. How come they're lettin' you work in the dinin' room, if you've got the sickness?"

"They don't know, and if they find out, I'll be in a heap of trouble," she cried. She hadn't thought about that. "I've been trying not to let them know, but it's getting worse every day."

"Damn it," Micah cursed. "I told you she'd be nothin' but trouble, but you had to bring her with us. Now, whaddaya gonna do? You believe her? You gonna take a chance she ain't tellin' the truth?" He waited a few moments for an answer. When there wasn't one right away, he said, "It'd be the best thing to just shoot her in the head and put her out of her misery, same as if she had rabies." Becky's heart almost stopped to hear his cold solution to the problem.

"I still think she's lyin'," Jesse insisted. "Look at her. She looks as innocent as a newborn lamb. Ain't that right, Becky darlin'? You ain't never been rode in your life, have you?"

"I'm not lying. I'm just trying to keep you from catching the sickness, too. Just let me go and I'll walk back home," she pleaded.

"Why don't you just hold your horses till we get to Doc O'Shea's?" Jesse suggested to Lucas. "We'll be in Durant tomorrow. Let Doc take a look at her and see what he says. If he says she ain't got no sickness, you can go to it."

"What about it, Lucas?" Micah asked. "Can you control your lust till tomorrow night?"

"You act like I'm the only one interested in takin' Miss Becky for a ride," Lucas replied. "Yeah, I can wait." He turned to look back at her again. "And if Doc says you're lyin' about this, you're gonna get a whuppin' after you been rode hard."

Fearful that she had succeeded only in delaying her torment by one night, Becky could only hold on to the packs she used as a saddle and pray for a miracle she was afraid would never happen. When they finally stopped to make camp for the night, she was not pressed into service as a cook for them. She had expected to be forced to do the cooking, but evidently, she had planted a seed of doubt, and they'd rather not have her handling their food. When they had finished their supper, Lucas gave her some bacon and hardtack before tying her to a tree for the night. She remained awake long after the four men had gone to sleep, fearful that one of them might decide she was lying and succumb to his lust. However, exhaustion finally claimed her, and she reluctantly closed her eyes and gave in to the urge to sleep.

When morning came, Lucas untied her after she pleaded that she needed to go to the bushes. "The sickness makes it extra hard to go and very painful," she said. "I can't go with you watching me. I don't want you to see the sickening mess I make."

It made him pause to think about that, but he was still not ready to accept her story about the sickness she claimed to have. Reluctantly, he finally let her seek the cover of the bushes by the stream. "But I better see you shake them bushes every time I tell you to. You understand?" She said that she did and just as a precaution, he made her go downstream to do her business. "What the hell are you grinnin' at?" Lucas demanded when he turned and saw the grins of amusement on the faces of Jesse and Micah.

"You, you damn fool," Micah answered him. "Get your little heifer saddled up and let's get started to Durant."

"You know, I ain't sure I'm gonna share my little heifer with the three of you, since it looks like I'm the only one willin' to take care of her," Lucas told them.

"Remember I ain't said nothin' about her bein' a bother," Leonard was quick to claim.

"I didn't see you offerin' no help," Lucas countered. Thinking of his captive then, he called out to her. "You better let me see them bushes shakin' down there." There was no response to his order, so he raised his voice to a shout. "You hear me? You better shake them bushes or I'm comin' in there after you!" There was still no visible response in the berry thicket Becky had chosen to shield her private functions.

"She's run," Micah declared. There was a pause of a few seconds while that thought sank in, then all four of them ran to the thicket to search for her.

Already fifty yards downstream, Becky could hear her

captors blaring out her name as they beat the bushes close to the edge of the stream. Along with the calling of her name, there were threats of all kinds, if she didn't come forth. More terrified now than she had been before, she ran for all she was worth. For she had decided that her torture would be the same whether she tried to escape or submitted obediently. And she had made up her mind that morning that she would rather die trying to escape than to surrender to their cruelty.

"You boys got back early," Ollie Dinkler greeted Perley and Charlie Ramey when they walked into the cookhouse in time for breakfast. Perley's brother John walked in behind them, having decided to have breakfast with them on this morning, rather than having breakfast with the rest of the Gates family at the house, as hc usually did. "Set down and I'll fill you a plate. Fred and Sonny can tell you the news."

"What news is that?" John asked.

"Four fellers robbed the bank in Paris and headed for Injun Territory," Ollie answered. Fred and Sonny rode with the posse. Sheriff McQueen came by here lookin' for riders to go with him, so Fred and Sonny joined up."

"You know 'em, Perley," Sonny said. "One of 'em was that feller you shot."

"I swear," Perley said. "I can't say as I'm surprised. Did you catch up with 'em?"

"Shoot, no," Sonny replied. "We didn't even get close. They had too much head start. We got to the Red and them fellers from town was ready to turn around and go home."

"What?" Perley blurted when he next heard Fred speak.

"I said they grabbed that little girl that works in the hotel dinin' room—the one named Becky," the soft-spoken Fred Farmer repeated. "They carried her off with 'em."

"What? How did they get Becky?" Perley sputtered, immediately in a panic.

"The sheriff said she was in the bank when they robbed it," Fred told him, aware now that it was news of a more tragic nature to Perley. "One of the robbers stuck her on his horse behind him to keep anybody from shootin' at him."

"And you came back without Becky?" Perley asked, unable to believe they could. "Where did you lose them?"

"Like I said, at the river," Sonny answered. "We followed the road right to the river, but we never went across."

That Perley was extremely upset at the news was painfully obvious, more so to his brother John than to the other men. He, and possibly Possum Smith, were more aware of the feelings Perley had for Becky Morris, although Perley claimed there was nothing more than a mutual friendship. John caught Perley's eye and asked, simply, "You goin'?"

"I've got to, John," Perley answered quietly.

"I know," John returned. "You wanna take some of the men with you?"

"No, I don't need to take anybody," Perley replied. "I'll take a packhorse with some food and such. Buck's rested enough. He oughta be ready to go."

"You're talkin' about goin' after four dangerous men," John protested. "You can't go by yourself, Perley. You'll need some help."

"I move better by myself," Perley insisted.

"Move to an early grave," John declared sarcastically.

"You need at least one man to back you up. I'm gonna tell Possum what you're fixin' to do and he won't let you go without him. And that's settled." He glanced down at the other end of the long table where Possum was just finishing his breakfast. It was plain to see by the way he was staring at Perley that Possum had already guessed Perley's intentions. While Perley hurriedly gulped down his coffee and crammed a biscuit in his mouth, Possum got up and walked up beside John. But before he could ask, John said, "It'll be all right for you to go. Take care of him."

"Yes, sir, thank you, sir. I always do," Possum said.

Perley looked up at him. "How come you always 'Yes, sir' and 'No, sir' my brothers, but never me?"

"'Cause he's the boss," Possum said. "Let's get saddled up. I'll get the packhorse, you're liable to forget the coffeepot."

"Saddle that little sorrel mare that Martha likes to ride, too. We're gonna need a horse for Becky." He looked at his brother. "That's all right, ain't it, John?" He asked because it was his sister-in-law's horse.

"Sure," John replied. "Martha would be glad to have Becky ride her horse. And you can put her saddle on her, too. It'd be more comfortable for Becky." Even as he said it, he worried that they might not be successful in catching up with the four outlaws. And if they did, it might be too late for Becky. He felt himself hurting inside for Perley when he found her. The chances were extremely slim that he would catch up in time.

In a matter of minutes, they were ready to ride, so they set out at an angle across the Triple-G range to intercept the north road where it ended at the Red River. There was no trouble seeing the tracks of the four outlaws and those of the posse at the south edge of the river. "If we're lucky, they rode straight across," Possum commented when they pushed on into the water. When they came out on the other side, they discovered that luck was with them because tracks were plainly visible of six horses leaving the water. It was only at this point that they slowed their pace as they carefully followed the tracks, still visible, though not as easily seen as before. And it was important to determine the general direction the outlaws had taken, so as to have an idea where they were heading. It was not as difficult as it could have been, however, causing Possum to declare, "They were so damn sure that posse was gonna stop at the river that they didn't even try to cover their tracks when they got over on this side."

There were three obvious trailheads heading out in different directions. They followed the tracks to one of them. "Looks like they're headed to Durant," Perley said. He was far more familiar with this part of the country than Possum was and he had ridden that trail into Durant before. "Fifty miles," he answered when Possum asked him how far it was to Durant. "No tellin' how big a hurry they were in to get there, but there's a good campin' spot almost halfway. They had to stop somewhere for the night. Dependin' on the shape their horses were in, they mighta stopped there. You think your horse is up to ridin' that far before we rest 'em? Buck seems to be all right." He tried not to think about what might have been Becky's fate when the outlaws had stopped for the night. The thought of it sickened him, so he attempted to keep his mind on the trail ahead and nothing else.

They reached the popular camping ground when the sun was directly overhead. A quick search led them to the remains of the outlaws' campfire. "I'll build us a fire," Possum volunteered, "and we can eat some of this bacon I brought unless you druther have beef jerky. I got both. I know you gotta be hungry. You didn't eat no breakfast but that cup of coffee and one biscuit."

"I'll make some coffee after we take care of the horses," Perley said. "I ain't really very hungry."

"Need to keep your strength up," Possum lectured.

"Is that so?" Perley responded. "Doggoned if ridin' with you ain't got to be like ridin' with my mama."

"Somebody's gotta look after you," Possum retorted. "Why do you think I came on this little trip with you? Worryin' about that little gal, you're liable to walk right into somethin' you can't handle."

Perley glared at his friend for a moment, preparing to tell him he didn't have any say about what he was liable to do. But he couldn't hold his resentment for longer than that one moment before his conscience reminded him that Possum was devoted to him. "I reckon you're right," he admitted. "I do need to keep my mind straight. But dang it, Possum, they've got too big a head start on us. They're most likely just about to Durant by now while we're sittin' here waitin' for our horses to rest up. I can't get it outta my mind what's happenin' to Becky while we're sittin' here scratchin' our heads."

Possum nodded his understanding. "Becky's kinda special to you, ain't she?"

"I reckon," Perley confessed for the first time Possum could recall.

"Well, all we can do is give it the best we can. These ashes ain't that old. It don't look to me like they're in any hurry to get where they're goin'. We've got a good chance to make up a little ground on 'em. As soon as the horses are ready to go, we'll mount up and keep on goin'. We're only as good as our horses. I know I don't have to tell you that."

"You're right, let's keep our mind on our business," Perley said.

They boiled up a pot of coffee and ate some beef jerky and a little hardtack and called that dinner, promising themselves to eat something more substantial for supper. When nature called, Perley, in fitting with his modest nature, walked downstream for some privacy. When he had finished, he walked down close to the edge of the stream and started back. He had taken no more than two steps when he was stopped dead still by a footprint in the soft sand by the water. It was a small footprint, from a lady's shoe. Stunned, he dropped down on one knee to examine it closely. It was a fresh footprint! He got to his feet again and looked in the direction the print pointed, then he splashed across the stream at the same angle. After a few minutes' search, he found another print where she had reached the other side. He looked ahead of him, trying to guess where she was trying to get to and decided she was trying to reach a cut in a low ridge a couple hundred yards ahead. *She got away!* was his first thought.

Anxious to tell Possum, he started to run back to their campsite when something else stopped him. There, on the other side of the stream, he saw hoofprints. They had chased after her! Hustling now to bring Possum the news and get the horses ready to go, he kept repeating over and over as he ran, "Run, Becky, run," as if it were happening now.

When he excitedly informed Possum of his find, his friend responded with, "I figured somethin' like that musta happened." When Perley asked why, Possum said, "'Cause while you were down the stream, I walked out to the trail we've been followin' and there ain't no hoofprints on that trail on the other side of this camp. So I knew they left here in some other direction."

The trail was fairly easy to follow through the trees and bushes hugging the stream, due to the broken branches and torn leaves that the outlaws' horses had plowed through. Once they left the stream, Perley and Possum had to look more closely to follow a trail across an open expanse of grass. But it was obvious the four riders had pressed their horses hard in pursuit of their runaway captive and the tracks led straight toward the cut in the low ridge Perley had determined at first.

"She musta hid in here," Possum said when he saw the disturbed dirt near the bottom of a gully running down from the top of the ridge. "I'd guess that she was of a mind to crawl up to the top of it. But they musta caught up with her too soon and she just tried to hide in the bottom of it."

"Looks like they found her," Perley stated soberly, and stepped back up into the saddle. "So there's no use wastin' any more time here." He didn't wait for Possum but gave Buck his heels and started out at an angle to intercept the trail to Durant.

"Reckon not," Possum murmured, got on his horse, and followed his distraught young friend. It seemed nothing more than wishful thinking to hope Becky had not been harmed at this point, and he was afraid it was going to destroy Perley when they found her remains—if they ever did.

* * *

With a rope looped around her neck, the other end tied to a tree like a dog in the yard, and her hands tied behind her back, she could only sit, helpless to even wipe away the blood running from her nose. She had tried to escape, hoping to run back toward the Red River, swim across, and find her way back to Paris. She had paid dearly for her attempt with a brutal beating at the hands of Lucas Sage. In her state of total despair, there was only one positive thing she could think of. He had beaten her so severely that he had lost all his carnal urges toward her for the moment. Even Jesse had no interest in her, but she knew that would not last. Already, they had decided her ruse about the sickness was just that, a ruse. Micah did not hide his disgust at his brother's treatment of her and was still in favor of putting her out of her misery. At this stage, she would welcome Micah's solution to their problem.

A great part of Micah's disgust for Lucas's infatuation with her was the fact that they could not ride on into Durant and take rooms in the Texas House Hotel and eat supper in the hotel dining room. Afterward, he would have gambled in the hotel's card room in the back. They had money to spend, and even though whiskey was forbidden to be sold in Indian Territory, it was bound to be available, if a man had the price. But instead of a trip into town, they had stopped and made camp a couple of miles short of Durant, and Leonard was going to go into town with Jesse to get Doc O'Shea to take a look at Jesse's hand.

CHAPTER 5

Myra Skinner, nurse, cook, and housekeeper for Dr. Oliver H. O'Shea, answered the knock at the front door to find the two men on her front step. Since it was right in the middle of Doc's suppertime, Myra was already irritated by their presence and said nothing while she looked them over. "I'm needin' some doctorin' on my hand," Jesse said.

"What's wrong with it?" Myra asked.

"I got shot," Jesse answered. "It happened while I was cleanin' my gun and it went off by accident."

"Can you pay for it?" Myra asked.

"Hah!" Jesse laughed at her question. "Hell, yes, I can pay for it."

She stepped aside and held the door for them. "Well, come on inside, then and let's take a look at it." She led them into the doctor's surgery. "Set yourself down on the end of that table." She turned toward a sideboard and picked up a pair of scissors to cut through his crude bandage. "Damn," she swore when she exposed the wounded hand to examine the puffy, pus-filled wound. "What'd you use to disinfect it with, horse manure?"

"We didn't have no disinfectant," Jesse answered, already growing tired of the skinny woman's caustic attitude. "Where the hell's the doctor?"

"He'll be in in a minute," Myra said. "Soon as he's had enough whiskey to steady his hand."

"Steady his hand?" Jesse responded. "I don't need no drunk workin' on my hand."

"Then don't come after supper," Myra told him. She continued her examination of the hand. "Went clean through," she said, "while you were cleanin' your gun." She shook her head slowly. "I'd be right interested to see how you clean a pistol, to shoot yourself in the back of the hand like that."

"It don't make no difference how I clean a pistol," Jesse remarked. "Go get the doctor before I die of old age."

"I gotta clean it up first, or he won't touch it," Myra said. "Just set there while I get a pan of water." She went to the kitchen, where they could hear her telling the doctor about the patient. When she returned, she was carrying a pan of water and a cloth and went to work cleaning the dried blood and dirt from around the wound. When she finished, she yelled, "He's ready, Doc." She then sat Jesse in a chair and told him to keep his hand steady on the table.

The little white-haired man with shaggy sideburns and tiny glasses astraddle the tip of a stubby nose reddened by a constant diet of alcohol made an unsteady entrance into the room. "What we got here?" he asked Myra, and she repeated what she had just told him in the kitchen. He didn't bother to examine the hand as closely as she had before giving his prognosis. "Nothing to worry about," he told Jesse. "You just didn't keep the damn thing clean. The bullet went right through." He took a probe and poked around inside the wound, causing Jesse to squirm to keep from yelling out. "Hand me a bottle," he said to Myra. She opened a cabinet, took out a bottle of whiskey, and handed it to the doctor. "Here, take a drink of this," he said to Jesse, and handed the bottle to him. Jesse, still in pain from the probing, eagerly took a big swig from the bottle. While he was smacking his lips, O'Shea took the bottle back and promptly poured whiskey into Jesse's wound, bringing forth a primeval howl from his patient. Doc then took a long pull from the bottle, himself, and handed it back to Myra. "Put a proper bandage on him, Myra." Then to Jesse, he said, "If you keep it clean, that wound oughta heal up all right. That bullet clipped that bone on your middle finger, so that's likely gonna stay permanently stiff after your hand heals. That'll be five dollars, three for the treatment, a dollar for the bandaging, and a dollar for the drink of whiskey—five altogether. You can pay Myra. Except for that middle finger, your hand should heal up fine. If it doesn't, come back to see me, and we'll amputate it." He turned around carefully and returned to the kitchen.

"Damn, that hurt worse than it did when I got shot," Jesse complained. "I coulda poured whiskey on it, myself, and it still hurts like hell. And he wants five dollars for somethin' I coulda done, myself."

"Look at it this way," Myra said. "You paid money to find out what to do for yourself next time you shoot yourself, and you got a drink of likker in a territory where it's against the law to sell it."

Leonard had to laugh. "I reckon she's right. Come on, Jesse, let's go back to camp."

* * *

"Possum! Look!" Perley exclaimed, and caught Possum by his elbow to stop him. "It's him, that fellow I shot in the hand, down near the railroad station! And that's the other fellow that was with him at the hotel back in Paris." It was rapidly getting dark, but there was still enough light for him to be sure of the two. The bandage on Jesse's hand made him doubly sure. Perley and Possum had been searching the businesses along the street and were now in front of the hotel. They stepped back near the entrance to the hotel to keep from being discovered by the two outlaws and watched them as they rode out of a small lane leading off from the main street. When they wheeled their horses toward the south road out of town, Perley and Possum ran for their horses.

As had been the case all day, the two outlaws seemed to be in no particular hurry as they walked their horses out past the end of town. The growing darkness made it possible for Perley and Possum to tail them at a distance while keeping them just in sight. In a short time, however, they suddenly disappeared. "They turned off the road," Possum said. "We must be close to their camp." They had not seen which way Jesse and Leonard had turned, but it was safe to say it was probably in the direction of the creek to the left of the road. "We'd best turn off this road right here," Possum advised. "Probably wouldn't hurt to go on foot up through those trees by the creek."

Perley agreed, so they turned off the road and dismounted. Both men pulled their rifles and checked to make sure they had full magazines. Then they started making their way through the heavy growth of oaks along the creek bank, leading their horses and moving cautiously lest they stumble into the camp. After they had covered about fifty yards, Perley caught sight of a thin ribbon of smoke, drifting up through the trees, and silently signaled Possum behind him. "I figure about another fifty yards," Perley said when Possum came up beside him. "I think it's best to leave the horses here and move close enough to get a look at their camp on foot. Then we'll decide what to do." Possum nodded his agreement. They tied the horses and continued on until they reached a spot where they could see the campfire and the four men around it. They could see Jesse and Leonard pulling the saddles off their horses while evidently telling the other two men about their trip into town. Perley's heart began to pound in his chest when there was no sign of Becky. Thoughts of what might have happened to her bombarded his brain relentlessly, and he felt every muscle in his body tense with anger and the fear that he was too late.

Sensing Perley's anger, Possum spoke softly, seeking to calm his young friend. "Easy, now, partner, don't let it get the best of ya. Let's watch 'em for a few minutes before we decide what we're gonna do. She mighta got away from 'em again." Possum was concerned. He had never seen Perley in a fit of rage before, and it worried him that he might abandon all caution and get himself killed in an attack on four hardened gunmen. "Hold on," he prompted when one of the men who had been sitting by the fire got up and picked something out of a frying pan, which looked to be a slab of bacon. He left the fire circle and walked a couple dozen steps downstream.

From their vantage point, Perley and Possum could just make out the man's form in the darkness. But it appeared that he stopped and bent over next to a tree on the creek bank. "It's Becky!" Perley whispered, suddenly realizing the man was talking to someone on the ground. He almost got to his feet, but Possum managed to grab his elbow to restrain him from charging blindly after her. "I'm all right, now. She's alive," Perley assured him then, and Possum was relieved to recognize the return of Perley's usual calm demeanor. "We'll watch for a chance to get to her. I think I can get her out of there if they don't move her."

"We gonna try to do anything about those four fellers?" Possum asked, thinking about the bank money in their possession. "Or are you just thinkin' about snatchin' Becky and hightailin' it?"

There was no question in Perley's mind about the right thing to do. "We need to take that money back to the bank," he replied. "But first, we have to get Becky away from there, and that's what I'm gonna do as soon as I get a chance. If we're lucky and get the jump on 'em, we might be able to put 'em in the jail here."

"There ain't no jail here, is there?" Possum asked. "I know there ain't no sheriff."

"There oughta be a Choctaw Indian policeman around here somewhere. Maybe he's got a smokehouse or something he uses as a jail—anywhere we can lock 'em up till they get a deputy marshal down here."

"Why don't we just find out if there's a Choctaw policeman around here and let him arrest them outlaws?" Possum wondered.

"Indian policemen can't arrest a white man," Perley said. "They just police their own people."

"I forgot about that," Possum admitted. He was not enthusiastic about the idea of capturing the bank robbers. Overpowering four hardened gunmen with a small fortune to protect did not strike him as a job easily done. He always preferred to leave the business of law enforcement to the men who were paid to do the job. He glanced over at Perley, lying a few feet from him, watching the dark figures near the creek. *Oh Lord,* he prayed silently, *I'd appreciate seeing daylight again after this night.*

"I brought you a nice fat slab of sowbelly," Lucas tempted as he bent low, grabbed a fistful of her hair, and yanked her head back. "You need to eat a little somethin' to keep your strength up. And I know you ain't took a bite of nothing ever since you joined up with us yesterday. You're gonna need all the strength you can muster up, so eat this sowbelly and if you don't give me no more trouble, I'll even let you have a little coffee. Here, take it." He held it out to her.

Without lifting her head to look at him, she rasped, "I don't want it."

He put his hand under her chin and forced her head up to look at him. "Ain't you learned yet that it's gonna hurt you bad when you don't do like I tell you? That whuppin' I gave you today was just a sample of what you'll get, if you don't learn to mind me."

"You're gonna kill me, anyway," she sobbed. "Why don't you go ahead and do it?"

"'Cause I ain't done with you yet," he snarled. "I'm gonna go finish my supper and then I'll be back to see you. You'd best think about how you're gonna act when I come back here. If you gimme a good ride, I might decide to let you live to see mornin'."

"I've got the sickness down there," she whimpered desperately.

He slapped her hard across her mouth. "Shut up, you lyin' bitch. You ain't got no sickness. You think about what I told you while I'm gone." He walked back to the camp-fire, where his brothers and Leonard were drinking coffee, and picked up the pan he had been using for a dinner plate.

"Didn't expect you back so soon," Micah remarked when Lucas sat down beside the fire and filled his coffee cup. "Did you feed your little bitch some scraps?"

"She's a little off her feed, but I reckon I read the gospel to her and I expect she'll start to find out what she was put on this earth to do, soon as I finish my beans and coffee," Lucas boasted.

"How 'bout some of the rest of us takin' a little ride before you send her to the promised land?" Jesse asked.

"Micah's the one wantin' to shoot her," Lucas replied. "Me and her might wanna get married when I saddle-break her tonight. And you know it wouldn't be fittin' for a woman to lie with her brother-in-law."

"How 'bout me?" Leonard sang out. "I ain't no kin."

"She don't cotton to men who ain't as handsome as a hog," Lucas japed.

"You'd best get done with whatever you think you're gonna do with her tonight," Micah said. "'Cause I ain't plannin' on sleepin' out here in the woods after tonight."

"Soon as I finish my coffee, brother," Lucas said.

She could hear their loud and boisterous boasts from where she lay captive, tethered to a small tree. With no hope of escape, still she strained at her bonds, even pulling against the rope around her neck, ignoring the rope burns until she was forced to rest. She knew it could be only minutes before he returned to call her bluff about the sickness. With that thought, she vowed to force herself to strain against her bonds again until they broke or she choked herself to death. Preparing to lunge against her tether, she was suddenly stopped with an arm around her chest and a hand clamped tightly over her mouth. Terrified that her horror had begun, she struggled to free herself. "Becky, Becky," the familiar voice whispered. "Be still. It's me, Perley. I've come to get you."

Thinking she was hallucinating, she fell almost limp in his arms, certain that she was in the initial stages of her death. Holding her in one arm, he cut the rope tied to the tree and quickly removed the loop around her neck. Because of her almost unconscious lack of response, he felt a moment of panic, thinking she might be dying as well. "No, no, Becky!" he ordered. "Don't go. I've got you. It's me, Perley. I'm gonna cut the rope around your wrists. You're safe now."

With the freeing of her hands, she suddenly realized she was alive and the voice ringing in her ears was really Perley's. She threw her arms around his neck and he picked her up in his arms. Backing carefully away from the tree, he carried her some thirty yards down the creek, where Possum was waiting with the horses. "Possum's gonna take care of you," Perley said as he shifted her over to Possum's arms. "I'll be back in a few minutes." Speaking to Possum then, he said, "Leave Buck here and you take Becky and the rest of the horses back out to the road and head for town. Find the doctor."

"What are you gonna do?" Possum responded.

"I'm gonna make sure you have a good head start, in case they try to come after you. So hurry now. I'll meet you at the hotel. You'll most likely have to find the doctor first. She's been beat up pretty bad."

"Doggone it, Perley, you be careful," Possum stated.

"I will. Now, go!" He turned and hurried back up the creek before Possum had time to try to talk him out of it. He wanted to be sure they got back to town before the outlaws had time to catch them. Their horses were all unsaddled and down by the creek on the other side of the camp, so that would ensure a little time saved right there. With no real plan, he decided to just see what happened next and react to it. That was pretty much the way he lived his whole life, had he stopped to think about it. So, when he got back to the tree where Becky had been tied, he sat down with his back against the trunk and his rifle across his lap and waited.

Seated there in the darkness, like Becky had been before, he could hear the loud voices of the four men around the fire. *Just keep talking,* he thought, for the longer they joked and laughed, the farther Possum and Becky would have ridden. Finally, however, the japing became extra loud and raucous, so he figured something was about to happen. He hoped all four of them didn't come for the girl. He wasn't sure he had a plan for that.

In a few seconds, he saw the form of a single individual approaching him, backlighted by the campfire. He realized the man could not see him in the darkness, so he sat quietly until he spoke. "Hey, there, sugar bottom, it's time for you to find out how it is to get rode by a real man," Lucas boasted.

"I can hardly wait," Perley replied, causing Lucas to

immediately reach for his gun. The report from the Winchester 73 announced the death sentence as the .44 slug tore into the startled man's chest. Lucas released his pistol, which was not even halfway out. It dropped back down in the holster as he sank to his knees. Expecting company right away, Perley scrambled up on his feet, his rifle trained on the man still kneeling before him, waiting for any sign of retaliation. There was none. Lucas remained in a kneeing position until Perley paused beside him to give him a slight push on the shoulder. Then he keeled over to land on his side. "Becky sends her regards," Perley uttered coldly, and hurried to circle back into the trees before the other three arrived. He didn't think about it at the time, but it was against his nature to kill with the sole intention of performing an execution. He had killed before, but it had usually been in reaction to an attempt upon his life. Instead of fleeing with Becky and Possum, however, he had deliberately waited to rid the world of the man who had harmed Becky. It might serve to give him pause later, but at the present time, he had to think about staying alive.

"What tha . . . ?" Jesse blurted when they heard the shot.

"Where the hell did she get a rifle?" Micah exclaimed as he scrambled to his feet, his first thought that it was Becky who fired the shot, for it was clearly a rifle shot.

Hustling to get to his feet as well, Leonard insisted, "He shot her. I knew he was gonna, but it sounded more like a rifle shot. Did he take his rifle with him?" They all looked at once toward his saddle where he had left it.

"Rifle's still there," Jesse said, then looked at Micah to decide what to do.

Although all three were on their feet and ready to react to the gunshot in some fashion, no one knew whether it was something that required action on their part or not. There was just the one shot and now everything was quiet. "Hell, I don't know," Micah said. "He might just be foolin' around with her, tryin' to scare her." There was still the question of the shot coming from a rifle, however. He paused, then yelled, "Lucas! You all right down there?" He waited, but there was no answer. "We'd best go down there and take a look." Following his lead, they drew their weapons and made their way down the dark creek bank. When they reached the spot where Lucas had tied her to the tree, Micah, who was in the lead, stumbled over Lucas's body and almost tripped in the dark. When he recovered and saw who it was lying dead there and the girl nowhere in sight, he cried out his rage. Right behind him, Jesse roared with anger.

Astonished as well, Leonard was stunned to find Lucas the victim, although he could not experience the pain Micah and Jesse felt for losing their brother. "That don't make no sense," he said. "Where the hell did she find a rifle?" While they wasted time trying to figure out how Becky managed to free herself and sneak around behind the camp to take one of their rifles, Perley took the opportunity to circle them, himself. While he did, he was close enough to hear their excited conversation and figured it would be good to feed their misconception. *I'll let them think Becky's running around out here in the woods with one of their rifles,* he thought. To carry out that hoax, he made his way around to the other side of their camp and took the rifle out of one of the saddles.

Just as he figured, they returned to their camp to check

on their rifles, mere seconds after he pulled a rifle out of one of the saddle slings and slipped back into the darkness. He took cover behind a low mound about twenty yards from the camp, where he could hear them talking. "My dang rifle's gone!" Jesse blurted. "She took my rifle!" Micah and Leonard both ran over to look at his empty saddle sling. Satisfied with their reaction, Perley decided to give them something else to worry about. Leaving the cover of the mound, he backed off another thirty or forty yards, so as not to be too close when he fired. Then he took dead aim on Leonard and squeezed off one round that caught the unsuspecting outlaw in the shoulder.

The shot had the desired effect on the three outlaws. Leonard dropped to the ground right where he stood while Micah and Jesse dived out of the circle of light provided by the campfire, seeking any cover they could find. For a little added incentive, Perley placed another couple of shots in the dirt close behind Micah's heels as he disappeared from the firelight. *That ought to give them something to think about for a while,* he thought, and withdrew from the assault. He made his way quickly back to the spot where his horse was waiting. Then he led the bay gelding back to the road and headed to town.

Behind him, Micah and Jesse hugged the ground in the darkness outside the light of the fire, ignoring Leonard's moans for help. "Micah, I'm shot," he called out. "I'm bleedin' bad. I need help."

"Where are you hit?" Micah called back to him. Leonard said he was shot in his right shoulder. "That ain't so bad," Micah said. "You oughta be able to move outta that damn firelight. If we come to help you, she's gonna shoot us. So you've gotta come outta there and we'll try to help you."

Afraid to move, but desperate to get out of the firelight, Leonard began to inch his way toward the darkness, expecting another shot to come at any time. Finally, when he could stand it no longer, he suddenly got up on all fours and crawled as fast as he could to the safety of the darkness beyond the fire circle. When he reached his partners, he collapsed and rolled over on his back. "Thanks for nothin'," he gasped between breaths.

"That wouldn'ta been too smart for me and Jesse to go paradin' out there to give her a shot at us, too," Micah responded. "That wildcat can shoot. Besides, you're just wounded in the shoulder, you made it outta there all right. There's some rags in the packs. We'll make you up somethin' to stop it from bleedin'. But we ain't gonna do much of anythin' till we chase that crazy woman down and slit her throat." He paused to take a look around him in the darkness as if checking to make sure no one was sneaking up on them. "I swear, he's my brother, and it grieves me to lose him. But if he hadn't had to have that crazy lunatic, he wouldn'ta got us into this mess."

"What I can't understand is, if she got herself loose and circled around behind us, why didn't she steal one of the horses and make a run for it?" Jesse asked.

"'Cause she's crazy as a bat," Micah answered him. He paused to tell Leonard to hold the makeshift bandage in place while he tied it around his shoulder. "Lucas beat her up so bad she's thinkin' more about gettin' even than gettin' away."

"Well, we're gonna have to do somethin'," Jesse said. "We can't lay around here on the ground all night waitin' for daylight. We need to find her. Did you see where those shots came from?"

"No," Micah replied, a little testy. "I was busy gettin' my butt outta the firelight, just like you." Finished with his emergency care of Leonard's wounded shoulder, he said, "I ain't got no intentions of staying pinned down in this camp all night by a little slip of a woman."

"She sure as hell had me fooled," Jesse remarked. "She looked like she was about to faint after Lucas worked her over. I figured she was about done for."

"She fooled us all," Micah said, "so we need to run her down and make sure she's done for. These damn woods are dark as the inside of a boot, so I expect she'll stay close to the creek, so she can hide. We're gonna have to keep a sharp eye. Jesse, you go down one side of this creek and I'll go down the other. And we'll check every bush and gully. Leonard can stay here and guard the horses in case she's got around behind us again and decides to steal one of 'em and takes the money with it." No one offered any better plan, so they began their two-man sweep of the creek banks.

While the two Sage brothers were sneaking cautiously along the creek bank, the woman they searched for was waiting patiently on Dr. O'Shea's front porch while Possum pounded on the door. It was late, but there was a light in the back part of the house, so he figured there was some-one in the kitchen. Finally, after a continuous knocking, he saw a light coming through the front window, approach-ing the door. A few moments later, he heard the bolt slide on the door and it opened to reveal Myra Skinner holding a lamp.

"Office hours are over," Myra informed Possum in her typical callous manner. "Come back in the morning and Doc'll take a look at what ails you."

"It ain't for me," Possum said. "It's for her. She's been kidnapped and beat up pretty bad." He stepped aside, so she could see Becky sitting on the top step.

Myra opened the screen door and pushed by Possum. Holding the lamp up so she could see the young woman, her harsh attitude softened immediately. "Oh my goodness, honey, what happened to you? Is what he said the truth?" She glanced back at Possum just long enough to take another look at him. "Is he your pa?"

"No, ma'am," Becky replied softly. "He's one of the angels who rescued me. What he said is true. Four men robbed the bank in Paris, Texas, and grabbed me when they made their getaway."

Myra set the lantern down and took a close look at Becky's battered face. "It looks like your nose is broke," she decided as she gently turned Becky's face to one side, then the other, looking at the swollen eye and the bruises on the side of her jaw. "Are you hurt anywhere else?" she asked.

"My shoulder hurts and one side of my ribs hurts," Becky told her.

"Anywhere else?" Myra asked discreetly. "Down below your ribs anywhere?"

Becky understood what she meant and answered, "No, ma'am, he hadn't got around to that before Perley found me and shot him."

"Good for him!" Myra responded, and turned to give Possum a nod of approval, thinking Becky was talking about him.

Seeing that Myra was in a more receptive state of mind now, Possum said, "I know it's late, but I weren't sure how bad she was hurt, so I brung her to the doctor on the chance he might take a look at her."

"Tell you the truth, Perley . . . Is that what she called you?"

"No, ma'am, I'm Possum. Perley's the one who rescued her and shot that feller."

"Perley Possum," Myra repeated, confused, then looked at Becky. "What's your name, honey, and if you say Posey, I'm going back in the house."

"No, ma'am," she replied in all seriousness, "my name's Becky Morris."

"Good," Myra said. "Like I started to say, Doc don't usually take any patients this late unless it's an emergency, like a gunshot or something. But I'm gonna take you on inside where we can get a better look at you." She smiled as she gave her a helping hand up. "And if he's too far into the bottle to take care of you, I'll do it myself."

CHAPTER 6

It had been quite some time since he had been to Durant Station, and Perley could see sure signs of growth in the little town on the MKT Railroad. He remembered the general store and the Texas House Hotel as well as the stable. He decided to try the stable first to see if Possum had left the horses there before finding the doctor. So he rode up to the end of the street, where he found Otis Black still working in the barn.

"Evenin'," Perley greeted Otis. "I'm lookin' for a man and a woman that mighta left some horses with you just a little while ago."

"Yep," Otis replied. "They was here. They said they hoped you'd be showin' up in a little while. They left a packhorse here, then rode out to see Doc O'Shea. That lady looked pretty beat up, so I told 'em I'd be here till they got back."

"Where's the doctor's office?" Perley asked. "I'll go see if they're about ready, then we'll drop the horses off. 'Preciate you waitin' for us."

"That ain't no bother a-tall," Otis said. "I sleep right here in the barn. Doc O'Shea's place is back the other end of town, out past the railroad station."

"Much obliged," Perley said, and climbed back in the saddle. As he rode back down toward the other end of town, he decided it might be a good idea to get a couple of rooms, so Becky could rest as soon as she finished with the doctor. The hotel owner, Sheldon Tate, was manning the small check-in desk and he was happy to accommodate Perley with a room for Becky and another for Perley and Possum to share. Since business was a little slow at that particular time, Tate would have been pleased to rent him the whole second floor. Perley assured him that the two rooms would be enough. Then, with two room keys in his pocket, Perley went to find the doctor.

Past the railroad station, on the opposite side of the road, he came to the lane that led to Dr. O'Shea's office. It was the same lane where he and Possum had spotted the two outlaws that led them to their camp and Becky. When he approached the house, he saw Possum's gray horse tied out front next to the sorrel. Anxious now to see how badly Becky was hurt, he reined Buck to a halt in the yard, dismounted, and dropped the reins on the ground. He took the two steps to the porch with one leap, knocked on the door, and went in without waiting for anyone to answer his knock. There was no lamp in the front room, but he could see light shining around the closed door for what he guessed was the examining room. So he headed for the kitchen, which he figured was the open door down the hall, with lamplight shining through it. That was where he found Possum. He was seated at the table, drinking a cup of coffee. Perley relaxed at once. "Well, she must not be too bad off," he remarked.

"Perley!" Possum exclaimed. "Boy, am I glad to see you! What happened back there?"

"When I left, they were busy runnin' around in the dark lookin' for Becky. How's she doin'?"

"She's just fine," Possum said. "Tougher'n she looks. She's more worried about you than anything else."

"Did the doctor say if she could ride right away?" Perley asked, thinking Possum might not be as concerned as he should be.

"The doctor ain't said nothin'," Possum replied. "He's been layin' in the parlor, passed out on the sofa, the whole time we've been here. You musta come right by him in the dark when you came through the room. Myra, she's his nurse, she's in there with Becky. She's been doin' all the doctorin'."

Just as he said it, they heard a door open back up the hall and a few seconds later Myra walked in. "She's doing just fine," she announced. "Putting her blouse back on and she'll be out in a minute, wanting a cup of coffee, I expect." She paused then to look Perley up and down. "You'd be Pearly, then?"

"Yes, ma'am," he answered, "Perley Gates. I wanna thank you for takin' care of Becky."

Myra's lips parted in a great big grin, as if in on a charade. "Pearly Gates," she repeated, laughing. Then she looked hard at him and asked, "Pearly Gates, you ain't japing me?" She recalled that Becky had said she was rescued by a couple of angels.

"No, ma'am, I ain't." He was accustomed to having people make fun of his name, but it was usually in the atmosphere of a saloon or dance hall. But this lady looked truly astonished by his name. He thought to spell his first name for her, so she could see the difference, but Becky appeared in the doorway at that moment and Myra interrupted him.

"Here's Posey, I mean Becky, now. You want a cup of coffee, honey? I know I'd like to have one. And I'll bet Pearly would like one, and Possum's already drinking one. I believe we could use a fresh pot." Laughing happily at the similarity of their names, she picked the big pot up from the corner of the stove and went to the pump. "I'll make a pot for Pearly, Possum, and Posey," she joked delightedly. "Doc ain't gonna believe this when he wakes up in the morning." While she was fixing the coffee, she said, "I knew there was something I didn't like about those two saddle tramps that were in here. The one with the hole through his hand said it was an accident that happened when he was cleaning his pistol."

"Perley's pretty good at causin' accidents like that," Possum remarked.

They finished another pot of coffee, and since it was too late to eat in the hotel dining room, Myra insisted on making some corn cakes in the frying pan and frying some bacon to go with them. "I bet you don't get that kinda service at any other doctor's office," Myra cracked. They all agreed that it was much like a banquet, celebrating Becky's rescue from her abductors. Although festive, it didn't last long because Becky wasn't up to it and needed some rest. "You're gonna be fine, young lady," Myra insisted. "That baboon broke your nose, but the bones are lined up pretty straight now. You may have a little bump in your nose that wasn't there before, but you'll still be pretty as a picture when you get all healed up. You're gonna have to breathe through your mouth for a day or two. Leave that packing in there for as long as you can stand it. It'd be good if you could let it stay for a couple of days. You'll be a pretty little lady again in a few days, won't she, Pearly?"

"Yes, ma'am, I expect she will," he answered. "I reckon we need to settle up now. How much do I owe you for all the doctorin' and the supper?"

"Well, you didn't have the doctor to work on her. You had to settle for a nurse. But I did exactly everything he would have," she felt entitled to say. "So I'm just gonna charge you half price for the medical attention. I'm charging you nothing for the food because I ain't enjoyed an evening like this since I don't know when." After Perley paid her, she walked them to the door and became serious for a minute. "You folks be careful. From what you told me about those men who carried Becky off, I'd say you might have them looking for you. I'm sorry we don't have any law enforcement in town yet. You can go to the railroad station and have them send a telegram to the U.S. marshal in Fort Smith. That would at least get a deputy marshal on their trail."

"That sounds like a good idea to me," Possum said. "I expect that's what we'll do. They're carryin' a whoppin' big load of cash money that belongs to the bank, but that ain't our concern. We got what we came for." He gave Becky a big smile. "We'll let the U.S. marshals worry about the money. That's their job, right, Perley?" When Perley failed to answer right away, Possum repeated the question. "Ain't that right, Perley?" He wanted to know that Perley wasn't harboring any thoughts about trying to do the Oklahoma marshals' job for them. "All we wanna do now is get Becky back home safe."

"I reckon so," Perley finally answered, and stepped down from the porch to help Becky. "This sorrel is Martha's little mare," he told her. "John thought you'd be more comfortable on her." She smiled and nodded, pleased to hear his family had concern for her.

While Perley was helping Becky, Myra caught Possum's elbow to stop him from going down the step. "Just thought you might like to know," she whispered, "there ain't nothing happened to that little girl below her belt. Understand?"

"Yes, ma'am," Possum replied. "I'm glad to hear that and I 'preciate you tellin' me." He decided to wait for the proper time to pass that information along to Perley. He watched Perley lift Becky up and place her in the saddle, then they rode into town to the hotel. Perley insisted on standing guard outside the washroom while Becky prepared for bed, then walked her up to her room, which was next door to his and Possum's room. He gave her the room key, so she could lock herself in, then he went to his room for the night.

Morning brought a feeling of optimism for the new day. Possum and Perley awoke early as usual but decided to wait for Becky to have breakfast. Possum decided to make no mention of the fact that he was awakened in the middle of the night when Perley sneaked out the door of their room. Since he was awakened again during the wee hours of morning to discover Perley sneaking back into bed, he had to figure Perley had spent most of the night sitting outside Becky's door. When it was closer to their customary time to get up, Possum woke him from a deep sleep.

They agreed that Becky might sleep a little late, since she no doubt needed the rest. So they went to the stable to collect their horses and settle up with Otis Black. Then they took the horses back and tied them at the hotel. There was some discussion about the remaining three outlaws they had left on the creek bank south of town and the odds that they might encounter them again. There was the matter of Lucas Sage's death at the hand of Perley. Becky had told them that two of the men were his brothers. So Perley and Possum had to consider the possibility that they would come after him to avenge his death. There were other factors to think about, however. Two of the three outlaws were wounded, one in the hand, and one in the shoulder. Added to that was the possession of a large sum of stolen money that should discourage them from hanging around town. There was no way to be sure, but Perley and Possum came to the conclusion that the three outlaws would most likely strike out for a more remote part of Indian Territory. So, there was no reason to rush out of town. They would give Becky all the time she needed to get ready to ride. All their discussion about her needs was wasted, because when they went back inside the hotel, she had left a message at the desk that she was waiting for them in the dining room.

"I declare," Possum remarked when they joined her. "Here we was outside waitin' for you to get up and come to find out you're waitin' for us to get here. How you feelin' this mornin'?"

"Like I ran in the back door but forgot to open it first," she replied. "Myra forgot to tell me it was gonna feel like my whole face has a toothache. I guess I'm feelin' better than when I went to bed last night, though. I slept real good. I'm just sorry you two have to look at this face while you're tryin' to eat."

"It's a pretty sight for us," Perley said. "We were afraid we'd never see that face again."

"Didn't Myra give you no medicine for the pain?" Possum asked.

"She did," Becky said. "She gave me a little bottle of laudanum, but she said not to take any more than a teaspoonful at a time, so I was afraid to take any, if it's that strong." She was still thinking about Perley's remark. She wished she knew what he really felt in his heart, hoping it was more than just sympathy for the pain she had endured. Further thought on the subject was interrupted then by the arrival of Fanny Wallace with coffee for Perley and Possum.

"I see your two gentlemen friends finally got here," Fanny said. "I told the cook to go ahead and start on yours, honey." She looked at the men and asked. "What kinda breakfast are you thinkin' about?"

"A big one," Possum answered.

"Have you got eggs?" Perley asked. Not every dining room did.

"Sure do," Fanny replied, "and the hens that laid 'em. How you want 'em cooked? The eggs, not the hens," she added, and chuckled at her humor.

"I like 'em scrambled," Perley said, "about three of 'em with bacon, potatoes, and biscuits."

"That oughta suit me, too," Possum told her, "but make it four eggs." He looked at Perley and said, "Those little corn cakes Myra cooked last night gave out a long time ago."

They had a long way to ride, so Perley thought Becky would be anxious to get started. However, he was surprised to find that she seemed inclined to enjoy the big breakfast, obviously feeling safe in the bright light of a morning already late by his standards. And since her two companions had seen no trace of the men who had abducted her, she felt like taking her time to embrace being alive. Having a waitress bringing her food was a big difference for her. She was almost reluctant to get started back.

It was an entirely different mood that hung over the camp just south of the little town of Durant. Like the heavy fog that hovered over the dark creek water, the activities of the night just passed cast a shroud of defeat and the loss of a brother by the acts of a seemingly fragile little woman. When the sun penetrated the canopy of leaves that lined the creek, the three outlaws sat beside their campfire, no longer concerned about any more rifle shots. For they had combed the banks all night long with no luck, and they were in agreement that the woman had fled long before sunrise. Bitterly fighting frustration and anger, Micah Sage sipped away at the hot coffee in his cup. "We need to bury Lucas," he announced to no one in particular. It was uttered more as a thought spoken aloud. "I reckon I'll have to do the diggin', since both of you ain't got but one arm."

Feeling his brother's contempt, especially with the way his wound occurred, Jesse offered, "I can do a little work with one hand, fillin' in the grave maybe."

"I don't need no help," Micah snapped. "I can do it by myself, like anything else that gets done in this gang." He was especially disgusted with the manner in which they were shot; Lucas shot point-blank by a slip of a woman he had tied to a tree, Jesse shot in his hand by some yokel by the name of Pearly Gates, and Leonard sniped in the shoulder by the woman again. It seemed impossible, but there was no other explanation for it. He was certain any posse from Paris had not followed beyond the Red River. Had it been a posse, they would have surrounded the camp and shot it to pieces. It was this one innocent-looking little witch that it had been Lucas's folly to abduct.

Troubled by Micah's reaction to his brother's death, Leonard was worried about what he planned to do about it, if anything. Each of them was even wealthier now as a result of the woman's elimination of Lucas. The thought of his share of all that money was weighing heavily on his brain. He was afraid to suggest splitting the money at this point, but he was strongly in favor of doing just that and let each of them go their own way. He watched the distraught brother as he worked to scratch out a hole in the creek bank with a small spade he carried on the packhorse. After a few minutes, Leonard asked, "Whaddaya think we oughta do now, Micah? I mean, you reckon that little witch has gone to tell the sheriff where we are?"

Micah didn't stop digging. "There ain't no sheriff in Durant. There ain't no kinda law except Injun law, and that ain't no good against white men. The only law is what I'm packin' on my hip and I'm fixin' to use some of that law on that damn witch."

"You reckon we oughta go ahead and split up that money, so each one of us can look out for their share?" Leonard asked.

"You worried about your share?" Micah paused and asked. "You thinkin' about splittin' up? We'll be better off stickin' together, so we can make sure nobody gets any ideas about our money."

"Yeah, Leonard," Jesse spoke up, "you thinkin' you don't like our company no more? Maybe you're worried about me and Micah cuttin' you outta your share."

"No such a thing and you know it," Leonard replied. "I've been ridin' with you boys too long for you to say somethin' like that. I just don't think it's a good idea to hang around this two-bit town waitin' for a couple of deputy marshals to show up to arrest us and take the money away from us."

"We know what we're doin'," Jesse insisted. "Micah's been callin' the shots ever since we started out, and we ain't done bad so far. He's the one who said hit the bank in Paris. That was a pretty good payday, weren't it?"

"Yes, it was, and I'd like the chance to spend some of it," Leonard replied. "But he's talkin' about goin' into town to try to find that woman. She might have that whole town fired up, gettin' theirselves ready to come lookin' for us— that or ready to cut us down if we show up. She's bound to have told somebody about the money we're totin', and that sure ain't a good thing. Hell, let's get on our horses and hightail it outta here while we still have our money. There ain't nothin' we can do to bring Lucas back." He paused and waited for one of the brothers to respond. "Don't that make sense?" he asked when there was no response to his plea.

"That'll have to do," Micah said, ignoring Leonard's question. "You two, take hold of a leg with your good arm, I'll tote his shoulders, and we'll lay Lucas in the grave." They did as he said, then they started covering him up, Micah with the spade, the other two raking dirt into the grave with their boots. When they were done, Micah turned to Leonard and said, "We'll pack up now and go into town. I expect you'll wanna go with me and Jesse, since that's where the money will be, all three shares." He waited to see if Leonard had any objection. When he made no protest, Micah said, "We can go by that doctor's office and let him take a look at your shoulder."

"That'd be fine, Micah, I'd appreciate it," Leonard replied, afraid to push the splitting of the money any further. He had seen Micah like this on other occasions and knew it best not to push him.

Micah had intended to go in to check the stores and the hotel first, but since Dr. O'Shea's office was south of the main street and they would pass it first, he gave in to Leonard's need to have the doctor look at his shoulder. He speculated that Becky would probably have gone to the doctor, herself, as soon as she reached town, and she might still be there. Jesse agreed, thinking the doctor might have taken pity on the young woman and kept her overnight.

Myra Skinner happened to be sweeping the front porch when the threesome rode up the path to the house. At once alarmed, she maintained her composure, however. "What can I do for you gentlemen on this fine morning?" she greeted them as cordially as she could perform.

"The doctor needs to look at his shoulder," Micah answered her. "He got shot last night by a low-down dirty sniper while we was in camp."

Myra looked at Leonard, then glanced at Jesse and couldn't resist remarking, "You fellows have a lotta bad luck with firearms, don'tcha?" When no one gave her as much as a smile, she said, "Well, come on inside and I'll get the doctor. Your two friends might wanna sit out here on the porch and enjoy the weather."

"We'll go inside," Micah said, and dismounted. He intended to find out for himself if Becky was hiding in there or not. They followed Myra into the front room, where she instructed them to take a seat while she went to fetch Doc.

In a short time, O'Shea came into the room. "Another gunshot wound," he commented when he saw the rather rough bandaging on Leonard's shoulder. "You were here yesterday when I fixed him up." He nodded toward Jesse. "You boys are mighty careless when it comes to cleaning your guns."

"He weren't cleanin' his gun," Micah replied coldly. "He was settin' beside the campfire when a low-down little witch took a shot at him. I don't reckon you mighta seen her, have you? She'd been in a little fight and got some cuts and bumps. Figured she mighta come here after she murdered my brother."

Doc shrugged as he replied, "No, I haven't treated any low-down little witches lately." It was a true enough statement, for Myra had not mentioned to him all the activity that had taken place there while he was deep in his drunken slumber. Back to Leonard then, he motioned toward his surgery. "Come on and let's take a look at it." He started toward the door and yelled, "Myra!" Knowing what he wanted, Myra immediately went to the pump with a pan for water.

Micah waited until Myra joined the doctor in his surgery. Then he walked down the hall to the kitchen and looked around, opened the pantry door and looked inside.

After that, he went from room to room in the small house and found no trace of Becky. So he returned to the parlor. "She ain't in the house, unless she's hidin' in there where he's workin' on Leonard. I'm gonna look in the outhouse." He walked out the front door, only to return in a few minutes to announce, "She ain't here." His patience already running thin, he worried that Becky might be leaving town even as he stood wasting time in the doctor's office. "You stay here and wait for Leonard. I'm goin' into town. Bring the horses with you. And, Jesse, make sure those sacks are safe. Keep your eye on Leonard, he's talkin' a lotta turn-tail talk. I don't trust him no farther than I can throw him."

"Oh, I'll keep an eye on him," Jesse replied. "I've been thinkin' it wouldn't be a bad idea to keep all that money in the family."

CHAPTER 7

Since it was the first business he came to, Micah stopped at Dixon Durant's general store, even though there were no horses tied at the rail. He figured Becky was still on foot when she fled to town the previous night. Leon Shipley, the clerk, greeted him when he came in the door. "Mornin', what can I do for you?"

"I'm lookin' for a young woman that shot my brother last night," Micah replied. "She's sick in the head, thinks all kinda things are happenin' to her. We was on our way to the hospital in Fort Worth. They got a doctor there that treats crazy people. She ran off from our camp after she put a bullet in my brother's chest, and I'm afraid she's gonna kill somebody else."

"Lord have mercy . . ." Leon drew out. "That is a sorry piece of news for you. You think she mighta come here?"

"I reckon she woulda been here when you opened up. I just wanna warn you if you have took her in, she can come up with some of the wildest tales you've ever heard. Then when you ain't expectin' it, she'll turn into a real she-wolf."

"Forever more . . ." Leon drew out again. "I ain't seen nobody like that around here."

Micah figured he was telling the truth. "Well, just thank your lucky stars you ain't. I'll keep lookin' for her."

After leaving the general store, he planned to check the Texas House Hotel next. There were three saddled horses and one packhorse tied at the hitching rail in front and they put another thought in his head. If she got to town last night, she would have been waiting for somebody to open up. And few businesses opened up before the stable every morning. Add to that, she would have been desperate for a horse. She had no money, but she had a fine Winchester rifle to trade for a horse. With that in mind, he rode past the Texas House and went straight to the stable up at the other end of the street. He dismounted and walked in the open door, oblivious of the two men and the young lady just coming out of the dining room at Texas House behind him to climb on the horses out front. The three riders rode south out of town, while he continued on to check the stable.

"Hey, anybody here?" Micah called out when he pulled up before the stable door.

"Back here!" Otis Black yelled from the back stall. "Be right there." A couple of minutes later, he walked out to meet Micah. "Howdy," he said. "What can I do for you?"

"I'm tryin' to find a young woman you mighta seen early this mornin'," Micah began, then told Otis the same story he had told Leon Shipley at the general store.

"I saw a young woman who looked like she mighta been beat up or throwed off a horse or somethin'," Otis replied. "She'd most likely been to the doctor to get bandaged up, but I don't think she's the one you're talkin' about. This young lady weren't crazy a-tall and she weren't by herself. She was with two fellers and they all kept their horses here last night. They stayed in the hotel and come got their horses this mornin'. I saw 'em when they left the hotel dinin' room. That was the first time I saw her, and like I said, she didn't act like she was tetched in the head."

Micah could feel the muscles in his arms and chest tensing immediately and he fought to keep Otis from seeing his reaction of anger. The picture was forming in his mind. Two men had come after her, stolen her away from where she was tied, then waited to kill Lucas when he came for her! To think he had been so stupid to have believed she had freed herself, killed Lucas, and shot Leonard made him even more angry. *That little witch,* he thought, *kill my brother then ride back to Paris with two dead men. And that's a promise, because I will kill both of them.* But where in hell were Jesse and Leonard? He was tempted to start back to Texas after the woman and her rescuers and ride his horse to death, if he had to, to catch up with the two men. If only he had brought all the money with him, he would have done just that, but he could not ride off without that money. Having been distracted by his thoughts of revenge, he glanced up at Otis, who was gaping at him, and realized the owner of the stable was puzzling over his sudden freeze. Without another word, Micah turned and stalked out of the stable.

"Odd feller," Otis commented, turned around, and went back to his work in the back stall.

At the south end of town, Perley, Possum, and Becky rode past the path that led to Doc O'Shea's house, following the road that led to the Red River. A few minutes later, Leonard and Jesse rode out to the end of Doc's path and took the road back up the main street of Durant to find Micah. The bullet was out of Leonard's shoulder and he was sporting a clean bandage. Never giving thought toward looking south when they reached the road, they didn't notice the three riders that had just passed. "I'da never thought that timid little woman had all that wildcat inside her," Leonard remarked as they rode side by side into town.

"I reckon ever'body is liable to turn wild when they know they're fixin' to die," Jesse replied. "And I expect she knew we was gonna kill her when we got done with her."

"If she had any sense at all, I reckon she shoulda knowed we weren't gonna take her into town with us," Leonard said. "I just hope if she ain't in town this mornin', that Micah will just say to hell with her and we can get goin' to some other part of the country."

Jesse cocked his head around to glare at Leonard. "Micah ain't the only one that's wantin' to find that woman. Lucas was my brother, too, so I wanna see her pay for what she done, same as Micah."

"Oh, I know that's so," Leonard was quick to assure him. "I'm just sayin' it might be a mistake to hang around this part of the territory while there's most likely some deputy marshals already on their way from Fort Smith."

"It's a long way from here to Fort Smith," Jesse said. "I'll go with whatever Micah decides to do. He's my brother. You don't understand what it's like between brothers."

Leonard didn't say anything for a couple of minutes, then he quietly begged to differ. "I had a brother."

That was a surprise to Jesse. "You never said anythin' about havin' a brother before." He thought about it for a minute, then asked, "You said 'had.' What happened to him?"

"He got shot in a gunfight over a pinto pony," Leonard answered.

"No foolin'? Who shot him?"

"Me," Leonard said. "I claimed that horse before we even went after 'em. There was other good horses for him to pick in that herd. He had his pick of the rest of the whole herd."

"Well, I'll be . . ." That was as far as Jesse got before he sighted Micah's horse tied at the hitching rail in front of the hotel dining room. A moment later, Micah came out the door. "Yonder's Micah!" he blurted, and gave his horse a kick. Leonard followed at a lope.

"It's about time you two showed up," Micah said. "She was here, all right, but she ain't on her own. She's joined up with two men and they were still in town till just a little while ago. They took her to the doctor last night and he fixed her up."

"Why, that lyin' son of a . . ." Jesse started. "He said he didn't treat no beat-up women lately. Maybe we oughta go back and see if we can't help him get his memory back."

"I'm thinkin' the same thing," Micah said, "but we can't take the time to waste on him right now. Miss Becky and her two friends just left here a little while ago, and if we hurry up, we oughta be able to catch up with 'em."

"Which way'd they go?" Jesse asked, as eager to catch them as Micah.

"Ain't nobody admitted they know which way they went," Micah answered. "But they're bound to be takin' her back home to Paris. And that trail we followed over here from the Red River is most likely the way they went back, so we'd best get goin'."

Leonard was disappointed to hear their decision to go after Becky and her rescuers and he couldn't resist speaking his concern. "I hope we ain't makin' one big mistake after another," he said. When both of the Sage brothers paused to see if he had more to say, he went on. "I mean, first off, we was just lookin' for trouble when we carried that woman off." He looked directly at Micah. "You said that, yourself, Micah. We shoulda let her go as soon as we was clear of town. If we hadda, Lucas would still be alive. If we catch up with that woman and kill her, it still ain't gonna bring Lucas back. But it'll sure give the Texas Rangers and the Oklahoma marshals more time to track us down. We're totin' more money than I ever thought I'd get to see in my lifetime. Why don't we say to hell with that woman and get outta this Injun Territory while we've still got that money? You're right, Micah, that woman's bad luck."

"Maybe it's hard for you to understand," Micah responded to his plea. "It don't matter to Jesse and me whose fault it was. One of those jaspers ridin' with Becky killed our brother, so they've got to answer for that with their own lives. An eye for an eye, that's just the way it has to be. And although the woman didn't kill Lucas, she caused him to get killed, so she's got to die, too." He paused for a moment and asked, "Hell, ain't you wantin' to go after the jasper that put a bullet in your shoulder?"

"Not if it costs me the chance to get away with the money," Leonard replied before giving his answer much thought. When he saw the judgmental look in the eyes of both brothers, he began to worry about the possibility they might be thinking about eliminating him and keeping all the money for themselves. "I just wanted to throw that out there, if you weren't sure what's the best thing to do. Me? Hell, I'm for whatever you boys wanna do."

"Good. Let's get goin', then," Jesse said impatiently, and turned his horse to follow the main road out of town to the south. Micah followed at once with Leonard after him, leading their packhorse. When they came to the trail that led back the way they had come from crossing the Red, they stopped only long enough to confirm fresh tracks made fairly recently. Then they pushed their horses hard, gambling on the idea that they weren't that far behind Becky and her friends. Micah planned to catch them when they stopped to rest their horses. He seemed to have no concern for the fact that Leonard's right arm was in a sling, nor the fact that Jesse could not grip his pistol with his right hand. He had confidence in his ability to take care of the situation by himself.

They had gotten off to a late start and held the horses to a steady pace in an effort to push them a little farther than they normally would have. According to Possum's railroad pocket watch, it took them six hours to reach the same place they had stopped to rest their horses on their way to Durant. It was also the same place where Becky had attempted her escape. Thoughts of that unsuccessful flight caused her to ask her traveling companions if she could select a spot for their fire on the opposite side of the small clearing from the one used on the reverse trip. It made no difference to Perley or Possum, so they built a small fire sufficient to heat up a pot of coffee while the horses were watered and rested. While they waited for the coffee to boil, Becky decided to take a short walk downstream to answer a call from nature. While she was gone, Possum thought it a good time to talk to Perley about an important aspect of their journey. "You know, we've been thinkin' we ain't likely to see those three outlaws again. They didn't show up in town this mornin' like we figured they might. So it sure looked like they decided to head for parts unknown."

"I figured they sure mighta come lookin' for us last night," Perley said, "after Becky told us that one fellow I shot was the brother of two of the other three."

"Right," Possum said. "So you're thinkin' what I'm thinkin'. We'd best make sure we ain't got those jaspers on our tail."

"That's what I'm thinkin'," Perley allowed. "I didn't wanna say too much about it in front of Becky. And it's the real reason I didn't wanna stop at that stream about five miles back. I didn't wanna make it too easy for anybody to catch up with us. I think now we can rest the horses up good here, then push 'em again and make the Triple-G tonight, so we won't have to camp overnight. Becky can stay at the ranch tonight and we'll take her into town in the mornin'. Whaddaya think?"

"I think that's a damn good idea," Possum said. "These horses can make the trip in one day. That's about sixty miles, but we've already gone over half of it right here. Hell, they're in shape to make it. Late as it is, though, it's gonna put us in the dark for the last part of it."

"We've gotta make sure they're rested up good before we start out from here," Perley stressed. "So I think I'd best go back to that ridge we passed about a quarter of a mile back there where I can keep an eye on our back trail, just in case those three pushed their horses as hard as we did."

"Shoot, I can do that," Possum volunteered at once, "and you can keep Becky company."

"I know you could, but I think it'd be best for me to do it, and you can help Becky cook something to eat while we're waitin'." When Possum insisted that wasn't fair for him to sit up on that ridge the whole time, Perley had to confess. "It's better for me to do it because my eyes are younger than yours and I can see farther. And if I see three riders comin', I can run faster than you can to get back here."

Possum poked his bottom lip out and looked a little hurt for a moment, but then admitted, "I reckon I can't argue with you on that. But when I was your age, I could run like an antelope."

"I'll bet you could," Perley said. "But now, you're packin' all that wisdom you picked up over the years and wisdom will slow you down."

Possum couldn't keep from smiling. "You think you're japin' me, but what you said is the truth. My wisdom let you talk yourself into settin' up on a ridge while I'll be down here by the fire, drinkin' coffee."

"I didn't think about that," Perley pretended.

"Didn't think about what?" Becky called out as she walked back into the clearing.

"Didn't think about maybe you wantin' to fix the coffee, in case I made it too strong," Possum answered her.

"No worry about that," she said. "I like it strong as blackstrap and any coffee will taste good today." They knew what she meant and that was the reason they didn't want to ruin her mood with thoughts that they might still be in for a visit from the three outlaws.

"I'll wait long enough for that coffee to finish boilin', so I can take a cup of it with me," Perley said aside to Possum. "If I see any sign of 'em on that trail behind us, I'll fire one shot in the air. Then I'll come runnin'. I think if that happens, we won't have any trouble outrunnin' 'em 'cause their horses will be exhausted." When he said it, he realized that it depended upon how soon after they left Durant that the outlaws came after them. Had he known that the time lapse between their leaving the town and the three outlaws coming after them was only a matter of minutes, he would have tried to come up with a different strategy.

When the coffee was ready, Becky filled three cups and sat down at the fire with Possum. "I'm gonna take a little walk back up the road a ways," Perley announced. "I'll just take my coffee with me." He turned and walked away before Becky had a chance to comment or ask a question.

After he started walking, he figured the ridge was probably less than a quarter of a mile behind them. *Good,* he thought, *I won't have to run as far.* When he got to the treeless ridge, he climbed up through the short grass to the top, where he took a long look around before seating himself to finish his coffee. It was a good lookout spot, he decided, because he could see the trail they had just ridden for perhaps half a mile or more.

As he sat there watching their back trail, he thought about the plans he and Possum had discussed to make it to the Triple-G that night. He wondered now if those plans were realistic. The afternoon was already approaching evening and he knew their horses were not ready to start out on a thirty-mile ride yet. Even Buck might quit on him before they reached the Red River. He stood up and peered back along the trail, straining to see any sign of movement that would indicate the three outlaws were catching up to them. When the evening shadows began to lengthen, he decided they were evidently in the clear, so he descended from the ridge and walked back to the camp.

"I've been thinkin' about what we decided to do tonight." Those were the first words Possum greeted him with when he walked back to the campfire.

"Me, too," Perley replied. "It might not be such a good idea. The horses ain't had enough rest to go that far yet and it's gettin' pretty late already. You think we oughta just camp here till mornin'?"

"I was kinda thinkin' that way," Possum said, "and Becky said she don't mind waitin' till daylight to go back." He glanced at the young lady and she confirmed his statement with a nod of her head. "But 'stead of campin' here," he continued, "I think it wouldn't hurt to ride on a little bit farther tonight before it gets hard dark—say, five or ten miles—whatever it takes to find some water for the horses. If those jaspers are just a little ways behind us, they might think we've gone on the rest of the way when they see this fire. And their horses will be tired out. They'll have to rest 'em, so they'd more than likely decide it wouldn't do no good to try to catch us tonight."

"I reckon it wouldn't hurt to put a little more space between us and them," Perley allowed. He looked at Becky and smiled. "So, if that's what you two decided, it's fine by me."

With that agreed upon, they put out the fire and mounted

up to continue following the trail leading them back to their original Red River crossing. Possum's memory of a stream somewhere around eight to ten miles farther proved to be accurate, so when they reached it, they unpacked again and prepared to make camp. Soon, the coffeepot was bubbling again and there was bacon frying in the pan. It was difficult not to feel as if they were safe at this point, but Perley was still of a mind that it didn't pay to be careless. So when it was time to turn in for the night, he suggested it might be a good idea to be alert for any unwelcome nighttime visitors.

The unwelcome visitors Perley was concerned about were, at that moment, approaching the campsite Perley and his companions had vacated a little over an hour before. "They finally had to stop and rest their horses," Jesse commented. "I was 'bout to think they were gonna ride 'em right into the ground."

Micah quickly dismounted and knelt by the remains of the fire. "These ashes ain't but about an hour old." The irony of what had just happened occurred to him and was enough to inflame his anger again. "Damn," he swore as he stood up and kicked violently at the ashes. "They was restin' their horses the same time we was restin' ours and we wasn't five miles apart." The three of them had agreed that it appeared Becky and her two friends were going to ride until the horses quit of their own accord before they rested them. Thinking that to be the case, Micah had decided to stop and rest their horses about five miles back. Then they would overtake the three of them on fresh horses when their horses were worn out, he thought.

Now, it infuriated him to find that the woman and her two friends were on fresh horses as well.

"Now what?" Leonard asked, hoping this setback would be enough to cause Micah to quit the chase. "Looks like they're fixin' to ride all night."

Micah didn't answer him for a few moments while he considered that possibility. "I ain't so sure," he finally said. "They ain't got no way to know somebody's chasin' 'em. It's gettin' awful dark. They might just be figurin' on pushin' on a little bit farther, so it won't put 'em so late gettin' to Paris tomorrow." He looked at Jesse and nodded, convinced. "If we step it up, we might have a chance to catch 'em when they do decide to stop for the night." He climbed back on his horse. "Let's not waste any more time here." He gave his horse a kick and started out again without waiting for any comments from Jesse or Leonard.

Leonard looked at Jesse, about to speak, but Jesse cut him off. "Ain't no use to complain. When Micah's got his mind set on somethin', you might as well keep shut and go with it."

They rode for more than an hour when Micah pulled his horse to a stop and pointed toward a line of trees that indicated a stream ahead. When Jesse pulled up beside him, Micah said, "Smoke. I told you so." Jesse squinted, trying to see what he was pointing at in the darkness. He couldn't see the smoke at first, but then, some little sparks caught up in the smoke gave it away. "I told you so," Micah repeated. "There's a campfire down that stream up ahead. We caught 'em.

CHAPTER 8

"We can ride a little closer, then we'll leave the horses and go into that camp on foot," Micah directed. "If we're lucky, maybe we'll catch 'em all sleepin'."

"We just gonna shoot 'em all?" Jesse asked. "I'm thinkin' we might wanna keep that little woman alive— for a little while longer, anyway."

"No, hell, no!" Micah responded. "Draggin' that woman with us is what killed Lucas and what's causin' us to be ridin' around in the dark down here in Injun Territory. We'll go into that camp and shoot every last one of 'em."

"Then we're gettin' to hell outta here, right, Micah?" Leonard asked.

"That's right," Micah answered. "Now, let's go get it done."

Since the camp appeared to be thirty-five or forty yards downstream from the trail crossing, they dismounted and tied their horses next to the trail. Then, with guns drawn, they made their way cautiously along the side of the stream in single file, with Micah leading. Close enough now, they could see a small clearing with a fire burning in the center. Micah dropped to one knee to look the camp over. Pulling up on either side of him, Jesse and Leonard did the same. "Ain't that nice of 'em?" Jesse said. "They're all rolled up in their blankets asleep."

"Maybe they are and maybe they ain't," Micah said, staring at the three almost identical bundles, lying like spokes on three sides of the fire. "They all look too much alike to suit me, with the blankets just throwed over their heads and ever'thin' else. They're playin' it cute, waitin' for somebody to come walkin' in there and shootin' up their blankets. I ain't that dumb." He pointed beyond the clearing toward the stream. "That's where they're sleepin', where that bank rises up. That's the best place for cover and that's where they're waitin'."

"How you reckon they got onto us?" Jesse wondered.

"Maybe they ain't got onto us," Micah said. "They just ain't takin' no chances. They gotta be behind that bank yonder. There ain't no other place to give 'em cover. You and Leonard circle around and see if you can get a clear shot at 'em. I'm gonna walk right through that clearing and put a shot in each one of them blankets, just to be sure. When they hear them shots, that'll get 'em outta their holes. You keep your eye on that bank, and as soon as a head pops up, knock it down." Even as he said it, he knew he was the only one he could really count on, since both of his partners were carrying their pistols in their left hands. He felt sure he could get a shot off faster before one of the men with Becky could raise up and fire. And his two left-handers should be able to throw enough lead at them to make the other one duck.

He waited until Jesse circled around to the left and Leonard did the same on the right. When he saw they were in a position to fire, he left the cover of the trees and stepped into the light of the circle. When he was within a few feet of the first decoy, he put a shot in it. Then he walked to the next one and put a bullet in that blanket just as the blanket on the third decoy was flung aside and Perley sat up, his six-gun blazing. Micah sank to one knee when Perley's first shot caught him in the side. Jesse turned to throw a left-handed shot at Perley, only to drop his gun and bend over double when a shot from Possum's rifle struck him in the stomach. Leonard turned frantically toward Possum, then back to Perley, both with their weapons trained on him, waiting for him to commit. Knowing he was outgunned, he tossed his six-shooter aside and put his hands in the air. "I reckon I know when I'm whipped, boys," he said in surrender. "We walked right into that one, didn't we?"

"Reckon you did," Possum responded, and walked up from the bank to pick up his gun.

"I swear," Leonard had to comment, "Micah said there wasn't nothin' in them blankets, that it was a setup, and we still walked right into it."

"Looks that way, don't it?" Possum said. "Set yourself down at that tree over there and put your hands behind you." Leonard did as he was told and Possum quickly tied his hands together around the tree.

Perley and Possum both watched Micah intently as he remained on one knee, his shirt soaking up blood from the wound in his side. His Colt .44 still in his hand, he looked from one of his assailants to the other, like a wounded buffalo. "Looks like you're tryin' to make up your mind which one of us you're gonna shoot at," Perley said. "Whichever one you pick, the other one is gonna put a bullet in your head. But you got a choice. Throw that gun down and we'll let you live—even try to see if we can treat that wound. Right, Possum?" Possum nodded, never taking his eyes off the hand that still held the gun. "I can't make any promises for your friend lyin' on the ground over there. He's gut-shot and it don't look too good for him."

Micah remained in his kneeling position, the Colt in his hand, his brain still reeling from the sudden collapse of his plan to kill all in the camp. He was sure the burning wound in his side was serious, probably fatal. His second brother was dying at the hands of the men who killed Lucas. A fortune in bank money was on his packhorse, never to ensure his future. Since he was dying anyway, he decided to take at least one of them with him. He chose the one who had been bold enough to lie in wait by the campfire with nothing but a blanket for protection. His hand was halfway around toward his target when Perley's bullet slammed into his forehead, killing him instantly.

"I swear," Possum said, exhaling, and went over to take a look at the body. After a few seconds, he looked at Perley and said, "That wound in his side weren't that bad a-tall. The bullet went right on out the back." He walked over to join Perley, who was checking to see how bad Jesse's wound was. Perley looked up at Possum and shook his head.

Obviously in great pain, Jesse cursed them and forced out through clinched teeth, "You kilt me this time," recognizing Perley as the one who shot him in the hand. "Did you kill Micah?" Jesse struggled to ask through the blood coming from his mouth.

"He committed suicide," Possum was quick to tell him.

"If you hurry up, you can catch the same train to hell with him." When Perley gave him a scolding look, Possum responded, "What? They was of a mind to kidnap Becky, then came to shoot me and you. Hell is where folks like that go." Perley might not have worried, for Jesse was gone seconds before Possum answered him.

"It's all over, Becky," Perley called back toward the stream. "Why don't you just stay where you are till Possum and I take these bodies off in the trees?"

"Are you all right?" she called back to him.

"Yes, ma'am, we're both all right. I'll give you a holler when we've cleared them away," Perley answered.

Once the bodies were removed from their campsite, they had to decide what to do with their one captive. "For what it's worth," Leonard told them, "right from the start, I tried to talk Micah and Jesse outta comin' after you folks, but they wouldn't listen to me."

"Well, it ain't worth much, 'cause you came, anyway," Possum replied. "Where'd you leave your horses?"

"Back by the trail," Leonard answered. "You know, like I said, comin' after you folks weren't my idea. If you'd just let me take my horse, I'd be obliged to ride as far away from you as I could. You wouldn't never see me no more. Then you wouldn't have to bother with takin' me back to Texas."

"Well, now, that's somethin' to think about, ain't it, Perley?" Possum stroked his whiskers as if thinking it over. "But you know, puttin' a bullet in your head would work just as well." He reached in his pocket and pulled out a coin. "We wanna be fair about it, so the least we can do is flip a coin, I reckon. Heads, we take you back to jail. Tails, we just shoot you right here."

Seeing the look of panic appear on Leonard's face, Perley decided Possum's japing had gone far enough. "We'll be takin' you back to Paris to turn you over to the sheriff," he said. "If you don't cause us any trouble, we'll take it as easy as we can on you, but you're gonna have to spend the rest of this night tied up."

"Oh, you'll see," Leonard insisted, "I ain't gonna cause you no trouble. I'm done runnin' with robbers and killers. I was already fixin' to leave Micah and Jesse, but they made me ride down here with 'em. I told 'em I didn't want a share in that bank money they stole, I just wanted to leave the territory and start over."

"And maybe start up a little church somewhere and you could do the preachin'," Possum mocked, unable to resist the urge. "If you'da cut out before you rode down here to kill us, you coulda built a regular cathedral with your share of that bank money." Leonard didn't bother to protest, since it was obvious that he wasn't likely to convince them of his innocence.

With Leonard left with his hands behind him and tied around the tree trunk, Possum walked out to the trail to bring the outlaws' horses back to the camp, while Perley went to check on Becky. "Might be the best thing for you to just stay right here in your blanket and try to go to sleep," he suggested as he knelt beside her. "Our prisoner is tied to a tree, and Possum and I will drag the other two off away from the creek and maybe bury 'em. Anyway, there ain't any use for you to have to see 'em again. Will you be all right?"

"Yes," she answered. When he started to stand up to leave, she caught his arm. "And Perley, I knew if anybody came to save me, it would be you."

"Well, I'd surely always try," he responded. "I hope you don't ever have as close a call as this one again, though. I'll go help Possum with the bodies now." She sighed, disappointed, as she watched him walk away. What, she wondered, was she going to have to do to get him to express his feelings for her? She was afraid to be blatant about her feelings, afraid he didn't really have any such thoughts about her.

Possum and Perley carried the two bodies off into the trees far enough to be out of sight of anyone who might pick the same spot to camp as they did. There was a short spade on the outlaws' packhorse, so they considered digging a grave, but not for long. "Hell," Possum said, "critters gotta eat, too."

"I reckon you're right," Perley said. "No use in inter-ferin' with nature's natural cycle."

As they walked back to the camp, Possum confessed, "We gotta take the saddles offa their horses and unload that packhorse. I'll have to admit I had to take a little peek in those sacks on the packhorse. I swear, Perley, I ain't ever seen that much money at one time in my whole life. Makes a man think about walkin' on the other side of the line."

"That's strange talk comin' from a man who owns a hotel," Perley joked.

"Half a hotel," Possum corrected. "Besides, it's way to hell down there in Bison Gap. Emma might be cheatin' me blind while I'm wastin' my time up here lookin' after you."

Perley laughed. "Is that what you're doin'?"

"Yeah, and it's a full-time job," Possum answered. Then he got serious for a moment. "I'll tell you one thing, though. I'll feel a helluva lot better when we get this money back to the bank. I'm thinkin' about that poor devil over there tied to a tree. Ain't no tellin' what a man like that would do to get his hands back on that money, especially now, when it ain't a three-way split no more. I'm thinkin' I'll just set up and keep an eye on him. By the time we take care of their horses, there ain't gonna be much left of this night, anyway."

"You're right about that," Perley agreed. "Tell you what, why don't we both watch him? You take the first watch for a couple of hours, then come wake me up, and I'll take a couple of hours. It oughta be daylight by then, and we can get started back." Possum agreed, so that's what they did.

Young Link Drew stopped on his way to the barn when he spotted what appeared to be a group of riders approaching from the north. It was hard to tell at that distance exactly how many there were. So he continued on across the barnyard to the corner of the corral and climbed up a couple of rails to give himself a higher perch to look from. He was hoping it was Perley returning home from his search for Becky Morris, but he couldn't see the small figures in the distance well enough to identify anyone.

Now they were close enough for Link to determine there were four riders and they were leading some extra horses. His pulse suddenly quickened when he realized that one of the riders was a woman. *Becky Morris!* he thought. Immediately after, he recognized the familiar figures of Perley and Possum. He didn't wait any longer to yell out, "Perley's back!" and ran to the barn to tell Fred Farmer and Ralph Johnson. They both ran back outside with the boy, to greet the returning searchers.

"By Ned, they found her," Fred marveled. "And it looks like they've brought back one of the men who took her."

"I declare, I do have to admit that I didn't give 'em much of a chance to catch up with the girl and no chance a-tall to find her alive," Ralph confessed.

Hearing the conversation outside his cookhouse, Ollie Dinkler stepped out the door to see what they were excited about. When he looked in the direction they were looking, he uttered, "Well, I'll be . . . I'd better roll out some more biscuits and make sure I've got enough beans to feed a few more at the supper table."

"Link, run up to the house and tell Rubin that Perley and Possum's back," Fred told him, and Link was off at once. In a couple of minutes, he was back with Rubin Gates. "Looks like Perley's back, Boss," Fred informed him.

"Yeah, that's what Link told me," Rubin replied. "Did he say they had a prisoner?"

"Looks that way," Fred answered. "Leastways, it ain't nobody I know."

A minute more, and Rubin's wife, Lou Ann, and John's wife, Martha, came out the kitchen door and walked across the barnyard to join the men. "Thank the good Lord," Lou Ann offered. "They did save her."

At the edge of the barnyard now, the rescue party could be clearly seen. "Oh, dear me," Martha said, "she's been beat up something bad. That poor baby." They stood by and waited to welcome the rescue party. As soon as the horses were reined to a stop, Martha and Lou Ann rushed to Becky's side to help her dismount. "Are you all right?" Martha asked, her face twisted with concern.

"Yes, ma'am, I am now," Becky answered softly.

Both Gates women turned to glower at Leonard Watts,

seated quietly on his horse, his hands tied together. "Is this the sinful scum that did this to you?" she demanded as if about to do something about it, if he was.

"No, ma'am," Leonard answered before Becky had time. "It was some of that other scum I was ridin' with. I ain't never laid a hand on her. She can tell you that." Convinced that he was in the hands of captors not likely to cause him any physical harm as long as he made no attempt to escape, he didn't hesitate to speak on his own behalf.

With Rubin, however, it was a different matter. "She wasn't talkin' to you and I'd advise you to keep your mouth shut unless somebody asks you something." He looked at Perley then. "Is he gonna be trouble? 'Cause if he is, we'll hang him from the hayloft until you're ready to take him into town."

"No, he ain't gonna be no trouble, are you, Leonard?"

"No, sir, no trouble a-tall," Leonard replied.

Rubin studied the reticent prisoner for a long moment before asking Perley, "What are you plannin' to do with him? You gonna take him into town right away? It's suppertime already. I don't know how far you've come today." He glanced over at Becky, who had been led several yards away by the two Gates wives. "She looks like she'd be better off stayin' overnight here at the ranch, and you can take her to town in the mornin'." He looked at Possum for confirmation and Possum nodded in agreement. It was his opinion that Becky needed a little more time to get her emotions under control.

"I was thinkin' that, myself," Perley said. "She's been through more in the last couple of days than any woman oughta ever go through in their whole lives. I don't expect her to get over it right away." He didn't get a chance to tell her of his decision, however, before Lou Ann informed them of the final judgment.

"Becky is going to stay here tonight," Lou Ann said. "There are some things she needs, and one of them is a good supper. Martha and I will help her bathe and change her bandages, and she can sleep in the spare room. Perley, you can take her home tomorrow, if she wants to go. She's welcome to stay here as long as she needs to." Without waiting for any response from him, Lou Ann and Martha turned the young woman around and marched her to the house. Becky turned her head back to give Perley one helpless look as she was led away.

"Sounds to me like the big bosses done spoke," Leonard saw fit to comment.

Rubin looked at Perley, then turned to Possum and asked, "Does he understand that he's a prisoner and you're takin' him to jail?"

"I thought we explained it to him pretty carefully," Possum replied, amused by Rubin's frustration with Leonard's behavior. "We thought he'd figure it out for himself after we had to kill his three partners and he decided to surrender."

Rubin shook his head, exasperated. "So whaddaya gonna do, Perley? Take him on into town tonight, or wait till tomorrow? If you wanna wait till tomorrow, we could just lock him in the smokehouse tonight. Did you recover that stolen bank money?"

"It's in those canvas sacks on the packhorses," Perley said. "And to tell you the truth, I don't think they even had a chance to spend any of it."

"He's right, Mr. Gates," Leonard volunteered again.

"We never got to anyplace where we could spend any of it, except at the doctor's office for my shoulder and Jesse's hand. Your brother was responsible for both wounds. And they was both pretty good shots, too, I was . . ."

That was as far as he got before Rubin exploded. "Shut him up, if you have to do it with a bullet to his head!" He turned to follow the women to the house but paused long enough to tell Perley to secure the bank money if he decided to wait till morning to go to town. "And make sure he's locked up tight." He walked away, taking long forceful strides and mumbling to himself, "Cow pie!"

"I'll tell you the truth, boys," Leonard announced, "I was hopin' we'd decide to stay here tonight. I figure I'll get a better supper here." Perley and Possum exchanged looks of disbelief and both grinned. "Won't I?" Leonard asked when neither of his captors said anything. "I mean, you're gonna feed me, ain'tcha?"

Fascinated witnesses to the whole discussion about what Perley was going to do with his prisoner, Fred, Link, and Ollie remained speechless until Fred said he'd help Link put some hay in the smokehouse for Leonard to use for a bed. "I'll fix him up with some chuck," Ollie said. "I reckon he'll like it. I ain't sure what dodo birds eat."

"I'll bring you the lock for that smokehouse when I bring the hay," Fred said. "I'll draw him a bucket of water and give him another bucket for slops." He looked at Leonard and said, "It'll be just like you used to have it at home."

"Maybe better," Leonard replied, "except I don't cotton to sleepin' in a smokehouse. I get confused in the dark. It'd be all right with me to just sleep in the bunkhouse with your ranch hands."

"It would, huh?" Possum responded. "It's too bad Becky's gonna be in the spare room in the house. We coulda put you in there and you coulda et with the boss's family."

"I can just eat in the cookhouse with the rest of your hands," Leonard replied. "No need to put yourself out on accounta me."

Possum and Perley exchanged glances of disbelief again. "Leonard, have you ever been in jail?" Perley asked.

"Sure have," Leonard replied. "I was in the Arkansas State Prison for four years. That's where I got to be friends with Jesse Sage. I got to know some other fellers there, too, but me and Jesse got to be real friends."

"Well, we ain't got no other prisoners here but you," Perley said. "So you'll be locked up by yourself, and the best place we've got for that is the smokehouse. It'll be dark in there, but, if you close your eyes, you won't know the difference. We'll bring you something to eat and you'll be fine till we let you out in the mornin'. All right?"

He hesitated a moment before answering but finally said, "I reckon. It's gonna be dark pretty soon, anyway, and I always close my eyes when I'm goin' to sleep."

"There you go," Perley responded. "Now slide offa that horse and we'll put 'em away for the night." While Leonard watched, his hands still tied together, Perley and Possum pulled the saddles off the horses with Ralph's help. When Fred and Link brought in enough hay for Leonard's bed, Perley marched him over to the smoke-house and locked him in. "We'll bring you some supper in a little while." When he walked away, he could hear Leonard mumbling to himself. He imagined it being much like how a small child afraid of the dark talks to himself.

The saddles and packsaddles, except for the canvas sacks containing money, were taken into the stable for the night. The bank money was taken into the bunkhouse to stay with Perley and Possum. Additional protection would be provided by the rest of the Triple-G crew. Perley felt it couldn't get much better protection than that. He had supper in the ranch house with the family, since these were special circumstances. He was made aware of that when the cook, Alice Farmer, sent her son, Jimmy, with a message from Rubin's wife, advising Perley that he should join the family for supper, since Becky was there. Perley had been considering doing that and the summons made up his mind. As it turned out, he didn't have much conversation with Becky. His sisters-in-law hovered over her like mother hens and his communication with Becky was very little more than wistful glances. Perley wondered if they had told Becky that the spare room she was occupying was actually Perley's room, even though he never used it. When supper was finished, they swept her off to help her prepare for bed, concerned that she needed rest to recover from her ordeal. Perley talked to Rubin and John for about an hour before retiring to the bunkhouse. They were very much interested in hearing all about the chase and the ultimate showdown. Both brothers knew they would get many more of the details when they talked to Possum in the morning.

CHAPTER 9

As was his usual custom, Perley slept in the bunkhouse with the rest of the men. He had breakfast in the cookhouse, where he was entertained with the various plans to abscond with a canvas sack of money during the night. "Good thing you didn't," he told Sonny Rice, "'cause Possum would most likely have shot you."

They brought Leonard out of his makeshift jail cell and Link Drew and Jimmy Farmer were given the job of taking the buckets out and cleaning up anything that wasn't there when they put Leonard in the smokehouse. Blinking against the light of the rising sun, he came out of the smokehouse looking much like a puppy that had just been released from a cage. "It got so dark in there till I got mixed up," he volunteered. "I weren't sure if my eyes was open or closed. I had to stick my finger in my eye to tell which way it was."

There were half a dozen men standing around, waiting to get a look at the prisoner. As one of the four robbers that stole all the money from the new bank, he was worthy of their gawking and something to crow about the next time they visited Patton's Saloon in town. Although the men gathered around him were rubbernecking, they were also charged with the responsibility to make sure he sat right there on the doorsill of the smokehouse. "Here," Ollie said as he pushed through the little circle of men and set a tray of food down in front of Leonard. "You'd best get busy and eat your breakfast. Perley's already got the horses saddled and ready to go." Leonard didn't hesitate to accommodate him. There was no real need to hurry, however, for Perley was still in the kitchen up at the house, waiting for Becky. He was in no particular hurry to get started, although he was looking forward to ridding himself of Leonard and the bank's money, too. He took advantage of the delay and had a cup of coffee with Alice Farmer.

"They oughta be just about ready to turn that sweet young woman over to you," Alice said. "Martha and Lou Ann have been fussin' over her ever since you brought her here. I think they wanna be sure her mind ain't been warped by whatever mighta happened to her when those filthy bandits had her captured."

"She seemed all right to me and Possum," Perley replied. "Just acted like she was glad to see us when we showed up."

"Well, she's a fine young lady, I don't care what mighta happened to her," Alice declared. "Some lucky young man will realize that one day, I suppose."

"I reckon," Perley agreed. "Any coffee left in that pot?" Alice shook her head, exasperated, and started to go to the stove to see, but Perley stopped her when the hallway door opened. "Hold on, Alice, I think she's ready."

Lou Ann and Martha led Becky into the kitchen as if presenting the queen of England, then stood watching Perley and Alice for their reactions. Perley, honest as ever, was the first to remark. "My goodness, Becky, you sure look a lot better'n when we brought you in last night."

"Thank you, Perley," Becky replied, and favored him with a warm smile. "I hope you haven't been waiting too long."

"Didn't make any difference," he said. "It ain't but five miles to town, and we've got all day. I wanted to ask you if you'd rather have me hitch up the buckboard to take you in. Or would you rather ride Martha's little mare in and I'll bring her back?" He glanced at his sister-in-law. "That all right with you, Martha?" Martha said that, of course, it was.

"Then I'd rather ride the mare," Becky said. "I'll ride beside you and Buck."

"Good," Perley said, grinning. "You'd make Buck proud, if he heard you say that."

She laughed happily. "I'll tell him that," she said.

"I reckon we're ready to ride, then. The horses are saddled"—he paused to give her a grin—"includin' the little mare." He went to the back door and held it open for them and they all filed outside to see them off, with Becky still thanking them for their kindness. She saw Possum standing a little apart from the other horses, holding the reins of Leonard's horse. So she went toward the big bay gelding and the little sorrel mare. Perley started after her but stopped when Rubin told him to hold up a minute.

"What are you thinkin' about doin' with the money?" Rubin asked. "You gonna turn it over to the sheriff, or are you gonna take it back to the bank? I don't know if there's any reason to tie Wilford Taylor's money up any longer than it already has been. It's his money. There ain't much doubt about that. I'm afraid if you turn that money over to Paul McQueen, he won't know what to do with it and he ain't got anyplace to put that money but in the bank, anyway."

"Yeah," Perley said. "I'd wondered about that, myself, whether the federal people had to be involved or not. I decided, like you said, it's the bank's money. I'll just take it back to them." He was about to say more but was distracted when he heard Possum shout.

"No!" Possum yelped.

Then Perley saw what had caused him to cry out and started running as fast as he could, repeating over and over, "No, Becky! No." But it was too late to stop her. The unsuspecting young woman already had her foot in the stirrup. And hearing Perley rushing up behind her, she threw her leg over and settled in the saddle before turning the big bay around toward Perley. She pressed her heels against Buck's sides and the big bay gently walked to meet Perley.

Stunned, Perley stopped before reaching her. Becky, smiling playfully, reined Buck to a halt beside Perley. "He's such a handsome devil," she said. "I just wanted to see how it felt to have this big horse under me. You don't mind if I just wanted to ride him, do you?" Perley was still in a severe case of shock over witnessing what she had just done. And when he didn't answer her, she prodded, "Do you?"

"What?" he blurted, then, "Oh . . . no, I don't care if you ride him. I just ain't ready to believe what I'm seein'."

"I'll take him back," she said, turned Buck around, and trotted back to the corner of the corral where the little mare was tied. Perley trotted along behind her on foot, his arms extended slightly, looking as if he was prepared to catch her when Buck threw her. She pulled up beside the mare and hopped down from the saddle with his help to catch her. By this time, everyone out in the yard was staring in disbelief, with the exception of Leonard, who was as clueless as Becky.

Sonny got to her first and exclaimed, "I ain't sure I believe what I just saw. I ain't never seen that before." When she reacted with only a puzzled expression, he said, "Ain't nobody but Perley ever been able to ride that horse," he explained, excited even more to hear himself say it. "That's the reason Perley named him Buck—'cause he does. But he don't just buck, I mean, can't nobody but Perley stay on him and there's lots of men tried. Even John, Perley's brother, can't stay on Buck, and breakin' horses is John's specialty. Tell her, Perley," he said when Perley just stood there, thinking about what he had expected to happen.

"I'm sorry," she said at once, thinking she had done something wrong. "I just stroked his neck a little and told him how handsome he is. Then I just took a notion to see how it felt to you when you were riding him. I hope I didn't make you mad."

"Becky, I ain't mad at you. I was just afraid you were gonna get hurt," Perley said. Like Sonny and everybody else who witnessed it, he found it hard to believe what he had just seen with his own eyes. "It's just that Buck don't like anybody on his back but me. That's the way he's always been, and he's thrown a lot of good men."

She turned and stroked the bay's face. "I can't believe he'd ever hurt anybody, he's so gentle."

Perley took Buck's reins from her and looked the horse in the eye. "You might have more sense than I've been givin' you credit for." He turned then and called, "You ready to ride, Possum?" Possum said that he was, and promptly got Leonard up on his horse. Perley politely gave Becky a hand up on the mare, thinking that, if she could climb up on Buck, she should surely be able to get on the mare without help. They started out for the short ride into town with just the four horses. The other horses Perley and Possum had acquired on their way back from Durant remained in the Triple-G horse herd. The only cargo they carried was in the canvas sacks filled with money. Rubin had suggested that they might want to take a couple of the men with them as extra guards, but Perley and Possum were confident they could safely transport the prisoner and Becky over that short distance.

Back at the foot of the kitchen steps, where they had witnessed the drama of Becky's amazing ride on Perley's horse, the three women were speechless until Alice spoke. "I declare, if that ain't a sign, I don't know what is. Even the damn horse is tryin' to tell him."

Thomas Deal ran back into Wilford Taylor's office without knocking first, causing Taylor to wonder if the bank was being robbed again. *They're out of luck,* he thought. *There isn't any money left to steal.* He had a big new vault scheduled to be constructed next week and he hoped to convince the customers who had banked with him before to return when they saw the new safe. It was not going to be easy to persuade the customers who had lost their savings in the holdup unless he could give them some kind of guarantee. "What is it, Tom?" he asked the excited young bank teller.

"You've gotta come see, Mr. Taylor! Perley Gates and

Possum Smith are riding down the middle of the street and they've got Becky Morris with 'em!" Taylor got up from his desk immediately and followed Tom out to the front door. "And that's not all," Tom continued. "They've got one of those robbers with 'em, too!" That was the news Taylor wanted to hear, and as a result, encouraged him to run.

Perley and his party had already attracted a growing crowd of curious followers as they approached the jail, and Paul McQueen came out to meet him. Becky seemed to be in no particular hurry to reunite with Beulah and Lucy in the hotel dining room, so Perley turned Leonard over to McQueen first, with a brief account of how he came to be captured. He told the sheriff about the money and said he was going to turn it over to Wilford Taylor. McQueen agreed that it was the proper thing to do. "I'm mighty glad to see you back here, Becky," McQueen said to her. "The whole town's been grievin' over your kidnapping."

"Thank you, Sheriff," Becky replied, but she was thinking that, while they were grieving, Perley came to get her.

"After I take Becky to the hotel, I'll come back and tell you the whole story," Perley said. "I don't know if I coulda done it without Possum." Possum reacted by merely stroking his chin whiskers, but it was obvious that it pleased him. They were interrupted then by Wilford Taylor yelling something as he ran down the street to join them.

When he got a little closer, they could make out what he was asking, even though he was gasping for breath, having run nowhere in the last forty years. "Did you find any of the money?" he panted. "Please tell me you did!"

"I expect we found pretty much all of it," Perley replied. "We caught up with them before they got to anyplace where they could spend it. It's all in those canvas bags tied onto the horses."

"Praise the Lord!" Taylor cried out, then hung his head as if in a prayer of thanks. When he lifted it again, he said, "Now I can restore everybody's account who lost money when they robbed us." He raised his voice, so the people gathered around them could hear. "And when you folks see the new safe I'm having built, you'll see that it won't ever be that easy to rob us again. We're gonna employ bank guards, too."

"You tellin' me that I ain't lost that money I had in your bank?" someone shouted from the back of the crowd.

"You bet you haven't," Taylor answered him. "And you never did lose it to begin with. It was just temporarily unavailable. The bank was always gonna make good on that. The bank is the safest place to keep your savings."

"I don't know, Ebb," another man in the crowd japed. "Maybe you'd best get you a good mattress to hide your money under."

"Or maybe you oughta give it to Perley to hold for you," another spectator joked.

"You're all invited to come into the bank to see the improvements being made. Everything is being done to prevent this kind of thing from happening," Taylor announced. Then, anxious to drop the subject of bank robberies, he asked Perley, "Can I have my money back now?"

"Yes, sir," Perley replied. "Right after I see Becky back to the hotel."

"You don't have to take me back, Perley," Becky said. "I reckon I can walk from here to the dining room by myself.

I think it's pretty important that you get that money locked up in the bank."

"I reckon I just wanna see you back home safe and sound," Perley replied. "That's more important than any bank money."

"You take Becky to the hotel," Possum said. "I'll take the money to the bank. If it'll make Mr. Taylor feel any better, maybe Sheriff McQueen will go with me after he locks his prisoner up."

"That sounds like a good idea," McQueen said. "Won't take me a minute to lock Mr. Watts up in a nice clean cell." The sheriff was as good as his word and was back outside right away. He locked the door of his office and accompanied Possum and Wilford Taylor to the bank while Perley rode to the hotel with Becky.

Unaware of the small parade coming up the street to the bank, Lucy Tate almost dropped a stack of dirty dishes balanced on her arm when she looked toward the outside entrance to the dining room. "Becky!" she exclaimed loud enough for Beulah to hear her in the kitchen. Caught with an armload of dirty dishes, she was helpless to run to welcome her. She was about to make a decision when Beulah ran by her.

"Don't you drop them dishes!" Beulah warned her as she breezed by to welcome Becky back. Giving the beaming girl a crushing hug, she then stepped back to look at her. Holding her by the shoulders, she said, "You poor thing. They beat you pretty bad, didn't they?" She gave her a great big smile then and said, "But we thought you were surely dead. Praise the Lord," she offered up in thanks.

She paused then when they heard the sound of an armload of dishes landing roughly in the kitchen sink.

A moment later, Lucy rushed from the kitchen to give Becky a second bear hug. Becky was fairly astonished by Lucy's show of affection, for she never thought Lucy was that fond of her. Like Beulah, Lucy confessed, "We thought we would never see you again. We were both blubberin' around here like a couple of babies."

"Perley saved me," Becky said. "They carried me all the way over in Indian Territory, but Perley found me. Possum came with him, but Perley came into their camp and got me."

"Well, we all owe you for that," Beulah sang out, and turned to him, preparing to administer another bear hug. Perley, not quite sure he could stand up under such an assault as the one she just gave Becky, was careful to step aside, putting Becky between them.

"Welcome home, honey," Lucy whispered sweetly, and gave her a gentle hug.

For the first time, Becky felt that she truly was returning home, so overwhelmed was she by the show of affection from the two women she worked with in the dining room. She had always been grateful that Beulah had taken her in when she was an innocent girl of fourteen, trying to take care of an ailing mother while her father was serving time in the Texas state prison. Left with no roof over their heads, Becky and her mother moved into a small room behind Beulah's little restaurant, where they lived until pneumonia took her mother when Becky turned fifteen. To earn her room and board, Becky went to work in Beulah's little eating establishment. Now Becky had her own room in the hotel, just as Lucy did. There had been no contact with her father since his incarceration for robbery and attempted murder. Her whole life was centered upon the dining room, Beulah and Lucy, and the little town of Paris, Texas . . . and Perley Gates.

Perley watched for a short time while the two women captured Becky, anxious to hear any details of her abduction she was willing to divulge. Figuring she might be more comfortable if he wasn't present to hear the whole story, he announced that he had best get over to the bank to see that everything was all right with the money. When Becky cast an anxious glance in his direction, he said, "I expect Possum and I will be back here for dinner before we're all done."

"We'll be lookin' for you," Beulah told him. "Your dinner is free of charge today. Possum's, too."

He gave her a grin. "Well, I know we can't pass that up. I'll see ya after a while," he promised, and took his leave, satisfied that they would take good care of Becky.

When he got to the bank, he found Possum and Sheriff McQueen standing in the back office watching Wilford Taylor and his two tellers count the returned money. "They're still countin', Perley," Possum said when Perley walked in. "All that money—we shoulda just kept ridin' north when we got our hands on it," he joked.

Wilford Taylor stopped counting his stack long enough to extend his hand to Perley. "I was so excited to see this money back, I swear, I don't remember if I thanked you or not. But, even if I did, you deserve my thanks again." Perley shook his hand and told him he and Possum were pleased that luck was running their way. "If the doggoned safe hadn't been open, they would have had to settle for what there was in the tellers' cash drawers," Taylor added.

"I don't know," Possum commented. "These boys played pretty rough. I expect they'da started shootin' one of you at a time, till somebody opened it."

"Well, if we can guard the safe until we finish the vault, there'll be a time lock on the door, installed by the S&G mechanical lock company and nobody will be able to get in there till the clock opens the door."

"That is indeed a wonderment," Possum responded. He looked at Perley and asked, "Is there really such a thing?"

"Reckon so," Perley replied, "if Mr. Taylor says so."

"That's a fact," Taylor said, "and I'm hopin' we'll see you open an account with us, Perley."

"I ain't really got any money to open an account with," Perley replied. "Any little bit I have fits nicely in the toe of my boot. Possum's the one you wanna talk to, he owns half interest in a hotel in Bison Gap."

"Is that a fact?" Taylor said, looking at Possum with more interest.

"It ain't nothin' a-tall," Possum answered. "That's just somethin' Perley likes to jape about." He didn't like to advertise that fact around Paris and Perley knew it. Truth be known, Possum didn't know whether he had any money or not. He trusted his partner, Emma Slocum, to handle his interest in the hotel, and at the end of the year, she would let him know. "I reckon Perley's gonna need to buy a bigger pair of boots after the cattle drive to Ogallala this comin' spring," he came back at his friend. "If that's where he keeps his money."

Perley had to laugh. "I reckon both of us oughta come see you after you get that vault built with the fancy time lock on it." Curious to see how much of the stolen money was returned, he and Possum stayed until the counting was done. It was amazing to him to discover the returned money was less than thirty dollars short of the original sum. Again, Taylor found it to be a miracle and thanked Perley and Possum profusely for the money's return.

"I don't recollect if there was a reward offered for the return of that money," Possum remarked. "If there was, it'd be a good amount to open those bank accounts with, wouldn't it?"

Taylor squirmed a little when he answered. "No, that is a shame, I'll admit. We hadn't gotten the chance to report the robbery to the government yet, so there wasn't a reward posted, either."

Perley laughed and said, "You and I just don't have any luck a-tall, Possum. Come on, I wanna pick up some .44 cartridges at Stallings Dry Goods. Then it oughta be about time to get some dinner at the hotel dinin' room. Beulah told me it was free today for you and me." He looked at Taylor and winked. "Kind of a little reward for savin' a woman's life."

CHAPTER 10

Redmond Quinn gave Lucy Tate a friendly smile as he paused to look at the sign above the table by the outside door of the dining room. Then he unbuckled his gun belt and carefully coiled it around his holstered Colt .44 before laying it on the table. "I don't see any other firearms on the table," he said. "I hope that doesn't mean that I'll be the only unarmed man in the room."

Lucy returned his smile with one of her own. "You don't have to worry about that. You're the only stranger in the room. Everyone else is either a guest in the hotel or some of our regular customers and they all know they won't need a gun. So they don't bother to bring 'em." She turned to survey the room. "Plenty of empty tables. Do you have any preference?"

"Just wherever you think you'd like me to sit," he replied. "Wherever you're my server will be fine with me."

"My, my, you're easy to please," she said. "In that case, I'll seat you close to the kitchen, so I won't have to walk too far with your food." She was well aware of his close scrutiny of her person, and in fact, she would have been disappointed had he not been looking.

"To the contrary, my dear, I'm rather hard to please," he responded in English precise and softly spoken. "I don't say that to be difficult or rude, it's just a nature I'm cursed with."

As much as she hated to admit it, she was impressed by the confident gentlemanly approach from the stranger. He was certainly a far cry from the typical cowboy, farmer, or drifter she was accustomed to bantering with there in the dining room. When she asked if he would like coffee, he said he would prefer tea if they served it, but he could drink coffee if they didn't. "Coffee it is, then," she announced. Beulah had some tea, but Lucy was not of a mind to go to the trouble to fix it. Besides, she could certainly recognize a game to charm her and she was determined to let him know she was not that easily impressed.

He shrugged in response to her denial of tea and asked, "What are you serving for dinner today? Is there any choice?"

"Today, we're having meat loaf for dinner. If you come back for supper, you can have a choice between pork chops and beef stew. We don't offer a choice at the midday meal."

"Meat loaf?" he replied with no show of enthusiasm. "I expect coffee would go better with meat loaf, so I guess we'll have meat loaf."

"You won't regret it," she said, and turned immediately to fetch his coffee. Inside the kitchen, Beulah and Becky were filling plates for one of Becky's tables. "You sure you wanna be in here today?" Lucy asked Becky when she walked in. Becky had insisted she wanted to go back to work right away when they tried to persuade her to take a day of rest. Already back to her teasing ways, however, Lucy said, "I don't suppose it has anything to do with Perley comin' back here for dinner."

"Maybe it does and maybe it doesn't," Becky said, much to Lucy's surprise.

"Did you hear that, Beulah?" Lucy said as she poured a cup of coffee. "Our little gal is getting some spunk." She chuckled delightedly. "Good for you, girl." She paused then to tell Beulah she needed another plate filled. "You oughta see this dandy I'm waitin' on now. He talks like he writes poetry or something. And he's dressed like a lawyer or a professional gambler—which is about the same thing." She winked as she went out the door. "And he's got his eye on ol' Luceee!"

She placed his coffee on the table and told him his dinner would be there in a minute. "Thank you, kind lady," he replied. "I'm new here in town . . ."

"You didn't have to tell me that," she interrupted.

He smiled. "Yes, well, I am a stranger, so I was wondering if you could tell me something. When I came out of the hotel, I didn't come through the inside door. I walked in from outside and came in that door, as you saw. Out on the street, I saw what appeared to be a small demonstration or parade that ended at the bank. I noticed one of the participants wore a badge. Was it for the opening of a new bank or something?"

Lucy had to chuckle when she thought about it. "Yeah, you might say that's what it was, all right." She went on to tell him of the recent bank robbery, the abduction of Becky, and the return of both Becky and the money, plus the one surviving bank robber. "See the young lady waiting on those other tables? That's Becky and she's already back working."

"Is that a fact? I noticed the bruises and swollen nose. I wondered if she might be in a bad relationship with some unprincipled man. And you say this fellow—what did you say his name was? Pearly Gates? He rescued her and killed two of the outlaws?"

She nodded rapidly.

"He must be a real gunslinger."

"I wouldn't call Perley a gunslinger," Lucy insisted. "He's really fast with a gun. Everybody around here knows that, but he doesn't like to brag about it."

"He sounds like an interesting man. I'd like to meet him."

"Well, I know he said he was coming back here for dinner," Lucy said. "Maybe you can talk to him then. Perley's real easy to talk to."

"I might even be willing to pay for his meat loaf," Quinn said, pronouncing *meat loaf* as if it were a tainted meat.

"You won't have to do that," Lucy said. "Beulah's already told him he didn't have to pay for his dinner today because he brought Becky back to us."

"Well, lucky for me," Quinn said. "Maybe I can buy him a drink later at the saloon up the street."

"You might have to buy two 'cause Possum Smith's with him. He's the other fellow I told you about who went with him to get Becky. Possum shot one of the outlaws." The conversation about Perley was interrupted then when Becky came out of the kitchen with his meat loaf plate.

"Thank you, Becky," Quinn said, surprising her. She looked at once to Lucy, knowing she had been talking about her to the smooth-talking stranger. "I'm glad that you were able to return safely after your ordeal."

"Thank you, sir," Becky returned. "I hope you enjoy your dinner." She quickly turned around and started back toward the kitchen but stopped when Perley and Possum came in the door. She immediately went to meet them when they paused to park their guns on the table beside the one lone weapon already there. "I was beginning to think you two might have changed your minds about eating before you started back to the ranch," she remarked.

"No, ma'am," Possum replied, "not when Perley told me it was free chuck in the dinin' room today. What did Beulah cook for dinner?" When Becky told him it was meat loaf, he said, "Meat loaf, good, one of my favorite things."

"I see you didn't change your mind about goin' back to work right away," Perley said. "Don't you think you oughta take a day or two to rest up? You've been through a heck of a lot."

"I'd much rather be out here working than sitting around in my room," she answered, her gaze remaining upon Perley when she spoke. "Besides, I didn't wanna miss seeing my two most favorite people in the whole world." Detecting a slight blush on his face, she was not sure how she should interpret it.

With Possum, however, there was no question. "Well, now, I don't reckon I've ever been anybody's favorite person before. I kinda like the idea, don't you, Perley? And Becky's our favorite little gal, ain't that right, Perley?"

"I reckon I couldn't argue with that," Perley answered, suddenly feeling self-conscious and awkward. "Reckon we'd best sit down if we're gonna eat."

"I guess you'd better," Becky said cheerfully. "How 'bout that little table by the window? Set yourselves down and

I'll go get you some coffee." She hurried to the kitchen, thinking that she could not be sure what Perley might be thinking about her. *I'm afraid I'm gonna have to hit him over the head and ask him outright,* she thought. But she feared, if she did, his answer might be no and she wasn't sure she could bear the humiliation of having asked and revealing her feelings toward him.

An interested spectator to the two men engaged in conversation with Becky, Redmond Quinn took another bite of meat loaf that he had to admit was not as bad as most others he had eaten. When Lucy came to his table with the coffeepot, she said, "You were asking about Perley Gates. That's him that just came in."

"I would have judged that, considering the way the young lady greeted them. Pearly Gates, eh? That's a tough name to defend and I'll wager that he's been called upon to defend it before."

"It does cause him some trouble sometimes," Lucy said. "His folks named him that after his grandpa. It sounds like the 'Pearly Gates' up in heaven, but his name is spelled different: P-e-r-l-e-y."

"I see," Quinn said, studying the two men intently. "He must have fast hands, especially for a man of that age. He's got a lot of gray in that ponytail hanging down his back."

Lucy couldn't suppress a laugh. "That's Possum with the ponytail."

Quinn was genuinely surprised. "The young fellow?" he asked. "He doesn't look like the violent type." He gave her a stern grin. "Are you having a joke on me?"

She chuckled, really enjoying Quinn's disbelief. "That's Perley Gates. Everybody makes that mistake when they first see him. You want me to go tell him you'd like to meet him?"

"No, no, thank you," Quinn replied at once. "I think it would be better if I introduce myself." He got up from his chair, walked over, and stopped in front of their table. The conversation between Perley and Possum went silent for a few moments while they both looked up at the stranger in curiosity. "I don't want to interrupt your dinner, gentlemen, but the lady over there told me that you two saved the little lady serving you from four outlaws and rescued the bank's money, to boot. I'd like to salute you on a job well done, and it'd be my privilege to buy you a drink after you've finished your meal. My name's Redmond Quinn. This is my first time visiting your little town." He paused a moment, waiting to see if they recognized his name.

Before Perley could answer, Possum spoke up. "Well, that's mighty sportin' of you, Mr. Quinn. I don't know about Perley, but you can certainly buy me a drink of likker. My name's Possum Smith, and I'm pleased to make your acquaintance." He reached up to shake Quinn's hand.

"Then you'd be Perley Gates," Quinn said as he shook Possum's hand.

"That's right," Perley replied, and accepted the hand Quinn offered when Possum released it.

"The other lady, Lucy, I think I heard her called, told me you took down three of the four outlaws and brought one back to jail. Are you two deputies or something here in town?"

"Gracious, no," Possum answered him. "Paul McQueen's the sheriff and the town ain't needed no deputies so far. Me and Perley work cattle for the Triple-G Ranch, 'bout five miles north of here."

"But you trailed after the bank robbers across the Red River, into the Nations, after a posse turned back. Was that to collect a reward?"

Possum looked at Perley and chuckled. "Nah, there weren't no reward offered. Me and Perley just went to get Becky and bring her home. We didn't care nothin' about the bank's money," he joked. "We just thought, since we was comin' back this way, we might as well tote that, too."

"Almost like a couple of knights riding off to save a fair lady," Quinn said, causing Possum to chuckle again.

"More like two punkin-heads that just got lucky," Possum said.

Quinn considered that for a moment, then turned his attention toward Perley and commented, "Perley, you don't talk much, do you?"

Perley shrugged. "As much as the next fellow, I reckon. When I'm with Possum, he don't leave much that needs sayin'." He couldn't help being curious about this stranger, who talked so precisely and was dressed to the nines. "What brings you to Paris, Mr. Quinn?"

"Glad you asked," Quinn replied. "I've heard this little town has been growing at a healthy pace, with both cattle and cotton businesses thriving. So I thought I'd take a look for myself before the rest of the business hawks discover it." He was interrupted then when Lucy called out to tell him that his dinner was going to get cold, if he didn't come back to the table. "First things first," he said with a confident smile. "We'll talk more over a glass of whiskey at the saloon. I'd best get back to my meat loaf."

"He's one smooth-talkin' jasper, ain't he?" Possum commented after Quinn returned to his dinner.

"I reckon," Perley replied. "Maybe I'd call him a slick-talkin' jasper. What does he wanna buy us a drink for?"

"'Cause we're heroes," Possum answered, enjoying the experience. "I ain't ever been called a hero before."

"You might have wanted to invite him to bring his plate on over here to eat with us, but he's just a little too slick to suit me. If you want to, we'll have a drink with him. Then we can tell him we've got to get back to the ranch. Whatever he's sellin', we've got all we need of it."

Possum shrugged, not sure anymore. Perley had razor-sharp instincts, except when it came to women, and he clearly had some suspicions about this Redmond Quinn dude. He only hesitated a few moments, however, before deciding. "Hell, there ain't a better way to top off a free meat loaf dinner than with a free shot of rye whiskey. So I say let's have a drink with him and give Raymond Patton a little extra business."

Quinn finished his dinner rather quickly. After he told Perley and Possum he'd see them down at Patton's Saloon, he walked out. Perley watched him when he picked up his weapon from the table. And it seemed to him that he appeared to be studying the two pistols remaining on the table. *Probably just natural curiosity,* Perley thought. Becky came over with the coffeepot right after Quinn left. "Does that meat loaf taste all right to you?" she asked.

"It's just right," Possum answered at once, "just like always."

She looked at Perley and he nodded his head in agreement. "Well, I don't think our fancy guest liked it very much," Becky said. "He didn't eat half of his. Maybe he won't come back to see us."

"I reckon he'll have to," Perley said. "There ain't no other place to eat in town, unless you count Patton's. And if Beulah's food ain't fancy enough for him, I don't know what he'll think of Sadie Bloodworth's cookin'."

"Maybe he just don't like meat loaf," Possum suggested. "There's lots of folks don't."

"You're probably right," Perley said. "I reckon it's foolish to judge a man before you even get a chance to know him. Let's finish up this fine dinner and go have a drink with our new friend."

"Now you're talkin', partner," Possum declared. "You better come on and go with us, Becky."

"I believe I'll have to pass that invitation up this time," Becky responded, knowing Possum was teasing when he invited her to a saloon. "Maybe when I haven't already missed so much work." She walked to the door with them and while Perley strapped on his gun belt, she placed her hand on his arm. "When do you think you might be back in town?"

"I'm not sure," he answered, "but it won't be long."

With her hand still on his arm, she said, "Perley, I want you to know I'll always be grateful for what you did for me. You saved my life, and I'll never forget that."

He felt his heart pumping against his chest as he looked down into her eyes. He wanted to say something, but he was afraid in his shyness, it would come out all wrong. "Becky," he finally stammered, "I . . ."

"Come on, partner!" Possum blurted, totally unaware of the critical moment in his young friend's life, having not been privileged to have heard the gentle exchange between them. Before Perley could protest, Possum grabbed his sleeve and pulled him toward the door. "A stiff shot of whiskey will finish cookin' that meat loaf in your belly."

Perley took one last look at Becky as he was dragged out the door, her eyes seeking his. "I'll be seein' you, Becky." It was all he could think to say, then silently cursed himself for his inability to say something more fitting to the way he felt.

Standing not very far away, Lucy, an especially interested observer, shook her head when Becky turned to go to the kitchen. "Possum Smith," Lucy said in disgust, "if I had a gun I woulda shot the dumb fool."

Benny Grimes, bartender in Patton's Saloon, greeted Redmond Quinn when he walked in after leaving the hotel dining room. "Back for another drink of that rye whiskey?" The dapper gentleman wearing the fine tailored clothes had been in for a drink just before going back to the hotel for dinner.

"Indeed, I am," Quinn replied, "and pour it from the good stock you and your boss drink. I believe you may find a bottle under the counter."

Benny looked surprised, not sure if Quinn knew what he was talking about or just guessing. But he spoke with such confidence that Benny decided he'd give him the good stock. He had been in earlier and spent some time talking to Raymond Patton. Maybe Patton told Quinn to ask for the good stock. So he promptly reached under the counter and pulled out a bottle, poured the drink, then quickly returned the bottle to the shelf under the bar. Quinn knocked the drink back and banged the glass back on the bar, smacking his lips, satisfied. Unfortunately, a couple of cowhands from a ranch west of town witnessed it and were immediately irate over what looked to be privileged service. They were already making quiet jokes among themselves about the fancy-dressed stranger.

"Hey, Benny," one of them called out. "We're ready for another shot. This time we'll have it outta the same bottle you just poured that peacock's out of."

"I don't know, Jake," his friend cracked, "maybe we ain't dressed up in fancy-enough clothes to drink outta that bottle."

Benny, already afraid Patton might catch him selling his special stock to every cowhand who ordered it, sought to dissuade him. "Ah, Jake, that's the same stuff you boys have been drinkin'. Just in a different bottle, that's all."

"That's a damn lie," Jake said. "We've been drinkin' your cheap likker for a long time. Then this prissy little pussycat comes in and gets special treatment."

"Jake, is it?" Quinn interrupted. "Well, Jake, don't complain to the bartender. I can take one look at you and that mongrel with you and guess you wouldn't know good whiskey from kerosene. It would be wasted on you and your friend."

"Mister, I don't know what fairy tale you come from, but you'd best be advised to keep your nose outta my business," the burly cowhand responded. "This is between Benny and me, but you keep on runnin' your mouth and I'll take the time to give you a good ass-whuppin'."

"Fancy pants looks like he ain't never had a good whuppin', don't he, Jake?" his friend joined in, thinking they might have a little entertainment at Quinn's expense.

"That's what I was thinkin', Bert," Jake replied. "How 'bout it, fancy pants, you ready to back up that prissy mouth of yours? 'Cause it's time you learned a saloon ain't no place for a woman like you."

Quinn smiled at him as if pleased by the actions of the two roughnecks, as Benny would describe it when telling the story to Paul McQueen later. "I don't wrestle with loudmouth saddle tramps like you and your overweight friend. I suggest you two can grapple with each other, if that's what you're in the mood to do. Or go back to the ranch and roll around with the hogs. That would seem to be a more natural environment for you."

Amazed by the eloquent stranger's gall, Jake answered Quinn's confident smile with one of his own. "Mister, you talked yourself into it, so now you can turn around and drag your sorry behind outta here, or I'm fixin' to break your back."

"Is there something wrong with your hearing?" Quinn asked. "I just told you I don't wrestle with hogs." He pulled his coat back out of the way of his Colt six-gun. "You're wearing a gun. Is it just for show, or can you use it? Because I've heard enough out of you. Pull it, or you and your friend get out of here. I'm sick of looking at you."

Jake, obviously taken by surprise, was not sure at this point if he had been drawn into a showdown with a professional gunslinger or not. But he was not inclined to turn tail and run. The stranger looked harmless enough, but he wasn't willing to take any chances. So he thought to distract Quinn, then get the jump on him before he knew what hit him. With the mocking smile still in place, he turned to his friend to remark, "Whaddaya think about this fancy pants, Bert? He's actually wantin' to commit suicide. You think I oughta give him what he wants?"

Bert was still preparing to answer his question when Jake suddenly spun around, whipping his gun out as he did. His pistol barely cleared the holster before he stepped backward with the impact of Quinn's bullet in his chest.

Before he sank to his knees, a second shot from Quinn dropped Bert, who was struggling to pull his six-shooter.

Moments before the double shooting, Perley and Possum approached the door of Patton's Saloon. About to push through the doors, Perley was suddenly jerked to the side of the doorway by Possum when they heard the shots. Thinking it foolish to rush into a gunfight, they hugged the wall beside the door, weapons drawn, and waited. After a few more moments with no further gunfire, Perley eased over to the edge of the doorframe, far enough to peek over the batwing doors. "It's Redmond Quinn," he said to Possum.

"Is he shot?" Possum asked, figuring that a good possibility.

"Nope," Perley answered, "other way around." He holstered his pistol and pushed on through the doors. They walked into a room still silent after the display of unexpected gunplay. In a moment, however, the rumble of barroom conversation resumed, but all with the same topic now. Behind the bar, Benny Grimes was still suspended in a state of shocked disbelief. The only person who appeared casual was Redmond Quinn, who was calmly replacing the spent cartridges in his pistol. Down at the other end of the bar, Perley saw the two bodies, one lying on top of the other. Both shots heard were evidently kill shots. *An efficient execution,* Perley couldn't help thinking.

Aware then that Perley and Possum had just come in, Quinn turned to greet them. "Ah," he said, "we'll have that drink now. Benny, pour my friends and I a drink of rye. You know out of which bottle." He dropped his revolver back in his holster and nodded toward the bodies on the floor. "A bit of unpleasantness, but that's been dealt with." Back to Benny again, he suggested, "Maybe you can have someone remove the bodies. But here's a man with a badge. Maybe he'll take charge of that chore." Sheriff McQueen walked into the saloon, and seeing Perley and Possum, automatically thought the shooting might have something to do with them.

Ignoring Quinn, McQueen asked, "What happened, Perley?"

"Don't know, Paul, we just walked in, too," Perley answered. "You'll have to ask Benny, I reckon."

"You can ask me, Sheriff," Quinn volunteered. "I'm afraid I'm the cause of this misunderstanding. The two expired gentlemen on the floor over there were evidently out looking for trouble. They were giving Benny, here, a lot of argument over what kind of whiskey I was drinking. Then they turned their mischief upon me, insisting they were going to thrash me for being different from them. I'm afraid it escalated into a life threat. I think Benny can tell you that the fellow on the bottom drew his weapon first. I had no choice but to defend myself. The poor soul on top had no better sense than to pull his weapon, too, again leaving me no choice." He turned to Benny then. "Is that about the way it happened?"

Benny hesitated for a moment before verifying Quinn's accounting of the incident. "Pretty much like he said, Sheriff. There ain't no doubt about it, Jake pulled on him first." He decided not to tell McQueen at that point about the way Quinn goaded Jake into a gunfight with the clear intention of killing him, it seemed.

McQueen walked over and took a look at the two bodies, then he looked back at Quinn. "Both center-shot in the chest," he said.

"I don't find it a game when a man attempts to shoot

me," Quinn said, "so I shoot to kill when I'm threatened. And a wounded man can still shoot you, so why take the risk?"

McQueen turned his attention back to the bodies. "Jake Bailey and Bert Watkins," he said. "They ride for the Rockin'-J. I've had 'em in jail overnight a couple of times before. Looks like they finally started somethin' they couldn't finish. I'll get Bill Simmons to come get 'em, Benny. Maybe they've got enough personal effects on 'em to pay him for his services." Back to Quinn once again, he said, "Looks like it was purely self-defense, so there ain't nothin' more I need from you. I hope you don't have any more trouble while you're in town."

"I do, too, Sheriff. I'm a peaceable man by nature. I'm about to have a drink with my friends, here. You're welcome to join us, if you're so inclined."

"I reckon not," McQueen replied. "Thanks just the same." *I ain't sure I speak your language,* he thought. *So I reckon I ain't so inclined.*

Perley and Possum were not sure they were still *so inclined* at that moment, but they had already accepted Quinn's invitation. So, they watched Benny pour three drinks from a bottle he took from underneath the bar. They knocked those back and Quinn insisted they should have another. "Two's my limit," Perley declared. "I drink more'n that and I get to actin' foolish." That was not really true. He had always made it a rule never to have more than two drinks, however, because he felt that he never wanted to experience real drunkenness. He had seen too many cases where drunken men lost control of their senses and reflexes. He couldn't help but wonder now if the two dead cowhands were victims of too much whiskey. As far as the smooth-talking stranger was concerned, maybe the consumption of whiskey by the unfortunate cowhands didn't have that much to do with their demise. Observing his casual demeanor immediately following the killing of two men, Perley got the impression that it was not that much out of the ordinary for Redmond Quinn. He was not upset in the least.

Bill Simmons, the town barber, sometimes doctor, and full-time undertaker, came in at that point. Seeing them at the bar, he spoke. "How you doin', Perley? I heard you and Possum brought Becky Morris back. Good work, man. Sheriff told me to fetch those bodies. Is this the fellow that done for 'em?"

"Sure is," Possum answered for him. "Benny said he cut 'em down like cornstalks."

"Well, then, thank you for the business, sir," Bill said, "I'll get 'em outta your way. Grab hold of his feet, boy." His son, Bill Jr., did as directed and they carried Bert Watkins out the door to a waiting wagon. When they came back for Jake Bailey, Bill said to Quinn, "Thank you again. I hope you plugged him before he spent all his money on whiskey."

Watching Quinn's casual indifference to Bill's remarks, Perley was beginning to wonder about Quinn's interest in Possum and himself. And he also felt sure now that there was a deeper character in Redmond Quinn than the one he exhibited for public view. It appeared to him that Quinn was constantly studying him, his every move, and once, he was pretty sure that Quinn tested his reflexes. It happened while they were still standing at the bar, answering Quinn's questions about the town. Without warning, Quinn suddenly tossed his empty shot glass in Perley's direction.

Perley was sure it was to see if he would catch it, which he did. But Quinn had waited until Perley turned his head partially away when Possum said something to him. That was the moment when Quinn tossed the glass toward him, knowing he would have only a split second to see the object coming toward him.

"You've got good reflexes," Quinn commented. "I would wager that you're quick with a gun as well as catching shot glasses."

"If I was really fast with a gun," Perley replied, "maybe I woulda drawn my pistol and shot the glass in the air. And I didn't do that, so I reckon I'm like every other cowhand wearing a gun, faster than some, slower than others. That's kind of the way life is, ain't it?"

Quinn laughed, good-naturedly. "And you're a bit of a philosopher as well, an unusual young man."

"Possum's the philosopher," Perley replied. "He's the one who does all the thinkin' for the both of us. And he's probably thinkin' about tellin' me we've got to get back to the ranch, if we want to keep our jobs. But, you know, you never finished tellin' us what brings you to Paris. You were about to when Lucy told you not to let your meat loaf get cold."

"Ah, the meat loaf," Quinn responded. "I have a strong dislike for meat loaf. I think it's an insult to cattle to grind good beef up like that. But that's another subject. You asked why I came to look this town over. Well, I want to determine whether or not it's worth investing money in."

"What kinda business are you thinkin' about investin' in?" Possum asked. "You thinkin' about cattle or farmin' or somethin' here in town?"

"I'm thinking about something right here in the middle

of town," Quinn answered, "something you haven't got—a saloon."

That caused the eyebrows of both Perley and Possum to rise. "A saloon?" Possum asked. "You're standin' in one right now."

"I mean a real saloon, a New Orleans saloon, with gambling, and sporting ladies. No offense to Mr. Patton, but this isn't a saloon. It's a water hole for drunks and the local shopkeeper's afternoon drink of whiskey before he goes home for the night."

"Patton's is like every other saloon in this part of Texas," Possum maintained. "You go in to get likkered up. Once in a while there's a gunfight, like the one you was just in today. From time to time there's a spoiled dove entertainin' the customers. There ain't one right now since Blossom ran off with a whiskey drummer, but one'll show up sooner or later."

"You've just made my point, Possum." He paused then to ask, "Is that your real name? Or is that just a nickname?"

"It's what I go by," Possum answered, showing a little irritation for the question.

Quinn shrugged and continued. "Anyway, Possum," he smiled when he pronounced it very distinctively, "that's just my point. Patton's is just like any of the other saloons in this part of Texas. I've got the money to make it the one saloon that stands out above all the others. And, gentlemen, when you have that, the business will come to you, and, of course, benefiting the town as well."

"Are you talkin' about buyin' Patton's Saloon?" Possum asked. "What makes you think he'll sell it to ya? I expect he's makin' hisself a pretty good livin'."

"A pretty good living is about the size of it," Quinn

agreed. "I have no interest in buying this building from him or pouring whiskey for the locals. I only invest money in myself. I am the magnet that will draw the extra business to this otherwise drab watering hole."

Perley was quick to identify the stranger then. "You mean you're a professional gambler? Is that what you're talkin' about?"

"I would have to say you are partially correct," Quinn said, a smug smile etched across his face. "I am a professional, but a gambler? No, I don't invest in losing propositions. In the next few weeks, you will see blackjack and poker tables arrive from Fort Worth, as well as a roulette wheel. To add to the customers' pleasure, there will also be some charming ladies to grace the saloon."

"Well, that sounds like an ambitious project, I'll say that for it," Perley said. "I reckon Mr. Patton will be right interested in hearin' about it."

The satisfied smile on Quinn's face remained. "Raymond has already heard about my plans for his saloon and he is looking forward to the nice little percentage he can expect, once we are in full operation."

That was a genuine surprise to them both, but Perley said, "We hope you have good luck with it. But there ain't anything Possum and I can do to help, so I expect we'd best hit the trail back to the Triple-G. Thanks for the drinks. It's been real interestin' talkin' to you."

"That goes for me, too," Possum said, and waited while Quinn shook Perley's hand. They left him standing at the bar and when they were outside, Possum said, "As full as a Christmas turkey. He ain't nothin' but a fancy-dressed card shark." He climbed on his horse and paused a moment to ask, "What's a roulette wheel?"

CHAPTER 11

Sheriff Paul McQueen looked up from his desk to see Wilford Taylor come in his office door. "Howdy, Mr. Taylor, what can I do for you?"

"Morning, Sheriff. I thought I should stop by and talk to you about what is to be done with your prisoner in there. Bank robbery is a pretty serious offense and you might even add attempted murder. Will there be a hanging?"

"I talked to the mayor about the prisoner already, and we wanna do what's lawfully right." Neither the mayor nor the sheriff wanted a public hanging in the town. "We were plannin' to keep the prisoner in jail until the federal marshals or somebody came to pick him up. Mayor Johnson wired the governor's office in Austin requestin' it, and they're sendin' a Texas Ranger here to take charge of the prisoner."

"I don't see why we can't have a trial right here and hang him after we find him guilty. That would send a message to any other outlaws that it doesn't pay to rob the bank here in this town." Taylor was obviously incensed over what seemed to him to be overtolerant treatment of one of the men who robbed his bank. "That'll take days for a Ranger to come get that man. Where's the Ranger coming from, anyway?"

"Why, I don't know for sure," McQueen replied, "I suppose Fort Worth. We ain't ever had to deal with this problem before."

Taylor was obviously disappointed to learn about the actions already taken by the sheriff and the mayor. "We're missing a golden opportunity to advertise to the outlaws in this territory that they won't be tolerated in our town. I'll have to discuss this with the mayor." He turned around and walked out, somewhat more abruptly than he had entered. McQueen shrugged, and since Taylor had brought the matter up, he went into the cell room to check on Leonard Watts.

"That feller sounded like he wanted to stretch my neck real bad," Leonard commented when McQueen walked into the cell room. "What's he got against me?"

"You heard that, huh?" McQueen replied. "He's the owner of the bank, the man you almost ruined." He was already accustomed to the simpleminded man's forthright approach with everyone. "I reckon I'd best keep this door closed tight if you can hear ever'thing that's said in my office."

"I always did have good ears," Leonard said. "Lucas Sage used to say I could hear the sun go down." He chuckled and added, "Course, the sun don't make no noise when it drops down, least, I ain't never heard it. I heard what you said about a Texas Ranger comin' to get me, though. What would he do, take me to get hanged?"

"He'd take you to trial and a federal judge would most likely decide what your sentence would be. Might not be a death penalty, might just be a prison sentence."

"I wish I could just stay here, if I gotta be in jail for a long time," Leonard said.

"They'll have to take you somewhere where there's a judge," McQueen said. "We can't afford to keep you here that long. Cost too much to feed you." He had to admit that Leonard was so simpleminded, he was beginning to feel sorry for him. "It won't be too much longer before dinnertime. Maybe they'll have some more of those biscuits you like. I'll be gone down the street to the hotel for a few minutes. I'll lock the front door. But I'll be back before it's time to feed you." He went out of the cell room and closed the door behind him.

"They're the best biscuits I've ever et," Leonard said aloud. "They never had any that good at Arkansas State Prison." He made up his mind right then that he wasn't going back to prison and he was damn sure he wasn't going to hang.

The sheriff walked past the bank to the hotel and when he went in the front door, he found Amos Johnson at the check-in desk talking to his clerk. "Sheriff," Amos acknowledged, "you lookin' for me, or are you headed for the dinin' room?"

"I came to have a little talk with you, Mr. Mayor," McQueen answered.

"Well, come on back to my office," Johnson said, and led the way through a doorway behind the front desk. "What's on your mind, Paul?"

"Wilford Taylor was just up at the jail bellyachin' about my prisoner. He's complainin' because he thinks we oughta hang him right here in Paris. Just thought I'd tell you, but that ain't what I'm worried about." He had Johnson's attention then, so he asked, "Do you know about this deal Raymond Patton made with that Redmond Quinn fellow?"

"Yes, I do," Amos said. "Patton told me about it," he said, then he emphasized, "after he signed a contract Quinn already had drawn up. Raymond seems to think it will be a profitable arrangement for them both, as well as new business for the whole town."

"Don't the idea of that deal bother you any?" McQueen asked. "He's talkin' about turnin' the saloon into a big-time gamblin' hall with prostitutes hustlin' the customers." He paused a moment, then asked, "Where are those whores gonna live? In your hotel?"

"It's my understanding that they are going to build an addition on the back of the saloon and that's where the women will live. I've already told him they won't be welcome here."

"So you and the town council are all right with the deal, then?" McQueen asked.

"Well, I don't see anything we can do about it." Amos shrugged. "It's his business. I reckon he can run it any way he wants to, as long as he's not breakin' any laws. What's your concern? You obviously have one."

"I'm thinkin' it's gonna bring a whole lot of the kinda people we don't want in our town. I'm already findin' it hard to keep up with my blacksmith business. And if that gamblin' hall does what they think it will, I think you're gonna have to be lookin' for a deputy to help me."

"I see your concern," Johnson said, "but let's wait and see if it turns out to be a problem before we try to fix it." He had been speculating on the number of rooms that might be rented by gamblers coming in on the train. Already benefiting from the arrangement he had made with Quinn for a two-room suite for his permanent residence there in the hotel, Amos was not likely to encourage McQueen's concerns.

"There's one other thing that don't set too well with me," McQueen said. "That Quinn fellow is pretty damn fast with a six-gun."

"I would think that in his business he would have to be," Johnson maintained. "And that doesn't automatically mean he's a gunslinger. Right offhand, I think about Perley Gates. He's fast as greased lightning with a handgun, but he's by no means considered to be a gunslinger."

"Yeah, but Perley don't ever pick a fight just to show how fast he is. I talked to Benny Grimes last night about that gunfight yesterday. He said Quinn kept pushin' them two cowhands till he made 'em go for their guns. He was just lookin' to kill somebody, and they were the unlucky ones."

Amos shrugged. "Well, that's hard to say. Maybe that's the way it happened, maybe that's just the way Benny saw it. Like I said, we'll just have to wait and see how things work out. There's nothin' illegal about what they're doin'."

McQueen didn't say anything for a long moment, since it was obvious Johnson was not interested in his concerns about Quinn. "Well," he finally said, "I wanted to see where you stood on it, so I reckon I got what I came for." He turned and walked out of his office, more concerned than when he went in.

Things began to move rather quickly around Patton's Saloon, starting the day after McQueen had gone to see the mayor. The carpenters who had built the new hotel were hired to begin construction on the bedroom wing of the saloon, with Redmond Quinn on the site to oversee every detail. The proper-speaking Englishman soon became a familiar sight around the fledgling town in northeast Texas, tipping his hat to the ladies and offering a friendly good-day to the men. Some found it hard to believe he could be the same gentleman who had shot two drunken cowhands down in the saloon. There were others who saw a different side of him, however, like Lester Graves, a homeless old drifter who helped Walt Carver in the stable from time to time to pick up a little money for a drink of whiskey and a biscuit.

Many times, when Walt had gone to the house at night, Lester would sneak back in the stable to sleep. He was un-fortunate to pick one such night when Redmond Quinn had decided that he wanted to check on his coal-black Morgan gelding, Midnight. He found Walt already gone for the night, so, never one to be dissuaded, he went in a small door he found unlocked in the back of the barn and entered the stable from there. He walked back in the stalls only to find Lester Graves relieving himself in Midnight's stall. "Who the hell are you?" Quinn demanded, straining to see him more clearly in the darkness of the stable.

"I'm just lookin' for a place to sleep, Mr. Carver," Lester blubbered pitifully, thinking it was the owner who had caught him. "I ain't doin' no harm, I'm just tired."

Irate that anyone would be relieving themselves in the stall with his horse, Quinn struck a match to get a better look at the intruder. In the glare of the match, he also saw the mess Lester had left in the corner of Midnight's stall. Disgusted, he uttered, "Why, you're just a pathetic old man." With his left hand, he reached over and drew his

Colt .44, aimed it at Lester's head, and pulled the trigger, still holding the match in his right hand. The old man jerked up when the bullet struck him in the forehead, then fell back against the side of the stall. Quinn blew out the match and holstered the pistol.

Knowing he had to leave before someone came to investigate the shot, he nevertheless took the time to calm the excited Morgan before grasping Lester's boots and dragging him out of Midnight's stall. He left the old man's body in the alleyway between the stalls, then made his exit out of the back of the barn as Walt Carver was coming in the front. Walking back to the saloon, Quinn reached the jail just as Paul McQueen came out of his office. "What was that shot?" the sheriff asked.

"I don't know," Quinn answered. "I heard it and I was just coming to alert you. If you need any help, I'd be glad to volunteer my services."

"Thanks just the same," McQueen said. "It was just one shot and it sounded like it mighta come from the stable. Maybe Walt was shootin' at a rat or something."

"All right, then, I'll head back to the saloon then and maybe see if there are any gamblers waiting for a good game of cards. It's a little early to turn in."

When McQueen walked up to the stable, he met Walt Carver standing out front. "I figured you'd get up here pretty quick after you heard that shot," Carver said.

"Yeah, I heard it," McQueen replied. "What were you shootin' at?"

"I wasn't shootin' at nothin'," Walt answered, "but somebody was. I found old man Lester Graves, a-layin' in there between the stalls with a gunshot wound in his forehead."

"Is he dead?"

"Well, I would have to guess he is 'cause he's got a little black hole right between his eyes," Walt replied. "And he didn't say anything when I poked him with the toe of my boot."

"You ain't got no idea who shot him? What was he doin' in the stable this time of night?"

"I got no idea a-tall who mighta shot him," Walt said. "He was just lookin' for a place to sleep outta the cold. He did it all the time. Didn't think I knew he was doin' it, but I kept that little door in the back of the barn unlocked, so he could get in when he didn't have no other place to go. I can't figure out why anybody would wanna shoot him. That's the fellow that worries me, the one who shot him. What was *he* doin' in my stable?"

McQueen scratched his chin thoughtfully. "Maybe somebody fixin' to steal a horse? Have you looked to make sure all the horses are here?"

"No, I ain't done that," Walt replied. "I didn't do nothin' after I found Lester. I just turned around and waited for you to show up."

"Well, let's go inside and take a look around," Mc-Queen suggested. "Maybe you're a horse short and maybe a saddle, too. That would tell us something." Walt lit another lantern for the sheriff to carry, then they went into the stable. Walt took him to see Lester's body first.

"This where you found him?" McQueen asked. "Out here between the stalls?" Walt said that was the case. The sheriff held his lantern directly over Lester's face. "You're right," he said, "shot him right between the eyes."

He looked all around the body then and it was pretty obvious that it had been dragged out of the stall beside it. "Whoever killed him drug him outta that stall. Whose horse is that in there?"

"That new fancy pants fellow that shot those two cowhands in Patton's," Walt replied.

"Redmond Quinn, huh? Wonder what Lester was doin' in there." McQueen walked into the stall, gently pushing the big Morgan gelding aside, and it didn't take long to discover what Lester was doing in there and the evidence that Lester left behind. "He must notta been plannin' to sleep in this stall," he commented, and walked back out of it. "Was Quinn here tonight?"

"Nope, not when I locked up and went to supper," Walt answered.

But anybody could have come in the back of the barn, just like Lester did, McQueen thought. It was quite a coincidence that he found Quinn out in the street when he came out of his office to investigate the source of the gunshot. *Said he was coming to tell me he heard a gunshot. How likely was that?* He thought about the man and wondered if he was coldhearted enough to shoot an old tramp because he took a dump in the stall where his horse was. "I don't doubt it, but I can't prove it," he mumbled.

"How's that?" Walt asked.

"Nothin'. Let's take a look around the stable and the barn to make sure there ain't anything missin'." They conducted a search of the whole place and found nothing missing or out of order, so they dragged Lester's body up by the front door of the stable and left it there for Bill Simmons to pick up in the morning. "I'll tell him first thing, so you can get him outta your way," McQueen told him.

Walt thought about it for a moment as they walked out the door, then said, "If you'll gimme a hand, we can put Lester up in the wagon and I'll take him to Bill in the mornin'. There ought nothin' bother him layin' out there tonight."

"I reckon not," McQueen said, so they laid Lester's body in the wagon sitting beside the barn. "Reckon you'd best start lockin' that back barn door now," the sheriff said as he walked away.

Just for the hell of it, McQueen decided to stop in Patton's Saloon on his way back to the jail. He was pretty sure he would find Redmond Quinn there, since it was still fairly early in the evening. When he went inside, he found it moderately busy, and some faces he knew, some he hadn't seen before. Quinn was sitting at a table with four other men, playing cards and carrying most of the conversation, himself. McQueen walked over to the bar to talk to Benny. "Evenin', Sheriff," Benny greeted him. "You drinkin'?"

"Yeah, you can pour me a little shot of corn likker to help settle my stomach," the sheriff answered. "I see your boss's new partner is sellin' some of our citizens on the joys of gamblin' that'll soon be available for 'em."

"You got that right," Benny said. "I'd kinda like to see that wheel he keeps talkin' about, myself. Just like the big gamblin' houses in New Orleans have, he says."

"You got some new buildin' that's supposed to get started pretty soon, ain'tcha? Are any of the big plans Patton and Quinn have gonna affect your job?"

"If they are, Raymond ain't said anything about it," Benny said. "Has anybody said anything to you about it?"

"Just that you're gonna have to start wearin' them

blousy-sleeved shirts with lace collars and knee pants with silk stockin's, like they wear at the king's palace," McQueen said, but he couldn't maintain a straight face. "Nah, I ain't heard nothin' about any changes in your job."

Just then noticing that the sheriff had come in, Quinn said, "Deal me out of this hand, gentlemen, I have to discuss something with the sheriff, but I'll be back." He got up from the table and walked over to the bar. "I see you're back already. Nothing serious, I hope. Benny, pour the sheriff a drink out of the good rye stock."

"He's drinkin' corn whiskey," Benny replied, causing an instant expression of disapproval from Quinn.

"One's all I needed," McQueen said. "Thanks just the same."

Curious to know the sheriff's reaction to the body in the stable, Quinn asked, "Did you find the source of that gunshot we heard?"

"No, I didn't," the sheriff replied. He wanted to see how much Quinn really knew about the shooting, so he decided to play it a little coy with him.

"It sounded as if it might have come from the stable," Quinn continued to press.

"That's what I thought, too," McQueen said.

Quinn waited for the sheriff to go on with details. When he didn't, he asked, "So, it wasn't in the stable after all?"

"Reckon not," McQueen said. "Me and Walt took a couple of lanterns and searched every inch of that stable, the barn, too, didn't come up with anything. You know, those woods are pretty close behind Walt's corral, somebody mighta took a shot at a coon or something back there." He could see by the expression on Quinn's face that the usually unperturbable gambler was wholly confused.

Enjoying the smooth-talking gunman's puzzlement, McQueen couldn't resist taking it a step further. "We found one thing you might be interested in, though. It looked like somebody had picked one of his stalls for an outhouse. Walt said it was the one your horse is in." He chuckled and added, "Walt said whoever it was, he was glad they didn't pick a stall with one of the purebred horses he's got in the stable now."

Unable to let that pass unchallenged, Quinn retorted, "It's obvious that Mr. Carver isn't the expert he claims to be. My horse is a registered, purebred Morgan gelding . . ." He was about to continue but stopped when it struck him that he was being baited by the sheriff, toyed with, in fact. *He suspects I shot that old tramp,* he thought, *but he has no way to prove it.* He formed a patient smile on his face. "But then, Mr. Carver is nothing more than a custodian of a stable. One cannot expect him to be a judge of horses." He had thought to ultimately control the sheriff once he was in full operation in the town, encouraged in the beginning when he learned that the sheriff was really a blacksmith who was filling in as sheriff. Now it occurred to him that he was going to have to replace him, if he was going to be a problem. He knew a couple of men he could contact for the job, if he decided to make that move. It would take a little more time to sell the mayor and the town council on the replacement of the sheriff. But once they realized the increase in money, he didn't expect any opposition from them. So, Paul McQueen's days as a lawman were limited. If he was lucky, he might go back to the blacksmith's forge full-time. If necessary, however, he might take the same treatment the old tramp took.

"I told Walt he'd best start lockin' that back door in the

barn, if he expects to keep tramps and saddle trash outta his place," McQueen said, and placed a coin on the bar for his drink. "You folks have a nice evenin'." He left them with that.

"Yes, you, too, Sheriff," Quinn responded. *Your days are numbered, you smug mongrel.*

thought me and my posseman could stand a good meal before we start back."

"That's a good idea," McQueen said. "And I know for a fact that your prisoner will be happy to have one more meal before he goes. He's gotten spoiled by the hotel dinin' room, I'm afraid. And that's the place I recommend for you and your posseman to eat your dinner." Prince seemed pleased by the recommendation. "You wanna take a look at your prisoner now?"

"Might as well," Prince answered, "then I'll take the horses back to that stable we just passed and leave 'em to rest up." Before they opened the door to the cell rooms, Prince asked, "Has he given you any trouble?"

"No, he ain't been any trouble to speak of. In fact, he does his best to cooperate with whatever you want. I'd be surprised if he caused you any trouble a-tall." He lowered his voice and added, "He's about a bucket short of a full gallon of brains, but he don't cause no trouble." He opened the door and led Prince into the cell room. They found Leonard standing at the door of his cell, having heard the sheriff talking to someone in the office. "Leonard, this is Corporal Grady Prince of the Texas Rangers. He's gonna transport you to Sherman, to the courthouse there for your trial. He brought a jail wagon with him to take you there in style." He winked at Prince, but the somber Ranger didn't respond.

McQueen's remark brought a grin to Leonard's face, however. "I reckon that's because I was ridin' with the Sage brothers," he said.

"Mighta been," McQueen replied. "And this time you

CHAPTER 12

Another day brought another stranger to town, this one in the form of Texas Ranger Grady Prince from the city of Sherman, a thriving town about sixty-five miles west of Paris. A tall, gangly man with a drooping black mustache, riding a white horse, Prince arrived in the late morning, accompanied by Willie James, driving a jail wagon. They rode into town at the north end, past the stable, and went directly to the sheriff's office and jail. "Sheriff McQueen?" he inquired when he walked in the door. When McQueen got up from his desk to receive him, he said, "Corporal Grady Prince, Texas Rangers. I've got an order here to take one Mr. Leonard Watts off your hands." He handed McQueen the transfer papers.

"Glad to see you, Prince," McQueen said, and walked around the desk to shake hands. "You by yourself?" Then, not waiting for an answer, he stepped over and looked out the window. "Oh, I see you brought a jail wagon with you." He took a quick scan of the papers. "Grayson County Courthouse in Sherman. Are you anxious to start back right away?"

"No, not right away. I need to rest the horses, and I

won't have to be tied up to a tree at night like you were when Perley brought you to jail."

Prince was not inclined to win Leonard's gratitude and friendship. He was straight and to the point. "My job is to transport you to the county court of Grayson County. If you obey my orders and don't cause me any trouble, it won't be a bad trip. I'll provide your meals. They won't be fancy, but it'll be the same thing I'll be eatin', so it won't do you any good to complain."

"Oh, I ain't gonna be no trouble," Leonard insisted. "That's right, ain't it, Sheriff?"

"That's right, Leonard, at least not since you've been here in my jail."

"All right," Prince said to Leonard, "we'll be leavin' here right after dinner. We've got about sixty-five miles to Sherman, so you'll be ridin' in the jail wagon about three days."

"Yes, sir," Leonard replied. "I'll be ready to go." He remained standing there at the cell door after they went out and closed the office door behind them. *If I let them get me in that jail wagon, I'm done for,* he thought.

Although it was an important day in the life of Leonard Watts, his transfer to Grayson County for trial was not close to being considered the major attraction in the little town on this day. Construction of the new wing on the saloon was very much under way, but that, too, was secondary to the demonstration of the new time-lock vault and the new safe at the First National Bank of Paris. Most everyone in town was interested in seeing this up-to-date technology for keeping their money safe. Perley found it a useful excuse to spend a day in town, and as usually occurred, Possum saw fit to accompany him. They timed their arrival to coincide with the opening of the hotel dining room for the midday meal.

"Well, hello, boys," Lucy Tate greeted them when they walked in. "You come into town today to see the high-falutin new vault at the bank? Or are you more interested in the construction of the ladies' quarters that Redmond Quinn is building?" When one of them said the bank and the other said the saloon, she laughed. "One of you is lyin', but Possum, I believe you when you say you wanna see the ladies' bedrooms. It'll be the only time you get to see 'em without payin' for it." She just looked at Perley and winked, having a pretty good idea what attracted him. "Set yourselves down, and I'll see if we can get you fed."

She left them to choose a table and went into the kitchen. "Where's Becky?" she asked.

"She took those potato peels out back to put in the barrel for the hogs," Beulah answered. "Was that Perley that just came in?"

"Yep, him and Possum," Lucy said as she went to the back door and opened it. "Becky, you need to get in here. There's a little lost puppy in the dinin' room, lookin' for his mama. And there's an old hound dog, too. I can't wait on everybody."

"I'm coming," Becky answered her, and wiped the last of the peels out of the bucket. There was no telling what Lucy was talking about, so she never took anything she said seriously anymore.

When she came back inside, Lucy was pouring two

cups of coffee. "Here," she said, "they'll want these." Then she left them on the sideboard and went back into the dining room.

Becky picked up the cups. "What is she talking about? Did someone bring a puppy in the dining room?"

Beulah just shook her head. "Young people," she grunted. "Go see for yourself." Then when Becky went through the door, Beulah turned to reveal her devilish grin and went to the door to watch Becky's reaction upon discovering Perley there. She wasn't disappointed and chuckled at what she figured had to be the two most bashful people in the whole state of Texas. Then she glanced across the room to see Lucy, grinning at her. *I reckon we're gonna have to find one of them marriage brokers, if those two are ever gonna get together,* she thought.

"Hey, Perley," Becky said softly, trying to hide the excitement in her voice. "Possum," she said then, about to forget greeting him. "What are you doing in town today?"

When Perley was still trying to create his answer in his head, Possum said, "He came in so he could see you. Now, lemme have one of them coffee cups before they get cold." She flushed with embarrassment, having forgotten she was still holding them.

"What?" she finally asked when she was aware that Possum was repeating a question. "Oh . . . ham," she answered, still with her gaze focused on Perley. "We're serving ham. I'll go fix you a plate." She spun on her heel and hurried to the kitchen. When she got there, she gushed, "Possum said Perley came to town today to see me!"

"Well, ain't that a big surprise?" Lucy declared. "If that's what Possum said, tell me what Perley said."

"Well . . ." she said, "Perley didn't say anything, but he didn't say it wasn't so."

Lucy looked at Beulah and shook her head. "Possum told me that Perley Gates is the quickest-thinking, fastest-reacting, best shot he has ever seen. But when he gets around Becky, he turns into a six-year-old first grader."

"Here," Beulah said, handing Becky two plates, "take them their dinner." When Becky went out the door, Beulah said to Lucy, "Possum told me Perley's been forced to use his gun in self-defense more than his share of times. But he said he never saw Perley go out to kill but one man, and that was the man who beat Becky up."

Out in the dining room, Perley finally got his tongue untangled enough to tell Becky that he and Possum were going to see Wilford Taylor's showing of the new bank vault. "I'm supposed to tell Rubin and John all about it when I get back to the ranch. I thought if you wouldn't mind, I'd hang around town till suppertime."

"I think that would be real nice," she said. "Then we could visit some more."

"Well, forever more, it looks like you young folks might finally get around to decidin' you like each other," Possum announced, increasing the blush on both faces.

"Becky and I have always been good friends," Perley said. "Ain't that right, Becky?"

"That's right, Possum. Perley and I have always been friends," she replied, disappointed that there was no stronger relationship implied. She decided then that it was time to declare her feelings for him and she was just about to do that when Paul McQueen and two strangers walked in the door. Seeing Perley and Possum, they came right over to the table, all three ignoring the weapons table, since the rule didn't apply to lawmen.

"Glad to see you two here in town," McQueen blurted. "Like you to meet Ranger Corporal Grady Prince and his posseman, Willie James. Grady, these are the two men that brought Leonard Watts and the bank's money back. And this is the young lady they rescued. Becky, we'll be eatin' dinner, so you can get us some coffee, too. We'll just sit right here at this table next to them." He pulled a chair back and sat down, never noticing the irritated look of disappointment displayed on the young girl's face when she turned to do his bidding. "Grady's come to take Leonard to Sherman to stand trial."

"From what I've been told, you two tracked the four men that robbed the bank up in Durant, in the Nations, and killed three of the four when you rescued the young woman," Prince said. "Is that right?"

"Well, near 'bout," Possum answered him. "Perley had to shoot one of 'em when he rescued Becky. That was all we came for, so we cut out for home. The other three came after us and tried to jump us where we camped. That's when we shot the other two."

"Why didn't you shoot the last one?" Prince asked.

"'Cause he surrendered," Possum answered, "so we brought him to jail."

Prince nodded in response, then offered his congratulations. "I'd have to say you two did a good job. Anything you think I should know about this Watts fellow?"

Possum shrugged, shook his head, and turned to Perley. "Leonard will try to be as cooperative as he can, as long as he thinks there ain't nothin' he can do about it," Perley offered. "But I think he's desperate enough to try anything if you get careless with him."

"I'll keep that in mind," Prince said. "Any chance you two will attend his trial when the date's set?" Perley replied that they had no plans to, since Sherman was sixty-five miles away. "It might help speed the trial along if I could take a couple of signed statements from you, just swearin' to what you just told me," Prince explained. He looked at McQueen then. "There ain't no judge here. Is there a lawyer or somebody to witness the signin' of their accounts of it?"

"Nope, no judge, no lawyer, either, but the postmaster could witness it. I think he's a notary. Will that do?"

"I reckon," Prince said. "There ain't no question about the prisoner's part in the bank holdup. That'll get him a prison sentence right there, and there's the kidnappin' on top of that. I'll take a witness report from you, too, Sheriff." He seemed satisfied with that, so they turned their attention to the ham-and-potato dinner Becky and Lucy brought to the tables.

When they had all finished eating, Prince asked Perley and Possum to accompany him to the post office while McQueen saw to the feeding of Leonard Watts at the jail. As they were leaving, Perley managed to promise Becky that he would be back for supper, if he wasn't able to stop by sooner. "You promise?" she pressed.

"I do," he said, and hurried out the door after the others.

Edgar Welch, postmaster, prepared the papers that Grady Prince requested, and Perley and Possum both signed them. Welch affixed his notary seal and handed the papers to Prince. He took a look at them and promptly informed them that they should have signed with their actual names. He looked at Perley and said, "I need your real name, not a nickname. You didn't spell Pearly right at that." It took a few minutes for Perley to explain the origin of his legal name, an explanation he had made so many times in his young life. "Sorry," Prince said, "but it is an unusual name." He turned to Possum then and said, "I see you knew the right thing to do, Reginald. I reckon we can go get the prisoner now." Perley was struck speechless and continued to stare at Possum as he hurried out the door after Prince. He silently pronounced the name, making exaggerated motions with his mouth as he did so, and thought, *I own him now*.

Perley and Possum went directly to the jail, where McQueen was preparing Leonard for his journey, while Prince and Willie James went to the stable. Prince got a pair of handcuffs, then proceeded to the jail, leaving Willie to hitch up the jail wagon while he went to get the prisoner.

"It was mighty nice of you fellers to come to see me off," Leonard was telling Perley and Possum when Prince walked in the cell room. "Hey, Mr. Ranger, I done forgot your name. I ain't in no hurry to get to my trial, so if you wanna rest up tonight, I'd just as soon wait and start out in the mornin'."

Prince looked at Perley, who shrugged in response. "I expect I'll take you outta here right now, so step up to the door, put your hands together, and stick 'em through the bars." Even as he said it, he had to admit to himself that he had considered doing just what Leonard suggested, due to the late start.

McQueen stood by with the key to the cell and when Leonard was securely cuffed, he unlocked the cell and

Leonard walked out. He nodded politely to the sheriff as well as Perley and Possum. "I want you fellers to know I don't hold no hard feelin's agin any of you."

"All right, Watts," Prince directed. "We're gonna walk real nice up the street there and when we get to the stable, I'll take those cuffs offa you and you can ride in the wagon with your hands free."

"Much obliged, Mr. Ranger," Leonard said, and walked dutifully out the door before him. Perley and the others went along behind them. When they walked out on the street, a small group of spectators gathered to follow when they saw what was taking place. Redmond Quinn joined them as well. He walked up beside Perley and remarked, "So this will be the last of your bank robbers to answer for his crimes. I guess you'll be going back to raising cattle now, right?"

"I surely hope so," Perley answered him. He glanced over at Possum and asked, "Ain't that right, Reginald?"

"All right," Possum responded, frowning lest Quinn might have heard it, "that's one free one I'll give you. I don't wanna hear it again outta your mouth and I want your word that you ain't gonna tell nobody else."

"I'll take it under consideration," Perley said. "Right now, I wanna see 'em get Leonard off on his way to Sherman."

When they got to the stable, Walt Carver was leading Prince's horse out of the corral. He tied the horse to the corner post while Willie finished hitching his horses to the jail wagon. Walt went around to the rear of the wagon, unfolded the step, and opened the door while Prince unlocked Leonard's hand irons. "Much obliged," Leonard said when Prince stepped back to watch him climb in the wagon. He hesitated then, remembering his earlier thoughts that once that iron-barred door was locked behind him, he was a dead man. Then, as if a higher power—the ghost of Micah Sage, or the devil, himself—came to his rescue, he realized that maybe he wasn't destined to be hauled off in that jail wagon. There, standing almost beside him, was Walt Carver, the butt of his .44 within easy reach and resting so loosely in the holster that it seemed to beckon to him. It was now or never!

Always alert in any situations that might require speed of hand and accuracy, Redmond Quinn kept a sharp eye on the prisoner. When Leonard made his move, Quinn was ready to react. No one else saw it coming when Leonard suddenly jerked Walt's pistol from his holster and aimed it point-blank at Grady Prince. By the time Leonard cocked it, Quinn's .44 was out of his holster, but before he raised it to fire, he heard the shot that caused Leonard to reel sideways and crumple to the ground with a bullet in his chest. Stunned, Quinn turned to see Perley, his gun in hand, watching Leonard to make sure a second shot was not necessary. "Are you all right, Grady?" Perley asked. "Doggone it, that was unnecessary and it was all my fault. I started to tell Walt not to stand so close to him, but I never thought Leonard was crazy enough to try something like that."

Equally in shock, Walt said, "I don't know what I was thinkin'. I wasn't thinkin', I reckon." He reached down and carefully took his pistol out of Leonard's hand, then released the hammer and eased it back down. "I'm just glad you were here, Perley."

"That makes two of us," Grady Prince finally spoke, still not sure he had seen what just happened. "I wanna thank you, partner. You sure as hell saved my butt today. I'm beginnin' to think I'm gettin' too old for this work."

He looked over at Willie James, who was as much in disbelief as he was. "Well, we ain't gonna haul any prisoner back this time, Willie. Whaddaya say we stay over one night and start back in the mornin'? I owe this man a drink or two, or maybe supper at the hotel."

"That sure as hell suits me," Willie said. "We gonna take the body back?"

"I don't know," Prince answered. "That ain't no hearse you're drivin'." He thought about it for a moment, not really caring one way or the other after the free pass he had just been issued due to the lightning reactions of Perley Gates. "You wouldn't have to cook for him, that's for dang sure. I don't know. I think I'd rather pay to have him buried. Sheriff, you got an undertaker here in town?"

Perley was amazed how this somber man of so few words had suddenly turned into a regular chatterbox. He had to guess that a close encounter with a bullet that had your name on it would tend to loosen your tongue. McQueen told Prince that he would have Bill Simmons take care of the body. So Prince decided to stay in town that night and Walt told him he would take care of his horses at no charge, since he felt he was to blame for almost costing him his life.

With even a larger crowd of spectators milling about the stable to gawk at the body of Leonard Watts, the fourth casualty of the bank robbers, one man was prone to replay the events just witnessed. Redmond Quinn studied Perley as he talked to the sheriff. Was he really that fast? He thought back to the moment before he drew his own gun. Maybe Perley already had his six-gun out when Watts made his desperate move. That must have been it. There was no better explanation for the speed with which he fired. And if that was the case, then he drew faster than

Perley could have. The shot was well placed, too, but he was ready to believe that a lucky accident. Reluctant to do it but thinking it necessary to continue playing the part he had played from the beginning, he walked over to congratulate Perley.

"That was quite a shot, Perley," Quinn said. "It's a good thing you were keeping your eye on that fellow. We all should have had our weapons out to make sure he got on that wagon without any mischief."

Perley shrugged. "I reckon we wouldn'ta had to watch him at all, if Walt hadn't got so close to him. And I know he feels bad about that, but you can't really blame him. That fellow had all of us fooled, thinkin' he didn't want to make any trouble for anybody. I'm sorry I had to shoot him. He mighta just got some prison time, 'cause he didn't shoot anybody in that bank holdup."

Still probing for information that would confirm his theory, Quinn said, "You did what you had to do. You were smart enough to have your weapon ready for whatever happened."

"Ha!" Perley reacted. "I wish I could say that. Truth is, I was japin' Possum about something that happened when we went to the post office to sign some papers. I was yakkin' away with Possum, and when I looked back at Leonard he had a gun on that Ranger."

Damn! Quinn thought. *He won't admit he was waiting for him to strike.* He knew Perley was lying then. If Leonard already had the gun pointed at Prince, there was no way Perley could have drawn his weapon and fired before Leonard pulled the trigger. That thought was enough to restore Quinn's confidence in his ability to beat any man in a quick-draw contest. *Before this is over,* he thought, *you and I are going to settle it for everyone to see.* "Well, gentlemen," he announced then, "'all's well that end's well,' as the poet said. So I expect we'll celebrate over a drink in Patton's when you've finished up here." He took his leave then and returned to the saloon.

"Whaddaya fixin' to do, partner?" Possum asked Perley. "It'd be downright impolite not to go have that drink with Prince, don'tcha think? And it's a while yet before time to go to supper at the hotel, like you promised a certain young lady at dinner. Rubin's most likely gonna fire both of us for takin' the day off, anyway. So we might as well enjoy ourselves while somebody's willin' to pay for the likker."

Perley didn't answer right away. The fact that he had just killed another man was beginning to creep into his thoughts. Even though it was the life of a conscienceless outlaw, it was still a life. He had not made a decision to kill Leonard—there had been no time for decisions. He didn't even remember the act of drawing his weapon and firing. It happened just like it had always happened before on similar occasions. He just reacted to the threat. Possum studied his young friend for a moment and guessed what he was thinking. "Perley, you saved a man's life today, a good man at that, a man who stands for law and order. There ain't no sin in that."

After another long moment, Perley answered, "I reckon you're right. I just hate to think it'll be all over town. I wouldn't be surprised if it hasn't already gotten up to the hotel."

"It might have," Possum said, "but Becky knows you ain't no coldhearted gunman. You're frettin' for nothin' on that score."

"Who said anything about what Becky might think?"

"Yeah, right," Possum japed sarcastically.

CHAPTER 13

After turning the Ranger and his posseman's horses back in the corral, they remained there at the stable with Prince until Bill Simmons arrived to take care of Leonard's body. "Afternoon, gents," Simmons greeted them. Looking around the group standing there, he naturally asked McQueen who his benefactor was for this piece of business. "Who done for this one, Sheriff?" When told it was Perley who had done the shooting, he nodded as if he suspected as much. "This poor soul was your prisoner, wasn't he?" McQueen nodded, so Simmons said, "Then I reckon he ain't got anything on him of any value. Will the town be paying for his burial?"

"Yeah, I reckon so," McQueen replied, "since he was in the town jail. The usual fee for puttin' him in the ground."

"I appreciate that," Grady Prince spoke up. "I figured I'd have to pay to get a hole dug for him, but I reckon, since he never got inside my jail wagon, he wasn't ever officially in my custody." When no one disagreed, he said, "In that case, I'm sure I owe for a couple rounds of drinks." His statement was met with a welcome grunt of approval from the small group of men standing with him. "I know I especially owe Mr. Perley Gates a drink," Prince added.

Since Simmons's son wasn't with him, Possum helped Bill load the body onto his wagon. Then they started back down the street to Patton's Saloon, and Perley moved up beside Prince. "I 'preciate the offer of a drink," Perley said, "but if you don't mind, I'll take you up on it a little later. I promised a young lady I'd call on her just before supper and I don't wanna show up with whiskey on my breath. She's a real proper young lady and I don't want her to think poorly of me."

The stoic lawman looked at Perley in amazement. Then he couldn't suppress a chuckle. "Hell, good for you, Perley," he said. "Matter of fact, it's a good idea to let 'em find out about your drinkin' after you tie the knot. You know where we'll be when you're done." Prince continued on toward the saloon, still chuckling over the thought of the man whose lightning-like reflexes had just saved his life.

Raymond Patton was there to welcome them when they walked into his saloon, which was not that common a practice. No one was aware of that more than Benny Grimes, who told Possum that Patton was making his appearances more often since Redmond Quinn had arrived. And his guess was that it was because Quinn had come to represent the ownership of the saloon since he was there most of the time and he acted as if he was the official greeter. Benny said Raymond couldn't complain because they were selling more whiskey since Quinn arrived.

They pulled a couple of tables together to make one big one with Patton's help. Grady Prince, Willie James, McQueen, Perley, Possum, and Walt Carver all took a seat. Raymond Patton had Benny bring a bottle and some glasses over, and he took a seat as well. Before long, Redmond Quinn pulled out of a poker game and came over with another bottle. "This looks like a celebration," he said. "Mind if I sit in? I brought some more refreshments." He held the bottle up for them to see. "What are we drinking to? The fact that Corporal Grady Prince is able to be with us today?"

"That's as good as any," Possum replied. "Pour 'em."

That started the drinking party in earnest and it seemed to some that with all that had been happening in the normally quiet little town, it was time to celebrate some possible tragedies that were successfully avoided. Redmond Quinn, to no one's surprise, didn't wait long before getting into his sales pitch for what he called the future of gambling in northeast Texas. He wasted no time before extolling the classy gambling house Patton's was going to be. "You should be sure to come back to see the place when we've finished it," he told Grady Prince. "And bring some of your high-roller friends with you. Not just cards, there'll be dice tables and roulette, too."

Already tired of hearing Quinn talk, Sheriff McQueen had permitted himself one drink more than he had planned. It spurred him to needle the slick gambler a little bit. "That's a good idea, Grady," he japed. "And while your Sherman friends are shootin' dice and playin' the wheel, you bein' a lawman, you could play another game we got here in Paris."

"What's that, Paul?" Prince inquired, his speech only slightly slurred.

"We've got a little mystery game called 'Who shot Lester Graves in the head in the stable?'" He paused to display a wide grin before continuing. "The only suspect we've got, so far, is Redmond Quinn's horse, named Midnight. Lester left a big pile of evidence in the corner of Midnight's stall and he was found right outside the stall where he'd been dragged. What ain't been figured out yet is how a Morgan horse could shoot a man right between the eyes. And we ain't found where the blame horse hid his gun."

When he finished his little speech, there were a few long moments of silent astonishment. And the first thought for some was that the sheriff had had more than it was his custom to drink. Grady Prince, the intended recipient of McQueen's pitch, just grinned politely, having no idea what the sheriff was talking about. McQueen had talked to Perley about the suspicious circumstances surrounding the murder of Lester Graves. Another person aware of McQueen's intent, Redmond Quinn, maintained a painful smile on his face for the entire length of the speech. When it was finished, Quinn said, "I think our sheriff has had a little too much to drink. Even so"—he raised his glass in the air—"I propose a toast to Lester Graves, whoever that is." To himself, he thought, *You meddling fool, you just signed your death warrant.*

There was still some confusion for the others at the table, since Lester's death had not been generally known, nor had his existence by more than a few people in the whole town. So the lull lasted for only a few seconds, then the party was renewed. The only lasting effect was the mark of death fixed on Sheriff Paul McQueen.

McQueen remained at the table for another half hour or so, but he didn't drink anything more. He got up out of his chair and announced, "Well, I'd like to stay here and drink with you fellows, but folks don't like to see their sheriff drunk. So, I'll say thank you for the whiskey, but I've got some things I'm needin' to take care of." He turned and headed for the door, his walk steady as a rock.

Outside, Perley called to McQueen, who was walking toward the jail. "Paul, wait up!"

The sheriff stopped and when he saw it was Perley, he waited for him. "What's up, Perley?"

"I think I know what you were doing back there when you said all that stuff about Lester Graves and playin' a game to find out who killed him. I just felt like tellin' you to be careful around that fellow. Like we talked about that thing before with those two cowhands in the saloon, then that shootin' of poor old Lester Graves. Everything points to Redmond Quinn for both of those killings, but there ain't no way to prove what we think."

"I know it, Perley, but it just pesters my mind knowin' he's gettin' away with it—shootin' anybody that don't suit him just right. That man's as crooked as a snake, and Raymond Patton and Amos Johnson just eat up that manure he keeps feedin' 'em. Look how he's took over Patton's Saloon already. You mark my words, he'll be tryin' to take over the whole town before he's done."

"I don't mean to say I'm qualified to give you advice," Perley said, "but I think you'd do well to watch your back real close. I wouldn't trust that man anywhere outta my sight." He was speaking his mind when he normally would not, but he felt strongly about the threat Quinn might be. And Paul McQueen was a good man and a good sheriff. "I apologize for buttin' into your business. I hope I ain't gone too far."

"Not a-tall, Perley," McQueen replied. "I 'preciate your concern about me. You're right, I have to admit. I oughtn't not bait that badger like I did just now. I just wanted him to know that he ain't got everybody in town fooled. I just wish that damn horse of his could talk." He gave a little chuckle. "I'll watch my back, though. Thanks, Perley." He turned and continued on toward the jail. Perley turned around and walked the other way toward the hotel.

He had real concerns for Paul McQueen, but there wasn't anything he could do about it. Possum always thought Perley had sharp instincts about people and places, but Perley was not at all sure that was true. He just knew that he got certain feelings about some things. It was like his reaction to a gun threat. He didn't stop and figure out what to do. His brain just took hold of the reins and he would gee or haw as directed. As he approached the hotel, however, his negative concerns began to fade the closer he came to the dining room. It was too early for them to open for supper, but he had made up his mind that he would try to see Becky before she had to start working the supper crowd.

The outside door of the dining room had two small glass panes in the top half, so he walked up to it and peeked in to see if he might spy Becky doing something inside. There was no one in the room at all. He hesitated to knock on the door, for fear that Lucy or Beulah might answer. And he wasn't prepared to suffer the embarrassment of them having their fun with him trying to call on Becky. With no better plan, he decided to walk around the dining room wing to the kitchen door in the back on the chance she might be doing some chore there.

So he walked around the building, past the dining room and along a section with four windows. When he was beneath the third window, he heard some tapping on the glass. When he looked up, he saw Becky, beaming at him through the window. Then she raised the window and exclaimed, "Perley, where are you going?"

It was too late to beat around the bush, so he confessed. "I was hopin' I'd find you," he blurted. "But I didn't see anybody in the dinin' room and I didn't know where else to look for you. It ain't like I could just go knock on your door. Heck, I don't even know where you live."

"This is where I live," she said. "This is my room. Lucy and Beulah have rooms next to mine, so I reckon if you came knocking on my door, you might bring one of them out in the hall, too, with nothing but their knickers on." She chuckled at the thought. "But you came looking for me?" He nodded as if guilty. "There's a table with seats behind this part of the building. We could visit there, if you want to. I don't have to start getting ready for supper for an hour yet." When he nodded vigorously, she said, "Let me get my shawl. Wait right there!" She was gone only a minute, then came back to the window. "You're gonna have to help me," she said, then sat down on the windowsill with her feet outside. He stepped up to catch her, and she giggled as he almost stumbled when she launched herself into his arms. He held her in his arms for a long moment before she said, "You'd best put me down so you can close the window. If Beulah or Lucy come in my room, they'll think I got kidnapped again."

He reached up and pulled the window back down while she watched, thinking this the happiest day of her life. When he turned back to face her, she took his hand and said, "Come on, there's a good place to visit back here under a big old oak tree." She led him toward the back of the hotel to a little area that had originally been planned to be a picnic area for guests of the new hotel. "As far as I know, nobody's ever used it. I know Beulah's never made up a picnic basket for anybody."

The picnic table Becky took him to was one with a bench built on each side. She sat down on one side and he sat down on the other, so they could face each other, but she reached across to take his hand while they talked. "We already heard about the trouble that happened when the Ranger tried to put Leonard Watts in the jail wagon. I'm so glad you came to see me right away. I wanted to know if you were all right." She paused then when she realized she was doing all the talking. "Here I am clucking away like an old hen and you haven't said a mouthful of words the whole time. I'm just glad to see you're all right."

"I was hopin' you hadn't heard all about that before I had a chance to explain it, at least, my part in it," he said. "I was afraid you'd think I was always gettin' into trouble, and I ain't that kinda person at all."

"What I heard was that you saved that Texas Ranger's life when that crazy Leonard tried to shoot him," she said. She gave his hand a little squeeze. "Perley, I know what kind of man you are. If I didn't, I wouldn't be sittin' here at the table with you." She giggled again. "And I sure wouldn't have jumped out the window for you."

He was at once relieved, for he had been very much afraid that with all the gunfights he had found himself in, she might think that he was someone constantly looking for trouble. "I didn't have no choice, he was fixin' to pull the trigger."

"I believe you," she assured him, and continued to assure him for most of what remained of the hour before she reluctantly told him that she had to go help Lucy set up the dining room for supper. "Beulah's already been cooking the food, so it's time for Lucy and me to go to work."

"I 'preciate you takin' the time to visit with me," he said. "I reckon I'd better help you get back in your room."

She laughed and declared, "I think I'll just walk in the back door, if it's unlocked, instead of crawling in the window. I expect you and Possum are coming to the dining room for supper."

"We sure are," he answered as he walked her to the back door. "At least, I am, whether Possum does or not."

"I expect he'll be there, too," she commented, "seeing as how he's your constant shadow. How in the world did you get away from him long enough to come see me, anyway?"

"He was more interested in what was goin' on at Patton's. Besides, he was wantin' me to visit you. You know he likes you."

She stopped to search his face intently for a moment. "Yes, I do know that Possum likes me. And I like Possum. What I don't know for sure is how you feel about me."

Her statement baffled him. "You gotta know I like you," he said.

She shook her head, exasperated. "You like me, like you like Possum and you like Buck, and you like mashed potatoes and gravy? Or do you like me, like I like you?"

"I reckon I love you," he muttered as if it was a secret he didn't want anyone to know.

"There! Finally! You said it. You love me and I love you. That's all I wanna know." She went up on her tiptoes and gave him a motherly peck on the cheek. "Now, I've got to go to work. I'll see you at supper, and don't be late.

I miss you already." With that, she skipped up the back steps and went into the hotel, leaving him to wonder what had just happened.

His brain was flooded with thoughts of how the past hour of his life would affect the rest of his life. He realized that he didn't know what the next step was in his newly formed relationship with Becky. Marriage? That was a term that had always been foreign to him, an arrangement he could never picture himself in. He had to wonder if his brothers would identify this commitment he made today as another *cow pie*. "I sure as hell ain't ready to get married and settle down to raise young 'uns," he mumbled, causing a stranger he passed to ask what he said. "Nothin', sorry," Perley replied. "I reckon I was just talkin' to myself." *Maybe I oughta ask Possum what to do,* he thought, then immediately decided that was not a good idea. By the time he reached Patton's, he thought he was ready for that drink he had passed up before he went to see Becky.

Inside the saloon, the party was all but over, so he went straight to the table and poured himself a stiff shot of whiskey from the one bottle that still had some in it. Possum, who could always hold his liquor as well as any man, grinned at him when he poured his whiskey. "This party's about done, partner. I expect that's the last of the free stuff. Glad you got back from your little chore in time to get a drink."

"You look like you got your share, judgin' by that silly grin on your face," Perley replied. He looked at Grady Prince, who appeared to be staring at him, then realized the Ranger wasn't staring at anything. He was passed out with his eyes wide open. There was no question about Prince's posseman, however. Willie was fast asleep, his chin resting firmly on his chest. Back to Possum then, he asked, "You gonna be able to go get something to eat in a little while? I think you're gonna need it." He looked around the saloon, then asked, "Where's your host, Redford Quinn? I thought he'd stick till the end."

"Perley Gates," he heard behind him, and turned to see Quinn coming from Raymond Patton's office. "You're getting a little careless, aren't you? Letting someone come up on your back like that."

"Maybe so," Perley replied. "I reckon I wasn't expectin' to run into any back-shooters in here."

"Ah, but that's the thing about back-shooters, you can run into them anywhere," Quinn expounded. "You can never let your guard down."

"We'll try to keep that in mind, won't we, Possum? I reckon somebody shoulda told old Lester Graves that." As soon as he said it, Perley scolded himself for giving in to the same tactics Paul McQueen had chosen to employ.

Perley's response drew the same patient smile across Quinn's face as McQueen's had. "Everybody seems to be mourning that old tramp's death as if he was a great loss to this community. I have found no evidence to support that high regard for the pathetic old soul while he was alive." Perley noted that Quinn no longer claimed not to know who Lester was.

"It's kinda like cullin' the sick cows outta the herd, so they don't pass it on to the rest of 'em, I reckon," Perley couldn't resist saying.

"Exactly," Quinn replied.

Possum was not too drunk to recognize a feeling-out sparring session between two fighters before a challenge was issued by one or the other. His immediate fear was that

Perley didn't recognize it as such, because Perley's usual way was to avoid such tomfoolery. "Well, I'm ready to get outta here. Let's go, Perley, before all of the whiskey I drank starts pourin' outta me."

Perley, recognizing a signal from Possum, realized he might be talking himself into a confrontation with the slick-talking gambler, so he gave Quinn a big friendly smile. "Nice talkin' to you, Quinn, I better take ol' Possum outta here while he can still walk." He turned to join Possum, who was already on his feet, and they walked out the door, giving Benny a wave on their way past the bar.

Possum only hesitated a few moments to breathe in the outside air before starting down the street toward the hotel. "I swear," he confessed, "I ain't drunk that much whiskey since I can't remember when. And for a while there, I thought you was fixin' to talk your way into a showdown with Redmond Quinn."

"You oughta know better'n that," Perley said.

"I was beginnin' to think you didn't know better'n that," Possum came back.

"I don't wanna waste no more time thinkin' about Redmond Quinn," Perley said. He walked a little farther, trying to decide if he should tell Possum about his meeting at the hotel earlier. He found that he couldn't hold it in. He had to tell somebody, but he wasn't ready to tell everybody. "I'll make a deal with you, Reginald . . ."

That was as far as he got before Possum exploded. "Dad blame it, Perley! I told you not to ever call me that!"

"Just hold your horses," Perley said. "I said I'd like to make a bargain with you, and here's what I'll do. I won't ever call you that again, and I won't tell anybody else about it, if you'll promise you won't tell anybody what I'm fixin' to tell you."

"What?" Possum responded. "About you and Becky Morris bein' sweethearts?"

"How did you know that?" Perley exclaimed.

"I swear, partner, sometimes, about some things, you're dumber than a hammer. You musta got to see her this afternoon. Did you tell her you love her?"

"I did, but it wasn't easy," Perley confessed, thinking back on the episode. "She just kept askin' me questions till she drove me in a corner and flat-out asked me if I liked her or loved her. I couldn't tell her a lie."

"Well, it's about time. You two young people were a matched set ever since I've known you and most likely long before that. Don't worry, I ain't gonna say nothin' about it, not till you think it's time to tell everybody. But you gotta keep your word about that name my mama tacked onto me when I was a baby and couldn't do nothin' about it. Right?"

"That's right, partner," Perley said. "Now, let's go have supper with my gal."

CHAPTER 14

As often was the case, Lucy Tate greeted them at the door of the dining room. "Well, good evenin', boys. I got strict orders from Becky to make sure you two sat at that table right by the kitchen door. She doesn't usually care where anybody sits. Must be something going on with that gal. She's been acting kinda strange ever since we started settin' all the tables up for supper. She's all smiles." She paused to wait for them to deposit their firearms on the table, before asking, "That hasn't got anything to do with you, has it, Perley?"

"Ha!" Possum blurted before he thought to prevent it.

Perley reacted with a scolding look for his friend before answering Lucy. "No, ma'am," he said, "I ain't got no idea." Lucy favored him with a look that said, *I know a case of young love when I see one.* She had no time to tell him that because Becky hurried out of the kitchen just then to intercept.

"Where've you been?" Becky asked. "We opened fifteen minutes ago."

Her rebuff caused Possum to chuckle. "It's my fault,

Becky. Perley had to drag me outta the saloon. He was rarin' to go."

Lucy was still confused by a decided difference in Becky's manner while waiting on the two men. One thing she noticed that was blatantly different was the fact that when Becky stood by Perley, she placed her hand on his shoulder. It occurred to her then. *Something's happened. That's why she's been skipping around the dining room like a child waiting for Christmas.* She went immediately into the kitchen to tell Beulah.

In a couple of minutes, Becky came into the kitchen to get coffee for Perley and Possum and found the two women standing by the stove waiting for her. "You might as well fess up," Lucy informed her. "You did it, didn't you? You told Perley you're head over heels in love with him."

Becky just smiled coyly and proceeded to fill two cups with coffee while they watched her like two turkey buzzards eyeing a carcass. She picked up the two cups before she answered Lucy, and then with only one word. "Maybe," she said, and went out the door.

"I knew it!" Lucy exclaimed.

"Well, hallelujah," Beulah sighed. "It's about time somethin' good happened for that poor little gal. Maybe it's a sign that good things are comin' to this town for a change."

Beulah's interpretation of a sign of good things coming might have been reconsidered had she known of an occurrence of a more sinister nature taking place at the railroad station. At approximately the same time Beulah and Lucy were speculating on exactly when Perley and

Becky acknowledged their attraction to each other, the five o'clock train rolled into town. It was running only twenty minutes behind time. Back near the end of the train, Ebb Barlow was in the process of swinging the door of the one stock car on the train down to make a ramp for a passenger and his horse to disembark. When the ramp was down, Ebb greeted the man. "Howdy. Welcome to Paris. What brings you to town?"

Elam Burke took a long look at Ebb before answering, "Oh, one thing and then another," he said, and led the big buckskin gelding out of the train car. "Where's Patton's Saloon?"

Ebb turned and pointed to the buildings across from the railroad tracks. "Won't be no trouble findin' Patton's," he said. "It's the only saloon in town." Burke climbed up into the saddle, and without a word of thanks, turned the buckskin toward the main street and departed. "Ain't a very talkative feller," Ebb muttered as Burke rode away.

Redmond Quinn sat at a table in Patton's Saloon, idly amusing himself by dealing blackjack hands between himself and an empty chair. There were only a couple of customers in the saloon, since the drinking party to celebrate the unsuccessful transfer of Leonard Watts broke up. Ranger, Grady Prince, and his posseman and cook, Willie James, had come to and staggered up to the hotel to rent a room for the night. "Where are all the big-time gamblers tonight, Benny?" Quinn's question to the bartender was in sarcastic reference to the typical lack of citizens willing to risk their hard-earned money.

"Most likely gone to supper and the little woman put her foot down," Benny replied. "There'll be a few souls in after supper, though."

"When I get this place fixed up the way I want it," Quinn predicted, "we won't need the timid souls of Paris. There'll be real gamblers seeking this place out."

Benny looked toward the front of the saloon when someone came in the door. "Here comes somebody now. Maybe he'll turn a card or two, so you don't lose any more money to that empty chair."

Quinn looked toward the door and smiled when he saw who had walked in. "Elam Burke," he pronounced to himself, then repeated it loudly so that Burke could hear him. Burke saw him at the table close to the back of the saloon and came immediately to join him. "Benny," Quinn called out, "bring a bottle of the good rye."

Quinn got to his feet and shook Burke's hand. "Sit down, Elam. I heard the train whistle, but I didn't expect you until tomorrow or the next day."

"How you doin', Quinn?" Burke greeted him. "Your wire came at a good time. Another day and I wouldn'ta been there to get it. I was fixin' to leave Arkansas and look for some better pastures somewhere else. You got some work for me here in this little cow town? You usually like to handle any problems you've got, yourself. Hell, you're the fastest man with a six-gun I've ever seen. You must want me to do some ambush work or some back-shootin'."

Quinn paused to wait for Benny to leave a bottle and a couple of glasses on the table before replying. "That's exactly what I want you for. I can't do this one, myself, because I've got to make sure everybody in this town knows that I didn't do it. So I have to be right here where a lot of people can see me when the job is done."

"Who is this jasper?" Burke asked. "Why the ambush?

Can't I just call him out and settle his hash in the middle of the street?"

"No," Quinn replied. "You can call him out, but he won't come out."

"What? Is he a preacher or an old man or somethin'?"

"No. He's the sheriff," Quinn said. "And, knowing him, I can tell you he won't face you in a duel. He's more apt to place you under arrest." When that caused a raising of Burke's eyebrows, Quinn asked, "Do you have any problem with shooting a lawman?"

"Hell, no, they're my favorite targets. What's the matter? Is he puttin' the heat on you?"

"He's in my way," Quinn stated. "I've got big plans for this little town." He gestured toward the construction work going on outside. "You might have noticed the wing being built on the back of this building." He went on to tell him of his plans for his gambling hall. "If you take care of the sheriff for me, I might find a spot for you here in my town, maybe as sheriff."

"That'd be somethin'," Burke grunted, amused by the thought. "Might be somethin' I'd like to try out for once."

"You've known me long enough to know any sheriff I hire in a town I own is gonna be a very wealthy lawman. And this dull-witted blacksmith, who's also the sheriff here now, has it in his mind that what I plan to do here is not good for the town. And I'm afraid he's going to be standing in my way with everything I do to build this town up. He keeps pecking away at me because I shot some old tramp who was messing around my horse in the stable. The sheriff knows I did it, but there's no way he can prove it. But still he keeps annoying me with his thinly veiled little innuendos about it."

"His little whats?" Burke asked.

"Never mind," Quinn replied. "He just annoys me and I want to be rid of him."

"Well, that don't sound like any problem a-tall," Burke assured him. "It'll be a pleasure to take care of that little chore for you and you'll be clear to take over the town, especially if I'm the new sheriff."

"I'll almost be clear," Quinn said. "There is one more problem I'd like to get rid of, but this one I'll take down myself. He's pretty fast with a gun, and he's a friend of the sheriff. But this one's mine. He's watching his step around me right now, but I'll challenge him to face me, so the people in this town know how fast I am. And that should take care of any future two-bit gunslingers who want to buck me."

"Well, I reckon I'd best find out what the sheriff looks like, so I don't shoot the wrong feller," Burke said. "Does he come in here very often?"

"Once in a while," Quinn answered, then a thought occurred. He looked at his pocket watch. "I've let the time slip up on me. It's suppertime at the hotel and the sheriff usually eats there in the dining room. Might be a good chance to see him. Are you ready for some supper?"

"I surely am," Burke said, "and it'd be a good idea to put some food in my belly with the whiskey I just drank."

"You can leave your horse here, if you want, and we'll walk down to the hotel. We've still got time to make it before they close. While we're there, you can get a room," Quinn suggested. When Burke hesitated a moment, Quinn added, "Of course, I'll take care of the rent."

* * *

"Well, good evenin', Mr. Quinn," Lucy Tate greeted them when they walked in the dining room. "I see you brought a guest tonight."

"Ah, Miss Tate," Quinn responded, falling at once into his facade of gentlemanly charm. He turned to Burke and said, "Elam, this charming lady is Miss Lucy Tate. Lucy, this rather rugged individual is Mr. Elam Burke, a man I worked with in Arkansas quite some time ago."

"Good evenin' to you, Mr. Burke," Lucy replied. "Welcome to our dining room." She couldn't help casting a suspicious eye at the tall, rangy stranger who openly eyed her in return. They paused there at the weapons table while Burke untied the rawhide cord holding his holster to his leg after he saw Quinn place his weapon there.

Quinn and his guest attracted the attention of Perley and Possum, who had finished eating, but were lingering over coffee and Becky's frequent visits to their table. "Looks like Redmond Quinn has a new friend," Possum commented. "Must be a gunslinger, same as Quinn, the way he wears that holster."

"He sure doesn't look like he rotates in the same social circle that ol' Slick Quinn does," Perley said. When Becky came by again to ask if they wanted more coffee, he asked, "You ever see that fellow with Quinn in here before?"

"No, this is the first time he's been in here," Becky answered. "Lucy was near the door when they walked in. She said Quinn introduced her to him. Elam Burke's his name."

Across the room, Quinn commented to Burke, "We got here in time for you to see that other problem I told you about. See the two men sitting over there near the kitchen door? One of them is the man that I intend to take down in a fair fight, so that there's no question who the fastest gun in town is." Burke turned to look and started to ask a question, but Quinn stopped him. "I know what you're about to ask, so I'll save you the trouble. It's the young one. His name is Perley Gates, and he's the fastest gun around this little town—until now."

"Pearly Gates?" Burke responded. "Are you japin' me?"

"That's his name, Perley Gates, and he's got a little reputation around town. It's important for me to show there's only one fast gun in this town. So forget about him. He's mine. The older man sitting with him might be another target for you. His name is Possum Smith, and I don't know if he'll be a problem or not after Gates and the sheriff are gone. We'll see about that when the time comes, but it's my guess that we won't hear a squeak out of him when his pal Perley is gone." The outside door opened then and Quinn said, "Just what I hoped for. Here's your target right now, coming in so you can get a good look at him. Sheriff," Quinn acknowledged when McQueen walked by, having spotted Perley and Possum at the table by the kitchen door.

"Mr. Quinn," the sheriff returned, taking a moment to take a look at the man with him. Then he continued on over to join Perley and Possum at their table.

"You're late," Possum said. "We done et."

McQueen smiled. "Hope you left a little bit of it, whatever it is."

"Roast pork and Beulah's beans," Possum said, "and I'm tellin' you, those beans of hers will set you free."

"Who's the stranger settin' with Redmond Quinn?" McQueen asked. "Anybody you know?"

"Never seen him before," Perley answered. "Becky said

he's never been in here before. We were thinkin' that he might be somebody who's come to work for Quinn. But he's wearin' a quick-draw holster, so we doubt he's gonna be a card dealer." The speculation about the mysterious-looking guest at Quinn's table continued for a while until Perley announced that he and Possum had best get on their horses and head for the Triple-G.

When they got up to leave, Becky followed them outside to say good night to Perley. As before, she went up on her tiptoes to give him a kiss. It was a quick kiss, just as her first one had been. But this one was on his lips, and consequently, it delivered a lot more impact than her peck on the cheek, and he was left speechless. She giggled at his awkward reaction and told Possum to see that he got back to the ranch all right.

Finding his voice again, Perley said, "I'll come to see you tomorrow night, if that's all right."

"Of course, it's all right," she said. "You're welcome anytime, but I don't want you to go to a lot of trouble."

"It won't be any trouble," he insisted. "It ain't but five miles. I'm gonna be workin' in the barn tomorrow, so I'll jump on Buck right after supper and be here when you finish in the dinin' room. I won't stay too long, though, 'cause I'll have to be ready to go to work in the mornin'."

"All right," she said, beaming. "We can sit on the hotel porch and talk." They both nodded their agreement, then she hurried back inside, hoping neither Lucy nor Beulah realized what she had been up to. Thoroughly embarrassed now, Perley turned around to see Possum grinning at him. "Don't you say nothin'," Perley warned, "lessen you want me to shout your name all over town."

"I ain't said a word," Possum replied, his grin almost from ear to ear now. "Come on, we'd best get home."

"You'd better be careful steppin' outside without a shawl over your shoulders," Beulah said to Becky when she came back into the kitchen with some dirty dishes. "These nights this time of year can get a little nippy." She fixed her with an accusing eye and a teasing smile.

"Kiss my foot, Beulah," Becky responded. "I just said good night."

"I wanna know when you two are gonna get to doin' some serious talkin'. Has he said anything about gettin' married?"

"No, we ain't said anything about that, for goodness' sakes," Becky replied.

"What if he don't ask you?" Beulah pressed.

"I don't care if he doesn't," Becky declared. "He said he loves me and that's enough for me right now. We don't have to be in a big hurry."

"You just be sure nobody gets to sample any of your apples unless they buy the whole peck of 'em first."

"Beulah!" Becky scolded. "Hush your mouth! You oughta know Perley ain't that kind of man."

They were interrupted then when Lucy came back in the kitchen. "Redmond Quinn and his friend had me move their plates over beside the sheriff's table. But Bill Simmons told me that McQueen and Quinn didn't get along too good."

"Yeah, that's what I heard," Beulah replied. "Maybe ol' Slick Quinn thinks it'd be a good idea to get along with the sheriff."

Beulah's speculation might have seemed on the mark, judging by Quinn's initial remarks. "Sheriff McQueen," Quinn began, "I got the feeling earlier in the saloon that there might be a little friction between us. And that's certainly something I don't want. I'll admit I've got some ambitious ideas about your town, and consequently, I'm going to need to work with you the best I can. I don't know how you can really believe I'd shoot down a defenseless old man in that stable, though. If it's because I shot those two men before, I shot them to protect myself. They pulled on me first. I had no choice. But with the old man in the stable, I wasn't even in the stable. I'm just asking you to consider that fact and give me the benefit of the doubt." He cocked an eye to make sure the other patrons in the dining room could hear his plea. He nodded toward Elam Burke then. "This is a man I've worked with before. His name's Elam Burke. He's especially qualified to provide protective service—at least, he was for me when I had some trouble with outlaws in another venture. He stopped over on his way to Fort Worth when he found out I was starting a new venture here. I thought it would be a good idea to have him meet you, Sheriff. And if my investment brings more work than a one-man sheriff's department can handle, you couldn't get a better man to back you up as deputy than Elam Burke."

McQueen kept a straight face throughout Quinn's pitch for this stranger, who looked more gunslinger than deputy, even though he was amazed that Quinn could approach him with such an outrageous proposal. He was more convinced than ever that Quinn shot Lester Graves. As for the prospective hire for deputy, this Elam Burke was studying him as if he was trying to decide where he should start to carve him up like a turkey. "Well, that's a mighty interestin' proposition, I'll say that for it," McQueen said. He shifted his gaze back to Elam. "You done a lot of law work, have you, Mr. Burke?"

Burke hesitated, obviously not prepared to answer any such questions, so Quinn interceded to answer for him. "Elam did most of his law work up in Kansas. Isn't that right, Elam?"

"Right," Burke answered. "That's where I did most of my deputy work. Over around Dodge City."

McQueen looked at the man, absolutely convinced that he was lying. "Right now, there ain't no need for a deputy, so I reckon we'll have to ford that creek when we get to it. If we do get to the point when I'm gonna need some help, then I'd certainly wanna talk to you. Course, it means a lot when Mr. Quinn recommends you, so I'm lookin' forward to the day when we have a town big enough to support two lawmen." He hoped he had been able to veil the sarcasm he had felt while making his little speech.

McQueen didn't spend much time finishing up his supper, spurred on by his uninvited supper companions. When Becky came back to the table with the coffeepot, he refused the refill, saying, "Thanks, Becky, but I expect I'd best go take a little walk around town." He got up from his chair. "Gentlemen," he said, and took his leave.

Quinn and Burke finished their supper shortly after. Quinn returned to the saloon, and Burke went inside the hotel to rent a room for the night.

Chapter 15

"What the hell's goin' on here, Quinn?" Elam Burke wanted to know when he came back from the hotel to join Quinn at the saloon. "I got me a room like you said and they put me in one next door to a Texas Ranger! If I'da known there was a Ranger in town, I'da made me a camp outside of town somewhere."

Quinn couldn't suppress a smile of amusement. "Did you see the Ranger?" he asked. When Burke said that he made certain he didn't see him, Quinn explained, "He left this saloon just before you got here today, so drunk he had to be led out by a man he brought with him. And that man wasn't too steady, himself. They came over here from Sherman to pick up a prisoner the sheriff had in jail here. You don't have to worry about that Ranger. He just came for the prisoner and the prisoner was shot down when he tried to make an escape. When you take your horse to the stable, you'll see his jail wagon parked beside it."

"Well, I reckon that makes it a little better," Burke allowed. "I just don't like sleepin' in the same place with a Texas Ranger. Makes the hairs on the back of my neck stand up."

"Forget about him," Quinn said. "We'll just wait until he leaves town in the morning and heads back to Sherman. We'll let the sheriff enjoy one more night in Paris. No need taking a chance on having a Ranger stick his nose in our little private business, is there?"

"That's all right with me," Burke said. "I'll take my time tomorrow to get to know the whole town, might even talk to the blacksmith, get to know him a little better before I blow his ass to hell."

"Just be damn sure you let me know when you plan to take care of him, so I can be sure I've got plenty of witnesses for my alibi," Quinn reminded him. He wasn't worried about Burke ever trying to blackmail him by threatening to tell the authorities he had ordered him to kill the sheriff. If he ever threatened, Quinn would simply say he was a liar and call him out to face him, then Quinn would kill him. Burke was fast, but Quinn was convinced that neither Burke, nor anyone else, was faster than Redmond Quinn.

"I'm gonna take a little late-night walk around town tonight," Burke decided. "Maybe get an idea of what he does at night. I'm hopin' he makes regular rounds before he locks himself up in the jail for the night. There might be someplace I can catch him where there ain't nobody else lookin'."

"Just don't get caught following him around," Quinn told him.

Paul McQueen took his early nightly walk up and down Main Street, making sure all the locks were on those businesses already closed for the night. "Pretty quiet night," he muttered to himself as he returned to the sheriff's office. There was no one in the cell room, so it was an ideal time to fire his forge up and continue working on those wagon wheels for Clyde Masters. McQueen had been taking advantage of this time while his wife and son were at her parents' in Kansas City. Instead of going home at night, he had been staying in the jail and working several hours a night in his blacksmith shop. So he hung his sign on his office door, notifying anyone seeking the sheriff that he was at the blacksmith shop, then he walked the short distance up the street to his forge. Every time he did this, he questioned whether it was worth it to continue running his shop. And every time, he told himself that he made more money from what he produced in that shop than he ever could on the sheriff's salary. *Besides,* he told himself, *I like to work the iron.*

Kneeling in the short grass about thirty yards from the blacksmith's forge, Elam Burke smiled to himself and thought, *This is going to be too easy. If you do this tomorrow night, you're a dead man.* On this night, there was no need to find a tree or a gully for cover. It was so dark that he felt safe just kneeling there in the open, for he knew no one could see him from the street. Tomorrow night, it would be different because he would be concerned about his muzzle flash, but there were ample trees to take cover behind. Satisfied with the easy target the sheriff was kind enough to present, he was tempted to take the shot right then, but he knew Quinn would be enraged at him, if he didn't have his witnesses on hand. So, he took a practice shot, using his finger as the weapon. "Pow," he uttered. "See you back here tomorrow night."

* * *

"Somebody lit a fire under Perley's ass this mornin'," Ralph Johnson commented to Ollie Dinkler when he walked into the bunkhouse for the midday meal.

Overhearing, Fred Farmer said, "You notice that, too? I thought he was gonna rebuild the whole barn, the way he was goin' at it."

"Ain't he gonna even stop to eat his dinner?" Ralph wondered.

"He's already et," Ollie said. "He popped in here just long enough to pile some beans on a biscuit, then he was gone again. Said he had a certain amount he wanted to get done in the barn today."

"Well, I hope Rubin ain't fixin' to set that rate as the standard for all of us," Ralph said.

When suppertime came, Perley's behavior wasn't a great deal different. He wasted little time with his food before heading for the washhouse to get cleaned up. "Good chuck, Ollie," was all he said as he hurried out of the bunkhouse on his way to the stable.

All those at the table looked to Possum for the answer to Perley's weird behavior. "Whaddaya lookin' at me for?" Possum asked.

"'Cause you're the only one likely to know what's eatin' him," Fred answered for them all.

Before Possum had time to answer, Perley's brother John walked in the bunkhouse and stood for a moment looking over the room. Then he went to Possum and asked, "Where's Perley? I want him to take a couple of the men to go fix up that old line shack on Skeeter Creek."

"I'll tell him," Possum said.

John just stood there for a long moment, as if uncertain. "He is here somewhere, ain't he?"

"Yes, sir," Possum replied. "You know Perley. He's around here somewhere. I'll tell him about the line shack." He could have told John that Perley was in the washroom, getting ready to take a quick ride into town. But he knew Perley wasn't ready to announce to everyone that he was courting Becky Morris.

Elam Burke sat around Patton's Saloon after supper-time, watching a demonstration of Redmond Quinn's new roulette wheel. It had arrived just that day on the five o'clock train, and Quinn was offering free whiskey to those who had come to see the wheel. A few of the town's more adventurous citizens were trying their luck on the black and the red as Quinn operated the foot pump. It served to entertain Burke for a while, but he had more interesting things in mind for the evening. So when Sheriff McQueen stopped in for a short while to satisfy his curiosity, Burke slipped out the door after him when the sheriff left to continue his rounds. Burke sat down in one of the chairs on the porch of the saloon, took out his cigarette papers, and rolled himself a smoke while he watched McQueen work his way down the street toward the hotel. In a short while, the sheriff appeared on the opposite side of the street, coming back toward the hotel. Burke remained there, a casual observer, until McQueen finally went into his office. *Won't be long now,* Burke thought, and promptly got out of his chair, stepped across the street, and went between the jail and the harness shop, into the darkness behind the buildings. He walked unhurriedly along behind the shops, satisfied that no one could see him, until he came to the blacksmith shop.

Earlier in the day, Burke had picked out the spot he was going to shoot from that night. For his warped sense of entertainment, he had even stopped in the forge when he saw McQueen there talking to a man who wanted his horse shod. He waited until McQueen had settled on an appointed time for the man to bring his horse in for shoes. "Just thought I'd take a look at your blacksmith business," he had told McQueen. "After talkin' to you in the hotel last night, I reckon I just wanted to see if you was japin' or not when you said you was a blacksmith on top of holdin' down the sheriff's job." McQueen had explained that he had been a blacksmith a lot more years than he had been a lawman, and he reckoned he didn't want to quit the one job he knew how to do. Burke had laughed with him over his comment. "Be seein' ya," he had left him with, after taking a casual line of sight from the anvil to the spot by the big oak tree he had picked out.

Now, in the darkness, Burke continued walking until he came to that oak tree. He walked all around it, making sure it was his spot alone on this night. Satisfied, he drew his Colt Peacemaker from his holster and checked to make sure it was loaded. He would have preferred to use a rifle for the shot, but his rifle was in his saddle sling in Walt Carver's stable. It might have aroused suspicion if it was found out after the shooting that his rifle had been taken from his saddle. He was as accurate as anyone with the handgun, at any rate, and the shot would be no longer than fifteen or twenty yards at most. *Besides,* he told himself, *a pistol shot is distinct from the sound of a rifle and wouldn't cause as much alarm.* The first thought would likely be that some drunk cowhand decided to shoot a hole in the watering trough. It struck him funny when he thought, *When they hear the shot, maybe they'll run to get the sheriff.*

He figured it must have been thirty or forty-five minutes since he sat down against the oak tree to wait for McQueen, so he began to wonder if he had been mistaken in his hunch that the blacksmith would show up to work that night. But then, McQueen suddenly appeared. At least, he assumed it was the sheriff. The dark figure he saw moving around the blacksmith shop had come in from the front and Burke found he was not as easily identified as he had thought he would be. He swore silently, got up from where he was sitting, and advanced cautiously toward the man, who was now standing before the forge. He still couldn't tell for sure that it was the sheriff. With his Colt aimed at the figure, Burke called out, "McQueen!"

"Whoa!" McQueen blurted. "You scared the hell outta me! Who is it?" That was the last sound he made before Burke's shot ripped into his midsection and he crumpled to the ground.

"It's the boogeyman come to see you," Burke answered, and laughed as he moved forward, intending to put another shot into him to be sure. But he stopped at once when he heard someone yell.

"Paul! You all right?" Clyde Masters called out.

Not sure if he had inadvertently opened up a hornet's nest or not, Burke backed away toward the oak tree for cover. He could now hear two voices calling for the sheriff. He realized at once that there would be a gang of people running to that blacksmith shop within minutes, so there was no decision to be made. His job was done. Time to vanish into the darkness. Already hearing voices calling out in alarm, he started running, anxious to put as much distance as possible between him and the blacksmith shop. Crossing back to the other side of the street, he ran around to the rear of the saloon and went in the back door, where he paused for a few minutes until his heart stopped pounding in his chest. When he thought he was ready, he walked on into the busy saloon, where Redmond Quinn was still entertaining the customers.

Burke walked over to the bar and told Benny to pour him a drink, just as the first word of the shooting came in the door. "Somebody shot Sheriff McQueen!" Luther Rains shouted. "Anybody seen Bill Simmons?"

"I'm here!" Simmons cried out from a table in the corner. "Where is he?"

"In his blacksmith shop," Luther answered. "You need to come now!"

"Is he dead?" Simmons asked when he had to decide on finishing the bottle on the table or responding immediately.

"Hell, I don't know," Luther answered. "Dead or dyin'. All I know is Clyde Masters said to find you quick."

Having caught sight of Elam Burke when he suddenly appeared in the crowd watching the roulette wheel in action, Redmond Quinn had nodded slightly. And Burke had responded with a definite nod of his own. Now Quinn looked back at Burke, uncertain, a question in his eyes, and Burke shrugged. The crowd was rapidly draining toward the door, anxious to see what had happened to McQueen. "Oh Lord, please, not the sheriff," Mayor

Amos Johnson muttered to himself as he ran past the roulette wheel, heading for the front door.

Burke moved over to stand beside Quinn. "I didn't hear but one shot," Quinn said. "Is he dead or not?"

"Yeah, he's dead," Burke said. "I was gonna make sure, but when I started to go in there to finish him, there was a bunch of people all of a sudden. And I had to get the hell outta there."

"Did anybody see you?" Quinn demanded, not at all happy with the report.

"Hell, no," Burke answered, irritated as well by his attitude.

"Something's happened up the street," Becky said as she pressed her legs up against the railing around the hotel porch, trying to see where everybody was running to. They had heard the single gunshot a few minutes earlier. But since there were no follow-up shots, they guessed that someone with a drink or two too many had simply discharged his firearm, just to make the noise. It was not an unusual occurrence.

"Looks like they're headin' to the blacksmith shop," Perley said. They stood side by side at the railing, watching until they saw James Bedford, one of the bank tellers, running down the street toward the hotel.

When Bedford reached the hotel and bounded up the steps, Becky stopped him. "James, what's happened?"

"Somebody shot Sheriff McQueen!" James replied, and continued toward the door.

"Is he dead?" Perley asked.

"I don't know. I think so. I've gotta go tell Mr. Taylor.

He's not gonna wanna hear this news at all." He pushed on through the door and ran to the stairs to deliver the tragic news to the bank president.

Perley looked at once to Becky, who was clearly alarmed. "Paul's wife and son are in Kansas City," she cried. "I don't know when they're supposed to come back."

"I better go see if what he said is true," Perley said. "Maybe it ain't exactly like he heard it. Maybe Paul ain't been shot at all. I better go," he repeated, not sure, himself, if he would be of any help to the sheriff. She just nodded rapidly in answer, so he quickly escorted her back inside the hotel and left her at the hallway door that led to the kitchen staff's rooms.

"Perley, you be careful," she said after a quick embrace and peck on his lips.

"I will," he said. "Don't worry about me." Then he ran back out the front of the hotel, where Buck was waiting at the hitching rail, jumped on the bay gelding, and charged up the street to the sheriff's office, where he left Buck. Then he hurried over to the crowd of gawkers forming around the blacksmith shop. It was ironic to him that one of the first people he saw was Redmond Quinn, for in Perley's mind, Quinn would be his first suspect. Standing near Quinn was the recently arrived stranger, Elam Burke. Before seeing Paul McQueen or any evidence of any kind, Perley knew those two men were more than likely involved in anything that had happened to the sheriff. He began to work his way through the spectators to get a closer look.

"Perley," Bill Simmons called out when he saw him edging his way through the gawkers. He was glad to see him because he was going to need some help moving McQueen.

His son, Bill Jr., was home with his mother, and Perley was the next best thing, for Perley was always ready to give a helping hand. "Can you help me with him?" As he expected, Perley dropped down beside him at once. In answer to Perley's inquisitive expression, Simmons said, "He ain't dead, but he's shot pretty bad. If the shot had been about two inches over to the right, he sure as hell woulda been one of my mortician customers. It'd be best if we had a doctor, but since we ain't, I'll take him to my place and see if I can dig that bullet outta there. I'd take him home, if there was anybody there to take care of him, but his family's gone to Kansas City. I was in the saloon with everybody else when this happened, so I ain't got my wagon with me. And we're gonna have to carry him to my shop."

"I'll hitch up my wagon," Walt Carver, who was standing close by, volunteered. "Won't take me fifteen minutes." When Simmons replied that it would sure make it a lot easier on Paul, Walt left at once to get the wagon.

"What happened here, Bill?" Perley asked. "Who shot him?"

"I ain't got no idea," Simmons replied. "Clyde Masters and his foreman was with him. They came to pick up some wagon wheels Paul was workin' on. Clyde said they didn't see anybody in the dark and they were waitin' out front while Paul went back to the forge. Next thing they heard was the shot. They couldn't see nobody behind here." He nodded toward the darkness behind the shop for confirmation of the inability to see anyone. "I think I finally got some of the bleeding to stop, but we're gonna have to be real careful when we move him. Ain't nothin' to do now but wait till Walt gets back with that wagon."

"Did he say anything at all?" Perley asked.

"Not since I got here," Simmons said. "He ain't opened his eyes, but right now, he's still breathin'."

When Walt returned, Simmons, with help from Perley, Walt, and Amos Johnson, took great pains to transport McQueen to the wagon. The crowd of onlookers parted to make a path for them. Walking close behind Mayor Johnson, who was carrying the sheriff by his right leg, Wilford Taylor was already voicing his fears. "What the hell are we gonna do, Amos? We can't go long without a sheriff."

"There's nothing we can do about it right now," Johnson told him, knowing the bank president would be constantly worrying him about it. "We'll just have to work on finding a new sheriff as soon as we can and hope Paul recovers from his wound."

"It was a mistake having a part-time blacksmith as a sheriff in the first place," Taylor complained.

"Now, Wilford," Amos replied, "Paul McQueen has done a pretty good job for us ever since he's been the sheriff."

"I suppose so," Taylor grudgingly admitted when he thought about McQueen's diligence when it came to watching the town's businesses. Then he glanced at Perley, helping Simmons carry the sheriff's head and shoulders, and it reminded him. "But it was Perley Gates who went after the men who robbed my bank and rescued the young lady who works in the dining room. Why don't we appoint Perley Gates as the new sheriff? Temporarily, at least, until we find out if Paul is going to make it through this."

Amos realized at once that his suggestion had a great deal of merit and was about to say so, when Perley interrupted,

Taylor having made his argument loud enough for Perley to hear. "I ain't no candidate for the sheriff's job," Perley announced. "I've got responsibilities out at the ranch I need to tend to." There had been an occasion when he and Possum were down in Bison Gap and he was talked into taking that job temporarily. He found out then that he didn't care for that line of work.

"I heard that you had some experience as the sheriff in that town down around the central part of Texas," Amos said. "Bison Gap, wasn't it?"

"Well, yes, sir," Perley replied. "That was in Bison Gap, but it was for a very short time. And I'm home now, back workin' at the Triple-G, where I've got responsibilities."

Taylor's suggestion had been loud enough for Redmond Quinn to hear as well, since he was one of the spectators following closely behind the wounded sheriff. "I couldn't help overhearing your dilemma, gentlemen, and perhaps I could help with a suggestion. I can certainly understand Perley's reluctance to take on the sheriff's job. It takes a special kind of man to want to handle that responsibility. But sometimes things have a way of working out for the best interest of those who deserve a fair shake. As luck would have it, you have an experienced lawman in your town at this particular moment. I have worked with him in the past in Arkansas and found him to be qualified to handle any threatening situations that might arrive. It might be a fortunate turn of the wheel that caused this man to decide to stop here to visit me on his way to Arizona Territory." He paused his perfect English sales pitch when they were distracted momentarily while sliding McQueen into the bed of the wagon. When the patient was resting as they wanted it, Quinn continued, "What I really find truly ironic is the fact that Sheriff McQueen was discussing the possibility of interviewing this man for a future deputy's position here in Paris."

"Take it real slow, Walt," Bill Simmons said as he climbed up into the wagon with the sheriff. Wilford Taylor and Amos Johnson stepped back and watched the wagon pull away and Perley went back to the sheriff's office to get his horse. He stepped up into the saddle and followed the wagon to help unload the patient at Simmons's place of business.

With the wounded man taken care of, Taylor and Johnsôn returned their attention to the smooth-talking Englishman. Quinn motioned for Burke to join them, then walked to meet him halfway. "Don't say any more than you have to," he whispered to Burke. "They'll be more impressed if you're the strong, silent type. Gentlemen," Quinn said, addressing the two businessmen, "this rugged-looking man is Elam Burke. Mr. Burke, this is Wilford Taylor and Amos Johnson, the two most prominent businessmen in this fair town." And so the interview of Elam Burke, longtime lawless scavenger and murderer, was under way for the job of protecting the good citizens of Paris from lawless individuals who sought to rob, murder, and rape—individuals like Elam Burke. The interview was carried over to Patton's Saloon, where most of the questions to Burke were answered by Quinn, while Burke attempted to maintain a steely-eyed countenance with single-word answers.

At the lower end of town, across from the hotel, Perley and Walt waited while Bill Simmons did what he could to save Paul McQueen's life. "You're lucky you ain't dead," Simmons said to his patient when Paul finally opened his eyes. "That bullet was lodged right up against one of your ribs." He waited a few moments for a vocal response. When there was none, he asked, "Do you know who shot you?" Again, there was no response. "Can you understand what I'm sayin'?" No response again, yet McQueen's eyes blinked as if trying to answer. "I done all I know to do," Simmons then said to the two men watching. "Maybe a doctor would know what else to try. I got the bullet outta his rib cage. That oughta killed him, but he's still tickin'. I'll just keep him the best I can and see if he comes out of it. Or if his heart quits, I'll prepare him for burial."

It was not a very promising prognosis, but Walt and Perley understood that Bill had done all he could and would try to keep him alive. Thinking it might be tempting for Bill to help McQueen slide on into the grave in order to cut his costs, Perley told him he would pay some of his expense to keep Paul alive. Walt said he would kick in a little as well.

When they left Bill's establishment, Walt drove his wagon back to the stable while Perley climbed back on Buck and rode across the street to the hotel. Since the dining room had long since closed, he rode around behind it to the row of windows. He pulled Buck up beside the third window and stopped. Sitting in the saddle, his shoulders were level with the top of the lower pane. He tapped on the window and waited. When there was no response, he tapped again, a little more businesslike. In a few moments, he saw the edge of the window shade pulled back far enough for someone to peek through, then the shade rolled up and Becky opened the window. "Perley," she whispered, "I thought you must have gone home, so I went to bed."

"Well, that's what you oughta done," he replied. "It's bedtime for young ladies who have to get up and go to work in the mornin'. That's where I'm goin' now, but I wanted to say good night to you before I left town." Her smile told him that pleased her. He also knew she wanted to know all about the sheriff, so he told her about his condition and what Bill was going to do to try to keep him alive. "Paul's a strong man," Perley said. "I think he'll start comin' back when he's ready." She stuck her head out the window for a good-night kiss, then Perley wheeled Buck away from the window and rode back to the street, headed for home.

Riding north up the town's main street, he found that there were still plenty of spectators milling around, most of them in front of the saloon. It occurred to him that he, as well as everyone else apparently, assumed Paul's attack had been a planned murder. If that was not the case, there would have been some people concerned about the possibility of more shots fired. It brought the thought to his mind that he knew one person in particular who would very much like to see Paul McQueen out of his life.

When he rode even with the saloon, he was hailed by Carl Miller, who worked in Henderson's General Store. "Hey, Perley! Is the sheriff gonna be all right?"

"Hard to say," Perley responded. "He ain't dead. I think he's still decidin' if he wants to live or die."

"Well, he can take his time decidin', I reckon," Carl said. "'cause I think Amos Johnson and Wilford Taylor have already hired somebody to take his job." Interested in that for sure, Perley asked whom they had hired. "That friend of Quinn's, Elam Burke," Carl replied.

"That man's a total stranger," Perley said. "He just rode into town, just passin' through. Are you sure that's the fellow they hired?"

Before Carl could answer, Ebb Barlow, who was listening to their conversation, interrupted. "He wasn't just ridin' through town, he came directly to town on the five o'clock train and asked me where Patton's Saloon was. So I reckon he weren't just passin' through."

Doggoned if that doesn't have a rotten smell to it, Perley thought. It had to be Redmond Quinn's work. "Can Taylor and Johnson just hire somebody like that?" he questioned. "Wouldn't they have to have the whole council approve it?"

"I don't know. I think so," Carl replied. "Maybe, in emergencies like this one, with McQueen shot, the mayor can do it on his own."

"Danged if I know," Perley said, and let Buck feel his heels. As he loped on past the jail and the blacksmith shop, he had a bad feeling about the direction the town might be heading in. *It ain't none of my worry, I reckon,* he told himself, then immediately thought of Becky. It was going to be difficult to think about working cattle while all that was going on in town. *I'd better check to see how Paul McQueen's doing in a day or two,* he thought.

CHAPTER 16

Perley and most of the citizens of the small town were not the only persons concerned about the progress of Bill Simmons's patient. Two of these folks were the man who shot him down and the man who ordered him to be shot down. They sat at a table in Patton's Saloon and discussed the changes in the town just overnight. "I'd feel a whole lot better if Simmons had reported Paul McQueen deceased," Redmond Quinn grumbled to the temporary sheriff.

"I told you about that," Elam Burke stressed. "I hit him flush with that first shot. And I was goin' in there to put one in his head when I almost ran into two more that I didn't even know were in that shop with him. I was damn lucky to get outta there before anybody saw me."

"Now that damn barber is trying to be the big hero and save the sheriff's life."

"He's gonna have to come up with a bloomin' miracle," Burke insisted. "I wasn't twenty-five feet away from that fool when I cut him down. He's a dead man. The only reason I was gonna put one in his head was just so you wouldn't be worryin' about this very thing. There ain't no way he could still be alive. If he was, that undertaker would be jumpin' up and down, braggin' about it. Ain't no different than if you shot a deer. He's down and can't get up to run, even if his heart is still pumpin'.'"

"Elam," Quinn said, looking the new sheriff in the eye, "I don't know about deer, but we need to be sure this one doesn't get up and run again. We need to make sure Mc-Queen doesn't come out of whatever state he's in and start to get well. You need to pay him a call before his miracle has a chance to develop." He let Burke think about that for a moment, waiting for him to come to the same conclusion. "Elam," he continued then, "if you were as close to him as you say you were when you shot him, then he probably saw who shot him."

"Oh, I don't know about that," Burke quickly responded. "It was awful dark inside that shed where his forge is."

"Yes, I suppose it was," Quinn replied, "but you saw him well enough to shoot him. I would wager that it was easier for him to see you standing out in the open, holding a gun on him. Were you standing behind anything? Was the moon shining?"

Getting more and more frustrated as Quinn kept pressing him, Burke finally snarled, "Hell, I don't know, I mean, no, the moon wasn't shinin'. I'da noticed that. He never saw me."

Quinn cast a cold look upon the angry man before commenting, "Well, I'll tell you what, Sheriff Burke, I think it would be the proper thing to do for you to call on the ex-sheriff to wish him a speedy recovery. Maybe you might get to spend some private time with him."

Quinn's ice-cold gaze tended to remind Burke that the precise-talking dandy dresser was the fastest man with a six-gun he had ever seen. The thought served to settle his anger down to a manageable level before he was provoked further. "I reckon it don't pay to take a chance on him coming back to his senses. I'll go over to that barber's place where he works on the stiffs."

"Good idea," Quinn said. "But you're not going to find him there this time of night, so go to see him in the morning. If any miracles had happened tonight, we'd already know about them."

Redmond Quinn's plan to silence Paul McQueen could not have allowed for the one person in town no one could claim to figure out—Lucy Tate. For while Quinn and Burke sat in the saloon deciding what to do about sealing Paul McQueen's lips forever, Lucy was making arrangements for Bill Simmons to transfer the wounded sheriff to a room in the hotel. Not only a more encouraging environment, it would provide the sheriff a more comfortable place to recover under the care of the staff of the hotel's dining room.

"You did what?" Beulah had reacted when Lucy told her what she had done. "Amos Johnson let you put McQueen in one of his rooms? What got into your head to make you ask him?" She was at once suspicious of a personal relationship between Lucy and the sheriff, although, if true, they had never shown any outward signs of one. And Lucy flirted with practically every man in town. Still, McQueen was married and had a six-year-old son, and she didn't think Lucy would cross that line.

"I went over to Bill Simmons's place to see if he needed any help with Paul," Lucy confessed casually. "I mean, hell, he is our sheriff. He's always come here when we needed him. And Jenny McQueen is with their son visitin' her parents in Kansas City right now. Least we could do is to see he's gettin' treated all right."

Becky, who joined them in time to hear Lucy's last statement, had to comment, "Why, Lucy Tate, you never cease to amaze me."

"Well, if you two coulda seen the way Bill Simmons had Paul layin' up on a table in that shop where he prepares the dead people for buryin', you'da had to do something, too. I ain't faultin' Bill. He was doin' what he thought was right, but he sure as hell is not a doctor. I asked him if Paul was dead and he said he wasn't yet, but he was workin' at it. So I took a look at him and Bill was right. Paul was still breathin', but he musta been outta his head, so I told Bill we oughta at least put him on a bed to make him more comfortable. Bill said he didn't have any beds in his shop and he didn't wanna take him to the house without his wife and son there."

"So you went to ask Mr. Johnson for a room," Becky concluded for her. "Bless your heart, Lucy. That was sure 'nough the Christian thing to do. We can all help take care of him. Can't we, Beulah?"

"I reckon," Beulah answered, "since he ain't got no family of his own here right now. He deserves to be a little more comfortable in his last hours." She paused when a thought occurred. "I wonder if he'll even know whether he's on a table or a bed."

"I'll go see him after we finish cleanin' up the breakfast dishes and see if he's gettin' any better," Lucy said. "Mr. Johnson let Bill put him in that little room at the end of the hall downstairs."

"Room 100," Becky confirmed, and Lucy and Beulah nodded. "Well, that'll be handy to the kitchen, if he wakes up and starts eating."

Two regular customers of the dining room, since both had rooms in the hotel, Redmond Quinn and Acting Sheriff Elam Burke were talking outside after breakfast. "I reckon I'll go on over to Simmons's place now and visit the sick," Burke commented.

"I think that would be a mighty fine gesture by the new sheriff," Quinn replied. "I'll see you back at the saloon. I hope you have some good news." He paused to tip his hat to a lady with two children coming from the dining room, while Burke started toward Bill Simmons's mortuary shop.

Burke knocked loudly on the door of the windowless barn some twenty yards behind the white frame house where Bill, his wife, Francine, and young Bill Jr. resided. When it appeared the barn was all locked up and no one answered his knock, Burke's initial thought was that McQueen must have died. The thought brought a smile to his face. He figured that was all he needed to know, but then realized he needed to find out if McQueen had said anything before he died, so he walked around to the barbershop, which was built onto the front porch of Bill's house.

"Mornin'," Simmons greeted him. "Can I help you?" Like most folks in town, Bill knew that Burke was an acquaintance of Redmond Quinn's but a stranger to everyone else in town. He was taken aback a little when he saw the deputy's badge on Burke's vest, but he didn't ask about it.

"I was just at your place out back, where you take care of the corpses, but you was all locked up, so I thought I'd catch you here."

"You need to have somebody buried?" Simmons asked.

"Nah, I don't need nobody buried," Burke answered. "I'm the new sheriff and I just came by to see how Sheriff McQueen was doin', see if he was gettin' any better. Thought it'd be the proper thing to do, but with your place all locked up back there, I reckon he didn't make it."

"McQueen's pretty tough," Bill responded. "He's still tickin', but he ain't here no more." Seeing the confusion in Burke's face, he couldn't resist making light of the tragic situation. "He's checked into the hotel."

Being a man with no sense of humor, Burke responded normally. "What the hell are you talkin' about?"

Concerned that he had made a mistake with his attempt at humor, Bill quickly gave the surly-looking man a report on his patient. "We moved him over to the hotel, where he'll be a lot more comfortable. I don't even have a bed back there in my place. And he was makin' a little bit of progress, so we thought it best to put him where he can get better care." He could readily see that Burke was not pleased with the news. "See, over at the hotel, the women in the dinin' room will look in on him pretty often and when he's ready to eat, they'll handle that."

"Damn it, I just came from the hotel," Burke complained aloud, then jerked his head back to fix on Simmons. "What room is he in?"

"I don't know where they put him," Simmons lied, at

last getting the impression that this new sheriff was not that compassionate toward McQueen.

Perplexed, Burke turned and started for the door but stopped to ask one last question. "How 'bout his badge? I need his sheriff's badge. Have you got it?"

"No, sir," Bill answered. "He still had it when he was taken to the hotel." *And long may he wear it,* he thought. After Burke left, Bill went over to the door and watched him walk away. He had a frightening thought when he wondered how that stranger could be taking over as sheriff. There was no special meeting of the council to take emergency action. What if the stranger was the man who shot McQueen and now, he was simply taking over the sheriff's office? He had the look of a hardened gunslinger. "I better go see Amos!" he blurted.

Up the street at Patton's Saloon, another concerned individual expressed a need to go see Amos Johnson. "Are you telling me that Amos Johnson let them use one of his hotel rooms for a hospital?" Redmond Quinn demanded. "Why would he do that? They must have some idea that McQueen is going to survive the shooting. It's even more important that you get in that room and crush the life out of him, or you're liable to be wanted for attempted murder." He paused to think. "And our plan to run this town is going to take a lot longer time than I planned."

Not sure if it was time to panic or not, Burke asked, "You reckon I oughta just go on back to the hotel and ask 'em what room McQueen's in, tell 'em I just wanna make a proper call?"

"Forget about the proper call now," Quinn directed.

"Go down there and tell them you're trying to catch the shooter and you need to see if McQueen can talk yet, so he can tell you who to go after. Right now, you don't want to insist on being alone in the room with him. Just find out if he's talked. If he hasn't, you need to visit him tonight when everybody's gone to bed and you can make sure nobody sees you going into that room."

"Right," Burke responded. "They'll think I'm takin' over this job for sure when I tell 'em I wanna find the killer." He wasted no more time there in the saloon.

By the time Burke walked back down to the hotel, the dining room was opening for the midday meal. He passed up the entrance to the dining room and went directly to the front desk, where David Smith was working. "I need to know what room you put Paul McQueen in," he told David.

"I'm sorry, sir," David answered. "Mr. Johnson said it would probably be a good thing not to give out the sheriff's room number to anybody we didn't know."

Instantly, Burke became enraged. "Damn it, you jackass, I am the sheriff! What room is McQueen in?"

"I'm sorry, sir, Mr. Johnson gave explicit instructions not to give out that room number," David insisted.

"Are you stupid?" Burke fumed. "I'm the sheriff! I'm the one you tell everything to."

"Your badge says you're a deputy and that's not worth risking losing my job for. Mr. Johnson said not to give out the sheriff's number," David maintained.

In his frustration, Burke reached for the Colt Peacemaker riding below his hip and had it halfway out before he regained control of his temper and let it slide back to rest in the holster. "Where is Mr. Johnson? He's the one who gave me this job as sheriff. I wanna talk to him."

"You'll find Mr. Johnson in the dining room, having his dinner," David said coolly.

"I'm gonna be watchin' you, boy. I catch you takin' one wrong step and you'll be stayin' with me in the jail." He promptly turned and steamed away toward the dining room.

Inside the dining room, he stood by the weapons table, making no motions toward removing his, while he scanned the diners. His eye fell upon Amos Johnson sitting at a table set apart from the others at the back of the room. His dinner companion was Wilford Taylor. He started back to their table but was intercepted halfway by Lucy Tate. "Don't tell me to take my gun off," he growled. "I'm the sheriff. I keep it on."

"I wasn't going to, Sheriff," Lucy replied coolly. "I was just gonna show you to a table."

"I don't need you to show me to a table. Now get the hell outta my way." He pushed past her, spinning her halfway around when he bumped her shoulder.

Amos Johnson looked up from his plate when he became aware of Elam Burke charging toward him like a stampeding longhorn. "Here's our new sheriff coming this way," he said to Wilford Taylor.

"He looks mad," Taylor said, somewhat concerned.

Amos put his fork down and smiled at Burke as he announced. "Well, Wilford, here's our new sheriff now." Looking up at the irritated Burke again, he asked, "Sheriff Burke, how are things working out for you in your new position?"

Already inflamed from his standoff with David Smith

at the check-in counter and ready for more of the same from the mayor, Burke was instantly deflated by the mayor's gracious attitude. He started to stutter while trying to remember what he had planned to say. Thinking him a man of few words and remembering his one-word answers during his interview with Redmond Quinn, Amos invited him to join them. His confidence immediately restored, Burke responded, "Why, I don't mind if I do. That grub you're eatin' looks pretty good." He pulled a chair back and plopped his body down.

Lucy was still watching from the middle of the room and shook her head in surprise when she saw him sit down. When she walked over to the table, she asked, "You stayin' for dinner?" When he said that he was, she asked, "Want me to take your hat for you?"

"Forgot I had it on," he replied, and pulled it off, then hung it on the back of the empty chair. "Bring me some of that grub they're eatin'."

Both members of the town council began to wonder what species of caveman they might have just handed the job of sheriff to, but it was too late to think about the man's social graces. "What's on your mind, Sheriff?" Amos asked. "You looked like you had something you wanted to talk about when you came walking over to the table."

"I come to find out what room McQueen's in," Burke said, getting right to it. "I was wantin' to find out if he had ever got well enough to say what happened to him." He looked from one of them to the other to make sure they understood what he was saying. "You see, if he got a look at that feller that shot him, maybe he can tell me who it was and I'll arrest him." They both nodded as if to say they understood. "Course, I'd like to go in to see him, myself, just as the proper thing to do, but not by myself. It don't have to be by myself," he emphasized, remembering Quinn's instructions.

"I'm sure McQueen would appreciate your visit," Amos replied. "But it's not necessary, since you didn't even know the man. And right now, I don't think McQueen would know if you had come to visit him or not. If he comes out of this, I'll tell him you were concerned for him. Right now, he's in room 100, down next to the kitchen. That's convenient for the ladies who work my dining room to pop in and out to keep an eye on him and bring him anything he needs."

"And already, though, I think he's looking better," Wilford Taylor saw fit to remark. He chuckled then in appreciation of his next comment. "Of course, that barn that Bill Simmons does his funeral work in isn't really the best place for an injured man to try to come back from the dead. Not with so much dead around him. I think that was a compassionate thing for Lucy Tate to undertake. Whatever Paul's fate turns out to be, I'm sure Jenny McQueen will be grateful for the woman's thoughtfulness."

"And I'm hopin' I can make her just as thankful when I run down the low-down murderer who sneaked up on him and shot him down," Burke quickly responded. "So I'd appreciate it if somebody was to let me know when McQueen comes to. In the meantime, I'll be doin' some lookin' to see if I can find anybody who knows somethin' about the gunman." Content that he had found everything he had come to find, Burke turned his attention to the plate of ham and potatoes Lucy set before him. He knew which room McQueen was in, and he knew that the sheriff had not been able to talk yet. So he knew Quinn would be pleased to hear that. There was nothing to do now but wait till after supper sometime that night and pay McQueen a little visit. Consequently, his lack of conversational skills came immediately to the surface as he consumed the food before him.

It did not go unnoticed by the two members of the town council he was dining with. So, when he sopped up all the remaining gravy on his plate with the one biscuit he had held in reserve for that purpose and abruptly took his leave, he left Johnson and Taylor wondering about their new sheriff. Instead of a strong man of few words, as they had first labeled him, they feared he might better be described as a brute of a puppet who required the hand of Redmond Quinn to speak at all. Wilford Taylor was the first to express his doubt. "Damn, Amos, I hope we haven't been too hasty in replacing our sheriff."

Johnson shook his head slowly and answered, "Not a helluva lot we can do about it now. We'll give him a little time and see how he handles it. I think maybe we interviewed Quinn instead of Burke."

One with no uncertain opinion of the man they hired for sheriff, Lucy Tate, remained close enough to the table to hear their conversation. She shared her concerns with Becky and Beulah in the kitchen. "I don't trust that evil-lookin' son of a gun. Somebody told him we brought Paul McQueen to the hotel. And just now, I heard Amos Johnson tell him which room Paul is in. It's a wonder he didn't give him a key."

"Whaddaya think we oughta do?" Becky asked.

"There ain't much we can do," Beulah answered her. "Keep an eye on who goes into that room when we get a chance. I can't believe he told him the room number. He's told everybody in the hotel not to tell that room number."

"He needs to move Paul to another room," Beulah advised. "Whoever tried to kill Paul likely knows he ain't dead and he'll be comin' back to try to finish the job."

"That's what I'm thinkin'," Lucy responded, "and I also notice who the first one was who came in askin' which room Paul was in."

"I wish Perley was here," Becky fretted. "He always knows what to do." She was thinking about her own rescue from the four men who had abducted her, how he had come into their camp to get her, and how he had fought them on the way back home. Possum was there to help, but it was Perley who knew what to do.

Beulah and Lucy looked at Becky as if they could almost see what she was thinking until Beulah finally spoke. "Well, there ain't nobody else in town who can help us. Perley and McQueen were always pretty good friends. Why don't we send somebody to tell him what's goin' on?"

CHAPTER 17

Bill Simmons Jr., more generally known as Junior, rode his father's flea-bitten gray gelding into the barnyard of the Triple-G, where he saw Fred Farmer at the corral, watching one of the hands saddle-breaking a buckskin horse. Junior rode directly over beside Fred and pulled up. "What can I do for you, young fellow?" Fred asked, not sure if he should know the young man or not.

"I'm lookin' for Perley," Junior answered.

"Perley ain't here right now," Fred told him. "Is there somethin' I can do for you, or do you have to have Perley?"

"I'm Junior Simmons. My pa is Bill Simmons. He sent me up here to find Perley on account of some trouble they're havin' at the hotel, and Miss Becky Morris at the dinin' room said they need Perley."

Fred didn't respond right away, while he gave Junior a quick appraisal. "Becky Morris, huh?" he finally replied. "Is she in trouble?"

"No, sir, Miss Becky ain't in trouble. Sheriff McQueen's in trouble, and she said they need Perley 'cause there ain't nobody else to help."

"Perley's with some of the other boys, roundin' up some strays off the south range. You know where Goat Creek is?"

"No, sir."

"Go back the way you came from town. Just before you get to the gate that says Triple-G, you'll see a little stream. Follow that stream west and you oughta run into Perley and the other boys on their way back home. Or you can wait right here for 'em and watch Sonny get his butt throwed offa that buckskin he's been tryin' to ride for two days now."

"I'd best go try to meet him," Junior said. "Miss Becky said it's important." He wheeled the gray around. "Thank you, sir," he said, and rode back the way he had come.

"I hope that ain't another cow pie, waitin' for Perley to step in," Fred mumbled as he watched Junior ride away.

Junior didn't have to ride very far west before he saw the group of riders coming toward him. Off to one side, he saw Perley riding beside Possum Smith. They all pulled up when they saw the lone rider approaching them. "Junior," Perley called out, "what are you doin' out here?"

"Lookin' for you," Junior answered, then eagerly gave Perley the message he was sent to deliver.

After hearing about McQueen's transfer to the hotel, then the information about Elam Burke trying to find out which room the sheriff was in and getting that information from Amos Johnson, Possum remarked, "I reckon we're fixin' to ride into town."

"Yeah, I reckon," Perley said. "At least, I think I'd better. I don't think Becky and the other women woulda sent Junior out here, if they weren't pretty darn worried about something happenin'."

"I'm thinkin' the same thing, so I reckon *we'd* better

get goin'," Possum emphasized. "But we'd best change to some fresh horses. We've worked these pretty hard today."

"If you think there's some trouble in town, you want some of the rest of us to go with you?" Charlie Ramey asked.

"No," Perley answered. "I don't know yet what's really goin' on, but Possum and I oughta be able to take care of it, if they sent Junior out here to get just me." He looked over at Possum and said, "I was already thinkin' I shoulda stayed in town last night. Let's go swap these horses."

Junior Simmons rode on ahead of them while they threw their saddles on two fresh horses and Perley took a quick couple of minutes to tell Rubin that he and Possum had to go to town to help the sheriff. Rubin's reaction to his brother's plans was like that of a tired parent exasperated by the actions of a wild young son. But he was well accustomed to it, so he simply told him to be careful.

When they rode into town, it was already well into the supper hour. Taking no chance on being seen, they rode behind the buildings, all the way down to the hotel, where Perley led them to the little picnic area behind the hotel. It was the place where he had first spent time alone with Becky. They tied their horses there and went in the back door that led to the hallway where the women's rooms were located. They figured it best not to be seen walking into the dining room. Quinn or Burke or both could well be in the dining room, and Perley thought it best they didn't know that he and Possum were in town. And they were already assuming that whatever the trouble was, those two had to be involved.

On this occasion, it didn't occur to him that he was entering a section of the hotel that he would not have considered entering before. Tonight, however, there was little risk of surprising any of the three ladies who lived there. They would surely all be in the dining room, working. The hallway was dark already with the sinking of the sun outside, but they could see the lights under the door at the end that had to be the kitchen. As they neared the door, the sounds coming through confirmed it. Perley turned the knob and opened the door very slowly, hoping not to startle anyone. When he opened it just wide enough to see into the kitchen, he saw that Beulah was alone in the room. She was stirring something in a frying pan, her back toward him. He opened the door all the way and stepped quietly into the room, Possum behind him. Very softly, Perley said, "Beulah."

She let out a little yelp and dropped the big spoon in the iron pan. "Perley Gates!" she gasped when she turned to discover him. "You scared the liver outta me. How'd you get in here behind me?" When he told her they had come in the back hallway, she looked surprised again. "That back door wasn't locked?" He said that it wasn't. "Lucy," she speculated. "She's the one always forgets to lock the door again when she uses the outhouse."

"We'll have to remember to thank her for leavin' it open for us," Possum remarked. "We mighta made a little noise if we'da had to kick it in."

"Good thing you didn't," Beulah replied, "'cause the sheriff's settin' right outside that kitchen door and I'da called him to lock you up." She chuckled to make sure they knew she was japing. "Have you had anything to eat?" They both shook their heads. "Set down at the table, and I'll get you something. Pour yourselves some coffee while I signal the girls." She went to the dining room door and stood there until she caught Becky's eye. Then with a subtle nod of her head, she signaled her to come to the kitchen.

When she came into the kitchen, Becky rushed to Perley. "Junior found you," she gushed. "We were afraid he wouldn't, afraid you'd be off somewhere with the cattle and he wouldn't be able to find you. I didn't want to bring you into town for this, but we didn't know what else to do. There's really nobody in town to turn to, and I knew you could tell us what to do." She paused long enough then to say, "Thank you for coming with him, Possum."

"You know you can always call me for help," Perley said. "Now, tell me what's happened. Is Paul all right? Junior told us that Lucy had moved him here to the hotel and Elam Burke found out what room he's in. Is that right?"

"Yes, that's right," Lucy said when she came in the door and heard his question. "When he found out we moved Paul here where we could take care of him, he didn't waste any time askin' if Paul had started talkin' yet. Then he wanted to know what room he was in. What does he care what room Paul's in? He's tryin' to make sure Paul doesn't come to and tell everybody who shot him. That's what I think."

"That's what I think, too," Becky said. "I just know he's gonna try to kill Paul." She took Perley's arm and pleaded. "I didn't want to put you in any danger, but I didn't know what else to do. That evil man is going to try to finish what he started. But if we let everybody know that you and

Possum will be sitting in Paul's room with him, then Elam Burke wouldn't have any chance to kill him."

"We need to make that sorry snake admit he's the one who shot McQueen in the first place," Beulah said. "We all know he did it."

"Well, he ain't never gonna admit it," Possum said. "So, you can forget about that."

"Is he still in the room close to the kitchen?" Perley asked.

"Yep," Lucy answered. "Room 100. It's right down the hall from the inside door to the dinin' room. We can't watch it all the time, but we pop in as often as we can."

"Is there any other room we can move him to without anybody else knowin' we moved him?" Perley asked. Beulah said there was one vacant room on the back hall where she and the other two women lived. "That would be better than leavin' him in room 100," Perley continued. "I have to say I think you women are right. I think Burke is the one who shot Paul McQueen, and he'll try to make sure he doesn't come to and start tellin' everybody who shot him. So, if we move him to that room on the back hall, he won't be in 100 when Burke comes to call—most likely when he thinks everybody's asleep because he's gotta get in and out without anybody seein' him." Out of respect for Possum's opinion, he asked, "Ain't that what you think, Possum?"

"You pretty much painted the picture the way I see it," Possum answered. "We can take turns watchin' that room all night."

After they were all agreed on their plan to save Paul McQueen's life, they realized there was a minor problem to face. It was going to be sometime yet before the last customers left the dining room and the women closed it down for the night. Consequently, Perley and Possum had a lot of time to kill before they could chance moving the patient to a secret room. Not only was it necessary to keep the transfer secret from Redmond Quinn and Elam Burke, it was deemed necessary to keep the hotel staff in the dark as well. Since it was important that no one knew Perley and Possum were in town, they had to stay right there in the kitchen until it was decided the hour was late enough to make the move.

Beulah cleared off one end of the kitchen table and set two plates down for their two guests and Perley and Possum sat down to have supper while the two servers came in and out of the kitchen for the coffeepot or extra biscuits. Since it had been almost an hour since anyone had checked on McQueen, Lucy skipped out the hallway door and went to room 100. When she returned, everyone in the kitchen gathered around to hear her report. "Well, he's still breathin'," she said. "But he still just lies there like he was, although, I swear, I thought for a moment he was fixin' to open his eyes and say something. But he didn't." She looked at Beulah and shook her head. "He's gonna have to eat something before long or he's gonna die."

"I'm afraid to even try to make him drink some water," Beulah said. "He might choke to death. So when I check on him, I just wash his lips with a wet rag and hope he shows signs of wantin' to drink some of it."

"Maybe the least we can do is nail that low-down murderin' Burke," Possum said aside to Perley. "It don't look too good for Paul, and him with a wife and young 'un." He scratched his chin as he thought about the impact the news of her husband's death would have upon the young woman.

The discussion went on until the lamps in the dining room were out and it was decided a safe enough time to move Paul from room 100 to the room next to Beulah's in the back hallway. Becky and Beulah acted as lookouts in the hotel hallway while Lucy took the key and unlocked the door. She was inside for only a minute before she appeared in the doorway again and motioned that the coast was clear. Becky, in turn, motioned behind her in the dining room to Perley and he and Possum hurried out into the hallway, down to room 100, and passed quickly inside. "He moved," Lucy said when they moved up to the bed to take a look at the sheriff.

"He's fixin' to move a little farther," Possum replied, and pulled the blanket aside, anxious to get the swap done. Looking at Perley, he said, "You grab his arms. I'll take his legs, and we'll tote him like a wheelbarrow."

"Jenny?"

Like a voice from beyond the grave, the feeble outburst froze all in the room for almost a minute before they realized that it had actually come from the wounded man. The first to react was Lucy, who answered him. "No, Paul, it's Lucy Tate. Jenny's not back yet. You've been shot, and we're takin' you to a better room. All right?" He didn't answer. Lucy looked at Perley, questioning.

"Might be a little bumpy, Paul," Perley said, "but it won't take long. Let's go, Possum." They pulled McQueen off the bed. Possum grabbed his ankles, standing between his legs like the wheel of a wheelbarrow. Perley hoisted his upper body, and with Possum guiding, they headed back into the dining room, through the kitchen, and down the back hall to the vacant room.

When they laid Paul on the bed, his eyes flickered open, but it was obvious that he was having trouble focusing. "How bad?" he gasped after a moment.

"Bad enough," Possum answered him. "You remember what happened?"

"I got shot?" McQueen questioned weakly.

"That's a fact. Do you know who shot you?" Perley asked.

"No, too dark," McQueen dragged out, ". . . couldn't see."

Always concerned with eating, Beulah asked. "Are you hungry? You ain't had nothin' to eat in a spell."

"Thirsty," Paul muttered, sending Beulah hurrying off to fetch the bucket.

"It's up to you ladies to take care of him now," Perley said to Becky. "Possum and I will get ready to see if we can catch a rat in our trap tonight." He took the key to room 100 from Lucy and he and Possum returned to the room.

"I swear, it sure woulda helped if Paul hadda seen who shot him," Possum said. "You reckon he mighta seen who shot him, but just don't remember? He might recollect later, after he's had a chance to heal up a little."

"We'll see if Elam Burke shows up here before mornin'. He couldn't have but one reason to come sneakin' in here before daylight and that's to shut Paul up for good."

"I don't know," Possum hesitated. "With him in so cozy with that slick-talkin' Redmond Quinn. He's liable to convince Amos Johnson that he sent Burke down here to make sure nobody broke in Paul's room."

Perley knew Possum's statement was pretty far-fetched, but still, it caused him to consider how difficult it might be to convince Johnson and the town council that Burke came as an assassin and not as a guardian. "You know, partner, as unlikely as that sounds, there could be a possibility of that happenin'. Quinn talked his way into Raymond Patton's saloon and talked Amos Johnson into giving the sheriff's job to Burke. We need to catch Burke in the act of tryin' to kill Paul."

"I agree with what you're sayin'," Possum responded. "But are you suggestin' we go get Paul and put him back in that room?"

"No, heck no," Perley responded. "I'm sayin' I'm fixin' to crawl into that bed in this room and we'll catch Burke when he makes his play. He'll think it's Paul still lyin' there."

"Hell, no!" Possum exclaimed. "Are you crazy?"

"Think about it," Perley said, honestly convinced the risk was not that great. "He'll want it to look like Paul just died in his sleep. He ain't gonna shoot him. He ain't gonna stab him with a knife. He can't even beat him to death with a club. The only thing he's got left is to smother him with a pillow, or strangle him with his hands. Then he's gonna try to sneak outta here before anybody sees him."

Possum shook his head, not at all comfortable with Perley's logic. He couldn't argue with it because everything Perley said was probably true. But there was still that moment when the truth was exposed and that was the moment when he wanted to be sure to be in position to be ready to save Perley's life, if necessary. "I don't know, Perley, I think you're stickin' your neck out a little too far." Then it occurred to him to remind him, "It's the same crazy trick you talked me into when we were bringin' Becky back—you, layin' under a blanket by the fire when that joker walked through our camp, shootin' all the dummies."

Perley grinned. "It worked, didn't it? And this time it won't be as dangerous as that was. Burke can't afford to make any noise or leave any wounds."

Possum still wasn't sure he wanted to go along with him on this trap for Burke. "I'd have to be somewhere close to keep an eye on you in case it don't go like you think it will."

Perley looked around him in the small room with the single bed and decided. "There ain't anywhere you could hide in here," he said. He walked back to the door and stepped out far enough to look up and down the hall. "That'll do," he announced, and told Possum to take a look. "Down at the end of the hall, see that cart under the lamp? That's to haul bedclothes and stuff in. You can sit behind that cart and watch the door of this room. Blow that lamp out over it and nobody would see you back of it." Possum agreed but was still concerned because he wouldn't be able to see into the room after Burke went in. "That won't matter," Perley insisted. "You'll see him if he breaks into the room and that's enough to show he came with the intention of doin' Paul harm." He could see Possum wavering. "And if we could catch him coming after me with a pillow, we'd have enough to hang him right here, right now."

Possum thought about it for a few moments before committing totally. "It is a slick plan," he allowed. "But you better be damn sure you're ready when the time comes."

"And you be damn sure you don't shoot me when you come runnin' to the rescue," Perley said. "Now, I expect

I'd best see how much I'll look like Paul lyin' up in this bed." He sat down on the bed, then threw his legs up and started to pull the sheet and blanket up but stopped when they saw the bloodstains. "Turn it around," Perley said, and Possum pulled the sheet and blanket off the bed, swapped them end to end, and spread them back over Perley. Satisfied that he was more comfortable with the stains lying across his boots, Perley said, "That'll do fine."

"Everything all right?" The voice came from the hallway to startle both of them. Perley immediately pulled the covers up over his head as Possum turned to find David Smith at the door. "I didn't expect to find anyone in the room with Sheriff McQueen this late at night," David said. He knew who Possum was, but he was surprised to find him in McQueen's room. "I'm getting ready to close down the front desk for the night now and I thought I'd see if everything was all right down here."

"Yep, everything's about like it was," Possum said. "It was my turn to set up with Paul tonight, and he 'pears to be gettin' ready to go to sleep right now. So I was just fixin' to leave, myself. I think he'll be all right for the night. I'm fixin' to lock him up." He held the room key up so that David could see it and maybe assume he was supposed to be there. David took a step into the room to peer at the figure on the bed in the dim light of the lamp with the wick turned down. Even though the sheet and blanket were pulled up over his head, he could see a slight movement under the covers. So he stepped back into the hall as Possum pulled the door closed and locked it. "I expect I'll look in on him after 'while to make sure he's all right."

"Good," David said, "and I'll say good night, since it

appears that Sheriff McQueen has plenty of folks looking after him." He did an about-face and returned to the front of the hotel, where he started locking up the desk and check-in counter. He did not customarily keep the office open that late at night, but Amos Johnson had requested that he stay later while Sheriff McQueen was recovering. As he removed the cash drawer and took it to the safe, he paused when he recalled something that struck him as odd. *Why did Sheriff McQueen have his boots on? He would have been so much more comfortable with them off.* He decided he might tell Mr. Johnson about it in the morning. Wounded man or not, it was pretty rough treatment for the hotel's sheets.

CHAPTER 18

Elam Burke had to give Redmond Quinn credit for thinking of all the angles leading up to the killing of Paul McQueen. It was Burke's way to simply kick the door to room 100 in and choke the life out of the helpless man. But Quinn told him that the busted door he would leave could not be explained. McQueen's death had to look to be from natural causes and even if done quietly, it would still be obvious that someone had broken into the room. That seemed to be a problem with no solution to Burke, but Quinn showed him how to solve it. So, after they had eaten supper, they went back to the front desk, where David Smith was doing the night clerk's job.

Burke laughed when he found out how easy it was to get by the locked door. Quinn had told him to take a few cartridges out of his cartridge belt and drop them near the corner of the front steps. Then he was to address David Smith in his official capacity as sheriff and ask him to come outside to check on the mysterious cartridges he had discovered. It worked just as Quinn had said it would. David made no objection to accompanying him outside and was mystified to find the cartridges. Burke had explained that he was being extra cautious about anything out of the ordinary since Sheriff McQueen's shooting. David assured him that the citizens of Paris must surely appreciate his diligence. While all this was going on, Redmond Quinn slipped behind the check-in desk. Each room had extra keys and he took one for room 100. Holding the key in his hand now, Burke grinned to think how he and Quinn had pulled it off.

The hardest part was waiting until the entire hotel was shut down for the night. Quinn had been smart again to tell him to keep his hotel room and not move into the jail yet. Because of that, he didn't have to worry about sneaking in and out of the hotel. With no watch or clock to tell him the hour, he could only speculate on the time, but he was afraid if he waited much longer, it might start to get light. Eager to get to the task, he opened his door and took a long look up and down the hallway. There was no sign of life and no noises to indicate the hotel was awakening, so he quietly closed his door behind him and moved as quietly as a man his size could. Down to the turn at the end of the long corridor and on to the smaller hall where the cheaper rooms were, Burke walked silently and confidently toward the last door. The end of the hall was dark, the one lamp having evidently burned out. *Even better,* he thought.

He stood directly in front of the door and looked back the way he had come. When he was sure he was alone in the hallway, he inserted his key and unlocked the door. There he was, lying still and helpless in the dimly lit room, the sheet and blanket pulled up almost to his eyes, and he was staring up at him. In one swift motion, Burke grabbed the pillow with both hands, jerked it out from under his head, and stuffed it down over Perley's face with all the strength he could muster. In his killing rage, he never noticed the blanket rising up like a tent under his arm until the silence of the room was shattered by the report of the Colt beneath it. He gave out one painful grunt when the impact of the bullet caused him to take a step backward before he sat down heavily on the floor.

When Possum rushed into the room, he found Perley sitting on the side of the bed, watching the unmoving figure of Elam Burke, still sitting upright, although not moving a muscle. Possum looked again at Perley when he casually spit a small feather out of his mouth, the result of Burke's massive strain on the pillow. "Is he dead?" Possum asked, holding his pistol on him in case he wasn't. He went over and turned the wick up in the lamp.

"That would be my guess," Perley said, spit out another small feather, and added. "He liked to cram me through the bottom of the bed."

"Reckon how long he's gonna set there like that?" Possum asked, still watching the dead man closely, in case he was shamming.

"Till somebody comes and carries him outta here," Perley replied. "'Least, I hope he don't suddenly decide to get up from the floor and walk outta here. That would be unnervin'. What I'm wonderin' is how long it's gonna be before somebody comes runnin' down here to see what that shot was about."

"I sure hope to hell you don't get to worryin' now because you shot a man," Possum said. He remembered the little session of soul-searching Perley had suffered right after he had to shoot Leonard Watts. "Ain't no different than shootin' a mad dog. It's somethin' that needed to be done, and look here, you saved Paul McQueen's life. So don't go gettin' down on yourself for cleanin' up some of the world's garbage." He was beginning to get wound up in his favorite subject when the sound of excited voices reached them from the hallway. In a moment, several people were at the door but stopped cold when they saw Elam Burke sitting on the floor.

"What are you doing here?" David Smith asked, looking at Perley, seated on the bed.

"Tryin' to get some sleep," Perley couldn't resist answering.

Redmond Quinn pushed by Amos Johnson to get into the room. He took a few seconds to confirm that Burke was really dead, then gave the body a shove, and Burke keeled over to land on his side. Quinn turned his attention to Perley then. "I guess the real question is, where's the man who checked into this room?"

"I think he checked out," Possum answered him. "Reckon he didn't feel safe here in the hotel." He smiled at Quinn. "I don't know why."

Quinn ignored him and looked at Perley. "You were in the bed." It wasn't a question.

"That's right," Perley replied. "There wasn't anybody usin' it, and it was too late to get back to the ranch. So, I figured this room Paul wasn't usin' anymore would be a good safe place to spend the night. I reckon I was wrong."

His answer made Quinn smile again. "Are you in the habit of going to bed wearing your gun belt and with your six-gun drawn?"

"Not always," Perley answered. "Sometimes it can be a comfort, though, like when you're sleepin' in a den of rattlesnakes, or with a playful sorta fellow like ol' Burke, there, who likes to see if he can stuff a pillow down your throat."

Knowing it was time to perform again, Quinn turned his focus on Amos Johnson, who had remained in a state of confusion over what had just happened and why. "I feel I owe you my deepest regret over this inexplicable incident and my apology for my recommendation to fill your vacant sheriff's position with this man. As I told you, I have worked with this man before and had always been impressed by his zeal to perform at the highest level of honesty. I cannot imagine what could have driven him to this state of mind." He looked around at those standing in the room as if searching for an answer. "My first thought would be that he had somehow been set up by someone wishing to do him harm. And there was no telling what manner of monster he had been led to believe existed in this room." When he saw the doubting smirks on some of the faces, he knew he wasn't selling it. "Let me just say that I am truly sorry that I recommended the man and I'm grateful that no innocent people were injured." He shook his head as if deep in regret. "The horrible thought just occurred to me that Elam Burke might even be the man who shot Sheriff McQueen, so that he could take his job. And he used me to facilitate that despicable ploy, knowing I could give him nothing but glowing recommendations, based on my experience with him."

"I reckon there ain't no doubt in anybody's mind now that Burke, here, was the man who shot Sheriff McQueen," Possum saw fit to point out. "Then when he found out he hadn't killed McQueen, he decided to come back here tonight to finish the job. Ain't that the way you see it, Quinn?"

"I suppose that could be true," Quinn responded. "I guess we'll never know for sure." He shook his head for effect and added, "It's a shameful thing for a man as brave and principled as Elam Burke to get confused as to the correct side of the fight he's on."

"I expect he knew, Mr. Quinn," Possum said. "The shameful thing is that some of us saw it in him from the first. Makes you look kinda foolish, don't it?"

"I'm not sure I appreciate what you're implying as far as my person is concerned," Quinn charged, his dander obviously up.

Perley figured it was time to step in before Possum found himself in a duel with Quinn. "He ain't implyin' anything, Quinn. Possum ain't the implyin' kind."

"That's a fact," Possum said with a wide smile. "Let's just all be glad that piece of dung is dead and Paul McQueen is lookin' like he might make it back to bein' our sheriff again."

That statement served to shift Amos Johnson's mind from the bloody scene in his hotel room to the return of his problem as mayor. "I have to admit that I, and some of the other members of the council, had already begun to question the appointment of Elam Burke to replace Paul McQueen. And obviously, Perley and Possum were motivated to find out for sure if Burke was the man trying to kill our sheriff. So, I reckon we owe our thanks to them for having the guts to risk their lives to do it. So, Perley and Possum, thanks for saving us from I don't know what, if that man had remained as sheriff. Having said all that, however, we're back in the same situation we were in when Paul was shot. We don't have a sheriff." He turned to look at Quinn. "And we're already showing an increase in the number of visitors to town just from the rumors of the gambling casino that Patton's Saloon is supposed to become."

"I can relieve you of some of your worries on that score," Quinn spoke up again. "I plan to bring in some men to police the gambling casino and keep the peace."

"That right there oughta be enough to make you shake in your boots," the female voice came from behind them. They turned to discover Beulah Walsh standing in the doorway with a blanket wrapped around her robe. The three women in the hallway had not been noticed while the talking among the men had filled the room. "Seems to me Elam Burke was the first one he brought to town," Beulah continued.

"It's a shame Burke didn't know that Paul McQueen started talkin' again last night," Lucy remarked. "Paul said he knew he'd been shot, but it was so dark he didn't see who shot him."

Quinn winced slightly before he caught himself. His morning was getting worse by the minute. His natural inclination was to blame Burke for bungling a simple job, and if he could believe what Lucy had just said, one that was not even necessary to attempt. "Well, at least that is good news," he rallied to declare. "It sounds like our sheriff will be back on the job, as soon as he heals up from his wound."

"We're still gonna need a temporary sheriff till that happens," Amos stressed. "It ain't no tellin' how long it'll take Paul to recover from a wound that serious. In the meantime, there are still gonna be drunks and fights and who knows what. And somebody's gonna have to handle all that. I know we talked about a vigilance committee before Paul took the job, and that talk didn't go very far. The problem was, and still is, Wilford Taylor and Raymond Patton and Ben Henderson, certainly myself, and several others aren't really handy with a six-shooter. And we're past the age of learnin' to be. That said, I know one of our town who is handy with a six-gun, maybe the fastest in the whole state of Texas. So I'm turnin' to you again, Perley, askin' you to come to the aid of your neighbors in Paris." All eyes turned to focus on Perley, who reacted in obvious discomfort. When Amos saw his reaction, he quickly continued, "It would just be temporary, Perley, till Paul gets on his feet again. If you didn't want to be sheriff, we can make you a deputy. That way, you wouldn't be takin' Paul's job. Whaddaya say?"

"Doggone it, Mr. Johnson, I don't know," Perley responded, and looked to Possum for help. "I don't like the idea of shootin' people for a livin'. And I ain't ever had any notion about tellin' folks right from wrong."

Possum, his gaze locked on Perley's, understood the young man's aversion to minding anybody's business but his own. He also had complete faith in Perley's ability to react to trouble in a way to fix it. It might not be a conventional way, but it usually worked. He had been a witness to enough of these situations involving Perley to know they were not accidental. He also knew that, in a shoot-out, Perley's reflexes worked two steps ahead of his brain. There was no one faster with a gun than Perley Gates. The thought made Possum shake his head. Then he winked at Perley and said, "I think Rubin and John will be glad to get rid of you for a while out at the ranch." He looked at Amos then and said, "He'll do it." Amos looked quickly at Perley to confirm it, and Perley just shrugged his shoulders.

"I say that qualifies as an official acceptance of the offer of the position as sheriff," Amos declared.

"Deputy," Perley corrected him.

"Deputy," Amos confirmed, all smiles.

The smiles and nodding of heads continued through the half-dozen folks who had come from other rooms to investigate the noise. One alone was burning inside with the scalding fire of defeat. Although he was well practiced in the art of displaying a picture of grace, Redmond Quinn had to concentrate mightily to hide the anger filling his veins. With Burke as sheriff of this town, he had immediate control of the path the town would take from this point. With Perley Gates or Paul McQueen as sheriff, it would take longer. It occurred to him that he hated Perley Gates more than he could remember hating any man before, with the possible exception of his father. His ego was still chafing from the ridiculous reports of Perley Gates's lightning-fast speed. A hometown hero, Perley could not even imagine what it was like to face a genuine expert. He would get his chance to pull against one who had twelve decisions against other hometown heroes who were the fastest in the area. *I will have to make it legitimate,* he thought, *to defend my honor, just as I did when I shot my father down.*

"Anybody know what time it is?" Beulah asked.

Several of the men who had collected in the hall outside the room started digging for their watches. David Smith was the first to speak. "I have exactly four o'clock," he announced.

"I expect we'd best close this room up," Amos said.

"David, get word to Bill Simmons to come get the body when it's time to go to work." He turned to Perley then. "I suppose Sheriff, I mean, Deputy Gates will need to search the body for the jail keys and his weapons. Maybe you'll find enough money to pay Simmons for his services."

"Well, it's about an hour before I usually start to get ready for breakfast," Beulah said. "I've been threatenin' to get up early and roll out some dough to make some doughnuts. Might as well make this the day. I feel like we sure oughta celebrate this mornin' somehow."

"Amen," Lucy sang out. "I'll help you cook 'em. I reckon we'd best go put some clothes on first." She turned to follow Beulah down the hall.

"Ah, that's all right, Lucy," one of the regular guests in the hotel called after her. "Ain't no need to go to a lotta trouble."

"That's a good idea, Jack," Lucy called back. "I'll just bring a flour sack to pull over your head."

"Make sure you cut some eyeholes in it," Jack returned, but Lucy had already followed Beulah out the door to the kitchen.

Perley glanced toward the door and saw Becky still standing there, so he handed Burke's gun belt to Possum and stepped out in the hall. "You'd best run along and catch up with Lucy and Beulah," he said.

"I wanted to make sure you were all right," she said. "I was afraid when I found out what you did."

"It was all over then," Perley said.

"I was still afraid," she insisted. "You'd better not let anything happen to you. I don't know if I like you being the sheriff or not."

"I'm just the deputy," he reminded her. "If you don't

want me doin' the job, then we all better take good care of Paul, so we can get him back to work."

"When you get through here, you and Possum come on to the dining room. I'll have a big pot of coffee made for you, Deputy Gates." She looked to see if any of the other spectators were watching them, then gave him a quick kiss and hurried after Lucy and Beulah.

One of the last to leave, Redmond Quinn happened to see their embrace. He continued to stare at Perley when he went back inside the room. *So that's your weak point,* he thought. *I should have figured that when I heard how you heroically rescued the fair maiden from her kidnappers. Never hurts to know where your opponent is vulnerable.* He turned and walked back to the front stairs, heading for his two-room suite for a couple more hours' sleep.

When they were finished, they left David to lock up room 100 until Bill Simmons was contacted. The next thing on Perley's mind were the two horses they had left tied behind the hotel, still with saddles on. They hadn't left them with Walt Carver at the stable the night before because they didn't want anyone outside the dining room to know they were in town. At least he wouldn't have to explain his negligence to Buck, since he had worked the big bay pretty hard the day before and had picked out another horse to ride into town. Perley and Possum climbed on the two horses and rode the short distance up the street to the stable.

"I swear," Walt exclaimed when he saw who was knocking on his barn door. "What in the world are you two doin' here this time of mornin'? I ain't even got started yet."

"We need to leave a couple of horses with you," Perley said. "They need water and a portion of oats. Rest 'em up and we'll get 'em sometime this afternoon." Then, knowing they had no choice, they stayed long enough to tell Walt all about their little ambush they set up for Elam Burke.

"So ol' Burke went right in Paul's room to finish him off?" Walt marveled. "I swear, that's one man I ain't sorry to see gone. And I know for sure I ain't the only one feels that way. Whaddaya want me to do about his horse and tack?"

"Same as you would with anybody who left their horse with you and didn't come back for it, I reckon. Take it for the rent he owes," Perley told him. "I'm pretty sure Burke ain't gonna be comin' back to get his horse."

"That sounds fair to me, but Burke didn't owe me anything for keepin' his horse," Walt replied. "Amos told me the council decided that was part of the deal with Burke, no stable rent for the sheriff's horses. I think Redmond Quinn talked Amos into it on account we was gettin' such a highly qualified man for sheriff."

"Did you charge Paul to keep his horses?" Possum asked.

"Well, no," Walt hedged, "but it weren't because the council told me not to charge him. That was my idea to help him out a little."

"Possum and I will pay you for these two horses today," Perley said. "I'm just Perley today. Tomorrow, when I'm Deputy Gates, you can decide what the rate will be."

"I swear," Possum declared, "you sure ain't much of a negotiator."

Chapter 19

By the time they left the stable, it was a little past six o'clock, the usual opening hour of the hotel dining room. When they walked in the door, Becky came to meet them at the weapons table when they paused to take off their gun belts. "You don't have to take yours off anymore," she reminded Perley. "Now that you're the law, you can keep it on."

"That's right," Perley replied. "I forgot about that, but Possum, you have to take yours off. Ain't that right, Becky?" He grinned at the peeved look on his friend's face. "I reckon I'll take my gun off, too. Seems like the polite thing to do."

"Where have you been?" Becky asked. "I made you and Possum some coffee as soon as I got back here. I thought you were coming right away."

"Oh, oh, partner," Possum warned. "Little lady's already tightenin' the noose around your neck and you ain't even asked her to marry you yet." They both gaped at him in shocked astonishment, too embarrassed to speak. He looked back at them, first one, then the other. "What?" he asked. "You two are gonna get hitched, ain't you? Everybody in town knows it. They're just wonderin' what you're waitin' for."

Perley looked at Becky, and seeing her shocked look of embarrassment gradually replaced by one of delighted amusement, he said, "Don't pay any attention to him, Becky. Sometimes his mouth is quicker on the draw than his brain."

"Oh, he doesn't bother me," she replied. "But he did ask an interesting question. I was wondering about that, myself."

"Doggone you and your big mouth, Possum," Perley complained, then turned to Becky again. "Do you wanna get married?"

"Well, I don't know," she said. "Nobody's asked me. I thought I might, but since you asked me like that, I'm not sure if it's Possum's idea or yours. I think I woulda liked it better if you'd thought of it yourself."

"I ain't hardly thought of nothin' else ever since we rode back from Durant," Perley blurted. "I knew then that I just wanted to take care of you for the rest of your life, just wake up every mornin' and see your face. I just ain't good with words."

"Well, those are some pretty good ones," she said. "Are you asking me to marry you?"

"I reckon I am, if you'll have me," he replied. "Whaddaya say? Will you?"

"I will," she stated emphatically. "Now, you two come on and sit down and I'll get you some breakfast."

"I'm powerful glad we finally got around to gettin' that done," Possum said. "The breakfast part, I mean, I'm 'bout to starve to death." He was mightily pleased with himself for having pushed his shy young friend over the threshold of matrimony. Like Lucy and Beulah, he had feared that Perley was going to be wearing a long gray beard by the time he worked up the nerve to ask Becky, if left to act on his own.

Breakfast for Perley proved to be a time of nervous self-consciousness, starting even before Becky returned to the table with their coffee. For only seconds after she disappeared inside the kitchen door, both Lucy and Beulah appeared in the doorway, their faces beaming happily as they stared in his direction. His only defense was to confine his gaze to the breakfast Becky set down before him. Even then, he could feel the flush of his embarrassment turning his ears red. Possum's occasional chuckle when nothing humorous had been said contributed to his sense of unease. When Becky came to fill their cups a third time, Perley declared that two cups were enough for him that morning. "I expect I'd best get over to the jail and see what kinda shape Burke left the office in." Becky looked disappointed at once. Seeing her reaction, Perley sought to assure her. "I reckon you and I have a lot to talk over and a lot of plannin' to do and we're gonna take time to do that. They kinda dropped this sheriff's business in my lap when I wasn't expectin' it. So, I guess since the whole town will be dependin' on me to take care of things till Paul gets well, I'd best make sure I'm ready if I'm needed."

She still looked disappointed, but said, "I understand. Will I see you later this morning or at dinner?"

"Oh yes, ma'am, you surely will," he was quick to reply. "Then sometime today, I'll have to ride back to the Triple-G to let John and Rubin know what's happened.

And I've gotta get my clothes and such, 'cause I'll be stayin' here in town all the time now."

"That's right, you will," Becky replied, smiling anew. "I didn't think about that. You go take care of your sheriffing business." Perley was about to comment on the big grin on Possum's face when he was surprised to see Sonny Rice walk in the door.

"I figured I'd find you two here in the dinin' room," Sonny japed. "Fred sent me in with a wagon to pick up some things at Henderson's, so I thought I'd see what you and Possum had got into."

"Oh, there was a thing or two last night to keep us busy, Perley more than me, but nothin' much to talk about," Possum couldn't resist japing.

"Were you lookin' for breakfast?" Perley asked, knowing Sonny would use any excuse to eat in the hotel dining room.

"Nope, I et with the rest of the boys before I came to town, but if you and Possum are gonna be hangin' around till dinnertime, I might let myself get talked into eatin' dinner with you."

"I expect we'll be here awhile yet," Possum said, and proceeded to bring Sonny up to date on all the recent activities and changes in town.

"I swear, if that ain't somethin'," Sonny marveled. "You're the deputy sheriff now. Ain't Rubin gonna be surprised to hear that?"

"I reckon I'd most likely use another word to describe how Rubin and John will feel about it," Perley said, "but I sorta got trapped into takin' the job. And it's just temporary till Paul gets back on his feet. We were just fixin' to go up to the sheriff's office now and see if there's anything that needs to be done."

"Okay if I go with you?" Sonny asked.

With the keys he had taken from Elam Burke's body, Perley opened the sheriff's office. After he placed Burke's gun and gun belt in a cabinet behind Paul McQueen's desk, he and Possum did a general check on the jail cells and the office to see if anything needing to be taken care of was obvious. Before they had finished, Sonny pulled the wagon up to the rail and came inside to join them. There was nothing really to do. There was no prisoner in the cell room, and there was little evidence of Elam Burke's short time as sheriff. As Possum pointed out, it shouldn't have surprised them, for Burke spent all his time in Patton's Saloon. In line with his tendency toward neatness, Perley found a broom in a corner and proceeded to sweep up some dried mud particles probably left by Burke's muddy boots. Once he got started, he continued on to sweep the whole office area. His reason, he said, was to sweep out any trace of Elam Burke in the office.

Not one to participate in housekeeping, which he insisted was women's work, Possum amused himself by looking through the desk drawers. As he explained to Perley, there might be some official business that Paul McQueen was going to take care of before he was shot. "Ain't you gonna wear a badge, Perley?" Sonny asked when Possum held one up to show them.

Perley said that he would, but he wasn't in any particular hurry to put it on. "There's gonna have to be a lot of explainin' to the folks here in town. I expect it might be best to let the mayor tell everybody what's happened before I just walk in sportin' a badge and claimin' I'm the law in town."

Rummaging through a bottom drawer, Possum came upon a stack of wanted notices, most of them quite old. As he was flipping through the pages, some had drawings of the more notorious outlaws, but most contained no more than written descriptions of the outlaw wanted. "I reckon our little ol' town weren't big enough to attract the attention of any of these big-time outlaws," Possum commented, and handed the notices to Sonny to read. Sonny called off a few of the names and aliases. "I ain't never heard of 'em," Possum remarked, "and it looks like Paul hadn't, either."

"But it looks like he kept 'em," Sonny said, "'cause some of these near the bottom are four or five years old. Was McQueen even sheriff that long ago?" He flipped through several more while Perley swept, calling out names until he stopped suddenly, one name having caught his attention. "English Red," he called out to Perley. "Who does that alias remind you of?"

"Nobody in particular," Perley replied. "Who's it supposed to remind me of?"

Only halfway serious, Sonny suggested, "How 'bout English Redmond?"

Perley paused in his sweeping, thinking of Quinn's kill count in the short time he had been in town—two cowhands and one old tramp—and his seeming fascination with everybody's quickness. "What does it say about him, Sonny? What is he wanted for?"

"Murder," Sonny answered as he read the report. "It was in New Orleans. Looks like he shot some gamblin' casino operator and the other feller wasn't armed. Says he'd be armed and dangerous; killed five men in pistol duels; not known where he's from but speaks with a distinct English accent." Sonny paused after he read that. "Boy, that makes you wonder, don't it?"

Both Perley and Possum were interested now. "What's his real name?" Possum asked.

"They list Randal Quincy and Robert Quail. He's been known by both names," Sonny read on.

"Kinda interestin', ain't it?" Possum observed, "initials always *RQ*, just like the initials on ol' Quinn's fancy saddle." He looked Perley straight in the eye and waited for his comment.

"It'd be one heck of a coincidence, wouldn't it?" Perley responded.

"I'm thinkin' it would," Possum agreed, "and it wouldn't surprise me none if English Red turned out to be ol' Redmond Quinn, the big-time gambler."

"Seems to me that I oughta be able to wire the sheriff in New Orleans and find out if English Red was ever caught," Perley suggested. "They might not know, but they might, so I don't see how it could hurt to make that my first official act as sheriff . . . I mean, deputy."

"Whatcha gonna do if they say he ain't ever been caught?" Possum wanted to know.

Perley looked at him and shrugged. "I don't know," he answered honestly. "It'd sure give us something to think about, though, wouldn't it?" He thought about the possibility, but knew he had nothing to tie Quinn to that murder after all this time. "I'll send the telegram, just for the hell of it. Maybe they'll know some way to tie Quinn to that murder." That seemed to tickle Possum and Sonny, so

Perley decided to go over to the telegraph office and send the wire right away. "Maybe they'll get back to me by the time we finish dinner and we can get on back to the Triple-G this afternoon. I need to explain to my brothers how I stepped in another cow pie and I've got to take that sorrel back and swap him for Buck. I can satisfy John and Rubin with a story about how the town ain't got anybody else to hold the job till Paul gets well. But Buck ain't gonna stand for any excuses for leavin' him behind."

"You gonna tell 'em about you and Becky gettin' married?" Possum asked with a smug grin on his face.

"What?" Sonny reacted before Perley could answer. "You got married? You and Becky Morris? When?" His face lit up with the news.

"No, I didn't get married. Possum shouldn'ta said anything about that," Perley responded. "Becky and I agreed that it would most likely work out between us. But we haven't even started talkin' about when or anything else. It's too soon to be nailin' any dates down. I've got this sheriff thing to take care of, so whenever we decide we're gonna do it, it'll most likely be after Paul takes his job back."

"I declare, if that ain't somethin'," Sonny whooped. "I reckon you and her would live out at the Triple-G, then, wouldn't you? That'll be the end of your days ridin' all over the country for one thing and another, I expect. You'll be like Rubin and John now."

"I expect so," Perley said. Hearing it put like that, he realized he had not thought about how drastically marriage would change his lifestyle. No more saddling up on a moment's notice and riding down to places like Bison Gap to help friends like Rooster Crabb out of a jam. He glanced over at Possum and he could tell by the expression on his friend's face that he knew what was running through his mind.

"Driftin' about aimlessly gets kind of tiresome after a while," Possum said. "You might think you're livin' like a free man, but it don't bring the real peace and contentment that the right woman provides. Them that finds that out early in their lives are the lucky ones."

Perley and Sonny were both struck speechless for a few moments before Perley remarked. "That was pretty profound comin' outta you," he said. "Sounds like something you mighta read on a tombstone somewhere." And even though it was spoken in jest, he had a feeling Possum was reflecting on his own life. He suspected that might have been the motive behind his outright aggressive approach to unite the two young people in matrimony. Anxious then to get off that subject, Perley said, "I'm gonna walk on over to the telegraph office and send that wire." As expected, Possum said he would accompany him in case he needed help telling the operator what he wanted.

"I expect I'd best get on up to Henderson's store and get what I was sent into town for," Sonny decided. "I'll meet you back at the dining room."

It was a little early for dinner when the three of them met back at the hotel, but Becky came at once to unlock the door for them. "You can sit down at a table in the back and have some coffee while you wait," she said. "We won't open for twenty minutes yet." So they sat in the back of the room, where other early arrivals for dinner couldn't see them, and they talked about the possibility that Redmond

Quinn was once known as English Red. Sonny never failed to give Becky a big grin every time she approached the table. If she noticed, she didn't say so. Dinnertime came, and they took their time enjoying it. They checked the telegraph office afterward, but there was no reply from the New Orleans sheriff's department. And there was still none when Perley deemed it time to go back to the ranch to talk to his brothers and get his horse.

It was not until the next day that word came in reply to Perley's telegram. It stated that there had never been an arrest in the case against Robert Quail aka English Red for the murder of Bode Mathews. Perley knew that news would interest Possum, but he had nothing to link Redmond Quinn with that, or any other, murder, and that included the one he was sure Quinn had committed. Like Paul McQueen, Perley knew Quinn killed Lester Graves and he would like to see him pay for it. He considered the shoot-out in Patton's Saloon with the two cowhands from the Rocking-J nothing short of murder. Paul McQueen had told him about Benny Grimes's eyewitness account of that double shooting. Benny had said that Quinn was like greased lightning when he finally goaded Jake Bailey into pulling his weapon. And most important to him and Possum was, although the man who shot Paul McQueen was dead, the man who had paid him to do the job was scot-free. Even though those things didn't set well on his mind, Perley had to remind himself that he was in a temporary situation. Nobody expected him to investigate anybody, even if he had reason. His job was to try to keep the peace on the streets of the town and lock up the drunks until Paul McQueen was back on the job. This was what he had told Rubin and John after they pressured him to stay out of the town's politics.

It was obvious that Possum wanted to accompany him when he rode back into town that morning. Possum was intent upon keeping the pressure on Redmond Quinn, if for no better reason, at least to let him know he was under suspicion. But Possum was also aware of his need to show up for work at the ranch, since that was what he was drawing wages for. So it was no surprise to Perley when he said he'd wait and ride into town that night to see if he had heard any word from the New Orleans sheriff.

When Possum arrived that evening, he found Perley in the sheriff's office, putting some clean bedclothes on the cot that was to be his bed. "Makin' yourself right at home, are ya?" he said when he walked in. "Don't look like you've been arrestin' anybody."

"Don't expect to, since Burke ain't here anymore," Perley replied. "I hope you ain't plannin' on startin' any trouble."

"Nope, you know me. I'm a peaceable man. I just thought it would be fittin' for me to buy you a drink to celebrate your new job. But first, I wanna know, is English Red dead?"

Well aware whom he was referring to, Perley answered, "I don't know, but I do know that he was never arrested for that murder." Then he joked, "I'm awful busy. But on the other hand, it ain't that often that Possum Smith offers to buy anybody a drink." He took his hat off a hook behind his desk and plopped it on his head. "Just one, though," he said. "I can't have the good folks of Paris thinkin' their deputy sheriff's a drunk."

CHAPTER 20

"Evenin', boys," Benny Grimes greeted them when they walked into Patton's Saloon. "What you drinkin'?"

"A shot of corn likker would suit me just fine," Possum answered, and Perley said to make it two. Benny poured and when Possum said, "Here's to the new sheriff," Benny poured one for himself.

"I'll drink to that," he said, and they tossed them back.

"Damn," Possum swore, "that's nasty stuff. Pour us another 'un, and we'll take it to a table." He winked at Perley. "And you can tell me what you found out about English Red."

"You want a bottle?" Benny asked, thinking it sounded as if they were planning to stay awhile.

"No, just pour us another one," Perley said. "Two's my limit and I don't want Possum to fall off his horse on the way home tonight." Their entrance did not go unnoticed. Seated at a table with four other players, Redmond Quinn was dealing a game of poker. He nodded in their direction, but otherwise ignored them. "Who's that he's playin' with?" Perley asked, since he didn't recognize any of them.

"Some cowhands from the Lazy-D," Benny said. "Two

brothers, I think they are. They come in from time to time. I don't know the other two. They ain't ever been in before, but Quinn seemed to know 'em."

Perley and Possum picked up their drinks and walked over to a table on the opposite side of the room from the card game. As soon as they sat down, they were joined by Raymond Patton. "Evenin', Sheriff," Patton greeted Perley. "Possum," he acknowledged. "Mind if I join you?"

"Why, hell no, Patton," Possum answered him. "This is your saloon, you can sit anywhere you want to."

Patton laughed. "Well, I reckon it's a good idea to try to shine up to the new sheriff in town." He directed his comments to Perley then. "I don't think we could have made a better choice to stand in for Paul McQueen than you, Perley. I want you to know you'll have all my cooperation."

"Thank you, Mr. Patton," Perley replied. "I 'preciate that."

"Does that include your partner over there?" Possum had to say. "You know Elam Burke was one of his boys. He mighta wanted to bring in another replacement."

Patton was plainly taken aback by the remark. "Mr. Quinn is not an actual partner, Possum, although we are working together on the gambling operations we're planning. I think Redmond felt he had been cruelly deceived by Elam Burke, if that's what you're referring to." There was no doubt in Perley's mind that Possum's reference to Quinn was not something Patton wanted to discuss, because he didn't linger but a few moments more before saying there was something he had to do in the office.

"Now that we got rid of him, I wanna know what you found out about English Red," Possum said. Perley told him everything he had learned, which wasn't a great deal, but that he had never been caught after he murdered a gambler named Bode Mathews. There were no details of the murder and he didn't expect he was going to ride east to New Orleans to try to find out. "What did you say was the name he was goin' by?" Possum asked. When Perley told him, Possum repeated it several times. "Robert Quail, Robert Quail," as if memorizing it.

Finished with that topic of discussion for the moment, Possum asked if he had gone by to see Paul McQueen that day. "I did," Perley answered. "I went by to see him just before supper. He's still in that room next to Beulah and the girls. He's gotten better, but just a little bit. Bill Simmons thinks he might be recovered enough in a couple more days to make the trip down to Sulphur Springs to see the doctor there. Bill says he's done all he can do for him."

"You ever think that he might not want his job as sheriff back, even if the doctor can get him back on his feet again?" Possum wondered. "He might decide it ain't worth this kinda risk when he's got a good business as a blacksmith."

"There's always that possibility," Perley said. "But if you're wonderin' if I'd stay in the job permanently, the answer's no. We might have to ask Redmond Quinn to bring in another candidate for the job, since he seems to have a source for able-bodied men."

As if he realized he was being talked about, Quinn announced to the men he was playing cards with that he was going to sit out a couple of hands. "Don't worry, I'll be back to take all your money. I just have to speak to our new sheriff." He pushed his chair back and stood up, adjusted his gun belt to a more comfortable position, and walked over to the two men at the table across the room.

"Gentlemen," Quinn greeted them, "good evening. Mind if I join you?"

"Ain't nothin' we'd like better," Possum replied. "Take a chair." When Quinn did so, Possum said, "Me and Perley was just talkin' about something you might be interested in. Ain't that right, Perley?"

"I don't know if he would or not," Perley answered, already concerned that Possum might be getting ready to set himself up for trouble, much like Paul McQueen did before.

"Oh, is that right?" Quinn answered Possum, then said, "First, I'd like to officially congratulate you, Perley, on being named our sheriff. I'd like to buy you a drink."

"I'll just thank you for the congratulations," Perley replied. "You're too late for the drink, though. I've already had my limit, but I thank you for the offer."

"Well, I regret that, but the offer is open for some other time," Quinn said. "I wish you well in your new job. I'll get back to my poker game and you can continue your discussion."

He started to turn and leave when Possum blurted out, "We was talkin' about English Red." Perley knew it was too late to stop him then.

Quinn showed no visible reaction. He said nothing at first as he shifted his gaze to Perley and then back to Possum. "English Red?" he questioned, a puzzled look now upon his face. "English Red," he repeated. "I'm not familiar with that. Is it an English wine or something?"

"No, it's an outlaw's alias," Perley quickly answered, hoping to keep Possum from getting himself put on Quinn's list of annoyances. But Possum was like a bloodhound on a fresh scent.

"English Red," Possum said again. "He murdered a feller named Bode Mathews down in New Orleans four or five years ago. English Red, he was goin' by the name of Robert Quail then. He was supposed to be fast with a six-gun, but when he shot Bode Mathews, he didn't have to be too quick 'cause Bode didn't have a gun. Ol' English Red got away and they never caught him. But now they've got some new evidence and they think they might have an idea where English Red turned up."

Quinn maintained a faint smile as he patiently waited out Possum's dissertation on the outlaw English Red. "That sounds like a fascinating story, and I'm pleased that you shared it with me. I'm sorry I'm not familiar with the story, myself, but I'm glad the law has some new clues to follow. Enjoy the rest of your evening." He turned and went back to the card game.

"Well, that was a helluva show you just put on," Perley scolded Possum. "What are you tryin' to do, get bush-whacked like Paul did after he kept goadin' Quinn about Lester Graves? I'd sure as the devil love to arrest him for that attack on Paul, but I don't want you shot in the process."

"I was watchin' you," Possum boasted. "You was watchin' his every move, just as anxious as I was. I thought I saw a little bit of a hole in that blank expression of his when I told him they had new evidence against him. That got him to thinkin'."

"I don't know, Possum. I didn't see him crack at all."

"Hell, Perley, he's a gambler by profession," Possum insisted. "What kinda gambler would he be if he didn't have a good poker face?"

"I know how you feel, Possum. I wanna nail this fancy

pants killer just as bad as you do. Just like you, I know in my gut that he sent Elam Burke to kill Paul McQueen. But I'm representing the law now, so it would be best if I had something to arrest him on and maybe see him hang. As far as this English Red business, I wouldn't be surprised if Quinn is that man, but I ain't absolutely sure."

"Well, I'll guarantee you ol' English Red over there is startin' to think he ain't so slick after all," Possum insisted. "He might have a lotta folks fooled around here, but he ain't got me fooled. He'll slip up, just like he did with Burke. Then there won't be no doubt what he's up to."

"You just be sure you watch your back trail when you ride out to the ranch," Perley felt the need to caution him. As soon as he said it, he was reminded of another day when he had warned Paul McQueen to watch his back after he had baited Quinn before. In short order, Paul was shot down. There were some mysteries about Redmond Quinn, but one thing Perley knew for sure, the man had a giant ego and tended to act violently if someone offended him. All he needed for proof of that were the executions of the two hands from the Rocking-J and Lester Graves. "You listen to what I'm sayin', Possum. This coyote you're pickin' at doesn't take pesterin' too long before he bites. So, damn it, you be double sure you don't pick up a tail when you ride outta town tonight. I'm thinkin' it might be a good idea if I was to ride along with you."

Possum was genuinely touched. "You're lettin' your imagination run away with you, partner. I'll be careful. There ain't no need for you to escort me home like one of the ladies in the dinin' room. When we get to the Triple-G, I might feel like I need to escort you back to town. Besides, who's supposed to watch the town if the sheriff's gone?"

Across the room, the poker game broke up when the two brothers from the Lazy-D lost as much as they could afford and decided to call it a night. "Just as well," Quinn said. "I need to talk to you boys about a little job that needs taking care of."

"That's what we came up here for," Porter Shaw said. "I didn't think you sent for me and Shep 'cause you needed somebody to play poker with."

Quinn thought about what he was about to do, and for a brief moment, he questioned his decision. Would he be showing his hand if he silenced Possum Smith? Could any of that talk about the killing in New Orleans being under investigation again be true? It had to be all talk with no fact. If it wasn't, Perley would be attempting to make an arrest. And he had nothing to go on. That was obvious from the way he tried to temper Possum's brash talk. *They're only guessing,* he decided, *hoping to get a reaction out of me that would incriminate me.* Back to the problem with Possum, then, he was afraid the longer he permitted him to talk about English Red, the greater the likelihood people would start to listen. There was no risk, he concluded. Just like the silencing of Sheriff McQueen, there might be suspicions, but no way to connect him to the killing. *Besides,* he thought, *I want the loudmouth dead.*

"You see the old coot sitting at the table with the young fellow I was just talking to? His name's Possum. He looks like one, doesn't he? Well, he likes to run his mouth about things he has no business talking about. I'm pretty sure he'll be leaving soon to return to the ranch where he's supposed to work. I don't want him to arrive there. Understood?"

Shep King smiled. "You know you can depend on us. Right, Porter?" Porter answered with a smile and a nod.

"The young fellow is just a temporary sheriff, but I'm going to have to take care of him before too much longer. He has a way of annoying me, and he thinks he's a fast gun. I think it won't be long before I show him how fast he really is." He realized that he was letting his mind run on, so he concluded. "Tonight, it would be enough to rid us of the old loudmouth."

"I expect I'd best head back to the ranch," Possum declared. "Some of us have to get up and go to work in the mornin'," he japed. "I'll be careful," he interrupted when Perley started to remind him.

"I'll walk out with you," Perley said. They got up and headed for the door, pausing briefly to say good night to Benny.

They walked back to the sheriff's office, where Possum had left his horse. "I'll tell the boys back at the ranch that you're workin' hard keepin' the peace," Possum joked.

"You be careful," Perley reminded him, and stood back while Possum climbed up into the saddle.

"I'll be thinkin' about you when I'm out working on that old line camp and you're settin' in the dinin' room eatin' breakfast with Becky." He laughed and wheeled the big gray gelding he called Dancer around toward the north end of town.

Perley stepped up to the door of the sheriff's office, but instead of unlocking the door right away, he waited there on the small stoop and watched Possum as he rode up the street, until he disappeared beyond Walt Carver's stable. He pulled his keys out to unlock the door, but he hesitated when two riders pulled away from the hitching post at

Patton's Saloon and rode up the street. Peering at the two riders as they passed in front of the jail, he felt sure they were the two strangers who had been playing cards with Redmond Quinn in the saloon. Since he was standing in the shadow of his office doorway, he didn't think they noticed him. He was immediately alarmed. It was too much of a coincidence that these two strangers left the saloon so soon after Possum had, especially when Benny had said Quinn evidently knew them. Perley might be creating a situation in his mind that had nothing to do with reality, but he couldn't take a chance when it had to do with Possum's life. He stepped off the stoop immediately and ran to the stable.

It was already past nightfall, but not what he called a hard dark yet, so he soon caught up close enough to the two riders to make out their images in the dark while still hanging back far enough not to attract their attention. He guessed that, if he was right about their intentions, they were probably trailing Possum the same way he was trailing them. What troubled him most was not knowing what their plan for Possum was. If they were just intent upon riding within rifle range and shooting him down, how could he know in time to prevent Possum from being shot? The answer kept coming back to him—he couldn't. He realized that he was acting on an assumption that Redmond Quinn was arrogant to the point where he could order Possum's assassination, after doing the same to Paul McQueen. Quinn would have to be insane to be so cocksure. Perley thought about that for a brief time before deciding there was only one way he could be sure Possum wouldn't be shot in the back. So he gave Buck a firm nudge with his heels and shouted out, "Hey, fellows! Wait up a minute!"

Both riders reined their horses back immediately. "What tha hell . . . ?" Porter Shaw started and turned his horse around to face the rider coming at them at a lope.

When Perley got close enough, Shep King recognized him. "It's that sheriff that was settin' with the other feller," he said. "What the hell is he up to?"

Perley pulled Buck up to face the two strangers. "I thought I saw you two fellows sittin' with Redmond Quinn back there in the saloon. I saw you were headin' the same way I'm goin', so I thought if you were lookin' for the Triple-G, I could show you the way. That's where I'm headin', but I oughta tell you, if you're lookin' for work, Triple-G ain't hirin' right now." He hoped he could stall the two of them long enough to give Possum enough of a lead to reach the ranch safely.

"We ain't headin' to the Triple-G," Shep said, "We're just lookin' for a good place to camp."

His partner had other ideas. "You're the sheriff, ain't you?" He had just heard Redmond Quinn telling about his plan to eliminate the young sheriff because of his persistence to get in the way of his plans. Quinn had said that he would personally take care of the sheriff, but Porter figured the opportunity to take care of that problem right away would mean double the money from Quinn.

"Yes, that's right," Perley answered. "I'm the sheriff, and I'm always glad to help strangers in our town find their way around."

"Well, Sheriff, you're out of town right now, so it don't make no sense to try to ride after us just to give us directions, does it? That sounds to me more like stickin' your nose in somebody else's business. Now, that's why you came ridin' after us, ain't it? Well, you caught us, so now you're lookin' at two of us against one little ol' sheriff."

Uh-oh, Perley thought, *this ain't turning out like I expected.* "So far, you two ain't done anything to get arrested for, so there ain't no need to get rowdy. Why don't we just go on back to town, and I'll buy you a drink? Doesn't that sound more sensible than gettin' in trouble with the law?"

"We're goin' back to town when we finish what we came out here for," Porter said. "But you ain't goin' back. You made the mistake of gettin' in English Red's way, and when we're done with you, we'll get your friend with the ponytail." His and Shep's six-guns came out at the same time, a fraction of a second behind Perley's. They stood stalemated for a few long seconds before Porter pointed out, "You're outgunned, Sheriff. You might as well throw it down."

"You're gonna shoot me whether I do or I don't, but one of you is gonna die with me," Perley said. "Which one of you wants to volunteer? I'm a pretty good shot, so I'll make sure I hit you in the chest, so you won't suffer long. I'm kinda hopin' you'll do the same for me. Course, if you don't, and just wound me, I'll take a shot at the other one, too. So whaddaya wanna do? Count to three and fire?"

"Mister," Shep said, "you're crazy as a june bug. We're both gonna shoot you and we ain't gonna tell you which one of us you oughta aim at."

"I'll take the one on the black horse, Perley. I've got the front sight of this Winchester layin' right between his shoulder blades." The voice of Possum Smith came through the darkness behind the two strangers loud and clear. Their reactions were predictable. Porter aimed at once toward Perley but was struck in the back by the slug from Possum's rifle. His shot went harmlessly into the ground. Perley's shot caught Shep in the side when his reaction was to turn and fire at Possum, but he never got the shot off. He keeled over and slid out of the saddle, struggling to reach for his dropped six-gun, but Perley jumped down and kicked the weapon out of his reach. Porter's horse bolted when the shooting started. Perley thought the outlaw was escaping, but the horse ran only a dozen or more yards before Porter's lifeless body did a backward somersault and came to land on the ground. "I hope I didn't spoil your little cow pie party," Possum commented when he walked out of the shadows. "I didn't wanna interrupt you when you was busy arrestin' those two coyotes. I started to just wait and see how you was gonna talk your way outta gettin' shot."

"I swear, I ain't ever been so glad to see you draggin' your old behind to the party before," Perley confessed. "But I think they were almost convinced that I was gonna try to arrest 'em." On a serious note then, he said, "I thought you might be halfway home by the time they decided to settle the discussion with guns. When did you know they were followin' you?"

"Right after I left town. I remembered what you warned me about, so I decided to be careful, like you said. I went a ways and pulled off the trail to wait awhile. Pretty soon, sure 'nough, here they come. So I tied Dancer to a tree limb and found me a place to shoot from, if I had to. Then before they got to me, I heard you hollerin' like a lunatic. Tell you the truth, I thought you'd lost your mind. What in the world were you tryin' to do?"

"I was tryin' to just waste as much of their time as I could, so they wouldn't catch up with you. I didn't plan on tryin' to arrest 'em." He went on to tell Possum how he had tried to tell them he wanted to help them. "Then it turned out they were happy to shoot me, too."

"I reckon there ain't much doubt about Quinn's part in all this now, is there?" Possum wondered. "Or is it just like it was with Burke? Nobody said Quinn told him to do it."

"Well, there is one more thing that might bring about Quinn's arrest," Perley said. "The one you shot called Quinn 'English Red.' He said you and I were gettin' in English Red's way."

"Hot damn!" Possum bellowed. "I knew it! I knew it soon as I heard about English Red. You gonna arrest him now?"

"I think I am," Perley said. "I think I'll wire New Orleans and tell them first thing in the mornin' and let them come and get him."

"It'd be a lot more satisfyin' to hang the cold-blooded killer right here," Possum suggested.

"You sound like Wilford Taylor wantin' to hang Leonard Watts," Perley replied. "I don't care who hangs him, just so he gets what's comin' to him." Their arrest discussion came to a halt when they heard a painful groan from Shep King. "We'd best take care of our wounded prisoner." He went to the wounded man at once. "We might need his testimony to hang Quinn."

"I'll go make sure the other one is dead," Possum volunteered. "We're gonna have to catch their horses and take 'em all back to town. Looks like you've got yourself a deputy, 'cause you're gonna need a little help. You got an extra cot in your office?"

"No, you can sleep in one of the cells," Perley said. "It oughta feel downright natural to you." He rolled Shep over to get a better look at his wound. "No testimony from this fellow. I'm afraid that groanin' we heard was his dyin' gasps. Let's get their horses and load 'em up and take 'em to Bill Simmons."

"What about Redmond Quinn?" Possum asked. "You gonna arrest him tonight?"

"I'm thinkin' about that," Perley replied. "I don't reckon there's any reason to wait. He might get itchy feet when he finds out his two killers are dead. But from what we've seen of him so far, he doesn't seem to be inclined to run. Always relies on his alibi—he wasn't there when it happened. Maybe we'll just take these bodies to Bill tonight and tell him not to tell anyone until tomorrow. Quinn can just wonder all night if his killers were successful or not, and I'll arrest him in the mornin'. I really don't think there's a chance he'll turn rabbit and run, but on the other hand," he reconsidered, "why take the chance?"

"Now you're talkin'," Possum responded. "Let's go get his fancy butt tonight. I wanna be there to help you arrest that self-confident jackass. I wanna see if he can still keep that straight face when he sees me walkin' in."

"Well, I reckon you've earned the right to make that arrest. I'm kinda interested to see his reactions, myself. They might wonder why you don't show up at the ranch, though."

Possum laughed at that. "Hell, they know I just likely

had to take care of you. Rubin won't fire me. He'll just dock my pay. I don't think he ever figured me as a regular hand, just somethin' you collected."

"Maybe a little more than that," Perley said. "Let's take these bodies to Bill Simmons, then we'll pay another visit to the saloon."

CHAPTER 21

There was no one in the street to notice the two riders, each leading a horse with a body lying across the saddle, as they walked slowly past Patton's Saloon. Judging from the noise, there was a typical crowd inside, since the night was still young. Perley and Possum rode down to the barbershop to find Bill Simmons still in the shop. "Howdy, Sheriff," Bill greeted him when he and Possum walked in. "You lookin' for the barber or the undertaker?"

"Undertaker," Perley answered. "We've got a couple of customers for you."

"Oh? Anybody I know?"

"I doubt it," Perley answered. "Two more of Redmond Quinn's old friends who made the mistake of tryin' to bushwhack Possum. Just give 'em the no-name outlaw deluxe burial at the town's usual rate."

Bill's face immediately showed surprise for the casual mention of Quinn's name with the two bodies. "Right," he replied. "I'll take 'em around to the back." He followed them back outside. "You want me to take care of the horses, or are you gonna take 'em to the stable?"

"You take 'em, if you don't mind," Perley answered.

"We've got another chore we need to take care of right now. We haven't looked to see what they might have of any value, so I want the weapons. Anything else you find you can keep as payment for your fees."

Simmons nodded in response. "But I still get the usual fee from the town for buryin' 'em, right?"

"I would expect so," Perley said. "This is my first time doin' this, so you probably know better than I do about that." With that taken care of, Perley and Possum headed back to Patton's Saloon.

After drawing their rifles from their saddles, they paused just outside the batwing doors of the saloon to take a look inside before entering. "Looks like ol' English Red has his usual card game set up," Possum commented. "Look at that, he's got the postmaster and the owner of the dry goods store bettin' on his fancy roulette wheel. He's probably preachin' about how the town's gonna grow when all his dice tables get set up."

"I wouldn't be surprised," Perley said. "It might be a good idea to keep an eye on that fellow runnin' the roulette wheel. He came in on the train with the wheel, and he might object when we arrest Quinn."

"I swear," Possum responded, "it's gettin' to where every stranger that shows up in town is on Quinn's payroll. I'll keep an eye on him."

Perley pushed on through the swinging doors and walked into the saloon, his gaze fixed on Redmond Quinn. When Quinn looked up to see him, he showed only a slight expression of amusement. His usual air of indifference failed him, however, when Possum walked in behind Perley. It was the equivalent of seeing a ghost. He hastened to replace his blank expression of astonishment with one he hoped would convey confidence. "Sheriff Gates, did you decide to come back for that drink I offered you before?" He signaled Benny over at the bar.

Perley held his hand up. "Never mind, Benny." Then he leveled his rifle to aim at Quinn. "Redmond Quinn, or English Red, whichever you'd rather be called; you're under arrest for the attempted murder of Possum Smith, as well as Paul McQueen, and the outright murder of Lester Graves. I might add the murder of Bode Mathews, too." All conversation in the entire barroom came to a halt.

For all his suavity and coolness, Quinn could not hide the shock of the accusations. Sputtering to answer at first, he soon regained his bravado. "Perley Gates," he exclaimed, "have you lost your mind?" He looked rapidly, right and left, as if to summon the support of the players at his table. "Has the responsibility of the sheriff's job brought you to the point of outright hallucinations? Come to your senses, man. Listen to what you are saying."

"I'll be more specific, then," Perley replied. "Your friends, the two men who were here playing cards with you when we were here earlier, are both down at the undertaker's right now. Both died of gunshot wounds. Turned out they couldn't handle the job you sent them to do when they set out to bushwhack Possum Smith and shoot me while they were at it."

"That has nothing to do with me," Quinn protested. "I don't know anything about any attempt on Possum's or your life and I certainly didn't order it. Those two men were strangers to me. I'd appreciate it now if you'd point that rifle somewhere else. You're definitely barking up the wrong tree."

"That's where we have a different opinion," Perley

continued. "You see, just before your men were fixin' to shoot me, they were kind enough to tell me why I had to be killed and it was the same for Possum. They said I was gettin' in your way, same for Possum, so you ordered them to kill both of us." A small swell of conversation rose in the barroom at that point, but faded away again.

Quinn hesitated for a few moments, not sure what to do. He considered drawing his six-gun and ending the confrontation in the manner he had ended arguments before, but he was looking at the business end of Perley's Winchester 73, and since he was seated at the table, his hand action would be slowed down. Then it occurred to him. "You say the two men are at the undertaker, they're dead. You can claim they said anything. So it's your word against mine, and I'm calling you a liar. I don't know anything about those two men except they're not very good at poker. You've had it in for me since the day I arrived. I don't know why, but it's time we settled it. I'm willing to face you man-to-man and end this harassment of me and my plans for the town. What do you say, Perley? I hear you're fast, so why don't we settle this thing with six-guns?"

"That ain't the way we handle criminals here in Paris," Perley calmly responded. "Like I said, you're under arrest, so keep your hands on the table, palms down, and we'll make this as easy as possible. By the way, I oughta tell you, the one who said I was in your way, called you by your alias, English Red. I've already been in touch with the sheriff's department in New Orleans, and I'm sure they'll be anxious to come out to our little town to interview you. Now, hands on the table, please."

Quinn did not comply for a long second while he considered his options. When he didn't, Possum raised his rifle to his shoulder and took dead aim at Quinn, causing him to reconsider. Still his right hand began to quiver from the tension in his arm. "It would be a mistake," Perley warned him. "Possum's already lookin' for a reason to settle with you for sendin' two men to bushwhack him. So keep your hands flat on that table and stand up." Realizing he had no chance, Quinn did as instructed. "Possum, shoot him if he raises those hands off the table," Perley said, then walked around behind Quinn and lifted the .44 from his holster.

"You're making a big mistake," Quinn growled as Perley pulled his arms behind his back and locked on the handcuffs he had found in McQueen's office. "I'm calling you a liar again," Quinn challenged. "If you weren't a yellow coward, you'd face me in the street to settle this thing."

"As sheriff, I ain't supposed to have shoot-outs in the street with low-down murderers like you. To tell you the truth, though, I would enjoy puttin' a hole in your head, but I reckon I'll just have to settle for watchin' you hang." He pulled the chair back out of the way, then took hold of Quinn's arm and pulled him away from the table. With the muzzle of his Winchester pressed against Quinn's back, he started him toward the door.

Once the prisoner was walking, Possum returned his attention to the roulette operator. Before Possum even spoke to the man, he said. "You got no problem with me! He just pays me to operate the wheel and deal cards. I don't even carry a gun."

"What's your name?" When he told him his name, Possum said, "All right, Curly Tice, I expect you better talk to Raymond Patton to see if you still have a job," Possum told him.

Gripped by the unexpected disaster that had suddenly descended upon his promising takeover of this small town, Redmond Quinn was at a loss. Along with his disbelief that this could happen, he felt the indignation of being arrested like a common criminal, which he was vain enough to believe he was not. He felt the astonished looks from the gaping faces as he was being hustled toward the door, faces that he had captured with his grand talk about what he was going to do for their town. Making the spectacle worse was the fact that he was being arrested by a young local character who was only substituting for a real sheriff. With no other option available to him, he decided he would call the upstart's bluff. There was only one more table between him and the bar area. When he reached it, instead of continuing toward the door, he suddenly sat down in one of the chairs. "That's far enough!" he declared. "I refuse to go along with this charade you've made up— this whole pack of lies. I call on the good people of Paris to see what this confused young mind has created out of nothing but jealousy and fear."

"Get on your feet and start walkin'," Perley calmly instructed.

"I will not!" Quinn exclaimed. "You might as well shoot me right here and show these people the murderer you really are."

Possum spoke up then. "Hell, if that's what he really wants, is it all right if I do the honors? Seein' as how he sent those two jaspers to shoot me, I'd be glad to accommodate his request."

"I hate to disappoint you," Perley said to Possum, "but

thanks for the offer." He turned back to Quinn, who was posing upright and defiantly in the saloon chair. "I'm gonna give you one last chance to walk over to the jail quietly, so get up from there and let's get goin'."

"Go to hell," Quinn replied.

"Right," Perley responded, still calmly. "Possum, would you go out and get that coil of rope off my saddle? While you're at it, tie one end of it onto my saddle horn. I think there's enough rope to reach here. We might have to drag English Red over closer to the door, though."

Sporting a wide grin, Possum went out the door. "You're trying to bluff a man who's a professional at the game," Quinn said when Possum left. "Admit it, Perley, you have no evidence of anything you're claiming, and the people of this town know what you're trying to do. Surely, even you must know they're not going to stand by and see you railroad a man just because you fear him."

Perley didn't bother to debate with Quinn but continued to hold his rifle on him while he waited for Possum to return. In a few minutes, Possum came back in the door but stopped just inside it. Everyone in the saloon, including Sadie Bloodworth from the kitchen, had formed a semicircle of fascinated spectators behind Perley. Most of them were really anxious to see how this drama would unfold, knowing well Perley's lack of a violent nature. "You didn't have quite enough rope left on that coil," Possum said. "We're gonna have to drag English Red over here to the door."

"You wanna make it easy on yourself?" Perley asked Quinn. Quinn shook his head, still thinking it a bluff.

So Perley signaled Possum, and he came over to transport the reluctant prisoner. Each of them, with a rifle in one hand, grabbed Quinn up under his arm with the free hand and started to drag him out of the chair. Quinn tried to resist with his feet around the back of the chair until Benny hustled over from the bar. "Here, lemme give you a hand," he offered cheerfully. He took both of Quinn's feet and they carried the fuming man, cursing and struggling, to the door. Still, to get enough slack in the rope to tie it under his shoulders, they had to carry Quinn out on the front porch.

Possum and Perley took a few seconds to discuss the best way to tie the rope around Quinn, while Quinn remained uncooperative, convinced they would not have the guts to do something as barbaric as dragging him up the street. "If we tie it around his chest, he's liable to get his neck broke when we go over some of them deeper ruts," Possum pointed out.

"I reckon you're right," Perley said. "It'd be better to tie it around his boots, so his head will trail. He might get skint up a little, but that's better'n gettin' his neck broke."

"How 'bout we tie it around his neck and drag him that way?" Possum suggested.

"Reckon we'd best let the hangman have the honor of tyin' a rope around his neck," Perley said. He tied Quinn's boots together and tested the knot. "That oughta hold all right. You ready to ride, Quinn?" Quinn didn't answer, still sure that Perley wouldn't have the audacity to do what he threatened. His first jolt of reality came when Buck took up the little bit of slack in the rope and Quinn found himself suddenly in midair when he was jerked off the low porch, only to land with a hard thud when he hit the ground. His eyes barely registered the sight of the underside of the hitching rail as he was dragged beneath it and out into the street. But he was painfully aware that Perley didn't bluff, for the temporary sheriff walked along beside Possum, leading the bay gelding, and seemingly carrying on a casual conversation. They seemed oblivious to Quinn's bumping and scraping as he bounced along the rough street until he was brought to cries of surrender.

Perley stopped Buck and went back to untie Quinn's feet. "I gotta give you credit," he said to the shaken man. "You came close to makin' it. But it makes a whole lot more sense to just walk on over to the jail, since you're goin' one way or another, anyway. It's a shame about that fancy mornin' coat you're wearin', though. I expect that cost a lotta money. Whoa! Take it easy," he cautioned when he and Possum lifted him up on his feet and Quinn seemed to almost stumble. "We'll set you down on a nice comfortable cot in the jailhouse. You'll feel better after you settle down a little." He turned to address the small crowd of spectators that had followed the short trip to the jail. "I reckon the show's over, folks. He'll be treated like any other prisoner in the jail, no better, no worse."

He and Possum escorted Quinn into the office, where they confiscated all his personal possessions except his watch and his smoking tobacco. Then they put him in one of the two cells while they fetched a water bucket and a slop bucket and put them in the other cell. When that was done, Perley transferred him to that cell and removed his handcuffs. "I expect it's been quite a while since you saw the inside of a jail cell, hasn't it?" Perley asked.

Feeling as if he might survive now, Quinn was again recovering his fight. "I've tried to tell you, you dumb small-time gunslinger, you're dead wrong on every notion you've put in that simple brain of yours. I've never been in jail before, never been arrested for anything. And what you have done today will no doubt cost me some time and money because you have slandered my good name. Yes, I've killed before, but only when I have been challenged or attacked outright, like the two men who attacked me the first day I arrived in this town. As far as Sheriff McQueen is concerned, I can only imagine that he crossed paths with Elam Burke somewhere. It had nothing to do with me, just as the attack you claim to have suffered from those two drifters tonight. And I cannot understand why you decided to make yourself the champion for that worthless old tramp, Lester Graves, but you should know that I would not waste ammunition on a wretch of that caliber." He paused a moment to look at Perley and then Possum. "So now, what do you propose to do with me, since you've managed to incarcerate me?"

"To be honest, I don't know for sure, but I'm keepin' you here till the folks in New Orleans have a chance to decide what they're gonna do. I figure they have first claim on you, since you skipped out on that murder. But even if they don't choose to follow up on that case, I intend to see that you pay for the damage you've caused here in this town. We might have to take you over to Sherman to try you there. I'm gonna try to get you a fair trial. I promise you that."

Quickly regaining his confidence, just in hearing Perley's intentions, Quinn was more convinced than ever that there was no solid evidence to prove any part of what Perley claimed. So he responded, "And I promise you this. No judge or jury can find me guilty of anything. And when this is over, I will call on you to defend yourself against me, man-to-man, in a fair contest of our skill with a handgun.

And if you refuse to meet my challenge, I will hunt you down like the coward you are and kill you for slandering my good name."

"Wow!" Perley responded. "That don't sound too good for me, does it, Possum?"

"No, it sure don't," Possum replied. "That sounds like the kinda talk English Red would use." He pretended to be peering extra hard at Quinn. "You reckon you can tell when he changes into English Red and when he changes back into Robert Quail or Redmond Quinn?"

While Perley was securing his prisoner, the news of Redmond Quinn's arrest spread quickly through the small town. For some, it was a worrisome development. When Amos Johnson was informed of the arrest by Ken Stallings, who had been in the saloon when it took place, their initial thought was that Perley must have been out of his mind. Quinn had impressed them as being far too legitimate to have to resort to criminal activity like Perley accused him of. Raymond Patton was close behind Stallings in seeking the mayor's reaction to the arrest. "I don't know what we oughta do, Amos," Patton complained. "Redmond was planning to put some big money in my place. The roulette wheel is already up and running." He nodded toward Stallings. "You and Edgar Welch was bettin' on it tonight. Development of his plans for the gambling casino is gonna make us all rich. You're already seeing the increase in your hotel, aren't you?"

"This is troubling news," Amos admitted. He had complete faith in Perley Gates when he pushed to have him stand in for Paul McQueen. He still believed Perley was honest as the day was long, but Perley was young. Maybe he had gotten a notion about Quinn without any real evidence to back it up. "We'll call a meeting with Perley right away and see what he's got to back up his arrest."

There were other people in town who were just as amazed to hear of the arrest, but were not so quick to doubt Perley's motives. Walt Carver grinned when Ebb Barlow brought the news to him at the stable. "That don't surprise me none," Walt remarked. "That boy ain't that easy to fool by no slick-talkin' big shot."

Although Amos Johnson was quite concerned, the women who operated his dining room were almost giddy with the news that the self-impressed fancy talker had been dragged off to jail. Only one, Becky Morris, was concerned about any harm that could befall Perley because of his brash actions. When Beulah told Paul McQueen about the arrest, he was understandably grateful for what Perley had done, convinced as he was that Quinn was behind the attack by Elam Burke.

Only a small portion of the citizens of the town were on the fence, waiting to see how the issue ended. Some had been impressed by Redmond Quinn, but everybody knew Perley Gates as an easygoing, happy-go-lucky young man, who usually avoided trouble at all costs.

CHAPTER 22

Before breakfast the following morning, Amos Johnson and Raymond Patton walked in the sheriff's office to find Possum Smith sitting at the desk. "Where's Perley?" Amos asked, obviously surprised to find Possum there.

"Mornin', Mayor," Possum replied. "Perley will be back in a minute. He had to go over to the telegraph office. Somethin' I can help you with?"

The two council members were stymied for a few moments, then Amos asked, "Is Redmond Quinn in one of those cells in there?" He pointed toward the door to the cell room.

Enjoying their confusion, Possum answered. "Why, yes, sir, I believe he is. Least he was last time I looked."

"Are you working as Perley's deputy?" Amos asked. "I don't remember authorizing Perley to hire a deputy."

"Maybe that's the reason I ain't ever got no check from the council," Possum couldn't help japing. He was thoroughly enjoying the situation, but he came clean. "No, sir, I'm just settin' here waiting for Perley to come back, so we can go to breakfast. He's gotta make arrangements for your dinin' room to feed his prisoner, but he wanted to send a telegram first. He oughta be back any minute now."

Both visitors shifted nervously from foot to foot for a minute or two before Patton asked, "Can we see the prisoner?"

"I reckon that would be all right," Possum answered. "You ain't got no weapons on you, have you? Long as you ain't plannin' a jailbreak. Perley said I could shoot anybody that tried to break him outta jail." Both visitors opened their coats to show him they were not armed, so he walked over and opened the door for them, leaving it open so he could watch them.

Redmond Quinn was on his feet when they walked in, having heard them out in the office. "I hope to hell you've come to get me out of here!" he ranted right away. "That maniac locked me in here for no reason at all."

"Well, we've certainly come to investigate this unfortunate incident," Amos assured him. "We have to wait until Perley gets back, then we plan to get to the bottom of this and see on what basis he felt he was justified in arresting you."

"What basis?" Quinn exclaimed. "None, that's what basis. The idiot got a wild idea from wherever crazy people get their ideas and decided to take it out on me."

"It was on a little bit more than that," Perley spoke out from the doorway. They had not noticed his arrival. "I'm basing a lot of evidence on the word of a very reliable witness . . . myself. One of the two men Quinn sent to assassinate Possum last night, whose name was burned on his saddle skirt as Porter Shaw, called Quinn by his alias, English Red, and told me that Quinn sent him and his partner to follow Possum and kill him. He said Quinn, there, told him I was in his way, too, so he was gonna shoot me while he was at it. Well, that didn't set too well with Possum or me. Guns were drawn, but Possum and I were lucky enough to get the best of Quinn's hired killers. So that's why I arrested Quinn. I'm pretty sure he was responsible for Paul McQueen's attempted murder, as well as the murder of Lester Graves. But I think what happened last night is enough to take him to court."

His accusations left the two councilmen speechless for a long few moments before Quinn exclaimed impatiently, "Are you actually believing such nonsense? The man is insane. I don't know what his reasons are for standing in the way of progress for this town, but he has no reason to destroy my reputation with his lies." He glared at the two merchants, waiting for some response, but neither Amos nor Patton knew how to respond to such serious charges. When it was obvious that they were at a loss, Quinn said, "Look at the back of my coat and the cuts on the back of my neck! The man dragged me through the street with his horse! Is that the kind of man you want for your sheriff?" He concentrated his glare on Amos.

Amos blinked helplessly. "Well, I hear that you refused to walk to the jail."

"All I did was demand my rights as a law-abiding citizen," Quinn replied, unable to think of any legitimate excuse.

Caught between the two opposing versions of the facts, Amos wasn't sure what he should do. He looked to Raymond Patton for his thoughts, but Patton had too much to lose if what Perley said was true. Amos appealed to Perley then. "I don't suppose you could release Mr. Quinn until we have a chance to examine all the facts."

"No, sir, not a chance, Mr. Mayor. There's no way I can ignore the attack on Possum and myself last night. It's plain to me, and should be to you, that Redmond Quinn, or Robert Quail, or English Red—whatever he's callin' himself these days—is capable of causing more harm and killing in this town."

"He's lying!" Quinn exclaimed, just as Ebb Barlow stuck his head in the door.

"Perley," Ebb called out. "Grover said you'd wanna see this reply to your telegram soon as it came in, so I brought it over to ya."

Perley walked back to the door and took it from him. "Thanks, Ebb. Tell Grover I 'preciate it." Everybody in the cell room stopped talking, including Redmond Quinn, while Perley read the wire. He studied it for a long moment, then looked at Possum. "They're mighty interested, all right." He looked at Amos and explained. "This is from the sheriff's department in New Orleans. They were prosecuting Quinn for the murder of a man named Bode Mathews but Quinn slipped outta town on 'em. That's when he was called English Red around New Orleans. I thought they'd be interested in interviewin' him and they can definitely identify him as English Red. My guess is they're gonna want to transport him back there to stand trial, but I don't know if we wanna take a chance on ol' slick English Red slippin' out of their hands again. Might be quicker to contact the Rangers in Sherman and hang him, I mean, try him over there."

Amos and Patton were struck speechless. There was no doubt in either mind that every charge Perley had leveled against Redmond Quinn was, in fact, valid. They were left to suffer the sting of Quinn's farce, which they had eagerly accepted. On the other side of the bars, English Red realized that his charade was ended. Most of Perley's evidence against him was hearsay, but that damn sheriff in New Orleans could definitely identify him. He realized it was useless at this point to protest. He moved back to his cot and sat down, his eyes on the floor, trying to figure a way to escape this trap he now found himself in. He realized that he hated Perley Gates more than any man he had ever encountered in his life of crime. The most painful part of it was to be caught by such a seemingly guileless young man. Regardless of the final outcome of this failed venture to take over the town, he was determined to have his vengeance against this naive temporary sheriff. His total concentration would now be focused on a way to get his hands on his gun belt. With that strapped around his hips, he was invincible. If he got the chance, he would shoot Perley Gates down like a rabid dog, but if he had a preference, it would be in a face-to-face showdown. The problem facing him at the moment was not knowing how long it would take the people from the sheriff's department in New Orleans to get there. In the meantime, he would wait for the mistake Perley was bound to make. He reminded himself that he had always found a chance to escape. He would recognize it when it came. When he lifted his head again, it was to meet the wide-open eyes of Amos Johnson and Raymond Patton. "Well, what the hell are you two buzzards staring at? I would have made you both rich. Blame yourselves for hiring that young jackass for a sheriff when this mudhole you call a town dries up."

"I guess we're about through here," Amos uttered, and he and Patton turned to leave the cell room. "At least we found out who we were dealing with before we got hurt too bad." A thought occurred to him as soon as he said it. "I reckon you got hurt more than the rest of us, though. With all that construction you've got going on at the saloon."

"That was the first thing I thought about, too," Patton said. "The crook persuaded me to pay for all of it, but I'm thinkin' now I might go ahead with his big plans and run that gamblin' casino myself."

Possum heard him and commented, "Maybe you could run an honest operation. That would be different."

"Yeah, I like the sound of that," the mayor said, "an honest gambling casino." As they walked through the office past Perley, he said, "Good job, Sheriff."

"Thank you, Mr. Mayor," Perley answered. After they left, Perley said to Possum, "Let me take a quick look at the prisoner to make sure he's all right, then we'll go get some breakfast."

"Lemme take a look at that telegram," Possum said, and Perley handed it to him before going back in the cell room. "It sure came at the right time, didn't it?"

"Sure did," Perley answered, and went in to tell Quinn that he was going to have some breakfast sent down for him. "Either that, or I'll bring it back with me," he told Quinn. "Maybe they'll have meat loaf for dinner."

"You may think you've won this battle between us," Quinn replied, "but nobody's won until one of us is dead."

"Whatever you say, English Red, you're the poet." He walked out and locked the cell room door. When he went into the office, he found Possum still studying the telegram intently. Knowing Possum couldn't read, he asked, "Want me to read it for you?"

"Yeah, I'd like to hear the official version of it," Possum said.

"Official version," Perley announced, then read, "Sheriff Gates. Trial records of Robert Quail aka English Red vs State of Louisiana for murder of Bode Mathews all destroyed in fire in storeroom, 1/15/1877 STOP New Orleans Sheriff's Department no longer interested in reopening case STOP Good luck in your investigation. And it's from the sheriff of New Orleans," Perley said.

"Why, you sly old dog," Possum uttered, his grin extending from one ear to the other. Delighted, he threw his head back and chuckled. "This time, you left the cow pie and he stepped right in it. I always thought you'd lie if there was a good reason for it."

"What are you talkin' about?" Perley replied. "I never lied about anything. I said I sent the telegram and I did. I said they answered it and they did. That was no lie," he insisted as he locked the office door.

"What about when you told them the New Orleans sheriff wanted to come to interview Quinn? It didn't say that in that telegram you just read me," Possum reminded him as they began walking down toward the hotel.

"I never told them that," Perley insisted. "What I said was I *thought* they'd wanna come out here to interview him. And that was no lie. I thought they would." They argued the point all the way to the hotel with Possum finally conceding that Perley was honest even when he was deceiving.

When they walked into the dining room, they had barely

seated themselves at a table when it was surrounded by all three women who worked there. Anxious to get the news straight from the source regarding Redmond Quinn's arrest, the questions started before the women even offered Perley and Possum a cup of coffee. Becky had naturally been the one most worried, since she had not seen Perley since supper the night before. "I'm sorry," he apologized, "but Possum and I were kinda busy all night. There were a lot of things goin' on."

"We know that," Lucy interrupted. "We heard about it all secondhand. What did ol' Redmond Quinn say when you told him he was under arrest?"

"Well, he wasn't much in favor of the idea," Perley said. Then he left it for Possum to give them the details, which he was raring to do. "Can we get a little coffee before he gets started?"

"I'll fix you some breakfast," Beulah said, "but I wanna hear every detail about that arrest, especially the part about draggin' Mr. Fancy Pants to the jailhouse." Lucy agreed to save her questions until they gave the two hungry men some breakfast. Becky fussed over Perley to his embarrassment until she was finally forced to wait on some other customers. While she was gone, Perley told Possum to kinda skip lightly over the part about the shoot-out with the two men Quinn sent after him. He also stressed the importance of keeping the contents of the telegram secret until after Perley had made arrangements with the Texas Rangers to come for Quinn.

Once breakfast was served, Possum gave them a full accounting of what happened, minus the parts Perley had stressed. Now that Quinn's true identity was out of the bag, all the women were claiming to have seen it from the first day he walked in. "He sure had Amos Johnson fooled," Lucy said, then looked quickly around to make sure the owner of the hotel wasn't in the dining room.

Beulah came out of the kitchen with the coffeepot and filled their cups. "Whaddaya gonna do with him now?"

"When we leave here, I'm gonna wire the Rangers in Sherman to come get him and take him to trial," Perley said. "That reminds me, I need to take him some breakfast when I go back."

"Maybe they'll send ol' Grady Prince back over here to give him another try at transportin' a prisoner," Possum said with a chuckle. "That's one Ranger that likes a drink of likker. He passed out with his eyes wide open."

When they were ready to leave, Beulah brought Perley a plate of food and a small soup bucket filled with coffee for his prisoner. "Much obliged, Beulah," Perley said. "I'm sure Mr. Quinn will appreciate it." He gave Becky a little squeeze of her hand and said he'd see her later on in the day. On the way back to the jail, he asked Possum if he thought he had best ride out to the Triple-G and tell them why he never came back last night.

"I expect I should," Possum allowed. "But with everything that's been goin' on here with your sheriff's job, I kinda hate to leave you shorthanded, especially with that rattlesnake you've got locked up in there."

"I don't think I'll have any trouble now that he's settled down in that cell. You'd best go make things right with Rubin. You tell him I'm the one who caused you not to show up for work this mornin'. Tell him I needed your help, because I ain't lyin' when I say I don't know how I woulda pulled this off without your help."

Possum shrugged modestly, pleased to know his help was appreciated. "You fixin' to go send that telegram to Sherman after we give Quinn his breakfast?" Perley nodded. "Tell you what," Possum continued. "I'll stay at the office and keep an eye on Quinn till you get back, then I'll head back out to the Triple-G."

"I'll take you up on that, partner," Perley said.

When they went inside the cell room, they found Quinn sitting on his cot with his back up against the wall. He favored them with a sarcastic smile. "I thought you might have decided not to feed me," he said.

"Sorry to make you wait," Perley said politely. "I'll try to be more punctual tomorrow. Now, you sit right there on that cot while I put this inside the door. Possum's gonna hold his gun on you in case you decide to move before I lock the cell door again. Understand?"

"Oh, indeed I do," Quinn answered, showing a hint of his old self-confidence. "I won't move." He watched, seemingly amused, as Perley unlocked the cell door and set the plate and the coffee inside on the floor, then locked the door again. "I hope you gave the ladies in the dining room my regards," he said as he retrieved his breakfast.

"They sent theirs," Perley told him. "We'll leave you to your breakfast now." He and Possum went back in the office. "I'll walk on over to the railroad depot. Shouldn't be gone long."

"Take your time," Possum replied. "I ain't in any hurry. Rubin will most likely send me back out to work on that old line shack. I'm kinda gettin' used to bein' a lawman, anyway. Maybe I'll apply for the job of sheriff, if Paul don't want it when he gets well."

* * *

Perley hadn't been gone for more than a couple of minutes when Possum had a visitor in the sheriff's office. "Mornin'," the thin little man offered.

It took only a second or two, but then Possum remembered who the man was. "Curly, right? Curly Tice, ain't it, the feller runnin' the roulette wheel?"

Tice nodded vigorously, evidently pleased that Possum remembered. "What can I do for you, Curly?"

"I know you think that everybody who worked for Mr. Quinn is an outlaw, but that's not true for people like me who just happen to be good at dealin' cards or runnin' a wheel. He's always been very nice to me and the women who worked for him. So, if I can, I'd like to visit him just long enough to tell him I appreciate what he's done for me and to tell him how sorry I am that this had to happen to him. Would that be all right?"

Possum hesitated, not sure if he should or not. "You totin' any weapons?"

"Oh no, sir, I never carry firearms." He lifted his coattails and turned around in a circle to show he was not armed. "I do have this one thing, though." He reached in his coat pocket and pulled out a pipe. "Mr. Quinn always enjoyed smoking his pipe, so I brought it to him, if that's all right."

"I reckon he can't break outta here with a pipe," Possum allowed, "You got anything else on you, pocket-knife or anything like that?"

"No, sir, you are welcome to search me."

Possum settled for a quick once-over with the patting of his hands. Feeling nothing suspicious, he said, "Go ahead and give him his pipe, and I'll be watchin' you."

"Thank you, sir, I won't take long."

Possum opened the cell room door and stood there to watch him as he approached Quinn's cell. He found himself feeling a little pity for the timid little man who might well be out of a job with Quinn's arrest.

Still eating his breakfast, Quinn put it aside and walked to the bars to meet his visitor. "Hello, Curly. Didn't expect to see any visitors here. Are you still running the wheel, or did Patton shut it down?"

"No, I'm still running it, but it's not the same without you. Mr. Patton doesn't know how to operate a gambling hall like you do." He held up the pipe for Quinn to see. "I brought you your favorite pipe. I know how you must miss smoking it." He ignored the puzzled expression that remark brought to Quinn's face. "I was afraid I was going to drop it and break it." Then he started to hand it through the bars, but it fell out of his hand. "Oh dear," he squeaked, and stooped quickly to catch it before it struck the top of his short-cut boot. With his back toward the office door, Curly quickly pulled the Remington derringer from his boot and slipped it through the bars into Quinn's hand when Quinn, without thinking, had stooped to catch the pipe, too.

Both men stood erect again and turned to look at Possum. Curly gestured helplessly as he held the pipe up for Possum to see before handing it to Quinn, who was smiling with new confidence now. "Nice catch, Curly," he said. "I always said you had the fastest hands of any dealer I'd ever worked with. I expect you'll be moving along now that we won't be working the casino as we'd planned."

"Yes, sir, I expect I'll return to that place in Houston

right away. As a matter of fact, I'm all packed up and on my way out of town right now."

"Good idea, you'd best not tarry," Quinn said. "I appreciate your stopping by to bring my pipe."

"Good luck to you, sir," Curly said in parting, and quickly turned to leave, pausing for only a moment to express his thanks to Possum as he went out the door. Quinn stuck the pipe in his mouth and pretended to puff on it, having never been a pipe smoker.

CHAPTER 23

"Hey, Possum," Quinn called out a couple of times before Possum stuck his head in the cell room door.

"What are you hollerin' about, Quinn?" Possum asked.

"I'm through with my breakfast, so you can take these dishes out of my cell."

"They'll be all right where they are," Possum replied. "Ain't no hurry."

"I want to tidy up my cell," Quinn insisted. "You should know by now that I like things neat and clean, and I've decided if I'm going to be a prisoner, then I'll be a model prisoner. I should think you would appreciate that. I'll bet your friend Perley would." He paused, but when Possum showed no sign of moving, he said, "For heaven's sake, man, all I'm asking is for you to remove the dirty dishes from my cell. Is that too much to ask?"

Possum shook his head impatiently. "I swear, if you ain't somethin'. All right, just keep your shirt on. I'll take the blame dishes." He took the cell door key off a peg by the office door and went to Quinn's cell. "Well, bring the dishes over to the door," he ordered impatiently. When Quinn did that, Possum said, "Put 'em on the floor and back away from the door." When Quinn complied, Possum unlocked the cell door and reached in for the dishes.

Like a great cat, Quinn suddenly struck. He was immediately over the surprised man with the derringer pressed against his head. Possum started to reach for his .44, but Quinn warned, "Do it and I'll blow a hole right through your head. Now, if you want to live, you'd better do just what I tell you to do. Crawl on inside this cell."

Already down on one knee to pick up the dishes, Possum knew he had no choice. Feeling sick inside from having been tricked so easily, he crawled inside the cell, worrying most about having failed Perley. Quinn pulled his six-gun out of his holster as he crawled by. "That sneakin' little snake," Possum uttered, thinking about how easily Curly had played him.

"Yes"—Quinn chuckled, knowing whom he was referring to—"Curly Tice has fleeced more than a few dumb saddle bums like you with his sleight-of-hand skills." He stepped outside and locked the cell door. "Now, I'll be honest with you. I'd much prefer shooting you in the head like I did for Lester Graves, but I don't want to disturb this peaceful morning in your fair city. And I'd hate to scare off your naive friend. Where did he go?"

"To the telegraph office to put the Texas Rangers on your tail," Possum replied, hoping to encourage Quinn to run. He was afraid that Quinn would wait to ambush Perley when he walked in the door. He would probably kill him, too, after he'd done for Perley, but he had more concern for Perley's life than his own. "For all your big talk about wantin' to face Perley in the middle of the street, man-to-man. You're lucky you never got that chance 'cause you'da found out how fast Perley is with a six-gun. I've seen some gunslingers in my time, but Perley's the fastest man alive."

"Is that a fact?" Quinn responded, his ego too inflated to let that go unchallenged. "I doubt very seriously if you've ever seen a really fast expert with a handgun, and I've given your friend the opportunity to test his skill against a truly fast gun. But I have to say, he wisely refused the challenge. Had he not, he'd be lying in a grave up on that hill back of town. I dare say he is about to find out that he can't hide behind that badge forever. I will abide this sorry town no longer than it takes for Perley Gates to return to this jail. I will put an end to his arrogant young life, then I'll walk up the middle of the street to the stable, daring any man to stop me."

"If that's what you're wantin' to do, then you'd best ambush Perley, 'cause if you try to take him on face-to-face in a fair fight, you're the one that's gonna be sleepin' in the ground tonight. Anybody in town would tell you that."

Quinn forced a chuckle to show his opinion of Possum's claims. "Too bad you won't get the opportunity to see your friend in action, since he refuses to fight me fair and square. I'd enjoy more of this conversation, but I expect I don't have the time right now. I'll give you something to consider while we're waiting for Perley to return. I intend to complete the job Porter Shaw and Shep King were sent to do on you after I've taken care of Perley. I'd go ahead and take care of it now, but I don't want Perley to hear the gunshot and be frightened away. So I'll leave you to your thoughts now." He started to leave the cell room but stopped to say one last thing. "I'll tell you what, though, if Perley should happen to accept my challenge to face me in the street, I'll be happy to report the outcome to you before your execution."

Perley walked out on the railroad platform after a brief conversation with Ebb Barlow, who wanted to talk about the big arrest. He happened to notice a solitary figure on a horse and leading a packhorse heading out the south end of town. He didn't identify the rider at once, but then realized it was the roulette operator, Curly somebody, he couldn't recall the last name. *Guess he couldn't come to an agreeable arrangement with Patton,* he thought. Walking back to the jail, he went past the blacksmith shop and wondered if Paul was going to make a full recovery. He was wounded pretty badly. *One thing for certain,* he thought, *I'm not taking this job permanently.* And that was a fact even if Paul didn't come back. Thoughts of Becky entered his mind then. As soon as he could, he wanted to move her out to the Triple-G. Then maybe he could settle into a normal life like his two brothers. With these and various other thoughts taking over his thinking, he was fully unprepared for the reception awaiting him at the sheriff's office.

The first thing he saw when he stepped inside the door was the muzzle of Paul McQueen's shotgun staring at him. Behind the shotgun, Redmond Quinn sat behind the desk, his feet propped up on the desk. Perley started to reach for his six-gun, but thought better of it, and his next thought popped out of his mouth. "Possum," he muttered.

"Perley Gates." Quinn pronounced the name with the same tone he had used when pronouncing *meat loaf.* "You and I have a great many issues to resolve between us. I find it noble that your first concern was for your friend Possum. There's no need to be alarmed yet. Mr. Possum is safe and sound in the cell I once occupied. He'll stay that way as long as you are alive, which I'm confident will not be a great deal longer. But as you know by now, I am a gambler, so I'm willing to offer you the option of saving your friend's life by facing me in the middle of the street at twenty paces. If you do that, I won't go ahead and shoot him now, which I'll do if you refuse to face me. So, what say you, Perley Gates?"

"I don't suppose you'd consider another option," Perley answered. "You put that shotgun back where you found it and return to your cell and I'll see if Beulah could make you meat loaf for dinner."

Quinn grunted out a weak chuckle. "I'll give you credit for your sense of humor in the grave situation you find yourself. Bravo, but I'm afraid you still have but two options. Die like a man, or die like a cowardly dog."

"Don't you even consider the possibility that you might lose?" Perley couldn't help asking.

Quinn chuckled again, this one sincere. "I have been tested by the so-called fastest guns in the territory. It is the only activity in which I am not considered a gambler. But enough of this useless discussion. What is your decision?"

"No choice really, I'll take my chances in a duel."

"Excellent," Quinn reacted. "Now, I'll have to ask you to remove that pistol from your holster and lay it on the floor. I'll return it to you when it's time to see if you really are as fast as the local people think you are. Use your left hand, please, and lift it with one finger and a thumb by the handle." He watched carefully as Perley pulled the weapon and laid it carefully on the floor. Quinn got up on his feet then and walked over to confront Perley, the shot-gun aimed straight at Perley's stomach. "Here," he said, "these are the bracelets you placed on me when you dragged me through the street. Put them on one of your wrists." When Perley did so, Quinn told him to put his arms behind his back and he quickly clamped the cuffs on Perley's other wrist. "All right, now we'll go in and visit your good friend Possum." He prodded him in his back with the muzzle of the shotgun, guiding him through the cell room door. "Here's Perley, come to rescue you," Quinn goaded. "I'm gonna put him in the cell next to yours, so you can have one final visit."

"Perley!" Possum exclaimed when he saw Perley hand-cuffed and under guard. "I'm sorry, man. I messed up. I shouldn'ta let that little weasel, Curly, in here to see him. The little badger had a pocket pistol hid in his boot."

Possum's outburst brought another round of chuckles from Quinn. He pushed Perley into the other cell and locked the door. "Now, this is more to my liking," he said. "The whole sheriff's department locked up, and I've got the key. I'll let you two talk about all the good times you've shared while I tend to the publicity of the show we're going to put on for the folks." He left the room then and seconds later they heard him go out the front door of the office.

"What the hell's he doin'?" Possum wondered. "What's he mean, publicity?"

"Sounds like he wants to gather some spectators to see him and me try to outdraw each other. I think he's willin' to take a chance on one of the town folks shootin' him down just so he can show that he's the fastest gunslinger in Texas."

"That's crazy as hell," Possum insisted. "He coulda just shot us both and rode on outta town."

"I think he is a little crazy. He's got himself a reputation, and that's more important to him than anything else. I believe it's got so bad with him that it's taken over his brain. So here's the deal: I have to face him in a shoot-out, he says, or he's just gonna kill us both, anyway."

"Damn, Perley, I'm sorry I got you boxed in like this. You think you can outshoot him?"

"I ain't got any idea," Perley said. "He's pretty damn fast, to hear him tell it." Further talk was interrupted by the sudden report of two shotgun blasts, right outside the front door. "That must be the publicity." A few minutes later, they heard voices outside the building, the loudest of which was that of Redmond Quinn.

"He's makin' a regular carnival outta this killin'," Possum declared. "He's crazy as a hyena eatin' locoweed. We need to see if there ain't some way to get outta these cells!" He already knew there was no escape. They had checked the cells thoroughly when they put Quinn in the night before. "Damn, Perley, I'm . . ." That was as far as he got before Perley cut him off.

"You don't need to apologize any more about that," Perley interrupted. "It coulda happened to me if I'd been in the office. You just got slickered by a harmless-lookin' little man that makes a livin' cheatin' people with his hands. That's why neither one of us is any good at gamblin'." Their conversation was ended when the cell room door opened and Quinn made a grand entrance.

"It's showtime for the local fast-draw champion, Perley

Gates—sounds like those in heaven but spelled differently," Quinn mocked as he unlocked Perley's cell. "One funny move out of you, and there won't be any duel," he warned Perley. "I'll shoot you down like a dog." With his hands still cuffed behind his back, Perley was marched at gunpoint out of the jail and into the street, where a modest crowd of spectators had begun to gather, most of them not quite sure a real duel was about to be performed. There was an instant swell in comments when they saw Perley marched to the middle of the street.

Standing behind him with his gun pressed against his back, Quinn pulled Perley's pistol out of his belt and dropped it into Perley's holster. "Can I check to see if it's loaded?" Perley asked.

"Don't trust me, huh?" Quinn responded. "Sure, go ahead and check it. I don't need to cheat to beat you. Just remember this gun in the middle of your back while you check your load." Perley stood still while he waited for Quinn to release his hands from behind his back. Then he drew his six-gun out and checked the cylinder to make sure there were no empty chambers. Satisfied that he had a loaded gun, he dropped it back in his holster. "You ready now?" Quinn asked, and Perley nodded. "I hope your arms and shoulders didn't get stiff being locked behind your back like that," he suggested in order to give Perley something else to think about. "Now, Mr. Perley Gates, you just stand right where you are and don't turn around till I tell you to. Because, if you do, I'll shoot you in the back. It's as simple as that. Understand? These good people deserve an honest contest."

"I'll do my best," Perley said.

Quinn laughed. "You do that, Perley, and maybe you'll

be remembered for this day. Hold still now until you hear me say *Turn around*. Don't worry, I'll give you time to get set before we draw." Quinn stepped away from him then, walking backward, counting his paces. When he had reached the distance he preferred, he eased his pistol up and down a few times to make sure it was riding easy. Then he called out, "Turn around, Perley, nice and slow."

Perley turned around as a hush fell over the growing crowd of spectators as word of the duel spread. Many of the late arrivals, unaware that Perley had been forced to participate, wondered why he would do that, take a prisoner out of the jail and execute him in the street. The two combatants stood there watching each other intently, neither making a move. "Whenever you're ready, Perley," Quinn encouraged, a smile of confidence on his face. "It'll be over in seconds." Still Perley did not make a move. It was not in his nature to attack. His natural reactions were triggered in defense of attack from an opponent, so he simply remained ready to meet any aggressive move by Quinn. Thinking him too scared to act, Quinn's smile widened as he thought, *He's making it too easy. I might as well end his misery*. His gun had not cleared his holster when Perley's shot struck him in his right shoulder, causing him to drop his weapon on the ground. Perley quickly moved to retrieve the fallen pistol while Quinn sank to one knee in total shock. Unable to believe what had just happened, he stared at the blood pumping from his shoulder. "You missed me," was all he could think to say.

"I didn't miss you," Perley said. "I just don't want you to miss your appointment with the hangman. Shootin' is way too easy a way to make you pay for all you've done, and you sure as hell don't deserve the easy way out. Now, get on your feet and let's get you back to your cell."

Still not positively sure what had just happened, he thought that someone watching the face-off had fired the shot before either man drew. That had to be the case, because it was not possible that Perley was faster than he was. "You cheated, you coward," he accused.

His accusation brought a few chuckles from those standing close enough to have heard him, and Ebb Barlow called out, "You just ain't as fast as you thought you was, English Red." His remark brought a bigger wave of chuckles.

Quinn realized then that he had actually been beaten, and the thought of it was almost too much for him to bear. "I'm wounded, I need a doctor," Quinn moaned. "You should have killed me," he said then. Perley knew why he said that. His reputation as a fast gun was more important to him than his life.

"There ain't no doctor in Paris," Perley said. "You oughta know that. I'm gonna take you back inside, and then I'll send for Bill Simmons to see if he can take care of it."

"I'm right behind you, Perley," Bill spoke up, having been one of the witnesses to the shoot-out. "I'll go get my medical bag. I thought I was gonna be totin' a corpse back."

Inside the jail, Possum was pacing frantically from side to side in his cell. He heard the one shot, but he had no way of knowing who fired it. He heard the raised voices of the spectators, too, but could not determine anything clearly enough to give him a clue. Then he heard the front door of the office open and someone came in. But it was not until he saw Perley helping the wounded Quinn through the cell room door that he could breathe again. "Hot damn!" he yelled. "I knew it! I tried to tell that damn fool he couldn't beat you, but he wouldn't listen. Hot damn," he repeated. "Perley, hurry up and lemme outta here."

"Let me get our guest down on his bed first. Bill Simmons is on his way with his medical bag to take a look at him. It ain't too bad. He's just shot in the shoulder. On second thought," he said as he locked Quinn's cell, "maybe I oughta leave you in there for a while for causin' me to have to shoot a prisoner."

"Ah, come on, partner, I told you how sorry I am for that," Possum pleaded. Perley laughed and unlocked his cell. "You shot him in the shoulder. How come you didn't kill the murderin' dog? He was sure fixin' to kill you."

"Like I told him," Perley explained, "shootin's too good for him. He deserves to hang." He shrugged and added, "That and the fact I just came from the telegraph office, where I requested the Texas Rangers to send somebody to transport a prisoner for trial. And I didn't wanna tell another Ranger that we killed the prisoner before he had a chance to take him to trial. I'm afraid Paris might start to get a bad name with the Rangers."

There were still a few gawkers standing around in front of the sheriff's office when Bill Simmons returned to examine the patient. "Patch him up good, Doc," Walt Carver sang out. "Maybe he'd like to try it again."

"Yeah, I'd like to see it again," Ben Henderson crowed. "I musta blinked the first time. I didn't see either one of 'em go for their guns, and then Quinn dropped down on his knee."

"I'll tell Perley you all want another show," Simmons said as he went in the door. Inside, he found Redmond Quinn sitting on his bed, holding his arm and rocking back and forth in obvious pain. Simmons took a quick look at the damage done by Perley's bullet and gave them a prognosis. "This looks a lot like a wound I fixed for John Bannerman last week. He accidently shot one of his sheep dogs in the shoulder, and the bullet broke the bone. That's what this one looks like." He turned to look at Perley. "You got a piece of canvas or somethin' to cover this cot? 'Cause it's gonna make a mess."

They had to settle for a couple of ragged old sheets when a search for canvas came up with no results. "I'll try not to make too big a mess," Simmons said, and went to work on Quinn's shoulder with Perley and Possum both standing guard. Although Bill's touch was far from gentle, Quinn remained silent through the whole process until the bullet was out and the shoulder bandaged with his arm in a sling. His only remark when it was done was to ask how the sheep dog was doing since he was subjected to Bill's rough treatment. "The dog died," Simmons said. "He hopped around on three legs pretty good for a week or two, though—lead poisonin', I reckon."

"You ignorant people in this town," Quinn couldn't resist lashing out. "You could have all prospered if you had not gotten in my way. I should have known better than to pick a town in north Texas with the name of Paris."

"Well, at least you'll get to enjoy some of our hospitality for a few days until a jail wagon gets here from Sherman," Possum told him. "Maybe the judge will rule in your favor, but I expect for your trial, there'll most likely be a wagonload of people from here wantin' to testify as witnesses."

A new sense of peace seemed to settle over the little town in northeast Texas almost immediately. Although Raymond Patton was still making noise about going forward with plans to create a gambling house, no one expected Patton to actually accomplish it. Redmond Quinn remained a guest in the town jail for four more days before Grady Prince showed up with his jail wagon to transport him back to Sherman. Perley continued filling in for Paul McQueen, visiting him every day to encourage his recovery and discourage any talk about his retiring from the business of law enforcement.

Perley was realistic enough to know that he did not present an imposing image to a drunken troublemaker. Consequently, he felt sure he was not an ideal candidate for the sheriff's job, even had he wanted it. While he had never ever recalled a feeling of fear in the face of unexpected encounters with dangerous individuals, in the days that immediately followed his farewell to Redmond Quinn, however, he was struck with a fear he had not considered before—matrimony. And the more he thought about it, the more he feared it. What if he was no good at it? When these thoughts invaded his mind, he would picture Becky and know that life would be worse without her. "Well, John and Rubin"—he laughed, thinking of his brothers—"looks like I'm clear up to my neck in this cow pie."

Keep reading for a special excerpt

National Bestselling Authors
WILLIAM W. JOHNSTONE
and J. A. JOHNSTONE

SAVAGE SUNDAY
A DUFF MACCALLISTER WESTERN

*Scottish cattleman Duff MacCallister staked a claim
for his life in America—and reserves a righteous anger
for those who break the law in this smoking six-gun
shoot-out from national bestselling authors
William W. and J. A. Johnstone . . .*

Thanks to a new line, the railroad has come to
Chugwater, Wyoming, bridging the gap between the
small town and the larger city of Cheyenne. Now Duff
MacCallister can transport his 250 Black Angus cattle
herd with ease by iron horse instead of enduring a
two-day trail drive. But the day after depositing
$15,000 in his Cheyenne account, Duff learns
that bank president Jeremy Brinks embezzled every
cent—totaling $65,000—and then guilt-ridden,
committed suicide.

Jeremy wasn't just Duff's banker, but his longtime
friend. The widow Brinks doesn't believe her husband
was a thief or that he killed himself. Duff agrees. And
after getting an appointment as territorial marshal, he's
aiming his barrel at putting every double-crossing
lawman, red-handed outlaw, and corrupt businessman
he can rustle up behind bars—or six feet under . . .

Look for **SAVAGE SUNDAY,** *on sale now!*

CHAPTER 1

Wyoming Territory

Duff MacCallister sat on his horse, Sky, with Bear Creek behind him, watching as Elmer Gleason, Wang Chow, and two other cowboys worked to round up the cattle he would be taking to market. Duff, who had arrived in America some time ago, had been a cattleman in Scotland. The cattle he raised were Black Angus, and he had introduced the breed to Wyoming.

Elmer, who was his foreman, came riding over to him. "You ain't moved in so long, I didn't know but what you was a statue someone put up here," he teased.

"Sure now, 'n what would be the need of my moving when there's a good man handling things?" Duff asked.

Elmer smiled. "I'm a good man all right, 'n I'm glad you could see it."

"I was talking about Wang."

"Wang Chow? Why, that heathen wouldn't know the difference betwixt a cow 'n goat iffen I wasn't here to tell him."

Duff knew that Elmer calling the Chinaman a heathen

was all in jest, for though he often used that sobriquet when referring to Wang Chow, the two men were actually very close friends.

"Perhaps Wang is a good man because you made him a good man," Duff suggested.

"Yeah, now, that's the truth of it," Elmer replied.

"What's the count?" Duff asked.

"We've got four hunnert 'n twenty rounded up so far," Elmer said. "I cipher that out to figure we'll need eighty more before we have the full gather. We'll have 'em all in before dark, so's we can leave first thing tomorrah mornin'."

"I've scheduled two special trains with fifteen cattle cars each, for the shipping of the cattle. One will be here at eleven, and the other at twelve. You'll have to see to the loading. The lass 'n I will be for taking the ten o'clock passenger train so we'll be in Cheyenne before the cattle arrive."

"So, Miss Meagan is goin' with you, is she?"

"Aye, 'tis a trip she's been looking forward to."

Elmer chuckled. "No more 'n you, I'm bettin'."

"Sure 'n 'tis a smart fellow you are," Duff replied with a laugh.

"Well, don't you be worryin' none 'bout them cows, on account of me 'n Wang will get the trains loaded," Elmer said.

Cabin, five miles west of Cheyenne, Wyoming Territory

The cabin had been abandoned when the four men found it, and it showed the disrepair from being a long time empty, with broken windows and missing doors. The only improvement they had made was to get the stove back in working order.

Bart Jenkins used his hat to protect his hand as he lifted the coffeepot off that same stove and poured coffee into his tin cup. There were three others around the stove. Moe Conyers, a cowboy who had been fired from the last three ranches where he had worked. Slim Gardner, whose honest work had been minimal, from teamster to mopping the floors in a saloon. The third was a black man, and nobody knew much about his background, nor did they even know his name. He identified himself as Black Liberty, but Jenkins was almost certain that wasn't his real name.

"How much money are we talking about?" Slim asked.

"It's hard to tell," Bart said. "It's a bank. How much money is in a bank?"

"I don't know," Moe said. "I ain't never robbed me no bank before. I mean, you can get yourself shot holdin' up a bank."

"You won't be holdin' up the bank," Bart said. "Neither you, nor Black Lib."

"What? Why not? You ain't leavin' us out, are you?"

"No," Bart answered. "I've got a job for both of you. Black, they's a saloon in Hillsdale called the Hog Waller in the town, 'n right acrost the street from it is Sikes Hardware Store. They's a bench in front of that store, 'n that's where I'm goin' to want you to be, 'cause you can tie your horse off right there. Don't worry none 'bout bein' colored. They's two, maybe three families of colored people in town, so nobody will pay you no never mind. You sit there while Moe goes into the saloon.

"Moe, what you're goin' to do when you go into the

saloon is commence a-shootin' up the place, but you better watch out for the bartender on account of he's likely to have him a shotgun under the bar.

"Don't stay long enough for anyone to shoot back, then you run outta the saloon, climb up on your horse, 'n ride outta town, headin' north. They's only the sheriff 'n one deputy in town. Soon as they hear the shootin', they'll more 'n likely come a-runnin' after you.

"Black, soon as you see the two lawmen chasin' after Moe, you get on your horse 'n chase after them. Moe, after you've come out of town a little ways, find yourself a rock to get behind, 'n wait for 'em. With Black comin' up behind 'em, you'll have the sheriff 'n his deputy caught betwixt the two of you 'n you can ambush 'em. Oughta take no more 'n you two to shoot the sheriff 'n his deputy. While you two is takin' care o' them, me 'n Slim will ride in 'n rob the bank. Won't have no problem with it, cause the sheriff and deputy will more 'n likely be dead by then. Ever'one else will still be thinkin' 'bout the shootin' that happened in the saloon.

"We'll meet back at the cabin, but ride aroun' a lot so's to throw anyone that might be a-chasin' you off track. Don't be a-leadin' 'em to the cabin. That way we'll always have a place to hide out," Bart said.

"What time we goin' to do this tomorrah?" Moe asked.

"Right after noon. That way there'll be some customers in the saloon, but not likely so many as to cause you any problems when you commence to shootin' the place up."

"Damn if that ain't about the best damn idee I've ever heard," Moe said.

Chugwater, Wyoming Territory

Biff Johnson, owner and proprietor of the Fiddler's Green Saloon, was opening a little earlier than he did on most days. He had told Duff he would be there when they came into town this morning. As he reached for the coffeepot, he knocked something from the shelf, and reaching down, he retrieved the pennant. Holding the pennant in his hand for a moment, as if studying it. It was a symbol of his past, a thirty-three inch by twenty-seven inch, swallow-tailed flag of the kind that had been hand-stitched by New York City seamstresses during the Civil War. It featured a field of thirteen red and white alternating stripes and a blue canton with thirty-five stenciled gilt stars, forming a circle within a circle, plus four more stars, one in each corner of the canton.

As the former Sergeant Major Benjamin Franklin Johnson held the flag, Custer's last battle came to him with a clarity and intensity as great as it was on the day it happened.

June 25, 1876

Custer had already detached Benteen's Battalion, as well as the trains, then he continued north, along with Reno's Battalion. When they reached the South Fork of the Little Bighorn River, he held up his hand and stopped the column. "Major Reno!"

Reno came to the front, saluted, and reported to Custer.

"Major, I want you to take your three companies across the river and attack the village from the south. Maintain pressure against them. I will go a little farther north, cross

the river, and attack from the other side." Custer smiled. "This way we will have the devils between us."

"Sir, do you think it is wise to split your command?" Reno asked.

"Major, you will do as I have ordered," Custer said firmly.

"Yes, sir," Reno said with a salute then rode to the back of the column to give orders to his battalion.

"Sergeant Major Johnson!" Custer called after Reno left.

"Yes, sir?" Biff answered.

"I want you to detach yourself from Captain Keogh, and go with Major Reno."

"But, sir, I would rather be with my own troops."

"I know you would, Sergeant Major, and I would rather have you with us, but Reno is untried. I would feel better knowing that you were with him."

"Yes, sir," Biff replied, the disappointment obvious in his voice.

Custer continued toward the village, while Reno, as ordered, pressed against the bottom end of the village where the Hunkpapa Lakota were located.

After his first engagement with the Indians, Reno dismounted his men and had them form a skirmish line.

"Sir, the colonel ordered us to attack the village," Biff said. "We aren't attacking, we're defending. We're cavalry, sir, we should stay mounted."

"When you get your own command, Sergeant Major, you can make the decisions," Reno replied in a high-pitched, frightened voice. "But you aren't in command, are you? I am. Now form a skirmish line like I told you to."

"We won't be able to sustain a skirmish line," Biff said.

"Do as I tell you, Sergeant Major!" Reno ordered.

"Yes, sir."

The result of Reno's incompetent leadership was exactly as Biff had predicted. Because Reno's troops lost their mobility, the Indians were able to maneuver around the skirmish line. What was supposed to be an attack became first a defense line, then, as Reno couldn't hold it, he ordered his men to fall back toward the river, where their defense was even less effective. As the fighting intensified, he lost his nerve and ordered a retreat.

Reno completely abandoned his men, thinking only of his own safety. Instead of an orderly retreat, it became a rout. Many of his men did not make it across the river, where Biff, Lieutenant Tom Weir, and a couple of the other officers finally managed to establish a defense.

When Benteen arrived, Biff thought their units would merge then move forward to relieve the pressure on Custer. There, he saw the body of First Sergeant Frank Varden, Biff's closest friend in the regiment, and he felt a particular loss seeing Frank lying among the many wounded and dead. Biff dismounted and kneeled next to his friend.

"Biff, when me 'n you get out of the army, what do you say we open us up a saloon?"

"Sounds good to me," Biff replied. "What'll we call it? Johnson and Varden?"

"Nah, we'll give it a good name. We'll call it Fiddler's Green."

"My friend," Biff said quietly. "You're at Fiddler's Green now. Save a place for me. I'll be along one of these days."

As he turned over First Sergeant Varden's body, he found a guidon Varden had tucked into his shirt.

* * *

"This guidon," Biff said quietly in the saloon, looking at the one he was holding in his hand. As he put the swallow-tailed flag back in its place, the memories of that battle faded away, sight and sound, tone and tint.

He had opened his saloon and, as Varden had suggested, he called it Fiddler's Greene. Cavalry legend has it that anyone who has ever served as a cavalryman will, after they die, stop by Fiddler's Greene—a shady glen where the grass is good and a nearby stream of cool water provides for the horses. There, cavalrymen from all wars and generations will drink beer, chew tobacco, smoke their pipes, and visit. They will regale one another with tales of derring-do until that last syllable of recorded time, at which moment they will bid each other a last good-bye before departing for their final and eternal destination.

The front door opened and four people walked in— Duff, Meagan Parker, Elmer, and Wang.

"You mean the sheriff ain't closed this place as a health hazard yet?" Elmer called out.

"I've got my rats and roaches trained," Biff replied. "They run away and hide anytime a sheriff's deputy comes in here."

"Now, you see there, Wang? If roaches can be taught, why I bet even you could larn somethin'," Elmer teased.

"If I am walking with two other men, each of them will serve as my teacher. I will pick out the good points of the one and imitate them, and the bad points of the other and correct them in myself," Wang replied.

"That's one o' them things that heathen feller, Confusion is always sayin' ain't it?"

"Confucius," Wang corrected.

"Well, hell, ain't that what I done just said?"

Meagan laughed. "Elmer, I suggest that you stop now before you get yourself in any deeper."

"Yeah, well, I was goin' to stop anyhow. I thought we come in here for a drink.

"Use my table," Biff invited.

CHAPTER 2

Duff, Meagan, Elmer, and Wang sat at Biff's private table having a drink. There had been a time when a few of the customers had questioned Wang Chow's right to be in Fiddler's Green, but Biff had let them know, in no uncertain terms, that Wang would always be welcome. And because Fiddler's Green was a particularly nice saloon, no stigma was ever attached to a woman being there. Meagan felt quite comfortable in the environment.

"Listen, if you happen to see one of them silver hatbands, I'd like you to buy it for me," Elmer said. "I can give you some money for it now, or you can just tell me how much it costs, 'n I'll pay you when you get back. I think one o' them silver hatbands would make me look just real elegant."

"Elegant, you say. Aren't you displaying a bit of vanity there, Elmer?" Meagan asked, a little laugh showing that she was teasing.

"Well, here's the thing, Miss Meagan. If I don't brag on myself, who will? You know Duff ain't goin' to do it, 'n the heathen here, why he don't even know what braggin' is."

Meagan laughed. "You do have a point. I'll look for

it, for you, Elmer. I'm going to be doing quite a bit of shopping for my store."

"Thank you, ma'am," Elmer said.

"What about you, Wang? What could we be getting for you from the big city?" Duff asked.

"I want nothing."

"How long do you think you'll be gone?" Biff asked.

"Two or three days," Duff said. "You heard the lass. She wants to tarry a bit, 'n I'll be there with her until she's done."

"There's no need for you to stay with me, Duff. I can get home by myself," Meagan said.

"Ha, you don't understand, Miss Meagan. He ain't worried none 'bout you gettin' back by your ownself. He's worried 'bout him gettin' back by his ownself," Elmer said, and the others laughed.

Meagan glanced toward the clock. "The train is due within the next half hour. Don't you think it might be a good idea to go down to the depot now?"

"Aye," Duff replied. "I'll be for wantin' to check on the cattle one more time before we leave, so now's a good time to do it."

"Have a good trip, and don't be doing anything I wouldn't do," Biff said as they stood from the table to leave.

"Damn, Biff, you've just told 'em they can do anything they want to do, 'cause just what is it that you wouldn't do?" Elmer teased.

At that same moment, one mile west of Chugwater, Lou Martell, a man of some disrepute, and three others, just as disreputable, were breaking camp.

"You sure this fella we're lookin' for is in Chugwater?" Deekus Carlotti asked.

"I read about 'im in a newspaper that picked up a story from the *Chugwater Defender*. It said a Chinaman named Wang Chow worked for a rancher here, by the name of Duff MacCallister. 'N this Chinaman come from China, so you know it's the selfsame one."

Carlotti laughed. "Well hell, don't all Chinamen come from China?"

"Did you come from Italy?" Martell asked.

"What? No, I was borned in Arkansas."

"Yeah? Well most of the Chinamans here was borned here, too. But this here Wang Chow was borned in China, 'n he kilt some important people there. Now China has put out a reward of a hunnert thousand dollars to anyone who can bring him in, or kill 'im."

"Hey, Martell, if we capture this Chinaman, we won't have to be a-takin' 'im all the way back to China, will we?"

"No, they's these fellas in San Francisco called the Dongs, or somethin' like that. If we can get 'im to them Dongs . . ."

"I think it is *Tong*," Gabe Kellis said.

"Yeah, the Tong. Anyway, all we got to do is prove to the Tong that he's been kilt. We can do that by takin' his head back to 'em, 'n when we do that, they'll give us twenty-five thousand dollars," Martell said.

"Wait, I thought you said this here Chinaman was worth a hunnert thousand dollars." The protest came from a man named Emmet Willard.

"It's only a hunnert thousand dollars if we take his head all the way to China," Martell replied. "Do you really want to do that? Anyhow, when's the last time you ever had twenty-five thousand dollars?"

"I ain't never had me no twenty-five thousand dollars."

"Well, all we got to do to get it is kill us a Chinaman. 'N just how hard do you think that will be?"

"Here's what I'm worried about, though," Carlotti said. "If we just up 'n kill 'im, what about the sheriff? Ain't we liable to have to deal with him on account of we murdered someone?"

"We don't need to be a-worryin' none 'bout no sheriff," Martell said. He held up a piece of paper. "This here paper is a reward from China. All we have to do is show the sheriff this paper."

"How's the sheriff goin' to read it, if it's in Chinese?" Carlotti asked.

"It's in Chinese 'n it's also in American," Martell said.

Kellis laughed. "There ain't no such thing as an American language."

"What the hell do you think we're talkin' in now, if it ain't American?" Martell asked.

"English," Kellis said. "We're talkin' *English*."

"Hmm. I allus thought that was the same thing," Martell said. "All right, boys, put out the fire. We're a-fixin' to go into town, 'n make us a lot o' money."

As Duff, Meagan, Elmer, and Wang walked toward the depot, they could smell the closely packed cattle from Sky Meadow and hear the almost human bawling cries they were making because the change in their environment made them anxious. Five hundred head of Black Angus cattle had been crowded into the loading pens at the Chugwater Depot.

Duff had sold the cattle to a Kansas City cattle broker, who would take delivery of and pay for them in Cheyenne. The recently built railroad from Ft. Laramie to Cheyenne took its route took through Chugwater. What used to be a two-day hard drive of the cattle had been reduced to a little more than two hours.

The railroad would have put a caboose on one of the leased trains, and he and Meagan could have ridden for no additional cost had he wanted, but he'd passed on the offer. He wanted to be in Cheyenne before the leased trains arrived so he could see to their distribution there. He wasn't worried about leaving the cattle behind. Elmer and Wang, two of his best men and closest friends, were remaining. Duff was confident they would see to the shipment of the cattle.

"Elmer, as soon as you get the beasties loaded, you and Wang can be for taking a little time off while Meagan and I see to the business in Cheyenne."

"Now, just what do you think me 'n this heathen can find to do while you two is gone?" Elmer asked.

"Well, I don't know what you two might find to do, but perhaps Vi Winslow and Mae Lin would have a suggestion," Duff replied with a smile.

"Oh, yeah. I forgot about them," Elmer said.

"Elmer, you wouldn't want me to tell Vi that you had forgotten about her, would you?" Meagan teased.

"No, now, there ain't no call for you to go 'n do nothin' like that," Elmer protested. "She might not never let me have no more o' them pies she bakes."

Vi Winslow owned Vi's Pies, a small, but one of the

more successful businesses in Chugwater. She was an attractive widow in her early forties who had shown an interest in Elmer, and that interest was reciprocated.

"Train comes." Wang didn't engage in banter, not because he was aloof, but because English was a second language to him.

"What train? I don't hear no train," Elmer challenged.

"Train comes," Wang repeated. "Look." He pointed north.

There, barely discernable, and still out of hearing distance, was a thin ribbon of smoke.

"Oh, yeah. Well sure. I mean if you're talkin' about *that* train, now that you mention it, I see it too," Elmer replied. "I just didn't know which train you were talking about."

Half an hour later, with good-byes said and final instructions given, Duff and Meagan boarded the train, then took a seat in the day coach, all they would require for a trip less than two hours.

Meagan wasn't traveling with Duff only because they were friends, though indeed their relationship was quite close. Like Elmer, she was a partner in ownership of the cattle that were being sold, so even if their personal relationship hadn't been close, she had every right to represent her interest.

"Duff, do you think Elmer and Vi will ever get married?"

Duff chuckled. "I'd not be for knowin' that, lass, and you have to admit that Elmer is a cantankerous old chancer."

"'N here you are speakin' with a wee bit o' the unfathomable Scottish talk. What would chancer be?" Meagan asked, perfectly mimicking Duff's Scottish brogue.

"Bha mi a 'smaoineachadh gu robh thu ag ionnsachadh a' chànain," Duff said in Scottish-Gaelic.

"Tha mi ag ionnsachadh a 'chànain," Meagan said, getting exactly the roll and lilt in her response. Then she repeated in English, "I *am* learning the language."

Duff laughed. "Sure now lass, 'n your words make me think I'm back in the heather again. Chancer means that Elmer has a wee bit o' the chicanery about him. But even so, 'tis a good man he is."

"You're lucky, no, *we're* lucky to have two such"—she paused, searching for the right word—"remarkable men as friends."

"Aye, lass, we are indeed."

Shortly after the train left the station, Duff thought about the woman sitting beside him. Back in Scotland there had been Skye McGregor, the woman he had planned to marry. But on the very day before they were to wed, she was murdered by a dishonest sheriff, and that had caused Duff to seek revenge. His success in exacting vengeance forced him to leave Scotland, thus accounting for his presence in America.

He'd thought he would never meet another woman to fill his heart as Skye had done, but to his surprise, Meagan had done just that. Feeling her so close and breathing in her perfume, he could almost believe she was the only woman he had ever felt that way about.